Däm'Um:
Song of the Vam Pỹr's

LOVE IN VEIN

Book two of the One Blood series

Written by Stavros
Edited by Tara Lindsay Hall

CRAZY DUCK PRESS

Library of Congress Catalog Number: 2011917491

ISBN: 978-0-9828121-7-4

Published by Crazy Duck Press
www.crazyduckpress.com

"Howlin' at the Moon"
Written by Hank Williams, Sr.
©1951 Hank Williams, Sr.

"The Order of Death"
Written by John Lydon.
©1983 Public Image Ltd

Illustrations, Photography, and Graphic Design by Stavros
Cover Models: Kate Tsocanos & Joyce Larioza
Make Up & Hair: Kate Tsocanos
Typeset in Garamond, Blue Highway, and Scythe

Printed in the United States of America

Praise for Love in Vein

"Attn Vamp Lit Lovers – Finally a writer on par with Anne Rice."
-Crystal Gimesh, TN; Facebook Post

"New twist on vampires...I highly recommend Love in Vein if you are looking for something different in your vampire books or paranormal reading list. If you are looking for something that is just slightly different than your normal take on vampires, then Love in Vein is the book for you."
-The Avid Reader Review by Nancy Allen

"Once again the author creates a superior universe filled with an entirely new culture of vampires... In the previous novel, I compared 'Blood Junky' to a very rich dessert, but 'Love In Vein' is a full course meal. The series is a gift for those that love vampire fiction... It has some of the best vampiric characters ever written in a novel... Vampire novels of the past have included some very formulaic visions of simple blood exchange. Yes, there is an exchange of blood but this series adds more to the basic scheme. It breaks many molds and expectations of this being another generic story of immortal bloodsuckers. This series and more directly this novel is comparable with, and at times, surpasses the 'Vampire Chronicles' by Anne Rice." *-Living Dead Media.com Review by Lori Bowland*

"I MUST recommend this novel to my fellow fangbangers! As a lifelong lover of the iconic neck-bite, I'm always looking for a new and fresh take on the infernal bloodsucker, and I certainly wasn't let down here! ...It is believable. It is real!... The transformation from human to vampire is also entirely different in the One Blood series than anything I've heard, or thought of, and is nothing short of complete genius!!!"
-5 out of 5 Star Amazon.com Review by Danny C. Gay

*This book is dedicated, with love,
to my children: One & Story*

"Love is a serious mental disease."

- Plato, 428 BC – 348 BC

Däm'Um:
Song of the Vam Pyr's
LOVE IN VEIN:

No
Good
Deed

The song came crashing through the window. Before the roar and sputter of the '63 Cadillac's engine kissed Jared's ears and the screech of its white wall tires turned from the dirty, dry tarmac into the parking lot, the cold eye of the security camera displayed the baby blue vehicle on a tiny monitor. Jared's manager, Mukesh, couldn't hear the song, tucked away in his little office, grinding through paperwork. The monitor flickered silently. To the Guwahati immigrant the vintage luxury car looked innocent enough.

Jared recognized the song immediately: the Yeah Yeah Yeahs' *Date with the Night*, track two on Fever To Tell, only nine tracks shy of Modern Romance. He looked up from the newspaper rag, squinted, peering out of the large plate glass windows into the bright, white glare of oncoming headlights. A cold shiver washed over him and he followed the tail-finned Caddy as it pulled into a parking spot.

The article that Jared read in the trashy black and white tabloid was just a distraction. Something to keep him from thinking about the lyrics to Modern Romance, and by so doing...*thinking of her.* The Yeah Yeah Yeahs was her band, the one she always had playing whenever they made out, groping and grinding each other like bunnies in dry, panting humps. Amber had been on his mind a lot lately. Ever since he uploaded the song, Modern Romance, to his Facebook page and added a link to the band's video on You Tube he hadn't been able to get the girl off his mind.

The motor churned, bubbled and spat. The track danced, crushing like a hot crotch. The front license plate on the classic car read: ETRNL BTCH. The engine died unwillingly and big doors opened wide spilling their contents. The lead on the number 2 pencil Mukesh used broke. He looked up from his calculations and figures, turning to the display screen as the rough and ready hooligans stepped from the car. The corners of his pudgy cheeks twisted into a suspicious grimace.

Hard-soled boots connected with the concrete and carried what were, in Jared's opinion, two female punks into the four-pump gas station/convenience store. The bell above the glass door clanked its toll as the Hard-Rock chicks entered the Stop-n-Shop to appease their late night cravings. Jared watched them walk. Purposeful. Knowing. They moved up the aisles with practiced ease.

Jared Richter was twenty-two. White. Sandy red hair. Pimply faced. He wasn't an athlete. Skinny. He had an ole tabby cat he got in the tenth grade that he named after Fredrick, The Great because he was studying the reluctant King of Prussia in history class that week. Jared was a loner, mostly quiet, only had two girlfriends that he considered real, and of those two lucky ex-loves he only had sex with one of them. Amber was the girl that didn't sleep with him. He still keeps pictures of her on his iPhone: the ones they snapped together last summer while at a music store in Phoenix.

Usually, Jared worked the nightshift alone. He had his own key. Mukesh gave it to him along with his last raise a few years ago. It was a perfect night for gaming, and it was being wasted. Only a few trucks had passed along Highway 95, and fewer still had made the little store their pit stop. Jared couldn't help but feel a twinge of regret at agreeing to cover Allison Beck's shift. Any other night he would have been online with his phone, gaming and chatting, but not tonight. Tonight, no good deed went unpunished. Mukesh had come in to clear up some paperwork. His daughter was getting married in four months and things at home were becoming more pressing, harder for him to find a quiet moment alone without his wife interrupting about one thing or another on the upcoming nuptials. So, the industrious immigrant drank coffee and ground through his paperwork as Jared read the pop culture tabloid and waited on customers, trying desperately to ignore the weight of his cell phone tugging at his pocket.

Jared had been home reading his course book when Allison called. He set the large text down and knew he shouldn't have answered it the second he heard her voice. Frederick the Great sat on the windowsill looking out on the apartment's parking lot, swishing his tail back and forth as Jared paced. It was two hours before Allison's shift was supposed to start and she was lying to him.

"Really. I'm not feeling well." Her voice sounded fine, a shrill octave above annoying. Jared had never liked Allison.

"I have Wednesday's off for a reason, you know."

"C'mon," she whined. "I'd cover for *you*. It's not like your hookin' up with Amber anymore. I know you're free."

"That's not the point!"

"You're just gonna sit home and whack off to the computer with all the other Warcraft geeks."

"That's rich. And you think that's going to make me cover your shift?"

"You know I'd cover for you. C'mon..."

"It's just too late. Goodbye, Allison."

"What the fuck, Jared, you want me to get the customers sick?"

"You're gonna have to do *a lot* better than that."

He hung up. Allison Beck was supposed to work the graveyard shift. Her name was on the schedule. In blue ink. A cursive script - 11p.m. to 8a.m. It had been posted for a week. He knew this because he had made the schedule. His cell phone rang again. Frederick the Great turned from the sparse night to the synthetic chime and hopped down from the windowsill.

"What is it now?"

"Ok, look," Allison breathed heavily. "I'm not sick. I've just been running around ragged all day and am beat. Ok?"

"What you choose to do in your own time is-"

"That's not what I'm talking about. Lemme explain."

As Allison spun it, her grandfather, the one with Alzheimer's, wasn't in his room again this morning and no one else was in the house to answer the phone when the nursing home called. So Allison was forced to get it. That was 7:30 a.m. Head all woolly, blond hair a tangled rat's nest, the phone wouldn't shut up. She had fallen asleep around 5:22a.m. with her headphones still drawn over her head, pumping out silence, and a book resting in her lap.

Allison, without a shower or breakfast, wearing yesterday's underwear, found her grandfather two-and-a-half-hours later walking down Maple Street. The old man thought he needed to let Major out of the house and into the back yard so the dog wouldn't soil the sofa again. Muriel hated it when Major did that and Frank didn't want to upset her again because he had forgotten. Muriel was his dead wife.

Feet padding slowly and steadily, he was walking to where he remembered the doublewide rancher used to be. Major was the little Scottish Terrier he and Muriel owned back when Allison was a little girl. She liked the dog, but he'd been dead now for almost fourteen years.

Driving back to the nursing home Allison stopped at a little place and picked up some breakfast burritos. They both missed the morning meal and it was nice to sit with her Grandpap outside, on one of the old wooden benches, that is, until he forgot who she was. Holes in his memory as big as bicycle tires, Allison hated his sickness. It was a cruel thing. She had to wait until he remembered who she was again before she could coach him back into the car. He caused a scene, shouting that he didn't even know who his granddaughter was. The restaurant manager helped Allison convince him that it was okay.

By the time Grandpap was tucked back in his room at the nursing home her cell phone rang. Her Mom asked if she would pick up her little brother from soccer practice as she was running late for a hairdressing appointment. Then Allison had to fix him dinner because their Dad was delayed at the office and Mom still hadn't come home yet. Allison was halfway through the mac & cheese, hot dogs, and green beans she had made when Penny called, and well...she was having trouble with David again. Allison had to help there. Couldn't abandon her BFF in a time of need, could she?

Yacking 'til her cell battery died, Allison realized she only had two hours before her scheduled shift at the Stop-n-Shop. Allison Beck sighed heavily into the tiny speaker of the electronic device. She felt drained. Tired. She needed a day off. Running around doing everything for everybody else had worn her out. So, she called Jared.

Reluctantly, Jared agreed to cover her shift.

Now, he watched the tattooed beauty with the short-cropped raven hair make a beeline for the drink coolers in the back of the store. The other one, a tall, lanky punk with a brightly colored mop slunk stealthily through the chip aisle and household goods stopping every so often to look at the items on the shelves. Her loud dyed red hair kept falling in her face. Both of the girls were too pale for Jared's taste. He liked his women caramel flavored, a rich honey-brown like Amber. He stored an impressive collection of pornographic magazines under his bed that depicted naked black women with big butts. Amber was skinnier than what the women in his magazines were, but it was as close as he was going to get to the girl whose picture was on his iPhone. Jared returned his attention to the trashy tabloid sprawled open on the checkout counter like a hot buttered biscuit, doing his best to ignore the lyrics of Modern Romance.

Lin eased the glass door open. A blast of cold air hit her knees. Like the register jockey, she didn't want to be here either. The purr of the Cadillac's white walls on tarmac was soothing. The store lights hurt her eyes. She felt the veiny parasite wiggle deeper into her corneas as a strangulating pang jolted her skin.

"Yeah, yeah, you greedy bitch. I hear you." Between the restless Jadaraa Soo and Z clamoring in her ears to stop for a bite, Lin knew she'd never get a moment's peace. At least, that was what she told herself, pulling off Highway 95 into the dim light of the little store.

Staring blankly at the rows of cold, bottled liquids, all of which wouldn't solve her annoying little itch, she chided herself for being so obstinate earlier. She shouldn't have refused the business lunch that the tall punk had lured to their hotel room. Now she was starving. It made it easier for Z to get her way. Lin exhaled. All she had to do was grab something. It didn't really matter. *Coke? Pepsi? Mountain Dew.* At least they weren't in Vegas anymore.

Vegas. Lin sighed. *Las Vegas. Nevada. The city of sin. Where else could a vampire stay out all day and never see the sun? Those casinos are like tombs, windowless. Ever winding deeper inward, a catacomb of vice, rich with enticements luring one further and further into the trap. A bloodsucker could learn a thing or two from Vegas.*

Lin felt it down in the marrow of her bones: Bringing Z with her this time around was a mistake. It wasn't the fact that by noon the dyed red punk was out ten thousand dollars, or even the fact that she whined and complained until Lin steered the great big baby blue machine north toward the glitz of cheap eats, one-armed bandits, and garish monuments of carousal. It wasn't any one thing in particular that smacked as an affront to Lin's pity for the dying creature. It was just…*everything.*

Everything felt wrong. The glib, slap, dab of twinkling neon lights in broad daylight was unsettling. An abomination to the natural order of things, much like herself, Lin wanted to vomit. The dyed red punk just wanted to play on and on and on – *a constant merry-go-round ride.* Lin wanted off. But they had only just begun. One day on the road and already Lin was steering off course. She felt an urgency to get *there* bristling under her skin, under the veiny limbs of her Jadaraa Soo*, riding the edges of her bones unlike anything she'd felt before. But instead of cruising through the atmosphere, churning miles, she was appeasing Z. Driving the rails to Vegas, stopping for a habitual grab-n-burn. The rhythm of the road hadn't even gotten a chance to settle in. The mood between them felt like new shoes, tight and uncomfortable.

Sequestered in a darkened hotel room away from Z was the only time that Lin enjoyed while in Vegas. That was until the punk came crashing through the door with some balding joker in a brown business

*See Lexicon on pg. 437 for assistance
with definitions and pronunciations.*

suit. Lin hated to admit it, but it was true: she should have left Z back home in LA to deal with Ryan's corpse. She felt icky, the backside of flypaper; and you know what they say, *what happens in Vegas, stays in Vegas.* Well, for Harold T. Johnston that was most certainly true. He stayed in Vegas alright. He never left. A maid found him just after midnight wedged into the bar's mini fridge when she came in to turn down the room and refresh the liquor stock.

She found Harold naked and gaunt, cold, in full rigormortis and drained of all blood. She, like Lin, was amazed at how Z had managed to stuff such a big man into such a small, confined space. It was a thing of marvel, really. However, the awful sensation of Harold T. Johnston's bones cracking in her ears as he became more pliable, and that gleeful look on Z's beaming face didn't stay in Vegas. It had left the neon desert oasis with Lin. Sitting in the driver's seat with Harold's casino winnings crammed into her back pocket, the two raucous vampires barreled down the road.

And it was such a gorgeous night out, too. Clear. Dark. Stars ignited the pantheon of the sky. It was the kind of night that Lin wore on her shoulders. The kind of night that Lin could have driven all the way through from dusk 'til dawn. Thoughts drifting along the cascade pulse of the open road, painting the changing landscape. The quiet of the desert surrounded her, alive on all sides. Its dry breezes swept across her face through the open window as dormant frustrations lingering under the tapestry canvas of her dead skin lulled into the rhythm of spinning wheels and ironed her heady feelings out. She needed that. She'd needed it ever since she left Los Angeles – needed to drive, percolate her cerebral chatter to the surface so her musings could have palpable reason. It was exactly the kind of night that Lin had been waiting for. Yet, here she was letting cold, recycled air wash over her.

She grabbed a Mountain Dew roughly from its pristine advertising slot and imagined the hotel maid's scream shattering the blissful ignorance of the twelfth floor when she found Harold's twisted corpse in the mini refrigerator. Lin thought about how Sin City police would set about tracking Sally Kellerman, under whose name the room was registered, and follow the little breadcrumbs to a stale dead end. Because Sally died in 1972 at the tender age of twenty-three by the very same hands that had stuffed Harold T. Johnston into the tiny box. Lin wasn't with Z then when she ran into Sally. But the ole gal's identification had been floating around between the two of them for the past thirty odd years. Despite Lin's rank position with the punk riding shotgun, it gave the frustrated vamp a smug jolt to think about the head scratcher they had left crime scene investigators, trying to figure out how a sixty-plus woman had crammed a forty-two-year-old man into a mini fridge.

Lin caught her grin in the frost-coated glass door as it quietly slipped into its jam. Her short haircut, just over the eyes, tomboy Bob felt good. She liked the way it framed her pale, white face. Initially, she only intended to give herself a trim before she hit the road. *Got a little carried away with it.* Though she liked the cut, Lin missed the bounce and weight of her hair's full regal girth resting on her shoulders. The ghost of hair locks lightly brushed against the back of her neck. She passed her eyes over her curvy frame. Motorcycle boots, faded Levi's, a wife-beater under an old green tee shirt, and a black leather jacket. Her shoulders slumped. It'd been a long day. The ickiness of Vegas was still there in her back pocket, pulling her down.

Lin spied Z stuffing a few tubes of lipstick, eyeliner, and blush into the pockets of her denim jacket as she entered the candy aisle. *Why couldn't she have just stayed asleep?* Lin grabbed a Snickers and a Whatchyamacallit. *Could've reached Flagstaff.* Barely out of Nevada and the vampire nodded off in the stroke of a sentence like an aging narcoleptic.

Ever since Lin learned that Z's blood parasite was dying she'd been letting the punk get her way. It was wearing thin, her nerves were razorblades and pin needles. Worrying about Z's symbiotic existence slowing down, ebbing to its inevitable stop wasn't working. It took its toll. *No good deed went unpunished.* Lin didn't even think the poor girl knew it was happening. Z just woke and picked up the conversation, without missing a beat, as if she hadn't stopped hours ago in a previous state. Consonants and hard verbs, the vibrant punk was ready to rumble through the veins of some unlucky vagabonds; tear reason from the cold fabric of night, and fuel her lust with blood. Z joined Lin's nagging Jadaraa Soo to find a quiet locale, off the beaten path, a little country-side oasis to party. After all, it'd only been a decade since their last splash. Lin sighed. *Fuck. She's so young; barely crowned a century.*

Z raised her head just as the store manager, a short, balding North Eastern Gateway native, stepped from the small, unlit hall near the fountain drink station. She flashed an eye at him and smiled. He scrunched his brow. Walking over to the liquid dispensing nook, Z wanted to be closer to the pudgy little man. She tried not to think about it. Time was wreaking havoc in her soul. Black holes the size of bicycle tires were spinning in her head. She was missing moments and didn't know why. *Lin's been unusually quiet, that ball of spit missing from her fire. She's usually such a mess when we start out for New Mexico, gabbing like a tourist.*

He's watching me.

The corners of Z's mouth curved upward. The violent wench felt a hiccup of anticipation and stopped at a sunglasses rack letting the man's gaze linger on her slender form. Z liked being watched. She was a spectacle of god light and bullshit, packaged in a hot little body built for speed, a temple of carousal, and she began looking through the fruitful display of eyewear. She caught Lin's reflection across a dozen tinted lenses as the brooding vamp crossed to the checkout island, sizing the little man up for a meal.

Mukesh Priyaranjan believed. He believed his customers were robbing him blind. He believed that Allison was lazy and Jared was a good employee. He bought the little gas station on Highway 95 in '84 from a guy named Joe who voted for Walter Mondale. The Guwahati immigrant sold his first tank of gas three years before Jared was born. Mukesh's wife, Banhi, was pregnant then with their second child. Coming to America, purchasing the fuel station, and settling in the Arizona desert was something his family back in India never liked or supported. He went against family tradition because he wanted something better for himself than what his father had. He wanted the freedom of the West, fast food, MTV, and a shot for his son to become a doctor in the States. Mukesh believed. Mukesh believed all things were possible in the West and that a better life was out there for him. All he had to do was take a chance. It paid off and by the time his daughter was out of diapers and riding a tricycle Mukesh had built the tiny gas station into the convenience store that it was today.

The Stop-n-Shop was the central component that supported his family and he never regretted moving to America. Not once. Not even when his father lay dying in India and his sisters refused to tell him about it until after he'd already passed. Mukesh believed and his faith was rewarded. His son graduated high school in '96 and completed medical school nine years later. Mukesh was never happier. He was a proud parent living the American Dream. Bought and sold, he had the debts to prove it. When his son received a residency at the Johns Hopkins Medical Center in Baltimore, Maryland, Mukesh threw a lavish party even though he and Banhi really couldn't afford it. Jared was invited to the celebration, but he never showed.

Orcs had just ambushed Rune Shadow, Jared's then Elf Warrior, in a clever move led by the wizard Phantom Ze. It didn't look like Rune

Shadow was going to make it and Jared buckled in for a long night battling online. During a late night snack run to the Priyaranjan's convenience store he ran into a pretty girl named Amber, who also was out that night scurrying across the cold desert for junk food and soda. The two hit it off awkwardly, shy, but kinetic.

Mukesh turned from the brash vixen for a moment as the biker dyke set a handful of items on the counter. Jared didn't even have a chance to move the trashy tabloid from where it lay before Lin placed her purchase items down. Mukesh sighed. *What's wrong with these kids today, lazy and absent-minded, always dressing like a bunch of freaks?!* Mukesh moved to ring up the hooligans himself, but caught the tall, lanky punk shifting off to his right from out of the corner of his eye.

"In the mood for a little snack, huh?" Jared asked the pale, imposing chick.

Z laughed aloud and it popped like thunder. Lin smirked at the irony of the boy's innocent question and Mukesh turned to see the eyes of the cold-hearted killer heading straight at him.

"Yeah," Lin uttered, "something like that."

Suddenly, and quicker than the old man could ever imagine, the redheaded wench was on him and he was flying through the air. She merely placed a hand to his collar and he hit the coke machine with a bright painful crash, splurting beverage syrup and soda water all over the place. Jared turned in the direction of the loud noise. That was a mistake. He took his eyes off the maddening red veins that crisscrossed Lin's peerless spectrum and she pushed him back using both hands. It felt like he'd been hit with a War-Hammer, +5 Damage Bonus! He landed on the floor with all the breath knocked out of his lungs.

Lin bounded over the checkout counter, landing squarely on the old tiled floor banging on the clerk's eardrums. Straddling him like a graceful jockey over a downed racehorse, he tried to fight back by reaching up to push the alarm. The biker dyke stomped on his outstretched arm with her big-ass boots. It smarted.

"Tsk, tsk, tsk," the raven-haired harlot stroked with her tongue. "I don't think so."

"Please, take what ever you want and just go," cried Mukesh trying to find some reasonable way out of this abrupt nightmare. "We don't want any trouble."

The old man's cries filtered past Lin's ears.

"We aim to do just that," muttered Z to the frightened man. "Don't we, baby?"

Lin smirked. Z was in her zone. Every second the tall, vivacious coquette took breaking the law reminded her of the days when she was robbin' banks and shootin' it up with her husband Simon Ray.

"Yeah," Lin uttered coldly to the live thing twitching on the floor under her. "Just that."

Jared went white when he saw the tips of the gnarled fangs protruding from the gums of the smirking killer. He knew then that he was going to die. He quickly thought about what Rune Shadow 2.0 would do in a situation like this. He wondered who would feed his cat and it occurred to him that he wasn't even supposed to be here tonight. *Allison was scheduled. It was written in blue ink, a cursive script. It should've been her!* Before Jared could cry out, plead to God, or spit in the face of death the ashen woman was on top of him, tearing into his neck. He felt the harsh, unbelievable sting of his flesh being torn and couldn't get over how the sounds of his own screaming eclipsed the maniacal snarling brutality of his fate.

Mukesh pleaded for his life as he witnessed Jared writhing in agony, being ripped apart. *Such savage cruelty!* He turned away and his bulging, brown eyes fell on the cold, uncaring thing on top of him as she pressed her lithe frame into his trembling flab. He couldn't help Jared now. He couldn't even help himself. He thought of Banhi and how his death was going to ruin their daughter's wedding. He wondered why the bitch waited, why didn't she attack him like her friend had done to Jared? *Why is she toying with me?!*

Z inhaled Mukesh's fear as the store erupted all around her into a cacophony of beautiful music. She nestled her nose into the soft corner of the old man's shoulder and licked perspiration and soda from his dark mocha skin. His jugular vein pulsed rapidly under her tongue, a tiny ticking, and Z's ailing Jadaraa Soo jittered along her bones, dancing to the tune.

"I love Indian food," she exhaled in a panting lust.

The Maestro descended into the hot flesh of the eastern man

with an opened mouth. Hungry. She clasped her arms tightly around him and cracked three ribs, making his battered screams a constant treble. The vampiric veins that twisted into the shape of her fangs unwound, like a ballerina's pirouette, and drove deeper into Mukesh's flesh, breaking through muscle, wrapping itself around the carotid artery, squeezing, while Z suckled, draining the old man like sweet nectar from the stamen of a honeysuckle flower.

Lin pulled every last drop from the boy. His flesh shriveled, nestling closer to his deflated muscles and bones. It framed his deathly composure. The vampire rose off from him satiated on the vibrant liquid coursing through her Jadaraa Soo, and wiped the viscous fluid off her chin. The red stain of Jared's blood on Lin's pale white flesh slowly absorbed into the mesh fabric of her skin as the protruding vampiric tentacles writhed back into the shape of two extended canine teeth. The sentient blood parasite was efficient. No drop was wasted. The greedy veins under Lin's perpetually decaying epidermis drew down the warm liquid; it consumed all – every drop, except those beaded on Lin's silver locket. The vile, poisonous metal could keep those droplets. Lin's Jadaraa Soo purred, emanating soft gyrations of pleasure to its host.

From the cold, glass eye of the security camera in the back of the store, the video recorder witnessed the carnal crime and how the dark haired woman strode to the cash register, pressed a few keys, and emptied the drawer of all its paper bounty when it popped opened. Lin stuffed the loose cash into her front pockets and jumped back over the checkout counter like hopping a fence. She headed to the automotive section as Z slowly rose from her kill.

"I rode my horse to town today and a gas pump we did pass," the whimsical viper sang on blood-covered lips. "I pulled 'im up and I hollered whoa! Said fill 'im up with gas. The man picked up a monkey wrench and wham! He changed my tune. You got me chasin' rabbits, spittin' out teeth, and howlin' at the moon."

Z hovered over Mukesh's shriveled corpse a few seconds as her parasite absorbed the splattered blood that decorated her soulless face before sprinting to the Manager's office. There, she scurried to find the security camera's video recorder and spied Lin on a tiny monitor carrying an armload of containers to the ravaged cash register. Z hit the eject button on the ancient video recorder and continued singing the Hank William's song.

"Well, I took one look at you and it almost drove me mad. And then I even went and lost what little sense I had. Now, I can't tell the day from night, I'm crazy as a loon. You got me chasin' rabbits, pullin' out my hair, and howlin' at the moon."

The violent punk stepped from the short darkened hallway into the body of the store, full of vim and vigor, and raising the outmoded videocassette high above her head, shouted, "And the award for best performance in a dramatic scene goes to..."

"C'mon," Lin prodded wearily, wanting to leave.

The wily punk was having too much fun. She crossed to the sunglasses rack again as Lin tore open the tops and emptied the containers of several flammable items that she had acquired from Mukesh's fully stocked automotive section. She began dousing Jared's dry corpse and the checkout counter island, mixing a mean cocktail. The titillating pulse of the kill hadn't settled her any. The warmth of Jared's blood, though soothing to the beast beneath her skin, only added to the icky-Vegas flavor riding her bones.

The tiny red veins that mapped Z's eyes and dove down the black holes of her pupils pulsated. They had grown fat and engorged on another's forced charity as the vampire tried on different pairs of sunglasses, one after the other.

"You sure we gotta do this?"

Z tossed the unwanted eyewear to the floor, hitting Mukesh's corpse.

"Yup."

Lin grabbed a pack of smokes from the cigarette rack above the cash register.

"You know she hates me." Another pair of unneeded sunshades hit the floor.

"Yup."

Z turned her head this way and that, examining the hot Hollywood look that the dark rimmed spectacles gave her.

"It'll be her fuckin' funeral if she steps to me again."

Lin chuckled, an annoying huff. Her fingers plucked a Zippo lighter from a little impulse display, flipped open the top, and struck the flint. A beautiful orange triangle of flame lingered above the gas spout as the vampire lit the cigarette that dangled between her lips. She sucked the smoke in and remembered a time when birthing a flame was a lot harder to create than picking up such an everyday item as a lighter. Her Jadaraa Soo, Lin's veiny nightmare companion, jittered from the bitter tasting smoky nicotine.

Z pulled the hot Hollywood look off her face, tossed it to the floor, and scooped up yet another offering from the self-standing display. She modeled the sunglasses in the little rectangle mirror noticing her jaw line. Angular and cut like a Greek statue. Her Jadaraa Soo slithered over the bone. Lin tossed the easy fire over the counter and watched as it landed on Jared's dead body, igniting the rancid cocktail. Z liked the new look and pushed the rack over as she headed toward the door. The plastic display crashed to the floor with the finality of movement, cracking and spilling its vital low cost objects like a shattered coconut.

"Thanks for the good time, boys," eulogized Lin as she held the door open for her wild friend.

Now, at least, she might be able to get a break from Z and the vile parasite. Lin hoped. With a belly full of blood, fire at their heels, and dawn still miles away, the prospect wasn't certain. She would have to get over the fact that the young vampire was dying if she were ever going to stop derailing the ritual. It'd been at least ten years since they last passed this way and Lin felt the pull stronger than ever. As the two desperados climbed back into their getaway car and fired it up, the clank of the Security Tape hitting other past memorabilia in the cluttered backseat ignited the rest of Date with the Night blaring back to life.

The song's driving rhythm crunched from rolled down windows orchestrating wounded stars to look upon the murder of two more innocent souls. *Yeah, Yeah, Yeah.* The fire consumed Jared's picture of Amber as it ate his iPhone. The paperwork in the bin under the checkout counter crumbled to ash as it reached Mukesh's toes. The callused killers sped away into the dawning night as the hot horror blazed in the little store off Highway 95. Flames took root and climbed to the rafters of the roof like playful children up a treehouse.

Pulmonary Artery.
Semilunar Vein.
Right Ventricle, Left Ventricle.
Superior Vena Cava

Wednesdays are always a disaster.

Tricuspid Valve.
Septum.
Mitral Valve.
Pulmonary Vein.
Aortic Valve.

Sounds more like a carburetor than a heart.

"The outer covering is a thin, strong membrane called the Pericardium."

     Pericardium. Sarah rolled the word around her brainpan again, listening to the echo, as she looked up from her book and gazed out the bus window. It pulled away from the stop. A slow lurch, tugs and pulls, spitting out several puffs of black acrid exhaust, groaning into gear. Sarah's stomach felt like lead.

Pyloric Portion.
Fundus.
Hydrochloric acid.
Pepsin.

I should have taken a Tums.

     Prescribing her own medication and she wasn't even out of medical school yet! Wednesday's were *always* a disaster. Hard to focus. Test on Friday. Wednesday was when she went back to work. Sometimes she got both Monday and Tuesday off. But it was rare since they started helping her with tuition. Got her working more now.

That guy's looking at me again.

     Sarah ducked her head into the binding of the book, trying not to think about it. Today's not Tuesday. She'd have enough guys staring at her soon enough; gawking at her, whistling over watered down drinks, pulling faded wads of cash out of moldy pockets to toss at her like surrogate cumshots; sticking Washingtons down her brazier that should've gone home to their families.

Can't the fuckers wait?!

Right Ventricle, Left Ventricle.
Pulmonary Artery.
Hyrodchloric Acid…Shit!

Her heart felt like it was in her stomach! Sarah glanced up from the cold, hard pages of her textbook. *Yeah.* He was still doing it. *What's his malfunction? Probably lives with his Mommy.* Sarah's eyes grew calloused and bitter. *Men!* Bile formed in the back of her esophagus. She should have taken an antacid. She was almost at the Club.

Sarah turned back around, closed the book, and jammed it into her bag getting ready to depart the bus. *Today's not Tuesday. Test on Friday.* As the hard corners and the flat painted sides of the strip club loomed into the oncoming distance from Sarah's porthole window she dug her painted nails into the thick plastic cushion of the seat. *Another day, another dollar.*

Her thoughts collided with gritting teeth. *Time to shine. Bury the light, live the fantasy. Everyone's got a fantasy. It makes the hard and boring go down easy. Think of it in terms of medicinal. I'm doing them a favor. I'm the doctor. I'm helping them to live their tired, pathetic lives.* "Yeah…Right. Medicinal." Sarah huffed and sighed as the bus pulled up to the familiar stop, an insufflate cardiac wheeze. *Who am I fooling?*

That guy is still watching me. Sarah stood; head bent low, and shook the lies from the soft cotton curls of her light sandy brown hair. She walked the solid black plastic runner that divided the bus to the hiss of swooshing doors.

Men? It's like dancing for a bunch of fucking vampires!

On stage, she tried not to think about Derrick, mentally running through her notes on the human circulatory system, going through the motions. She didn't need him on her mind now. A test loomed like circling vultures. Her flat, sultry abdomen undulated in a sensual wave as she jutted her ass and breast to the meager crowd, dancing. She grabbed the pole and twirled, opening her legs like an autopsy, and inspired a few more dollar bills to hit the stage floor.

She worked the front of the crowd. That guy with "FREEDOM" tattooed across the front of his fingers just stared at her blankly, like he was at the zoo. His tattoo made her think of Derrick and Sarah felt gross. She rotated her ass and coaxed more crisp green paper into the bans of her scant leather panties. She looked up and noticed her boss, Tone, behind the bar counting out earnings against receipts. *Tone was an alright fellow.* Clean. Dressed nice. Sarah had no illusions about it. He was her pimp. *More or less.* If it wasn't for the fact that the Detroit born man had been paying for her semesters then she wouldn't be up here on this dance floor shakin' her ass or putting it into a seat at the

University. She justified it. Weighed the end against the means and did her best to push Mr. Freedom, and Derrick, from her mind.

Pulmonary Artery.
Semilunar Vein.
Right Ventricle, Left Ventricle.
Superior Vena Cava
Tricuspid Valve.
Septum.
Mitral Valve.
Pulmonary Vein.
Aortic Valve.

She was going to be a doctor.

Pericardium…Pericardium…

Hellbent and full of fury, if need be, she was gonna make it. She wasn't gonna to be like her Momma, subject to the whims of a constant string of loser boyfriends, barely able to make enough ends meet to keep her trailer tied to one spot. Sarah was going to be a doctor. So, if she needed to play the doctor of love for a little while to get her standing on her own two feet then that's all there was to it. Better this than some asshole that only understood I-Love-You if it was tattooed across his fist. *Fuck!* Sarah grabbed the pole. Feeling pride swell within her bare chest like Derrick's hardening cock, she twirled and slid to the front of the stage and buried her luscious round beauties in the face of a willing and eager customer. His twenty-dollar offering felt nice tucked between the leather ban against her ass.

It felt like success.

After the dance, Sarah hit the bathroom and went straight to the dressing room to change and clock out for the night. She'd already done three shows and still had a lot of studying to do. She was agitated. A jumbled ball, hard to focus, she needed to light a fire under her butt and catch the next bus.

"Eddie's looking for you," Brina said as Sarah slid into the portal beside her.

"Shit."

"Giirrrlll," the Latino lovely stretched as she saw her friend's face.

"You got more bags under those eyes than Zsa Zsa Gabor got luggage." She turned back around, applying her mascara in the lighted mirror. "But you know better than to make that man come lookin' for you."

"Yeah, I know," grumbled Sarah as she wiped makeup off her face. "I have a big test coming up and...."

"Ms. Thing!" Came Eddie's voice booming from the doorway. "You got a dance in room seven. You know you suppose ta' see me after each show."

Sarah's sigh pulled her shoulders down and she begrudgingly turned to the large, round manager wanting nothing more than to change back into her street civvies and hit the bricks.

"I have a test that I have to study for."

"So, you don't want your job then. That's it?"

The fat bastard stared at her puffing on a cigar blunt.

"I didn't say that..."

"Guess I have ta' go tell Tone you got betta' things ta' do than business with that tiny, little ass of yours." His eyes scanned her up and down like a three-day-old Prime Steak dinner. "Don't know why they even ask for you. You ain't got enough meat on them bones to wet my gorgeous appetite let 'lone pay us back. I told Tone not to give you a single dime in advance, 'cause you simply couldn't cut it."

Sarah bit her tongue, feeling trapped.

"Thought so," he gloated, filling the dressing room with damp Cuban smoke. "Now, get that skinny ass to room seven. Special Request! Or, pay me my money and get the fuck outta my building." He turned like he was going to leave, but stopped. "Oh...and yous gots ta' do another show."

Eddie's smile hit Sarah in the chest like a tattooed fist that read: *I Love You.* He waddled away leaving a thin, vapor trail of rancid smoke.

"Fuck!" Sarah swung back around and glared angry in the mirror.

"It's not that bad," Offered Brina trying to console her. "It'll be over before you know it."

The wanna-be doctor sighed heavily and picked up a makeup brush to reapply the costume she had just wiped away. Her eyes were red, swollen, and heavy with water. She caught her reflection in the silver-backed glass and the look of her Momma stared at her. Sarah threw the brush and pushed her makeup away, breaking into tears.

"How am I supposed to even pass the damn thing!"

"Hey. It's all right," Brina said as she took the young woman into her arms. "You'll work it out-"

"How?!" The task loomed over her like an impassable mountain. "When do I have the time to do anything?! I'm barely passing. Can't sleep..."

"Shit, ggiirrlll." Brina rocked the little dancer. "Sleep's overrated. You're young. Get all the sleep you need once yer dead."

Sarah laughed a little and sat up. Brina always had a way of making her smile. Even if she did want to drive her fists into the belly of that fat man, Brina was right. She'd work it out. She had too! The Latino lovely turned around in her seat, grabbed a tissue, and took Sarah's face in her hands and began wiping the dancer's tears away.

"You can do this," she encouraged. "You ain't like the rest of us here. You're going places, got things to do. You know it. Just hold onto that and don't let these bastards beat you down. They ain't got nothin' on you. You're doin' what ya need to do and that's okay. Just stay focused. You know all the answers already." She smiled and eventually Sarah smiled back. "Your nose is always in those damned books. And, shit girl, you always got me...I got your back."

"Yeah?"

Brina looked at the girl and it was solid in her eyes. "Yeah."

Sarah took Brina's hand, squeezed, and thanked her.

"Go on now," said Brina dissipating the tender moment. "Do this thing. We can bounce some questions later in between."

"You sure?"

"Suurrree," intoned the dancer as she stood and checked herself once over in the lighted mirror.

"Thanks," said Sarah again softly, meaning it from the worried bottom of her tired soul.

She picked up the makeup brush and stared at the black bags under her eyes.

"No problem," said Brina dismissing it with a wave of the hand. "How else I'm gonna get free heath care. Sure as shit ain't by shakin' my ass in this place."

The Latino lovely offered a quaint chuckle and Sarah tried to smile. The woman cocked her eyebrows, squeezed Sarah's shoulder, and exited the dressing room to take her turn on the pole. Once Brina was gone Sarah's body drooped. The hand holding the makeup brush fell to her side as she peered blankly ahead. Hate churned in her chest as she stared into her own eyes through the lighted mirror. This place was sucking the life right out of her.

Room Seven. Special Request. That meant leather.

Sarah quickly put her face back on and decided that whoever the client was in Room Number Seven he was going to get a special treat, all right. She was going to bring her whip this time around. And she intended to use it! He wanted a *special* dance. A leather-clad prom queen. *Okay. He was going to get one. And if that meant blood was gonna be spilled in this carnival meat factory then it sure as shit ain't gonna be mine!*

Sergeant John Wallace walked atop the charred rubble of the Priyaranjan's convenience store. The acrid smoke and false campfire smell couldn't cover up the scent of burnt human remains. *Putrid.*

"Hhrrmm," grumbled the leathery faced Sergeant as he stepped on a pair of melted sunglasses.

The whole thing had an all too familiar vibe tugging at the pit in his gut.

"M.O. appears the same," affirmed Lieutenant Mauldune as she stepped up to the veteran police detective in her smart shoes, holding her notebook open. "An accelerant was used, localized near the bodies; ignited for maximum incineration. Fire spread outward from the register. Most likely something from the store." She flipped her notebook shut and surveyed the grim remains. "We'll get the full report in a few days and know for sure."

"It's them," Wallace uttered from a stern face. "Got their stink all over it."

"If so," the detective announced. "Then that means they're back."

"Apparently."

Wallace picked up a piece of burnt wood that used to be a part of the building's roof.

"If they continue the pattern like last time," the Lieutenant declared, "that means they're heading East."

The bitter sergeant tossed the charred piece of wood completely unlike skipping stones across the ocean's surface. It landed with a tiny clank. Two ambulance attendants walked past them carrying the well-done husk of one of the two men that were trapped in the fire. Wallace's eyes dropped to the black plastic body bag. Its filled folds were all too familiar. Wallace lifted his gaze to the Indian woman crying with her daughter, arm-in-arm, just outside of the police line. *They don't need to see this.*

"Poor bastard," he muttered.

Lieutenant Mauldune looked up from the body bag to her partner. She wasn't with Phoenix Metro when Wallace worked a similar scene where his nephew, Stephen, was killed in exactly the same way. From what she learned around the water cooler Wallace found out for certain that it was his nephew in the blaze from the Medical Examiner's report. *Hell of a way to learn that you just lost kin.* Kate empathized with the man, but couldn't even begin to understand what he must be going through right now, reliving that horror. His eyes were like two glassy steel bars of rancor.

They'd gotten word about the fire over the radio. John went stark white and quiet and didn't tell her where he was driving until they were almost there. He had more years and experience with Phoenix than she did, but she had the rank. In the small town from where she'd transferred she had risen quickly through the department from a few lucky busts. She'd reached the glass ceiling there and wanted something more. A bit of excitement, really. Coming to the big city, working with the seasoned grumbler, gave her more all right. John had seen enough of the brutal underbelly of humanity to make him cold, make him blow jurisdiction to trek all the way to Bullhead City on a hunch.

From what little she knew of the case ten years ago, the Sergeant's nephew and two others were murdered at work. A possible robbery or drug connection to one of the other victims was pursued. Each of the casualties had their throats torn out and the convenience store was burned to destroy evidence. The killers were never brought to justice. That kind of unanswered crime was just the kind of thing that kept gnawing at a man if he let it. Could consume him if he wasn't strong enough. The Sergeant was never one to get too carried away with his feelings or even talk like he had them. But Kate knew they were there. She knew he was feeling something. That his stomach had to be pulling itself into tiny balls and knots about now.

"Maybe it's not even them," she tried offering an alternative view. "Maybe-"

"It's them."

Ignoring the Lieutenant, he walked back to the car. Mauldune sighed and looked at the black ground feeling stupid and followed him to the unmarked police cruiser. She had to do it. He couldn't button himself up like this. He was a big man, had the years on the force. He knew the score.

"You know it's not our concern, Sarge?" she hollered after him. "Locals got the lead on this and if you're right, they're outta State by now. Federal Jurisdiction. The Chief is all ready to haul our keisters in a sling for breaching city limits. "

"Hhhrrmm."

The Sergeant opened the driver side door and glanced up at the sky. He took a long minute staring at those slow moving Arizona clouds and felt cool breezes brush over him lightly. He pulled a grim face down and looked at the women who'd just lost their husband and father speaking with one of Bullhead City's finest. John thought about the look on his sister's face when he told her about Stephen and how she and her husband held one another as he delivered the news – *two lonely souls adrift in a sea of pain.* The Indian women held each other in the exactly same manner now.

"Kate," he said after a time. "You're a good cop. You don't want nothin' to do with this."

"Sarge?" she pleaded with him.

He only raised his eyebrows, saying to her in his silent reproach, *'I'm not letting these sick fucks get away with it again.'* He slid behind the steering wheel.

"Sarge..." *He had to see reason!*

He leaned across the seat. "You can get a ride from one of the other units."

Damn him! A ball formed in Kate Mauldune's chest. She knew what he was going to do. He was going to run off, be all cavalier and John Wayne, and bring in the two suspects that he'd been gunning for since his nephew Stephen had been senselessly murdered. It was macho and bullheaded, and she knew he knew it. And worse yet, she knew he didn't give a damn. This was exactly the kind of thing that she was hoping to avoid when she found out the circumstances of their two-hour drive across the desert. *The Chief is going to hand him his ass if I let him do this.* Against her better judgement Mauldune opened the passenger side door and slid into the seat and confronted Wallace's hardened gaze.

She stammered, nervous like a June fly, and then heard a different set of words tumble from her mouth than what she had planned to say. To her own surprise, Kate uttered, "Let's do it."

Wallace just stared at her. "Hhrrmmm?"

She stared back, but didn't growl. Any second now and she'd loose her nerve. She wished that he'd just start the car and get going. Kate closed her door and sealed the deal as a handful of codes and regulations that they were about to break flitted through her head. Wallace fired up the unmarked ride and together they set off like some great cowboy movie across the plains of a southwestern sky.

May 9, 1934.

The road ahead was impassable. The sky was a solid brown, twirling mess, revolving around some hidden stormy center creating a deathly wall of sand. It smelled of tilled earth and dry leaves. There was an electrical charge in the air. Jordan gripped the steering wheel. He bent his head low and a blond lock fell across his face as he accidentally drove into the gigantic wall of dirt. He'd thought the horizon was farther off than it was, moving at a pace that astonished the young vampire. Juliana, in the seat next to him, grabbed his thigh as a million pounding flakes of topsoil assaulted the Ford Coupe. It rocked back and forth so violently that Jordan half expected the tiny automobile to take flight. Even the smarmy comments from Prophet had fallen off and the brutish vamp was quiet in the back seat at the awesome power of the storm.

Jordan had hoped to connect with Highway 528 and take them all to a safe harbor around the storm. But deep in the thick of it, his only hoped was that the swirling madness would soon pass them by, moving along its enormous path across the Great Plains, and they'd come out the other side, continuing on their way unscathed. Yet, after a few moments, pounding gusts against howling bursts, jostled in their seats, the five travelers knew they were in trouble. He depressed the small metal gas pedal and hunkered down doing his best to keep the car on the road. After a few more minutes he was sure that he'd missed the turn onto 528. Now they were lost. Visibility was nil and he wasn't even sure if they were on the road anymore.

Juliana started to panic, pressing her hands to the edges of the windows attempting to keep the sand from seeping into the vehicle. Lin watched her with a feeling of growing dread as the vampire complained. Lin pulled her coat tighter around her shoulders, nestled tightly in the back seat between Prophet and Ramielle Eirinhas.

"Calm yourselves," Ramielle told Juliana. "Losing your head isn't going to help matters any."

They were returning to Los Angeles from New York, and had managed to get through most of the Midwest without hitting any sandstorms. They'd been lucky. But Henry's little engine wasn't designed for this type of weather and soon the carburetor choked as if strangled and pistons ground against mud in their chambers. The automobile sputtered and coughed, and eventually stopped.

Jordan hit the steering wheel. "That's it, she's dead. We aren't going anywhere."

"What are we going to do?" Juliana's voice cracked. "We can't stay here. The sand keeps pouring in."

"Relax," mouthed the cool, sultry voice of their coven leader. "Can you fix it when the storm passes?

Jordan turned around in his seat and looked Ramielle in her grave chocolate eyes and apologized. The Spanish woman leaned back in her seat, thoughtfully. Lin turned to her and saw real worry displayed on Ramielle's face for the first time since she'd known her. Though she had to admit it, the vampire queen hid it fairly well from her brood.

"This looks to be a doozy too," muttered Jordan, peering outside his window at the dark and unnatural air. "I think we're going to be here for awhile."

Prophet laughed, a soft, soothing chuckle that unnerved everybody, and Jordan's eyes flicked hard at him. Lin felt the Bohemian's body jiggle in the seat next to her as he combated the raging storm with his awkward sense of humor.

"The sun will be up in a few hours," commented Juliana.

"There are bound to be farmhouses near by," added Jordan, hopefully.

Prophet's laughter burst loud in the small shell of the Ford's cab. It stabbed their ears like a concussion grenade.

"I don't hear you offering up anything useful," chided the driver.

"Like it matters," the hyena voiced.

"Enough," ordered Ramielle.

Her men fell silent and the din of the storm clamored more violently. Ramielle didn't see any other choice. They had to abandon the vehicle and seek shelter. The storm wasn't abating; it was growing stronger. She could feel its electrical pulse bristling across her skin, raising the soft, fine hairs along her forearms. Even if they stayed in the car they wouldn't be able to drive it anywhere once the storm broke. They were going to get caught out in the open come dawn, one way or the other. *Best to keep moving. Find a place to hole up for the day.*

"We have a better chance out there than we do in here."

Nobody said anything to Ramielle's comment. The storm raged against their tiny shell, a havoc of noisy moments. A few short breaths passed between them and she ordered everybody out of the car with clear instructions to stay close by it. Already the vehicle was being buried where it had rolled to a stop. Bitter, hard, howling madness beat against them. Lin didn't believe that they'd find anything in this mess. She'd been through the tail end of the Midwest before. It was hard enough to find good shelter on a clear night. Farmhouses were stretched thin across long patches of flat nothingness. How then were they to locate a possible host in this crazy weather?

Surely, God had turned against man. These sandstorms that had been ravaging the country over the past few years were biblical in nature. Lin wasn't a devoted believer of anything. But witnessing the ground take to the sky and roar like angry bees was enough to make any honest vampire reconsider the Son of Man. When she stepped from the vehicle Lin knew she'd never see the little Ford again. It had that vibe.

They only had a few hours of night left. As strange as the storm was, its thick blanket of surging dust could shield them from the eventual climb of the sun if they were still in it come dawn. Lin figured that even if they were lucky enough to last until morning it wouldn't matter. They, like their auto, were going to choke. Even the Jadaraa Soo needed air to breathe. Sure, it prolonged their lives and gave them ungodly charms, but dirt never made for good oxygen.

Ramielle pulled her cloak tighter about her person and huddled close to Jordan and the others. "What do you think?"

Jordan looked through the black blizzard, dazed with no sense of direction or landscape. "That way's as good as any."

The tawny-skinned coven leader looked to her small brood. Now was the time for suggestions; Lin had nothing to stay. Prophet stood beside her, quiet.

"Okay," the tall dark-eyed mistress announced. " Let's do it. Everyone stay close. Tight group. Been through worse than this."

Confidently, she started walking in the direction that Jordan had pointed out. The others followed her. Jordan took Juliana's hand and held her close. She was frightened. The wind whipped around them, trying desperately to knock them over. A few feet away from the abandoned vehicle Lin tossed a look back. The coupe was practically buried. A few more steps away from the familiar shape of the two-door roadster and it was lost in the swirling thick.

They trudged on, wading through dunes as high as their knees and as low as a flat rock. Twenty minutes in and they were most definitely lost amid a turbulent sea of spiraling dirt. A stronger gale ripped through them, cold and bitter. Each had to duck into their shoulders, plant their feet, and block their faces from the sandpaper winds. In the gust, Jordan let go of Juliana's hand to block his face. He struggled to see and breathe as he continued on, coughing and choking on the meaty gusts. Lin stopped, unable to tell which way to move anymore. Prophet pulled along side of her and pushed.

"Keep moving! Don't stop!"

They plowed on, nestled against one another. It was hard to see a foot in front of one's own face. Pressing forward, Jordan looked to see Juliana at his back. But his dirt-laden eyes saw only twisting thick dusts, heavy and lonely, without Juliana's lovely form. Fear gripped him and he stopped cold in his tracks. He turned about, but she wasn't anywhere. Lin noticed him and stopped too.

"Juliana!" the vampire called, his voice crushed in the heathen winds. "Juliana!"

It took Lin a few seconds to piece it together. Juliana had vanished. Lin rent her voice to the deafening winds, joining Jordan's frantic calls to reconnect with his lover. Lin's long, dark hair beat about her face and neck as her impaired sight, ravaged by the blinding sand bore witness – *God's disaster and appetite had swallowed Juliana whole.* Prophet and Ramielle also stopped and began calling out for their wayward sister. Against the furious maelstrom the four vampires shrieked and cried, screaming out the poor girl's name. "Juliana! Juliana!" But she was lost. Lost in the cacophony of bitter, heavy winds…

Through the rearview mirror Lin watched the spirals of dust and dirt swirling around the back end of the Cadillac as they turned onto the little dirt road. Taillights cast a red hue to the spinning, dusty stew and ignited the memory of that night, so long ago. Z's rear-end was up in the air, bent over the front seat, digging through the backseat collection of junk in her capacity as Minister of Music. She was talking about something or other, but Lin had faded into the lush canvas of her thoughts. It seemed that the farther she drove away from LA the closer she got to reliving her past. The journey had finally set in and her hand wandered to the silver locket about her neck as the memory faded.

"What?" the preoccupied driver asked trying to reinstate herself into the conversation.

"How come we gotta stop by every time we pass this way, huh?"

Z turned right way around in the seat with a short stack of CDs.

"I told you," Lin reminded her. "She knows it if we don't. And if we don't she's gonna blame you. Neither one of us needs that kind of headache."

"Fuck her," Z blurted out as she tossed an unwanted CD into the backseat. "All of those ancient fucks are the same. Self righteous privileged pricks with their voodoo stuck up their ass."

Another CD returned to the chaos from which it came.

Lin leveled her brow. "And you wonder *why* she doesn't like you."

"What's not to like?" Z was serious.

Lin cocked a single knowing eyebrow and held her tongue. Z popped a CD into the stereo and leaned into the driver.

"You know I'm fun. I'll never grow old. I'll never die…and I'm sexy as hell." Z's words fell through Lin's gut like cold lead as the impetuous rascal drew near. *She doesn't know.* The crazy vampire coddled Lin's ear with her tongue and kissed the dangling lobe. The effect was sensual and brash and Z broke out laughing. "I am one hell of a party!"

Lin thought on it for a second, wiping her wet and sticky ear with her shoulder. *She doesn't know.* Finally, the brooding vamp conceded to the rascal's point of view, breaking her grim countenance and they both fell into the warm merriment of laughter. Though, the edge of Lin's giggle was nervous and uncomfortable, frayed by the knowledge that she alone held. Z cranked the volume on the stereo, filling the classic car with blistering tunes of modern decadence as she danced in the seat. Through the swirling haze of the dirt road that seemed to wind endlessly through untamed desert, taillights blared like little glowing devils vanishing into stark nothingness.

Ears of coyotes pricked up as the loud machine rolled past. Rabbits dashed under the false protection of sagebrush. Insects sacrificed themselves to the windshield. By the time dawn reared its nasty bright head they were nearly there. The square dome of Chateau le Rouge Mort rose in the distance and two helicopters were visible behind the bland adobe structure on the stone Helipad.

*She's throwing another party…*the warm feelings that Lin had worked so hard to muster quickly vanished as Dominique's Chateau drew closer. Sunlight crept across barren sandy dunes like a lover's hand on the hip of a woman. Lin sighed, *again?*

Inside, after narrowly escaping a sunbathing they parked in the above-ground garage and were led through the subterranean, hand-bored tunnel to the Chateau's buried chambers. Construction on the magnificent feat that was Chateau le Rouge Mort began in 1958 a few years after Lin took permanent residence in Los Angeles. It was completed in the winter of '67. Except for the solid protruding ground-level garage entrance the entire domicile was underground. The construction site was chosen particularly for its mass of hardened bedrock under the wispy desert. Lin knew Dominique had it built so that she could maintain a vigilant eye on her former consort and lover. Even after a hundred-and-fifty-some-odd-years since they first broke up Jaci still couldn't let her darling Linnet go. She had to remain constant, shining down like the moon, watching her. But the ardent Ex did not want to appear to be so obtrusive and so the southwestern retreat was the closest length of leash that she thought Lin would tolerate.

Dominique's Personal Assistant, Clyde, led Lin and Z to the main hall. Svelte and quiet, it appeared that she had been waiting for them. *Was Araci so predictable in her actions that Jaci could set a decade tide by her?* Dominique's arrogance was already too much too bear, and to be greeted with formal introductions, like they had never met, was putting Lin off. She had known the assistant for over a hundred years. She knew her habit to inhibit characters, but wasn't expecting it, or the party. The last time Lin had seen her former mistress's aide, she was going by Margaret, was fond of flower dresses, and had just shaved her head bald as a cue ball. Now, she was dressed in a snazzy business suit, had Margaret's haircut, was sporting decorative tribal tattoos across her dome, and carried herself with an air of disinterested confidence. If the girl wanted to be called Clyde now, what did she care. *Really, it doesn't matter.*

Lin frowned at her vulnerable common certainty. Dominique's dominion over her still seemed to permeate like an invisible vapor to even the farthest boundaries that Lin pushed. There was no escaping her former dark mistress. In this, Linnet Pevensey did not know if she should be thankful or rudely pissed. She owed the great monarch of night much and still had love for her, though it was not the disillusioned vibrancy it once was.

Lin noticed that several of the decorations in the quarter-mile tunnel had changed. Some of the same tapestries and statues remained, but there were many new additions, none recent or modern in design. Their presence spoke an uneasy undercurrent of longing in their owner.

Only one who had an intimate knowledge of the Lady De'Paul would be able to detect such pronounced feelings on display through the mere arrangement of artifacts. It was sad, and Lin was unsure if it was better to recognize these subtle cries and inquire of them with the mistress of the house or feign blissful ignorance. The shutters on her soul concerning the Vam Pŷr had been shut for quite some time. *Dusting them off now may not be such a wise decision.* Opening old wounds could hurt. Their days of basking in each other's light were over.

Yet, there it hung among the other additions to the entranceway collection. Master Reynolds' portrait of her. It spoke more loudly than the other pieces and drove the point home that Dominique missed her highborn lady from the Opera. Her mind was tempered from bygone days and like a staunch candidate waiting for death she lived in her memories.

"Awww," said Z, stopping to stare at the painting, drawing the sound out like southern fried chicken. "So cute! And with little bows too." The brash vamp laughed.

"Fuck off."

Lin found nothing funny about it. Dominique's heart was oozing all over the place! The portrait had not been hung since Lin abandoned her in São Paul, Brazil, after she returned from building her Council. It was shipped to France, covered, and placed in an attic among other painful treasures where it collected copious mounds of dust. Now here it was, restored to its former glory. Even the fire damage that her portrait received the night Inácio Braga attacked had been repaired.

To make matters worse chamber music began filtering up the sloping access from the main hall. The frank disgust awash on Z's face was a button for how Lin felt internally, though for completely different reasons. Z's distaste was simply in the music's style; too dull and baroque. Lin's distaste was in the message that the music carried. It was a continuation of all the visual uneasiness that she had so far endured. If Clyde's presence at the tunnel's entrance did not hint at Dominique's omnipresence then surely this choice of orchestration did.

It was the allegro to Antonio Vivaldi's L'estro Armonico, a concerto for two violins, cello, and strings in D minor. Lin recalled the first time she heard the piece. *Vienna, 1772.* She and Dominique had just attended a concert by Joseph Hayden for Prince Nikolaus, which was thrown by the Prince's personal physician and his wife Maria Anna. The middle-aged composer had performed selected works of his Sun Quartets and an after party had ensued at the Genzinger's estate. It was a wicked affair. One to remember and Lin smirked.

In the late eves of morning after compliments and wine led through the personality of flesh the Maestro revealed in part his inspiration for his six-string Opus to the sun. Vivaldi. Lin had never heard of him. The Red Priest had passed before her birth, but Dominique knew of him and of his works. It pleased the Lady De'Paul that such an aficionado as Master Hayden gave not only praise, but accreditation and love to this magnificent musician. Joseph had many of Vivaldi's Concertos with him abroad and birthed, from a leather satchel, his hand written copies for the pale lady to peruse. The Maestro was studying them, as he said, *"because there dwelt genius in his quill."*

Upon Dominique's request Master Hayden rousted a tangle of musicians from their rooms, pulled them as they lay barely clothed with their companions to take up their instruments and join him in his room. As the mostly naked ensemble played the symbiont's request she whispered in Linnet's warm, human ear.

"Of all the worlds, from all the lands, this song sang to me of your arrival in my heart. Now, here, on this night, I can no more outwardly express this love better than the collection of notes that do kiss thee."

As they neared the wide-open space at the mouth of the tunnel, and the allegro continued to wind its memory charm about Lin's waist, the bored-out walls of this underground palace began to feel as if they were closing in. The Vam Pŷr's daughter truly felt buried, suffocated by such garish displays of open longing and lost affections.

The main hall was mostly lit by candlelight, though intertwining strings of soft blue runner lights trimmed the ceiling, casting an angelic glow to the sky-painted canopy. The blue lights glinted and reflected off protruding metal chains and full-body leather suits that wound at their ends. Inside the sightless and soundless submissive garments were the party's unfortunate Sanglants. Sharp metal spouts punctured the blood-lender's vital arteries and filled the dangling thin, lengthy tubes with bright red fluid. Dominique's guests could easily replenish their appetites by twisting the valve at the end of the tube, enjoying hospitality and mirth, at the expense of taping the Sanglants like wine barrels. Lin wondered if The Council had sanctioned such abuse of resource. *Who am I fooling?* Dominique *was* The Council. *More or less, these days.* She created it. *Her control is flagrant.*

True to form, a nude blindfolded quartet played Vivaldi's

reminiscent score in one of the many alcoves that adorned the spacious room. Their wooden string instruments filled the great hall with lush song and Lin could think of nothing other than that night in Vienna, that beautiful night so very long ago. Though if Lin thought the additions to the collection and choice of audio accompaniment pointed to Dominique's heart and how she wore it on her sleeve, then the contrasting scene within the main hall conveyed tormented misgivings of the Vam Pŷr's darker nature and bitter age. *My former love is not herself.* In another alcove, two mortal women seduced a bound and gagged mortal man in a bizarre S & M show, and in still another alcove, actors improvised a divine comedy of lost carnality. Decadence and depravity, the rapacity of lust, flourished and were amply abound throughout the room.

A grotesque circus of callous opulence, it made Lin restless and she began tugging at the silver locket around her neck. Toward the back of the main hall was a magnificent arrangement of exotic fruits, lavish hand crafted cakes, and three special dishes prepared by the queen bee's personal chef. This delicious array was not just for Dominique's human guests, but for vampires with a nasty food fetish. Lin spied two gorged fanatics slinking away from the enormous spread of edibles, down a pink-lit hallway to where physicians waited to cram hoses up their bums and shovel them down their throats to eviscerate the chewables from their unmoving bowels.

Prominent vampires and humans littered the chamber, attired in various periods of dress from different continents and countries. It appeared that all those stored boxes of gowns and jackets, shoes and jewelry that had gone out of favor over the centuries were once again unearthed by their night-dwelling lords, and dusted off for the caprice delight. It was a spectacle of undead haberdashery, a monument to the onslaught of time and periods of Man. Both Lin and Z stood out from the crowd in their casual garb, looking as if they had just wandered in from a rock concert. Clyde took her leave as they entered the main hall and Lin saw the color in Dominique's cheeks rise upon seeing her.

Jaci wore an elegant black dress with an opened back. Her silky, dark Persian hair was done up and adorned with jewels. The mulatto tone of her soft amber skin was paler than what Lin remembered. Her complexion was aging white, reflective of the beasts that had transformed her. The Matron of Night even had her Jadaraa Soo pulled down so that its crisscrossing veins would not disrupt the unbroken tapestry of her sublime flesh. An immediate sadness welled up in Lin and she felt a flashing need to protect her former lover's perceived fragile condition.

"I mean it, Z," the dark haired belle whispered. "If you fuck with her I'll have to put you down."

The comment was flippant and unexpected. Z was shocked. And on top of it, to add insult to verbal injury, the queen bitch was walking over to them now.

"My child," Dominique offered with wide loving arms, speaking in French. "Oh my gentle spirit, you have come home."

She kissed both sides of Lin's cheeks in the European fashion and flashed hard eyes at Z. Dominique's Jadaraa Soo twitched in constant ado as she enveloped Lin in a gracious and warm embrace. Upon parting she took her former maid by the shoulders, saying "if even for a little while."

"How could I not," returned Lin, also in French.

It's called a gas pedal you stupid cow. Z had to stop herself from blurting out something crude and intrusive that would shatter the moment. The words danced on her tongue, but she did not use them. She was pissed at Lin, disliked being around Dominique, and this wasn't her type of party.

"Yes. Well..."

Dominique's eyes inflicted judgment as she viewed Lin's petite form. Her obvious displeasure of the vampire's choice of accompaniment was more than evident. She didn't even try to hide it this time. Instead, she played the stoic host and led her one-time lover into the grand hall, introducing her to guests as if she was a brand new prized jewel. It made Z want to puke.

"Friends. Vagabonds. Gate Crashers." The room drew silent. "This is my daughter, Linnet...and *her*...acquaintance." Several nods folded in their direction. "You will treat her as the lady of the house, without exception. The other is…game."

Z rolled her eyes as the queen bitch's pretentiousness smacked her like a vase of flowers. *At least the dislike is mutual.* Lin looked back at the vivacious punk as Dominique escorted her into the throng, feeling like she was abandoning her friend on an unsafe shore. *Why do I always have to stop and see Dominique? Why can't I just truly break it off and be done with her once and for all? Others have.*

Squeezed into traditions, proudly on display, Lin asked herself the same loaded questions that Z had asked earlier. But before Lin could define her questioning thoughts into painful answers Dominique introduced her to a pair of regal looking gentlemen from Nepal.

A smooth, velvety voice spoke from behind Z, thick with a Hungarian accent. "My...you do come to a party well dressed."

The vampire turned. He was beautiful. Suave. Devilishly handsome and taller than herself. Immediately, and for all these reasons and more, she didn't trust him. She wasn't game.

"I love your perfume," he gently offered. "What is it? Dirt and... blood?"

He smiled playfully, laughing at his own joke, and presented the newcomer with a goblet of warm sanguine fluid. *Gorgeous.* She refused the drink.

"Bite me."

She flashed him a curt smile and started walking away. But the devilishly handsome vampire merely chuckled again, and his frivolity irked the edges of Z's tense shoulders.

"You should not tease me with such a good time."

His voice was chocolate. Z stopped. Sighed. And turned around. "You couldn't handle me if you tried."

He stepped toward her with a confident swagger. "Would you believe that's exactly what Queen Maria the First, of Portugal, said to me in 1780 just before..."

The charming devil wiped the rest of the sentence away with the curl and flash of his hand, acting nonchalant. Z raised her eyebrows waiting for him to continue. The mysterious man only smirked.

"Before what?" Z finally asked, taking the bait. The hook was set.

"Now, there's an interesting story." He moved closer, passing the chalice of blood to the newcomer, and placed a pale hand to the small of her back. "I'm Edward, by the way."

Offering the rough edged vamp his other hand, she took it. "Z."

"Is that just the end of the English alphabet or is there some hidden treasure behind it?"

"Just Z."

"Ah, so mysterious," he enjoined, leading her through the room. "I do love a lady with hidden delights."

Z sighed. *God!* She hated parties where all the people did was talk. This was going to be an excruciatingly long daylight-trapped visitation. She tried to smile, though was absolutely sure that it came out crooked.

Sarah exited the class shaking her head. She pulled her bookbag tight against her shoulder and plowed through the yard to her next class ignoring the perfectly formed clouds that floated in the clear blue New Mexican sky.

"How'd you think you did?" came a familiar voice from behind.

Sarah grumbled. Friday's test was moved up, a pop quiz. Jimmy caught up with her. He was moderately handsome, had freckles, and a cleft chin. He wore an old T-Shirt that promoted drinking because he was Irish, even though Jimmy did not have a single drop of Irish blood in him.

"You know we could get together later." The young man nervously corrected himself, "and study, if...if that is, you know, if you want?

"Yeah," piped Sarah absentmindedly. "That'd be great." She stopped walking. "But I've got work later on. And hopefully sleep at some point in between. Would you believe they have me working back to back shifts?"

"Another all-nighter, huh?"

Sarah rolled her eyes and started walking again. She and Jimmy had been friends since his high school days. He was the first person her age that she met when she moved to Albuquerque. His cousin Angie introduced them when she dropped Sarah off in the desert city several years ago. She even arranged for Sarah to stay with him and his family for a few days while the girl found her feet. But she didn't stick around that long.

"You'll find your stride," he encouraged. "It's always crazy at the beginning of a semester." He bumped her with his shoulder. "You know that. It'll mellow out."

"Yeah. I guess."

"You ready for Grimblatt's test?" he asked with a smile.

Sarah stopped abruptly and went wide-eyed. "Is that today too?!"

The look on her face alarmed the poor boy. "Next week," he said, "next week."

Sarah exhaled a sigh of relief and Jimmy realized just how far out of whack she was. He tried to make up for scaring her.

"I have great notes from yesterday's lecture. You can borrow 'em if you want. Kinda noticed how you nodded off."

"Oh God, really?" Sarah blurted out with an embarrassed smile.

"Yeah," he admitted. "You look cute when you're drooling on your desk."

"Shut up!" She bopped him with her arm. "I am not."

Jimmy smiled shyly. "I'll make you a copy."

"Thanks. That'll be great."

She peered up at him with those beautifully full doe eyes of hers and his knees went a little weak.

"Really?" he asked as if it meant something.

Sarah just smiled and shook her head. His little boy come-ons were cute and innocent. He'd been tripping over his tongue since the tenth grade. She thought he was going to ask her to his Junior Prom, but he took Miley Reynolds instead. They spent the summer together after Miley dumped him. But nothing more ever developed between them than a platonic relationship. They did make out once at a party during Jimmy's graduating year. He was completely smashed and Sarah didn't think he remembered it, but he did. Jimmy thought about it often. He's just never had the stones to do anything about it.

"I'll call ya," the scared boy said as they neared the end of the yard. "Maybe we could get together one night; you know, go over the notes, that is…if you have any questions." The look on Sarah's face dropped and Jimmy started breaking down again. "When you have the time, that is. I…I know your busy…working."

Sarah stopped and looked up at him, offering her friend a weak smile and far away eyes. "Yeah. Maybe later. I don't know." She shook her head in a tight cage and breathed a heavy sigh. "I have another class."

The air held the girl's scent as Jimmy watched her go, feeling stupid. She was obviously a wreck and now wasn't the proper time to be trying to ask her out on a date. *Stupid. Stupid. Stupid.*

"Yeah, well…later then," he threw at her back as she crossed the courtyard. "I'll text you."

Sarah waved as she disappeared into the building unaware that she took with her Jimmy's failed attempts at hooking up. The reluctant Romeo back-pedaled the way he came. Having traversed the distance away from his next class he had to double time it or he'd be late. Along the way he decided that he was going to take it slow with Sarah. Maybe invite her on a small trip over Christmas break. *Yeah, right!* He'd been going slowly with her for almost six years now. Compared to him…snails led more fascinating lives.

Dominique leaned against the arm of the sofa stroking Lin's hair and mentioned how much she liked the short tomboy look. The compliment spurred a bad taste in the young vampire's mouth as she eyed an amorous couple on the couch beside her. They supped from the wrists of a small boy. He was no more than twelve, if he was that at all. The couple kissed after each helping that they took from the child, swishing his green blood around their tongues as the parasite absorbed the rich solution. Lin thought The Council had banned such use of children in Versailles back in 1883. There was so much about this gathering that was laden with dark history. The woman herself seemed fixed there. A moment in time, disillusioned and unattained, Dominique only spoke to Lin in the language of her second home: French.

"How long should I expect you to stay this time?" she asked, fingering the woman's short-cropped hair.

Lin gently brushed Dominique's hand away. "Just the day."

"Mon Ami? You tease me so." Dominique's hand wandered back to Lin's dark locks, curling strands of hair around her agitated digits. "Must you always bring that dog with you when you come? You could leave her outside...get a little sun. She looks as if she could use it."

Lin peered up at the dark mistress. Dominique's eyes were rigid candelabras intent on burning down the image of her companion. Again, she brushed the woman's fingers away from the tangle of hair and wondered why she held so fervently to the French tongue. They spoke so many languages together. Any could find the bed for a growing conversation. Yet when Lin used a different tongue the Vam Pŷr remained firm to that of her second home. *Language used to be a reason to reinvent oneself, she recalled.* When they were together the two lovers dived into strange dialects with abandon. It renewed and invigorated the parley of their romance. Being stuck to one country unnerved the old paramour.

"Be nice," Lin uttered and turned away.

"If you wish," the woman at her side sighed.

So rarely had Lin ever heard Dominique speak her native Persian during their years together. She avoided it. Sitting under the arm of the Vam Pŷr, Lin labored to recall the few phrases that she had coaxed out of Dominique. They did not well up. Too much time had passed, centuries withheld from the mouth and the tongue grew cold. Forgetful. *Had Dominique also finally gone so long without voicing her native tongue that France had become the birthplace of her speech? After all she was but a child when she was taken from her lands.*

Lin watched the night mother as she conversed with Joshua. He was their eldest, nearly two thousand and three hundred years old. It still boggled Lin's small mind to think that someone had lived so long. That perhaps she might reach that ripe old age. It irked her to think of Z. *She roughly had another five to ten years, tops.* Once the Jadaraa Soo entered its sleep cycle the symbiont was doomed. Lin knew she was going to have to confront Z about it sooner or later. Though she didn't want to. She wanted the vibrant punk at home in LA where she could figure it out for herself. Lin sighed and brushed Dominique's fingers away.

She peered up at non-aging old man. Joshua came from what is now called Morocco and was traditionally a Moor. He too, like Dominique, originally had dark sunburnt skin that had turned pale olive-drab by the perpetual death of their Jadaraa Soo. Though he was lighter than she was. More white. Luminescent. The parasite had reconstituted his flesh to appear closer to an Omjadda. His hair was a rich mop of ebony dreadlocks that fell past his strong shoulders and chest. Lin only met him once before and she did not care for him that time either. He was an odd, regulated man that diminished her vibrant spirit with a simple gesture, a carefully placed word. He was cold and calculating in a way that made Lin feel weak, and she hated that. She hated how he always seemed to suck the attention out of the atmosphere around him as if he were feeding.

Unlike Lin's dark mistress, Joshua was never a slave of the Omjadda nor forced to work centuries in the darkened hollows of dangerous mines. He was transformed by the blood of a member of the N'um Vala'Shiya J'in, and so was spared Dominique's brutal fate of slavery. The N'um Vala'Shiya was one of the Omjadda clans that migrated to India, found god or enlightenment or some shit. Dominique said that they were the original architects of the ancient Vedic texts and Hindu gods. Lin never found it all that interesting nor read any old scrolls about them. Eastern religion held no fascination for her in the slightest. All she knew about Indian mysticism was that Shiva was the Goddess of Destruction/Creation and Z got her tattooed on her back when they rummaged across Tunisia on a whim. The fiery punk liked the way the Goddess looked with all of her arms, dancing on a mountain of skulls.

Lin was only vaguely aware that the ancient clan was known as the Dalam Vala'Shiya before the Great Migration and that over issues of direction, in both land and choice to feed on human beings, the Omjadda J'in split into two distinct families: the Dalam Kha'Shiya and the N'um Vala'Shiya. From what Dominique told her, the splintered halves were polar opposites, day and night from one another and their impact on the world.

Dominique stopped trying long ago to get Lin interested in their history. When they were together the consort feigned interest for her mistress's sake, but once they were no longer lovers she gave up. The need to learn about the Omjadda to manage Dominique's affairs was moot. After all, she had only met one once. The English lass remained on the fringes of Dominique's affairs with The Council. For Lin, they were just creatures from old stories and blood memories that happened to somebody else. Without the grand matriarch at her center her interest in the ancient species waned. Even hearing about them in Dominique's letters ingrained bitterness on her heart as the grand matriarch toiled to build her Council, traveling throughout Europe and Asia. To Lin, back then, separated from the woman, pining for her from across the sea, dealing with her affairs in Brazil, she didn't care that the N'um Vala'Shiya was the first Omjadda J'in to recognize the authority of The Council. Nor did she care to learn that the Dalam Kha'Shiya was the last J'in to offer recognition. By then Lin and Dominique were arguing, tearing each other down, brick by brick, with hard words and cold shoulders.

Lin's fingers wandered to her oval necklace. Her Jadaraa Soo retreated from the vile silver mineral, diving farther from the vampire's pale digits as she rubbed the artifact slowly. She knew Joshua helped Dominique win the slave revolts. She understood how important he was to their kind and that without him Dominique would have never have escaped the Tien Däm Mu J'in. She would have died there among Ornn's great house and Lin would have wasted away in England taking care of her sick father centuries ago. Nothing would be as it is now. The existential thought was only vaguely amusing. Though Joshua was instrumental in freeing their race from the clutches of the Omjadda, the last time that Lin had heard anything about him he was occupying the bed of Isabela da Nóbrega. Lin couldn't forget what she had tried to do to Dominique and her son. So, there was *nothing* that she cared to converse about with Joshua, despite the fact that it appeared that he and her former lover had plenty to share at her elbow.

Isabela had plotted to kill the Vam Pŷr. She stole Linnet's son, William. She usurped Dominique's land holdings and disrupted the ownership of her mines at Minas Gerais with the bloody Portuguese. She was an unholy terror that deserved nothing short of a sword and the touch of the sun. Regardless that all of this happened long before she'd undergone her transformation to become a Child of Evensong, when she and the night mother were consummate lovers, it still made Lin hot. William was just a baby and that vampire bitch used him to lure Dominique into a failed ambush. Just thinking about Isabela made Lin's skin crawl. She would never forgive her. *Not ever!*

Thoughts churned, twisting knives in Lin's gut just as fresh as the day, over two hundred years ago. It angered Lin that Isabela had survived Dominique's assassination attempt at the turn of the Twentieth Century. Nearly burned the whole city of Baltimore to the ground to weed her out, but the Spanish Countess was resourceful. She'd escaped. *Damn waste that woman is still walking around breathing.*

As Dominique and Joshua's conversation continued, Lin grew increasingly uncomfortable, fidgety. Spying her former lover's posture on the edge of the couch, she noticed that even Dominique's body language seemed different then that of their last encounter. She too looked caged. Almost like metal that had been bent out of shape and attempted to reform to its former contour. The twisted ore never wore itself well again. *Perhaps it was the Moor's company that offended her and she was too modest a host to ignore the man?*

Their banter told Lin otherwise.

Perhaps Dominique drowned in history, tethered to her second home, that framed her caged thoughts and mood? Perhaps she recalled her old teacher Nicodemus Blouchard? He did, after all, save Dominique after she'd escaped the chains of the Tien Däm Mu J'in with the aid of Joshua and Ramielle Eirinhas. Perhaps that was why the old one was here instead of bedding the usurper? Dominique was drowning in the past, having no connection to this age. Was it not Nicodemus's manuscripts that I saw freshly mounted on the tunnel walls?

Much of that man, Lin supposed, was ingrained in Dominique. Just like she was composed of the woman who sat at her arm and played with her hair. *What would Nicodemus think of his pupil now?*

Lin's gaze swept across the main hall as her mind wandered. *How would he react to the vulgar exhibitions on display in this room?* From what Dominique told her of Nicodemus he was in his later years when she came to live with him at his home in the Ville de Nicé. The Mediterranean port city was known to the Barbary Pirates, with whom the recently freed slave kept company. If it were not for Monsieur Blouchard Dominique would have died at the hands of the seafaring ruffians. *Would he still have lavished love on the Vam Pÿr, just as Dominique lavished Lin, after so much heartache had passed between them?*

Lin was not unlike her dark mistress in this respect: she owed her teacher much. Blouchard was a scribe, mathematician, astronomer, and self-styled philosopher. He was nearly blind by the time Dominique met him and had a kindly disposition. During this time in the great matriarch's long life she had not donned the De'Paul moniker; that was yet to come. She was simply known as Fizza. And to the escaped slave of the Omjadda the kindness and warmth that she received from Monsieur Blouchard was akin to that of a father. Fizza could scarcely remember her own Papa, taken from her homelands by Bedouins when she was twelve.

Nicodemus taught her to read and write. He taught her the way of the stars and numbers, and held no disgust or bitterness toward the woman's fearful inclination and need for blood. Instead, the patron was fascinated by her rough hue and colored temperament and arranged for several butchers in the neighborhood to furnish his household with fresh sanguine fluid.

While under his care they crafted the persona of the Lady De'Paul and Dominique began establishing a small fleet of ships. She made the old man wealthy, opening resources to him so he could pursue his astronomical studies. It was a relationship of convenience that both student and teacher grew to love. For eleven years she stayed with the aging master until pestilence finally took him to his grave. He was the first person that Dominique ever thought to have changed by the blood of Ornn Däm Mu. But the old master would not have it. He longed for his earthly slumber and urged his pupil to rid herself of the wicked fluid of the Tien Däm Mu J'in Ankh and to brave the rest of her remaining days as a unique child under God.

This last request was the only piece of her teacher's advice that she would not heed. Dominique was already making plans to birth more of her kind in the world. So few like her had survived their war with the Omjadda J'ins. Even less had lasted as long as she had outside of the mines. Joshua's guidance did help, but she did not remain in his company long. Her companionship with Ramielle assisted Fizza to survive longer than she would have if she had been alone, but even that didn't last. Time consumed all things. The path they cut to the Atlantic Ocean together after fleeing the J'in gave them reasons to keep going, but as she soon learned her worldly pursuits were empty and vane.

Most of the Vam who'd won their freedom from the ancient oppressors found existence outside of the Omjadda strongholds too difficult, too bizarre. The world mostly held death in its bosom. They vanished into the sun or found some harsher end at the hands of frightened villagers. Upon Nicodemus's death, Joshua was in retreat in the mountains of Tibet, and Ramielle was embroiled with the Ottoman Empire. Dominique experienced such a vast loneliness that she too briefly contemplated walking into the sun. Eternity – *free or otherwise* – was no kind gift. Yet, the blood of Ornn Däm Mu was with her. She did not have to be alone.

Lin imagined that Master Blouchard would not have approved of what his pupil had wrought since his passing: establishing her Council; birthing the Children of Evensong onto the world. Lin recognized the parallel of Dominique's disapproval of her little "Stop-n-Shop" horror shows with Z, if she were to learn of them. The Council frowned upon killing humans for food. There was no justification in it, The Service had seen to that. *At least, the old man did not live to see his pupil surpass him and populate the earth with the hybrid species. He found his rest and comfort in six feet of dirt.* Dominique did not have his eyes on her back prodding as she set out into the world, but Lin still felt the unwanted machinations of her instructor. Dominique let her heart be felt whether Lin wanted it or not.

Lin downed a healthy dose of blood from the chalice in her hand. She sighed…and gently brushed Dominique's fingers from her hair as her own agitated digits wound around the silver chain and locket that dangled from her neck.

Z eyed the blokes in the full body suits. "What's with those guys in the corner?"

"The Bithtarans?" said Edward as he sipped from a blood-tube that hung down from one of the submissive Sanglants dangling from the ceiling in a leather containment suit.

"Yeah," said Z. "That's a sun-eater, right? I've heard about them." She stared garishly at the woven layered cloths covering the wearer from head to toe. "What's with the dashiki?"

Edward chuckled, a light flittering laugh. "That is the Bithtara, their sacred robe. It is from their garments that their name is derived."

"Looks uncomfortable to me."

Several members of the group that she and Edward sat with snickered at her ignorance. Z thought she made a funny and joined their chortling, not realizing that they were laughing at her, rather than with her.

"Yes. Well…" posted Edward. "In a manner it is. However, it is also our eldest known religion. Every one hundred years they walk into the sun to purify their spirits of all the souls they have taken. Those that survive are revered, even among the lower classes. The Bithtara shields them, protects them…and us…from the scarring."

"Until the skin grows back, of course," interjected a member of the small group.

"Of course," echoed Edward maintaining his knowledgeable air. "The skin grows back stronger. And they say that the elder, sacred priests are even able to walk in the light of day." He twisted the valve on the dangling tube and pulled a healthy dose of blood into his mouth and swallowed. "Personally, I have never known anyone that has done so. And I have been around long enough to know."

Z stared at the religious class thinking. *To willfully go into the sun! Feel the fire start inside as it spread to the outer layer of skin.* She thought of Cross crawling across the dew strewn grass of Rosehill Cemetery. Inching toward her as she cowered in the dark while the morning sun dried out his Jadaraa Soo and set him ablaze. She could still feel the heat of his flames as he ignited in paralysis; blind and deaf to his own screaming. She smiled. "Wow. That's heavy."

Dominique's laugh cut through the room and woke the rough rebel from her spell. Z glimpsed her as she tossed her head back in mirth and then leaned down and whispered into Lin's ear. Her flatmate looked as if she was having just as much fun as herself, which meant that her skin was crawling and she wanted to hit the road. Z made a face and stuck her tongue out at the sable hair vampire. From across the room, Lin cracked a smile.

"Would you care to sample me?" came the small voice at Z's side.

She turned to the well-dressed boy. "What?"

"I'm very sweet." He smiled nicely at her.

It took Z a few seconds for the young boy's invitation to sink in. When it did she was not amused. She pushed the boy away from her and told him to get the fuck out of her face. The child represented everything that she hated about the older ones. True, Z wasn't so high-minded as to actually respect the adolescent's life and judge his small service at the affair. She was wicked in her own way, but she never chalked up a kill of a kid or used one like a refrigerator. It wasn't like he was soliciting himself for execution; it was just that, well…he was a child, a mere boy. A mini-man. Z didn't like kids. She never had and she never would. Children and small people in general gave Z the willies.

When she finally reared her head again from her flashing disgust she spied Lin following Dominique out of the chamber. A hot rush of jealousy piqued her pale flesh and a malcontent mood overcame her.

"Can't we get some better music on?" she inquired loudly to the small party around her or to anybody that would listen. "I've farted more interesting notes."

"Sounds delicious," intoned Edward, liking where this was going. "What did you have in mind?"

Z snorted and laughed, rose from her seat and crossed to the unused stereo system in the center of the room. She procured a CD from her pocket that she placed there for such an occasion. She turned the amplifier on, opened the carousel, placed the home mix into its plastic mount, and hit the button.

"That's right bitches," she whispered as she turned the volume up. *The Minister of Funk is in da' house!*

A few seconds later a blistering guitar riff screamed through the room. Dominique's guests were jarred in their seats, caught unaware where they stood. Heads turned toward the "game" with rank dissatisfaction. A few seconds more and a gyrating bass grabbed Z's hip, underscoring the masterful lead. Then a heavy pulse drumbeat crushed the undead crowd with its rhythm. Z was the only one dancing until Edward rose from his seat and joined the rascally punk in the center of the hall. The blindfolded quartet put aside their instruments and quietly waited for the house music to cease.

The ripe shift in music hit Dominique and Lin in the back as they made their way to the night mother's bedchambers. Lin could scarcely contain a giggle for her friend. Dominique turned to her former love with a face that cried out for war. Lin's laughter broke open and she grabbed Dominique's hands to keep the enraged Vam Pŷr fixed to the spot, lest her party was rapidly reduced to a bitter family feud.

"It's of no concern," she deflected, pressing Dominique's ashen fingers to her bluish lips.

The regal lady sighed, displeased. Eyes a torrent of torpedoes.

"You know I love you," encouraged Lin hoping to avoid a scene.

"Yes," the patrician lady marked. "But you will tire of her, as you have *me*...one day soon."

That stung. The queen bee had venom for her creature of dawn. Lin tried to sway her from traversing down this heartfelt path, but Dominique would not have it.

"I already see it in your eyes," the matriarch truthfully spoke and all Lin could do was listen, her smile vanishing from her lips. "Your heart is ever wandering. It always has been. Time has only made you restless and I fear you will never settle. That you will keep falling down this dark path you are on. That you will lose yourself." Dominique's brow knotted. Her eyes enveloped Lin, soft and ancient, a chasm of deep remorse.

Blood tears welled on the edges of her lids and the Vam Pŷr's hands fell away. She sucked the brine love in and a moment later placed her fingers to her distant paramour's cheek. "Do not keep me waiting."

Perplexed, Lin watched the Persian beauty walk down the length of the tunneled corridor. The opened back of Dominique's dress glared at her, an oval of sublime olive-drab flesh. The shadow from the curvature of the Vam Pŷr's shoulder blades poked out like two hollow eyes and a voice from behind Lin bid her to turn around.

"She said you would come. Like clockwork. I did hope to speak with you."

It had been seventy-five years since Lin heard that accent, in the dark ravages of a desert that swam through the sky and tore at the flesh, blinding the eyes and weakening the body. Even before she turned around, Lin knew who spoke at her back, though she could scarcely believe her eyes. The last she heard, Prophet had entered the Order and gone into the sun. She didn't know what to say. He looked the same, though his black hair was cut shorter. His eyes were brighter and livelier than her nightmares recalled. He still towered over her with a striking presence. Only now he wore the official black and red robes of a Bithtaran Priest and smelled faintly of citrus oil. How unlike her memory, he smiled at her warmly.

"You never told her what happened."

"Why would I?"

He held her tenderly in his eyes before he spoke again, feeling the distance that the old lovers shared. It lingered in the corridor like smoke.

"She still cares about you."

Lin turned away. *Damn him! It's none of his business.* "I know."

Prophet placed a hand to her chin and lifted her head.

"It didn't make sense to me at first, when she told me how you kept coming out here every decade or so on some mysterious trip. You know, for a time she thought you were just coming out to see her." He paused for effect, watching guilt splay across Lin's face like a whore. "But that didn't last. You should tell her. It might make you feel better."

"Who said I felt bad?" Lin removed her chin from his grasp. "What happened, happened. It's over and done with."

He picked the locket up from around her neck and held it in his opened palm. "Is that why you still wear this?"

His nails were manicured, short, and urbane. Lin remembered them long, dirty and dangerous.

"Is that why you joined the Order?"

"Yes." He was completely frank and Lin hadn't expected that. "And I feel better because of it. It cleansed my spirit. I had to atone. I had to make amends."

"I don't see how getting a suntan is going help me forgive myself for what we did."

Prophet let the locket fall to the valley of her chest and his Jadaraa Soo moved back into the domain of his hand.

"You said it…not me."

"Said what?" Lin flashed angry. *Prophet was always so damned confrontational!*

"Forgive yourself." There was a true gentleness in his voice that Lin had never heard before. "No one else can." His brow creased and his expression dipped with genuine concern. Lin didn't know if it was for her or Dominique or for all those people they had murdered. "You should tell her. She's more sympathetic than you think."

Lin stared at the man. The veins of her parasite, agitated, crawled under the skin of her back. It wiggled over her spine and ribs, squeezing and pulling taught. Her hatred for Prophet renewed like a summer rain. She ground her teeth, turned, and started walking away.

"Jordan starved himself to death."

Lin stopped, huffed, and exhaled. But she did not turn around.

"Two years after that night," informed the priest, walking slowly toward the hard shoulders of the vampire's back. "He locked himself away and it took months. I saw him near the end. All he could talk about was the storm and what we did. He said he couldn't get the sounds of their screaming to stop. I watched him stab his ears with a knife. A knife that I'd given him when he'd joined the Coven. He was weak and could barely hold it. But he jabbed it into both ears regardless, and the screaming never stopped. Do you know what the last thing he said was before he died?"

Staring at the cold gray floor, Lin's fingers worked the locket, rubbing back and forth between thumb and forefinger. Prophet's breath brushed across Lin's neck just like the tresses of her ghost hair. The back of her throat was hot and dry and she could feel the veiny fingers of her Jadaraa Soo inching up her esophagus like bile.

"He said you were right. That you knew all along that what we did was wrong."

The raven haired vampire slowly turned around and looked into the serene composure of the one time murdering bastard. She'd heard that Jordan had passed, decades and decades ago, but did not know how until just now. Her face ached, twisted into confusion. She didn't understand. Jordan teased her so unrelentingly during the sandstorm. They both did. He and Prophet egged her to join them in their murderous merrymaking. They ridiculed her for sport in front of the frightened villagers. They were confident, viscous bastards. They were grinning sociopaths that tormented Lin for the sheer joy of it!

"I can see it in you," Prophet mentioned, staring through her as if she were vapor. "There are years of countless deaths burdening your soul." He grinned, falling back into focus. "What have you been up to?"

Lin flared and reacted, slapping Prophet across the face. Its thunderous clap boomed in the stone passageway. She hated him. She hated him then and she hated him now. Reaching her arm out she meant to tan his other cheek with the flat side of her hand, but the priest grabbed her wrist and stopped her, drawing her close.

"How do you think Ramielle passed?" he asked the angry woman. "She wouldn't talk about that night when we returned, and after Jordan starved himself she barely talked at all. In less than a decade she'd left the Coven she formed, abandoned her seat on The Council, and took to raiding the Tavistock Hamlets until the locals hunted her down, cut off her head, and burned her remains. She gave up, living in the forest like a wild animal, waiting for them to find her." The love Prophet had for his former Mistress was evident in the way he passionately tried to reach Lin. "What makes you think that what you're doing is any different?"

He let go of Lin's arm and stood there for a minute staring at her before he left. Lin could not look him the eyes. He knew too much. His gaze pierced her soul. The priest had not said hello, nor did he say goodbye. He just stepped past her in the corridor, leaving her alone with her thoughts, heavy and dank, dripping with blood.

Prophet knew what she was thinking about. The locket around her curvy neck told him all that he needed to know. He planted the seed. That was all he could do for now. That was all he had told Dominique that he would be able to do. Lin had to come to the Order of her own accord. She couldn't be coerced.

No one survived a Bithtaran passage if his or her heart was not truly set on releasing one's sin. The fire was a purification right. Flames became the tongue of forgiveness. Light was the cradle of God. *In Rah's divine eye we are all set free!* One had to let go to be reborn in the blaze and truly atone for the evil that they had wrought in their waking life. Prophet prayed for Dominique's daughter just as he prayed for the mother of night. They both were lost children and he would suffer their prayers until their hearts were baptized with fire.

⚬⚬⚬✹⚬⚬⚬

The entire class had emptied and Sarah still pounded zzzzs in her seat. Professor Roybal watched her for a minute before he woke her. Sarah was a pretty girl – *sandy chestnut hair with a wholesome face, green eyes, and a good complexion.* She jumped as if struck by a bolt of lightning when he tapped the desk. It was all the tendered instructor could do to keep from laughing at his sleep-deprived pupil.

"This is not a boarding house, Ms. Somers."

Sarah looked around, slowly getting the gist.

"Class *is* over," he said with a doughty finality. "You missed yet another riveting, educational lecture of mine. Keep it up and I can assure you that you won't pass this class. Or any other, if this is a sign of your current attitude on class participation."

"I'm sorry," Sarah emphatically started as she grabbed her books. "It's just that..."

"Please, spare me the excuses. Just read pages 323 to 367, and Ms. Somers..."

Sarah looked up at him earnestly. "Yes?"

"Do try to get some sleep...*at home.*"

"Yes. Thank you. Sorry. I will."

Sarah entered the hall cursing at herself for falling asleep again. She needed more free nights than what the Club was allowing her to take. *It can't continue like this or I'm gonna burn myself out before midterms.*

With the student gone Professor Roybal could finally release his stored chuckle and file the class papers away in a manila folder.

A knocking on the door permeated her mind.

It's rapping turned fearful eyes in her direction.

Stinging sand that bled her ears like bees burrowed into the back of her raven's nest.

A knocking permeated her mind.

Lin's fingers rubbed the silver ornament with unnoticed fury. Prophet had set her thoughts on edge. Her teeth were buzzing, anxious. Even the mercy fuck between the old lovers did not abate her constant agitation. Dominique noticed her distance in their touch and remained face down, lying on the bed, in all her gorgeous nakedness thinking of what she'd lost over the years.

Had the fire of the sun truly purified him?

Why do I always come this way?

Lin turned her head to Dominique's form stretched out behind her on the wide girth of the dark mistress's bed, enveloped in a cascading sea of fine black silk. *Why do I always stop to go through this row with her?* The addled vampire wanted to reach a hand out, lay her hot fingers on the woman's spine and ask her for forgiveness. Right here and now. *But... forgiveness for what?*

Damn that Prophet!

Lin slid her arms through the holes of her wife-beater tee. The scent of their mingled bloods crammed her nostrils. She felt a thousand miles away. Her mind kept reeling back to those two fateful days in 1934 when the Ford choked on sand and they continued on foot through the storm. Lin never even heard Juliana cry or scream. She just simply vanished. One minute she was there, the next she wasn't. A knocking permeated Lin's troubled memory. She opened the locket to stare again at the black and white portrait of the woman inside, and the knocking ceased.

Prophet found the village. He found us a safe harbor in the torrent of ungodly winds. The eyes of the portrait in the locket bore into Lin. *Prophet discovered a light so we could find our way. But at what cost?*

The curve of the woman's cheek in the portrait was as calcified and burned to memory as was the curve of the woman that lay at Lin's back. The pitch and timbre of the photograph's eyes were felt even when the locket lay closed against the cradle of her chest. The smile was dainty and sure. Her face beamed. She was in love. Lin caressed the antique photograph with a finger and her Jadaraa Soo twitched.

Now, only she and the converted Bithtaran Priest were all that was left of them. A few years after they returned from those wailing days of horror Jordan became a recluse and starved himself to death, never taking blood again. It was hard for Lin to fathom. His appetite was so ravenous. Ramielle went mad and was hunted down by a group of humans who vanquished the once reigning Council Member by burning her severed head and body in a shallow dug pyre during the safety of daylight. In Lin's memory Ramielle was always strong – a pillar of conviction that lifted Lin up and forced her to see herself for what she truly was.

What cost?

Lin recalled how Dominique fretted when she heard the news that Ramielle had passed. It was one of the only times that she had visited Lin in Los Angeles. Dominique arrived at her doorstep a caged flurry of sorrow, a melting snowflake on the shores of not knowing what to do. There were no remains, nothing for Dominique to hold onto. A member of Ramielle's coven had informed her that their leader had just upped and abandoned her position. She left LA. Even with Ramielle's consecutive absences at Council meetings piling up Dominique did not suspect that she'd gone off the deep end. So when the rumors of vampire-type murders began to surface throughout Southern England Dominique sent Deven St. Cloud to investigate. She never expected to uncover that Ramielle was the cause, that she was so incapable and uncontrolled as to openly attack a human village and expose herself so recklessly.

Nothing about Ramielle gave Dominique the impression that she would have done such a thing. Pacing through the living room on that pale October morning, the angst-ridden Vam Pŷr kept asking Lin why. Over and over again, voicing the irritating word to the indignity of cruel fate. Dominique had no inkling of what had transpired between Lin and Ramielle during the sandstorm. She was upset and venting. But the constant question bore through her darling Linnet with tenacity, plying her open like a pair of vice-grips.

Ramielle was the only other surviving blood slave from the Tien Däm Mu J'in that had lasted throughout those early days of freedom with Fizza. They traveled together for years and sailed the high seas inflicting piracy on unsuspecting merchant ships. Their blood was thick with love and time. *Ramielle was the key. She was not a mad woman!* They had collaborated together to bring about the fall of Ornn Däm Mu's great house and win their exodus from bondage and so inspired the blood slaves of other great Omjadda J'ins to rise. *Ramielle was a hero to her race. Not some monster!* She was akin to a sister of the Vam Pŷr. She helped Dominique build The Council. *She did not deserve what fate delivered. To be butchered and burned, an undistinguished end for such a thriving, guiding light.* It made no sense to the grief-stricken woman and Lin could scarcely offer her former lover any comfort or illumination as to why the Vam Däm Mu had snapped. The loss of Ramielle Eirinhas settled between Lin and Dominique like a fermenting secret, decaying all around them. It was a garden of filth.

Now the garden had been tilled by her little chat with Prophet. The filth began to stink. Lin felt greedy. As if she held all of the straws, saw the strings of the past with common clarity and kept them from the grief-stricken woman that lay at her back, waiting. Prophet said she was expectant. That she should tell her what happened. *Does she already know?* Lin bit the inside of her bottom lip and stared at the photograph in the locket again.

It wouldn't do any good to dredge it up now. The past is over. What happened, happened. It can not be changed. Better to have died like Juliana and vanish into the thick. Unknown. Unseen. Just simply…gone.

Lin closed the locket and tossed another look at the lovely creature behind her. *So sublime. So reposed and distant like a painting.* She recalled how the master artist, Sir Joshua Reynolds, wanted to fervently paint her likeness to discern the complexities of Dominique's fair skin, as he put it, when he was painting Lin's portrait. The vampire sighed, a long, grievous exhalation. She had already unraveled the complexities of Dominique's skin years ago. What secrets her flesh held were common knowledge and boring.

Dominique felt Lin's eyes on her back and knew she wanted to say something. She had known it for years, decades even. The Vam Pŷr never wanted to pry. She did not want to interfere. She felt the heft of her old lover's stare and wondered. Too many years ago she stopped hoping that Lin would just open up and spill what was eating at her soul, but she never had. Lin's secret remained sealed like a tomb and the eight hundred-year-old Vam Pŷr didn't want to have to ask what it was that troubled her about those bygone days. She wanted Lin to open up to her when she was ready. But waiting for Lin to be ready had turned into a hellish century of despondency.

It was obvious that the run-in with Prophet had shaken her up. *Good!* Dominique orchestrated the meeting between them to get that door swinging open, to get Lin to talk. Prophet had said that she just needed to be patient. Dominique exhaled into her ebony sheets. *Patience.* She had a lot of practice with that. It was probably the only thing she learned in the mines of the Rom Pŷr J'in that she cared to remember.

Prophet said he would speak with her if she arrived, and so he has. His tiny push. Dominique knew her lost love needed to expel. She could feel it! *All these insignificant inches forward. Why is it that the dead only speak slowly concerning the dead!*

Dominique stirred, thankful that the man had reached out to her raven haired darling. *He's a better man for joining the Order. Not all Bithtaran converts are as dedicated as he. And to think I was against his ascension initially.*

Ramielle sponsored him. A smile crossed Dominique's majestic lips as she thought of the Spanish widow. She missed her laugh and the sway of her dark walnut hair. Her fine wit was a lost treasure. Ramielle was fearless, a hellcat full of fury and adventure. Suddenly, Dominique's belly knotted and she imagined Lin succumbing to the same horrifying fate that befell her departed sister. *What happened to you?* The Vam Pŷr felt it in the marrow of her bones that it had something to do when Lin had moved out and stayed with the California coven queen. Though, Dominique wasn't sure. Certainty was a luxury that slipped through her fingers, so she guessed. Piecing little bits here and there, things just never quite felt the same after their time together. Both Lin and Ramielle appeared changed.

The Vam Pŷr ached to ask. To finally have it out with her former lover once and for all. *Perhaps that would be best?* But Prophet's words drilled through her head like a meat cleaver and the eight-hundred year-old blood slave feared pushing Lin away further than she already was.

Have faith. She's still here. "Are you alright?"

Lin turned away from her naked mistress. "Yeah. Fine."

Dominique did not turn to look at her. "You can always talk to me."

There was a long silence wherein she imagined Lin opened to her like she used to, shining her heart in a confidential embrace. "I hope we still have that, at least."

The hard sigh that escaped Lin's mouth sent angry ripples across the ocean of Dominiqe's flesh. She turned to her lost lover's bent back. "Whatever it is, you can tell me. It'll go no farther than this room. I am not a council member when I am with you."

"I know."

"Then tell me."

Lin's head sagged and she stood. The bed shifted to lonely. The jangle of her belt buckle clanked as she fitted into her jeans, one leg at a time. She grabbed her boots and shirt and started walking toward the door. Silence nested between them now, aging with the locked secret. It grew heavier with each and every step that Lin took away from her. Dominique's eyes burned.

"You know what sucks about being in love?"

Again, the parlance of France. Lin stopped, though she did not turn around.

Dominique sat up. "It's the knowledge that no matter how much you love someone, no matter how much you give to that one person, you know they could take it all from you, and you wouldn't even care. That you would do it over and over again just to hold them one more time, just to feel them...one...more...time."

Lin tilted her head back and looked at the ceiling. Chisel marks still grooved the contour of the circular room. *Always circular.* Ever since Lin had known the Vam Pŷr she'd been entombed in a circle and she, Linnet Pevensey, was nothing more than a mouse that ran around the constant ring as if it were a wheel. *Circles always return; always drag back in.*

Not this time.

The hardened vampire lowered her head and cracked a kink in the lovely jewel of her neck. She did not turn to face her old lover. Lin's

Jadaraa Soo slithered through her cold bare feet, galvanizing her to the spot. Dominique gazed into the icy stare of Lin's bare shoulders and had nothing more to say. A frustrating knot formed in the hole where her heart once lived. She crashed backwards on the bed, falling onto her pillows, and glared at the ceiling too. Lin crept from Dominique's chambers like a silhouette lover stealthily vanishing.

A great valley separated them now and the former blood slave didn't see any bridge to forge a crossing. She had hoped that all she had done for Lin would matter. That the love that was still there would open her mouth and free her tangled and barbed spirit, giving her words wings so that she could save her soul. The Matron of Night threw this party for her, asked Prophet to intervene on her behalf, and gave her a wide berth through her afterlife. But nothing seemed to satisfy; nothing seemed to mend the rift that had aged between them. *Love so fondly ripens to sour wine.* Even the mercy fuck was unforgivably bad. They had grown awkward with one another from the personal isolations they endured.

Ours is not a life after death. But a continual dying.

Dominique felt worse than before the raven haired beauty had arrived. It appeared that no good deed went unpunished. Dominique curled into a ball, closing the gap of her abdomen. Pressing her knees to her temples, she closed her eyes. Her own thread was badly in need of repair. She could not hold out for her darling Linnet any longer. Her dawn, her Araci was gone. Dominique knew it now with more clarity than ever. She had to awaken her own vibrancy or else the clattered, slow shuffle of time was going to eat her heels until she walked into the sun, like most of her kind did.

Prophet said he would council her if she so chose. The gulf of ache, bitterness, and sorrow gnawed at the maw in the Vam Pŷr's gut. She needed the Bithtaran priest. She had to let Linnet go. There was no other choice. Lin's fate was in God's hands now. Dominique picked up the house phone and called Clyde. She asked her transvestite secretary to send Prophet to her chambers. The phone clunked back into its handle, a purposeful knell. She rolled over and felt the full magnitude of her years weighing her down. She pressed her eyes tightly to hold back the flood, but it was of little use. Blood tears ran down the plum bowls of her whitening checks and stained her black silk sheets. All she could do now was pray.

Prayer was the cup of loneliness that begged to be fulfilled.

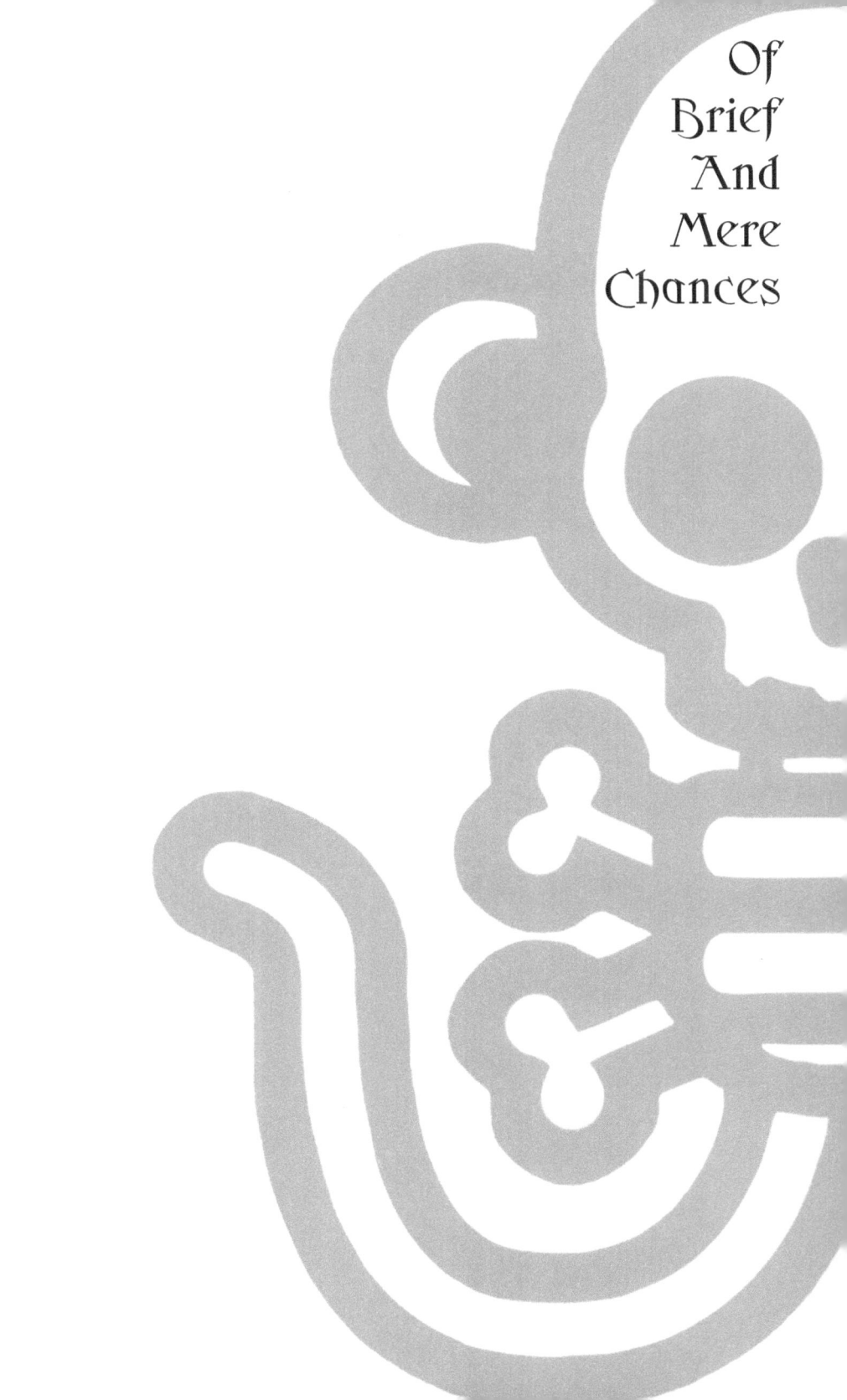

Of
Brief
And
Mere
Chances

It was simply an urge. A pulse. A bump in the road that made Detective Wallace go, "Hhrrmm."

The next thing she knew he was turning into the crowded parking lot of a southwestern bar and getting out. Mauldune hadn't recovered from the ear lashing she'd received from their commanding officer. She was just closing her phone and still felt a dent where her hearing had been when the elder detective had turned off the road.

"You are Phoenix Detectives, Gaddamn it!" yelled the bristly bearded Captain. They shouldn't have even left the city to case some burn site in Mojave. Now they were chasing some, as of yet, unidentifiable suspects toward the state border!

Kate played it hard and held firm, stringing together a long, impressive history of case files and incident reports that Wallace had collected over the years. He had made her read them when he stopped for gas, retrieving them from the trunk and tossing the tight bound stack of manila folders into her lap. He told her to "make yourself useful."

It was excellent police work, all those files. It gave ground to her argument and it was convincing enough that the Captain finally relented and gave them some leash, demanding regular updates. The spry Lieutenant felt like she had won the damn war, deserved a medal, or at least a hearty Thank you. But all she got was the bitter, old Sergeant storming away from the car toward the cattle rustler's watering hole.

The sky glared down on the two police officers as they entered the old style Honky-Tonk. Majestic and clear, the edges of night skirted the horizon. Dust clung to hydrogen molecules as the musky scents of hay and dung permeated the dirt lot.

Inside, the rowdy patrons soothed themselves with drinks, conversations, and Western tunes bristling from a Jukebox in the far corner of the room. The clash of pool balls, rolling on soft green felt, clanging against one another, excited the smoky atmosphere as the Phoenix detectives wandered across the wooden plank floor, and made for the bar. A regular barfly downed a shot of mud-colored bourbon, pushing the small glass to the lip of the bar to be refilled. An unshaven man in his mid thirties, wearing a black tee shirt, jeans, and boots refilled the shot glass with another $3.25 brew.

Wallace's gaze swept the crowd when he came in, looking for anything out of the ordinary. He could sense Kate's eyes on him, wanting to ask what he was up to, thankful that she hadn't yet. The bar's back mirror was littered with old wanted posters: A collection of southwestern unmentionables, a few Chicago mobsters, old FBI mugshots, and a lone faded black and white pic of Zia Jean Boyd from 1928, wanted in connection to a series of bank robberies in Florida and Illinois with her husband Simon Ray. Wallace took it all in. The crowd appeared to be locals, from what he could tell. Nothing out of place. Nothing at all. Just a local liquor spot. Pool Hall. Juke Joint. But something here made his gut twitch.

"Whatchya want?" came crashing from the bartender.

Wallace flashed him his badge, but the cocky, young man didn't even look at it.

"I know whatchya are," the bartender added, "Now whuddya want?"

Mauldune unfolded a photocopy from her coat and laid it on the bar. It was a snapshot of Lin and Z from a bit of refurbished security tape that hadn't completely charred from one of their earlier exploits. The sticky lock to the security camera equipment was a bastard to break, so Z had let that one go. That was also the night that she killed Sergeant Wallace's nephew, Stephen. He was a sweet kid. Literally. His blood tasted like it was laced with sugar. There was also an artist's rendition of both Lin and Z atop the video still and the detectives' phone numbers to call below. Kate had the idea of mixing the flyer up as she perused Wallace's case files. So, he found a Kinko's and scotch tape.

"We're lookin' for these two," Wallace muttered, giving the wetback a few seconds to look it over. "Anybody like this pass your way?"

The Bartender popped up from the photocopy and shook his head. "Naw."

"You sure?" asked Wallace, sliding the picture closer to the lazy barkeep. "How 'bout you look again."

The old man's eyes bore into the immovable glare of the thirty-something drink-tender. *He's done time.* Wallace was convinced; he had that cocky air. Slowly, the bartender's eyes shifted down. He picked the photocopy up this time and gave it a once over and let it drop arrogantly from his fingers.

"Like I said, I ain't seen nobody like this."

"Our number's on the bottom, here." Wallace pointed with one of his fat, stubby fingers, boring a hole through the guy's head with his eyes. "You hang on to it. Call us if you see 'em."

He stepped back from the bar, noticed Mauldune staring at him, but he wasn't gonna give her any space. The barkeep huffed and went to attend another customer, leaving the photocopy on the bar. Its glaring white paper burned in Wallace's eyes like it was a dead rat, a picture of his ex-wife fucking his best friend – *which of course she did* – or the smoking gun in a murder case. He wasn't gonna leave until the young criminal picked it up, gave it some attention, and put it where his fickle little brain could register it. Wallace didn't care if he had paid his county dues in the local pokey or been up state for real. In his opinion the cocky ex-con was just a stones throw away from a lifer and he was about to get his noggin thumped if he kept up the shenanigans.

A few customers and a dozen or so drinks later, the bartender returned to that spot where the photocopy lay like a pregnant elephant in the room. The cops watched him as taped it to the huge mirror. He hated their eyes on him. He never liked cops. *Bloated egos, the lot of 'em. Itchy to bust your balls over bullshit just to curb their own boredom.* As he mounted the photocopy next to the 1928 black & white wanted poster he never even noticed the resemblance of the mug shot to the artist's rendition or the grainy image from the convenience store's security tape. Blind ignorance and cops at his back, he sauntered over to another customer, just as a different song sprang from the antique jukebox.

Night framed the sky, a picture hanging on the arms of dusk. The big Cadillac boat slowly snaked its way through the rugged parking lot pulled by the tendril fingers of fate. Z finished the last strokes of Max Factor appearance enhancer, checking the normal, average, totally alive-looking gal face in the visor mirror, and turned to Lin.

"How do I look?"

Lin scanned the rascally punk over, port to starboard, reviewing the grade. "Alive and kicking." She moved to exit the vehicle, feeling a bouncy pulse to mingle among the muckrakers ripping through her bones.

"Here," said Z, keeping the sable haired vampire in her seat, "you need some."

Lin rolled her eyes, played it big, frowning a disapproving grin. Z ignored it and began applying a flesh tone base.

"Don't know of any cowboy necrophiliacs in this neck of the woods. So, just grin and bear it, sweet heart. Grin and bear it."

Lin chuckled, exposing her fangs.

"On second thought…we don't want to scare 'em away. Well…" shrugged Z, "not until much later anyways."

The vampire's laugh was dry and lonely. It made Lin smirk. She was surprised at how eager she was to go out this night, instead of spinning the Caddy's wheels on the busted tarmac. She was downright anxious and Z told her to stop squirming. Annoyed at the ritual make-up application, Lin sighed and decided to beat the need to the punch.
Concentrating, she pulled her Jadaraa Soo down - just below the layer of skin so that she would pass as a regular looking gal. Riding the curvature of her muscles, quiet and docile, its darkened reddish hue added a bit of color to her thin pallor. It had taken the elder vampire awhile to learn how to communicate with the veiny blood parasite and pull the trick off. She learned it from Dominique. It was rather simple to do once you got down to it.

Z's body caved in with envy. "You gotta teach me that."

She's never able to make her veins recede

"Maybe if you treated the 'lil fella better it would do it for you," encouraged Lin as she exited the car.

"That's bull and you know it." Big doors thudding, farmer stink and arid night settling around them, they headed toward the honky-tonk. "So, whaddya do?" Z asked. "Concentrate real hard; hold your breath? I've tried everything."

Lin chuckled, shaking her head no.

"Bribe it? Ask it pretty fucking please…"

The vampire was reaching for straws, and though funny, the undercurrent of it was that Z's Jadaraa Soo was dying. She would never be able to make her veins recede under the ceiling of her skin, and any day now she might simply drift off to sleep and never to wake up again.

"No. Nothing like that," stroked Lin, avoiding the truth.

"Command the little fucker?"

"Definitely not."

"Promise it an Olsen twin? C'mon, what?"

Lin's laugh bubbled up from between the parked cars just as Sergeant John Wallace and Lieutenant Kate Mauldune exited the smoky bar, walking toward their vehicle. John patted himself down, looking for something.

"What is it?" Kate inquired, glaring at the man like he'd gone senile.

"Think I left my smokes on the bar?"

"Can't say I've ever seen you smoke, Sarge."

"Hhrrmmm?" grumbled the seasoned detective suddenly aware that he'd stop smoking two years ago. "Guess I quit."

He continued walking toward the car, still feeling the nagging twang of nicotine addiction.

"You wanna go back in, renew the habit?" teased Kate. "Make it official…" She stopped and gestured toward the saloon just as their primary suspects spilled out from the scant protection of parked cars. "I could run in and pick ya up a pack?"

"I will shoot you, ya know," Wallace warned, eyes off her, as he kept walking toward the unmarked police cruiser.

The Lieutenant followed him with a mirthful grin. Behind her, ten feet away, was the cause of the trouble, the dynamic duo of death, grab and burn specialists, murderesses of hapless men and faint-hearted women, walking up onto the saloon's porch! Kate felt good. She didn't know that she should have turned around. Fate was messing with her. She hadn't a clue. The old man was easy pickings, hard on himself, humorless. Kate found that she finally had something she could ride him about. But her good cheer vanished as her cell phone exploded in her pocket. She pulled the little device out. It was the Chief calling. She answered the call, blank, doe-eyed, as her joy vanished.

The vampires entered the cowboy bar.

People danced. Conversed in clouds of cigarette fumes. Fiddled with the Jukebox. Drank. Played pool. But no one was riding a mechanical bull. Z wanted to ride one. She'd assumed that all redneck bars had 'em. It was the whole reason why modern cowboys wore those ridiculous looking hats. She wanted a tumble. She wanted something huge and powerful between her thighs. Tonight was about something more than just blood. Both of the girls felt it. In their own way. They didn't speak on it, per se, but it was there like hands up their asses. It felt natural.

The vampires crossed to the bar like they owned the place. Arrogant, an occupational hazard of the dead, they leaned against the thick maple bar, backs to the mirror, almost mimicking the cops from earlier as the bartender moseyed up.

"What can I get for you two?" His demeanor was polite, interested.

Lin slightly turned, eyes casing the joint. It was an old habit; memorizing exits, assessing threats, trolling for meat. "Two double whiskeys. Two beers."

Z bounced to the music oozing out of the Jukebox. It sounded like wheat, swaying and easy. The bartender nodded and turned, sloppily filling whiskey glasses next to the photocopy of them that the Phoenix detectives had pressed him to post.

"That'll be fifteen with the beers," he said, placing the drinks behind them, and wiped his hands.

Z scooped up her whiskey and tossed it down the back of her throat in a single throw. *Mmmm, fire water. Good.* She slammed the empty shot glass down like she was banging a drum. "'Nother."

It burned and her Jadaraa Soo bitched violent blood memories, a shudder throughout Z's whole body. It caused her makeup to ripple. Lin tossed a crisp fifty dollar bill onto the wet bar top as the alcohol jockey loosely filled the vampire's request.

Z grabbed her whiskey up as the barkeep held the fifty to the light, checking for the United States Treasury Seals that told him the bill was legal tender. Lin spooled a finger around the opened fat mouth of her beer bottle, turned around, and took a swig. Her eyes splayed across the crowd.

"Take that you little bastard," Z informed her incessant symbiote and threw the whiskey down her gullet. "Mmmm. Sweet bliss."

Lin tapped her wild friend on the arm and pointed at two young cowboys shooting pool at the back of the room. They were handsome, rugged for their age, wearing dungarees, leather boots, button up shirts, and 9-gallon hats. One of them bent over the table to take a shot. Z sucked in a breath of cool, smoke-filled air as Lin rolled the fermented hops lazily over her tongue.

"Ride 'em cowboy," the rascally vamp uttered in a slow, soft drawl.

Z set the empty whisky glass down and picked up her beer, liking the feel of the cold, hard shaft in her hand. She was feeling horny and was about to procure a ride. *No Mechanical Bull dammit! So, this young buck's gonna do!*

The quiet sound of paper, behind Lin, hit the bar. She turned around and grabbed her double shot and tossed it back, letting the sting settle in, all of the way through her dead, transformed flesh to her porous bones, drilling river stones, pock marked and snaking with an overbearing blood parasite. She set the wet, empty glass on the loose change and told the bartender that he could keep it.

The vampires, filled with liquor and curves, cold intentions and wonton lust creaming their jeans slunk up to the cowboys playing pool. One of them noticed the girls right away and stepped up to meet and greet, lest they were just fooling and were going to veer away from their table. After all, pool was cool, but broads were better.

"Ladies, ladies…" the slick, cleaned up local oozed, all hard consonants and slow 'esses, tipping his hat like a gentleman.

He smelled of after-shave and cheap deodorant and couldn't stop staring at Lin's rack, snug and luscious in the manly tee, under a locked winged heart tattoo.

"Whatchya drinkin?" cooed Lin, propping a billboard smile on her face.

She moved to sip her beer and hide her uneasy grin, but the playful man grabbed her cold bottle of brew and took a swig, answering her question.

"You."

If fate has a mouth, it's laughing. He never took his eyes off her. Now, she couldn't hide her slap-happy face. The upturned frown felt hollow and weird as the irony played her like a symphony. It had been too long since she last twisted her lips in the harmonious affirmation.

Z eyed the tall guy in the back, who looked them over from the security of his pool stick. Braving up, he stepped toward the girls, busting his friend's balls.

"You have to forgive him. He was raised in a barn with pigs."

"Shit." Darryl pursed his lips. "By your Momma."

Z, tightening her grip around the shaft of her beer, grinned and wet her lips. Politely, the tall hunk extended his hand and introduced himself. He was cute, fingers warm, the palm of his hand wide, it told the vivacious vampires that he didn't have an office job.

"My name's Jake. This here's Darryl."

"Lin. Z," the raven haired beauty announced.

Darryl got obvious. "You all ain't from around here, are ya?" He pulled another swig from Lin's beer.

"Uh oh," piqued Z.

"Looks like he found us out," affirmed Lin.

"Sharp as a cue ball, this one," said Z, cocking her hip at a dangerous angle.

"What are we gonna do?" Lin asked as she retrieved her beer from Darryl's hand.

"I don't know," confessed Z, picking up the eight ball, and turning to Jake, all serious eyes and vibrant, "What do *you* wanna do?"

The look was lusty. It read like a cheap pulp novel. Harlequin in her eyes that smacked of a budget motel, dirty sheets, and bumping uglies. Jake feigned a smile, nervous like a little boy, and dipped his head to the side as his friend laughed. Neither one of them had ever met such forward girls as these before. *Must be city chicks.* It made them feel awkward and uneasy, but in a way that they liked.

Jake reached out for the ball. "We were in the middle of a game." Z pulled the ball just out of his reach and devilishly grinned. "C'mon. Give me the ball." He stepped toward her.

"Hey," spoke Darryl, getting an idea. "If, ah, you know…it looks like they, ah, wanna play too."

"Yeah," Lin chimed. "We wanna play."

Her innuendo was weaker than Z's. She never had the punk's gift for gab.

"You ain't getting out of it that easy," Jake relayed to Darryl. Then turning to Z, "he was losing fifty."

"I was just setting him up," he lied through his teeth, trying to keep his manly façade going a bit longer. No one believed him.

"So, ah…the ball?" Jake held his hand out, working hard to keep his focus on the money at stake.

"You a bettin' man," Z claimed.

"We got a lil' money on the game, is all."

"Tell ya what…" The vampire spoke as she stepped toward him, close enough to breathe his oxygen. "I've got a bet for you."

His heat was palpable. His scent stroked her tongue.

"What's that?"

"You. Me. These two, *big* sticks. One game." Z paused for dramatic effect. Both Darryl and Lin watching them, cocooned in the bristly sexuality that ebbed from the edge of the pool table. "And, if you win…I'll let you fuck me."

Darryl busted up laughing. Thinking he was dreaming, he had already begun to compose the letter in his head to Penthouse Forum as Z leaned into his childhood friend. "Any way you like," she whispered in her best Marilyn Monroe and could tell the young man was embarrassed. "I win…" Z added with curt objectivity. "And you're mine. For the rest of the night. To do with as I please."

She pulled from her beer, looking the man over as he considered her proposal. It didn't take him long to think it through. "I'm flattered. Really. But, I don't think my girlfriend would appreciate that too much."

Z was awed. Two strikes with the lonesome dove and Lin chuckled behind her brew as Darryl guffawed.

"Aw man!" He crumpled the letter to Penthouse Forum in his mind. "I don't believe it. You're the biggest pussy I've ever met. She don't even like your ass anymore."

Now Z's shame was complete. *He lied about a girlfriend to cover his dislike.*

"I told you to shut up about that," Jake flared, real anger twisting his face.

Darryl ignored him, trying to pick up the pieces, and smooth the letter out. "Ladies, you'll have to forgive my boy here. He's just a little scared is all."

Jake tossed his pool stick onto the table, jostling the balls, and stepped toward his childhood friend. "How 'bout I whoop your lyin' mouth."

"Gettin' hot now!" chimed Z, ready for fury, eyes blazing, enjoying the hicks more than Cable TV. "I mean it. I love watchin' guys duke it out. All fists and fury; sexy as hell, but if your goin' for all that homo-erotic glory, then let's get those shirts off and get you in a mud pit; 'cause I gotta tell ya, I want to be entertained. I want a thrill."

Her enthusiasm killed the testosterone quicker than a cold shower and conversations about shoe shopping. Jake, embarrassed, just laughed.

"Yeah," piped Darryl, liking the vixen's wild spirit. It was a breath of fresh air from the same ole, same ole. "That's what I'm talking about! A little fun. Let's have some fun." He dug down deep into his pocket and pulled out the fifty-dollar bill he had stuffed there and threw it on the table. "Here fool. I was losin' anyway. Why don't you go get us some drinks." He turned to the girls. "You want drinks?"

And they did, answering him with smiles, wide over sharp tipped fangs, silent like grave robbers. Jake scooped up the fifty and retreated to the bar as Darryl racked the table for a little tag team action. He was excited and ready. He wanted to play. The girls were paler than those around these parts, a little kooky, sure, but they seemed more exciting and imbibed life better than the girls that he'd grown up with. Tonight, he thought, loading the small, hard balls into the rack, tonight was shaping up to be something spectacular.

Lin looked to her quiet co-conspirator, easy in the knowledge of what they had in store for these two rough-around-the-edges gentleman. She was ok with it. She was enjoying herself and was instantly reminded of something that Z had said to her a long time ago.

Murder is contagious. It's a fanciful disease.

She watched her dying, violent friend, thinking back over the years. Her wild cavorting nature had seeped into her like slow syrup, steady and thick, and Lin realized that it was true. Murder was contagious.

Her eyes splayed across Darryl's fine muscular structure and she felt nothing for him. He was meat and a lazy good time before the meal. Her cold expanse usually filled her with some sort of regret for the sacrificial lamb. But tonight it didn't. Tonight, she felt free and clear – absolved from all the sin that she'd earned, finding beauty in the god awful. Tonight, she felt like she could get away with anything, anything at all. Especially murder.

May 9, 1934.

The sky was alive with cancer. Thick and brown. Buzzing and choking all around the four of them, a stampede of dust and endless disaster. They were wandering. Could have been walking in circles. Time was as distant and incredible as the horizon, lost in the tempestuous dirt sea. Prophet drew close to Ramielle, huddled near Lin's hunched shoulders, his black hair wild in the gale.

"This wind will rip the flesh from our bones," he shouted above the bombastic din, its vibrant quake barely making him audible. "We need shelter!"

"The ground will uncover us," Ramielle yelled from behind the cowl of her hood. "We can not take the chance."

"At least allow me to scout ahead."

"No! We must stick together." Ramielle's hand shot out of the sleeves of her cloak grabbing Prophet's arm. Dirt instantly pooled between the folds of her fingers. "I do not wish to lose you like we lost Juliana."

Prophet looked about. The storm was ravenous. Nothing was ever so clear. "I don't think we have much of a choice."

Lin stared up at the Vam Däm Mu, the question hanging between them like a river of thieves, dark and brooding, tunneling through their ears like a crashing freight train. Ramielle's fingers released him before she silently shook her head, yes. Lin watched the man run off into the black blizzard. Five steps and he was gone.

Prophet wasn't all that bad. A little crazy. Lin had only met him during this visit, and it seemed odd to her now that she would probably never see him again; that just like Juliana, the storm swallowed him whole and delicious, like he never existed in the first place.

"Stay together!" Ramielle shouted to her remaining charges as the dense grime attacked her mouth. "Keep it tight!"

Jordan pulled closer to Lin. There was no other place to go. He despaired; his face was twisted in pain. He loved the vampire that the storm had consumed. His feet moved like anchors and Lin wrapped an arm around him to keep him tethered. He fell into her, a shipwreck, and she was stacked between the ancient bloodsucker and her brood. Ramielle turned toward her, the countenance of her face unbroken.

"Not to worry, Little One." She sounded strong. "I promised Dominique you'd be safe and so you shall be."

"I'm not worried Mistress." Lin was at peace with the knowledge that she'd never walk out of this storm.

"Good." The dark countess patted Lin's hand. "That makes two of us."

Lin wasn't sure if the council member was just playing strong or if she really was that confident. Dominique spoke highly about her many years ago. But up close and personal, in a hellfire of dry wind and topsoil nothing seemed to make much sense. God was having a go at Man. For all the advances civilization had achieved throughout the eons mankind's eldest craft, farming, had returned with seasons of vengeance. These black storms brewing in America's heartland were destined since Man's first spade ripped the earth in those primitive days of the Fertile Crescent. On the heels of World War I to feed American soldiers in the Old World the Great Plains of the New World had been used like a ragged doll. Stripped of her Buffalo grasses, tilled in ignorance and over-seeded with wheat, harvested fields were razed and left barren over winter months. Agricultural arrogance and decades of drought were biting them all in the ass.

Lin looked to Ramielle, her cloak tight about her waist, hood up, head down, shuffling one foot in front of the other through the sweeping tempest as if she knew exactly where they were going. Lin felt the woman hadn't a clue where she was leading them. Betting on blind luck and the will of the damned, Lin knew where they were going. She figured it out hours ago when Jordan drove into the gigantic wall of silt. They were heading toward their deaths. Plain and simple. Lin didn't mind the thought of dying. Death is an inevitable feast. She had a one hundred and eighty year run of it. Her Mother only lived to the ripe ole age of thirty-eight. Lin surpassed her by one hundred and forty-two years. Any year past thirty-eight was considered a blessing in her book. At least she'd done things in her life, seen things that other people never saw, visited places that others only dreamed about or never knew existed. Hers was an incredible life, so she readily followed the Vam Däm Mu toward their inevitable slow burn and windy burial.

Watching Prophet disappear into the twirling thick, Lin was reminded of an old nursery rhyme that her mother used to sing to her as a little girl. Softly, Lin mumbled the childish, homespun tune to the raucous, bastard winds.

"The trees in the forest fall one by one. One by one. One by one. The trees in the forest fall one by one. All...day...long. The trees in the forest fall chop, chop, chop. Chop, chop, chop. Chop, chop, chop. The trees in the forest fall chop, chop, chop. All...day...long."

As she sang and walked, Lin recalled the first time that Dominique told her about Ramielle. Such vivid stories they shared then, so rich and thick, much like the sands that ate her now. Ramielle was only a blood slave of the Tien Däm Mu J'in for a very short time before the slave revolts swept her up in its turbulent fists. The night mother told Lin about how instrumental the Spanish woman had been to her survival after the Eras of Slavery had ended. The Vam Pŷr noticed her, a favorite Mar among the guard quarters, and took pity on her wretched condition. The poor woman had been captured in a raid, her village burned to the ground, men killed. All the females stolen. She was one of the last survivors of the raid, and at the rate the Omjadda guards were abusing her, she wasn't going to be around much longer. Using the captured woman like a pleasure doll, they passed her amongst their brood – feeding and fucking. The widowed female was nothing short of sport.

"This was long before I came to the Villa de Nicé and lived with Nicodemus Blouchard," explained Dominique to Lin one evening while they lounged in the Vam Pŷr's chambers, under their house in São Paulo, Brazil. "I found Ramielle close to death one night, naked and unconscious on the stone floor of the guardhouse. She reeked of the ancient creature's sweat and semen. She'd been beaten, was malnourished. They fed off her so often that the puncture wounds from their teeth did not have time to heal. I absconded with the woman and nursed her back to health in the privacy of my chambers."

"You had such freedom among the Tien Däm Mu?" inquired Linnet draped under the woman's arm.

"Not at first," the former slave explained. "Ele Däm Mu, Ornn's wife, was not pleased that he placed me among the house servants when I arrived. She wanted me put within the mines like I was at the Rom Pŷr J'in. So, to test my mettle she sent me to the kitchens. Having spent my early years as a captive of the Rom Pŷr I knew the Omjaddas regularly subsisted on blood. Vranac Pŷr's monthly consumption of my sangreal fluid as I grew to adulthood was common among the kindred. Once I matured though, they only consumed blood from bites, either on the neck, my wrists, sometimes my breasts or thighs. All this I have told you before. The only time that they did not feed from me was when we were too busy in the mine quarries constructing new temples and chambers for the palace or when they forced me to breed. Once I had undergone the Ja Rů Tộk, having been transformed into a Vam, they never took sustenance from me again. So, I was fully aware of their feeding habits when I came to the Tien Däm Mu, or so I thought."

Lazily, Dominique stroked Linnet's long, dark hair as she spoke. The scent of candle wax, burning wicks, and incense imbued the Vam Pŷr's chambers with soft aromas and a demure light. It comforted Lin to think on it now, surrounded by the stinging dark.

"The Tien Däm Mu J'in were known as the Clan of Blood. This was an honorific moniker, having some claim to the royal bloodline of the Jadda Asli Roh by some celebrated cousin. So…"

"But I thought you changed that?" interrupted Linnet.

"I did. Listen."

The consort nestled quietly into the nook of the woman's arm.

"The clan was also known for its distribution system of human blood and the use of human beings as a source of meat."

The young girl wrestled around the woman's arm again, propping herself up, and stared at the Vam Pŷr, shocked, not saying a word.

"In the kitchens it became my job to flay the meat off the bone. Another slave had the job of terminating the prey. And yet another slave had the responsibility of boiling the bones for broth. They did this for all meats, not just those that came from humans. You must understand, they saw no clear distinction between people and an animal from the forest. The bony remains were processed; some crushed and used in powders, some used in the construction of catacomb walls, while others were used for decorations. It was all very orderly and efficient. The Omjadda did not waste a single thing. To them every part of an animal was vital to the survival of the clan. To waste any of the beast was a disrespect to Gai'Anâka. It was a tribute to the sacrifice of spirit that all parts of flesh were used for the benefit of the people.

Ele thought to break me by placing me in the kitchens. Surrounded, days on end, in slaughter, stinking of death. Instead she fortified me! She gave me more than enough reason to break my bondage and flee the Omjadda Keep. Upon close inspection I saw exactly what they were. How they lived. They had plenty of dirty secrets. I do not think they realized that I spoke their language. Having come to the Rom Pŷr so young I learned it quickly and kept it to myself. The Omjadda cooks did not even consider us when we were in the room…talking away as if we were invisible." Dominique paused and looked down at the woman nestled across her chest, whose heart thudded rapidly against her ribs. "Even for all that I have just told you, it wasn't the worst of it. The worst was the Chaya Ip."

Linnet stirred. She couldn't imagine anything worse than skinning people to feed to the ancient race. She slid her hand across Dominique's flat belly and rolled over so that she could see her face. Candle wax dripped onto the stone floor delicately as she listened.

"The Chaya Ip was something altogether ugly and barbaric and the Tien Däm Mu were renowned for it. Ele made sure that I assisted the Chef in preparing the hellish meal and then served it to her guests at her functions. The Chaya Ip was a tower of six human beings, three women and three men. It was my job to coerce each one of the unlucky participants to imbibe a sweet wine that not only made them compliant and listless, but it enhanced the flavor of their meat, or so I was told. Then we stripped them naked, bathed them, and shaved each one of all their body hair, and finally scented their skins with a mixture of herbal oils that the Chef had prepared. Once they were ready the Chef bound them together with seasoned leather straps that he'd marinated for at least three days in a pungent solution. He arranged the humans to his own musings and what emerged was an intertwining tower of torsos and limbs bound together by the soaked and dripping leather straps. We, that is, the servants of the kitchen, had to remain attentive lest the Chef called for us as he constructed his monstrous sculpture. Usually, the sweet wine made them docile enough. But on occasion we were forced to hold the unlucky victims as the Chef tied the straps together."

Dominique sighed, a long-winded gale that swept across Linnet. "In the center of this living sculpture was usually set an array of exotic fruits. The fruits varied depending on who it was that prepared the Chaya Ip. And always in the center of the collection of the soft delicacies was there placed a precious gem. A diamond or a ruby, a sapphire or emerald, again, the nature of the stone was indicative of the artistry of the Chef that prepared the grand meal.

Once the Ip, the jeweled centerpiece, had been placed and the fruits and seasonings arranged and the living tower of flesh constructed we carried the whole mass into a large standing oven. There, the Chaya Ip was roasted to perfection as the men and women that comprised the grotesque meal slowly burned to death in agonizing pain. Their screams filled the kitchen as the sweet wine in their bellies and veins boiled, seeping its sugary water into the coarse fibers of muscle tissue. What emerged from the stone hearth of the concealed oven was a torturous mountain of twisted bodies, their faces golden brown in the last moments of horror as they were slowly roasted alive. The Chaya Ip was traditionally served during celebrations and feasts wherein Ornn and Ele entertained dignitaries."

"How many of these things were you forced to make?" asked Linnet solemnly from the crook of Dominique's arm.

"Too many." The Vam Pŷr fell silent for awhile as the story nested between them. "It was considered an honorable prize to the one that breached the outer wall of the Chaya Ip and found the roasted jewel."

"Barbaric," Linnet spat.

"The Ip was considered the eye in the mountain, the center of Gai'Anâka, to which the tower of flesh, the Chaya, was dressed. It symbolized the hidden nature in all things. The beauty that dwells at the heart of all creation."

"God, you sound as if you admired the thing."

"What have I always instructed you?"

Linnet thought on it, stroking her dark mistress's belly with the tips of her fingers, feeling chastised. "To know your enemy…"

"As yourself," finished Dominique.

The former Persian captive rose, jostling Linnet to the side, and crossed to a small chest that was resting on a shelf within the armoire. Unlocking the chest, she pulled an item out. Linnet could not see what it was. The Vam Pŷr closed the chest's lid and turned around. The item was covered in a raggedy, old red cloth. Dominique sat on the bed next to the raven haired beauty, holding the object in the flats of both hands between them.

"During my first Chaya Ip I was instructed to dispose of the remains of the meal. Among the leftover mashed fruits and bits of half eaten flesh I noticed a sturdy thigh bone that had not been cleaved in two for its juicy marrow. I stole it and hid it on my person." Dominique unwrapped the first layer of cloth from the object. "Over time I ground the large bone down and carved it into this."

The Vam Pŷr lifted the last layer of ruby cloth from the object and lying across her opened palms, in the red brilliancy of the antique wrapping, was a decorative bone knife. Linnet stared at the deathly instrument held aloft in Dominique's hands. It had been painstakingly carved with thick symbols that Linnet recognized as Omjadda, but she had a hard time deciphering the script. It was a dialect that she did not readily comprehend. The knife was a solid piece about twelve inches in length and the ivory blade curved outward from the hardy hilt to a gleaming, sharp point. A dull, dark reddish hue stained the tip of the knife, running down its fine edge. Dominique handed the artifact to Linnet. It had a calcified weight and when the young maid curled her fingers around the hilt she felt instantly how powerful the blade was for killing.

"It took me years to craft the bone into this blade. It kept me sharp. I feared growing complacent in the J'in Ankh's home. I had been a captive for nearly three hundred years by this time and life among the Omjadda was all I knew." Dominique sighed. "Something in me died in those kitchens and in its place something dark sprouted wings and I knew I had to escape…or die trying." She placed a lithe hand to her deadly creation as Linnet looked up at her. "Finding Ramielle and nursing her back to health allowed me to remember what it was like to be human again. My ire was raised anew when I found her and when I showed this knife to her one evening as it rained, I vowed to free her from her tormenters and take us both far away."

Dominique gently lifted the bone blade from Linnet's dainty hands and slowly wrapped it back in its cloth. "You are now the third person that I have shown this knife too."

The Vam Pŷr crossed to the opened armoire and lifted the chest's lid. The rusty hinges on the tiny box squeaked, sounding much like the wine that infiltrated her ears.

"Who was the other person?" Linnet remembered asking her bygone lover as she glared at the ancient woman by her side. "If Ramielle was the first and I am the last, who else besides you has seen this knife?"

Dominique turned, still holding the covered blade. "Ornn Däm Mu."

"You mean..."

"Yes." Dominique shook her head solemnly. "He saw this knife just before I slit his throat with it."

Linnet climbed off the bed and stood. She had heard the tale of how Dominique had killed Ornn, but never dreamed that she still possessed the instrument of his death or grasped that the virulent artifact had such a torrid and sadistic history. She paused, glaring at the cloth-covered bundle, the tumblers of her mind franticly working.

"This is the knife that you killed Ornn with?"

Dominique nodded and Linnet crossed to her dark mistress. The young maid peeled the red cloth back and looked again at the decorative carvings inlaid in the hilt of the knife that slew the Omjadda lord and his wife. Linnet slowly ran her fingers over the sacred weapon.

"It is his blood that you intend for me to drink so that I can become as you?"

Dominique wrapped the knife back up. "If it is what you will...then, yes."

"Did not Ele see the knife before you killed her too?

"No." Dominique placed the ancient bone back within the chest. "She was running away from me when..."

Her words ran out of air as she returned to her perch on the broad covered bed. Linnet stood, an island between the chest that held a link to her dark mistress's past and the woman herself, who lay afloat on a downed raft amid a sea of sensuality and brutal imagination.

"You still have not told me," chided Linnet, as she returned to the steady roost, "how you came to have your own quarters within the Omjadda Keep."

Dominique lifted her eyebrows and moaned, a throaty acknowledgement, caught in the delicate trap she had laid within her own stories.

"I have wanted to tell you for some time, but have always avoided it." She paused while Linnet sat next to her. "Ornn took me as his lover."

"I suspected as much."

Dominique smirked. Her darling Linnet was always keen to her even without explanation. "He arranged for me to have private quarters so that he could visit whenever it pleased him to do so."

"Did he force you?" asked the attentive maid.

"No." Dominique shook her head tightly. "I cultivated it as much as he." The Vam Pŷr felt the heft of her lover's stare. "For all his differences, he was a very regal and powerful creature. He was refined, even though his people were brutal. He possessed an alluring mystique that harkened back to the primordial days when his ancestors lived within the Lanz Gur Mae. He was handsome enough, yes. Tall; and could be very delicate when the moment arose." She paused remembering. "He was a gentle lover. Kind. In private he treated me with the utmost respect and appreciation. And there were times that I thought that he actually cared for me."

Linnet could see the hurt within her dark mistress as she spoke. Whether or not Ornn had loved her was not the issue that the caused great matriarch's brow to furl into painful worry. It was evident to Linnet that Dominique had come to love the Omjadda J'in Ankh, but to win her freedom she had to murder him, face to face.

"He would linger in our bed after coital passions instead of running back to Ele. He gave me presents and told me a great many things about his people. Their history, their customs and way of life; their laws, and after a time I shared with him that I spoke his tongue and he taught me to write it." Dominique's face drew up into a sour position.

"What is it?"

"It is his words, spoken to me, that I carved into the hilt of the knife. *Born of Moon, you are my eternal night, my beautiful end.*"

Linnet made a face. "Do you think he knew that you would one day be his death?"

Dominique shook her head slowly, up and down. "Yes. He saved me from my execution when I was but a girl. He sent orders to the Rom Pŷr instructing them to educate me in how to live among their household, instead of having me killed. From that day foreward I was groomed to live among the Tien Däm Mu J'in by *his* will. Fedah Maalj was with him on the balcony when they brought me to see him."

"The Jaddat?"

Dominique nodded. "Ornn told me that she brought him there that day to save me. That I was the one that would carry the Omjadda seed to the other end of time. That I had to live in order for their race to survive."

Linnet felt a heaviness descend within her chest. "Do you think she meant for you to use Ornn's blood as you have?"

"I do not know. Personally, I do not believe in the sight of the old witch and I'd rather see all the Omjadda dead before I pass anything of theirs to the other end of time."

Linnet felt Dominique's callused words roll across her shoulders in hard gusts of silty winds. The chaos that swirled around them was as dense as Dominique's old rhetoric. The memory lent a wicked bitterness to the cascading sandstorm. Linnet feared that all her former lover would recall in her absence was the harsh words that they recently shared before she had left to go to New York.

"What of this woman?" Linnet remembered asking.

"Ramielle?"

"How did she play into all of this?"

Dominique's brow knotted. "Despite her fevered and battered condition, her loss of family and friends, and the upheaval of all she knew, she clung to life. She reminded me of myself before the Ja Rǔ Tôk and I couldn't take myself away from her. I knew that if I were caught giving her aid I would be killed. But in Ramielle I saw hope…and a way to escape the bondage I had so far endured."

Linnet peered at the huddled coven leader, searching for the hope that Dominique had seen. She wondered if the woman still possessed the strength and will to outlast the jaws of the storm, as she had done against the Omjadda.

"The main house of the Tien Däm Mu J'in was not adjacent to the slave quarters or near the mines where most of the Vam worked," recalled Lin's memory. "There was no contact between any of us. There was no foreseeable way to orchestrate a strike and unhinge the operations of the great house. They kept us isolated. I'd come to learn through bits of news here and there that other clans had suffered slave revolts, but the Omjaddas always quelled them quickly. This was mostly due to two offensive weaknesses. The first being able to organize a synchronized attack to the entire structure of the Keep, and the second was the assistance of an outside force. With each failed attempt of the Vam the Omjadda cleansed the slave population to a fifth and restocked their ranks to avoid any possible repetition of offense. This left any resistance too thin to effectively manage a revolt. It was shrewd, but it kept the status quo.

Now, I have told you briefly, on occasion, about one of us: Joshua of Mauretania. He was born by the blood of Uraal Shiya, of the N'um Vala'Shiya J'in, when he and his traveling companions sought refuge among the Berber kingdom. Joshua, his father, and sisters took the three Omjaddas in. Uvii, Uraal's wife, was injured. Joshua, then only a young man, along with his family nursed the injured kindred back to health before the villagers grew restless, having the strange creatures amongst them. It was not long before an armed rabble descended upon his home and took the Omjaddas by force. They killed them of course, and in their own savagery feasted upon them and were transformed. But hellishly. Not properly or indicative of the Children of Evensong. Joshua slew the villagers that had killed them, and in his arms the dying Omjadda revealed many secrets, bequeathing a quest of the mortal man. Which was for him to collect their bloods and return with it to their J'in over the seas and mountains in India, far away."

"But why?" Linnet asked.

"As I have told you, Omjadda blood retains a sentient quality. When they imbibe the vital fluids of their fallen brothers and sisters they relive that life. They gain all of the knowledge that either he or she had acquired during their long tenure on Earth."

"Though, it is not like that with you?"

"No it is not. When the Omjadda blood absorbs our fluids it becomes something altogether different."

"But you see visions of the past from the blood that the Omjadda has experienced."

"It is distorted. Broken. A way for the blood to communicate its intentions of hunger; nothing more."

"It is hard for me to understand such a state," confessed Linnet. "I guess I will just have to wait until I receive Ornn's blood." Linnet paused, a bit shocked by her fresh thought. "Do you think I will see you with him? Or, the moment when you killed him from his eyes?"

Dominique looked nonplus. "I do not know. You may." She scrutinized her consort for a second. "Will that disturb you?"

"No. I should think not." She smiled a sly sideways grin. "I have already seen you in the throws of passion." Linnet leaned into her dark mistress and kissed her. "I am not so easily offended or made to feel jealousy."

"You are a remarkable young woman," breathed Dominique, her whole body humming from the moist warmth of the live girl's lips.

Linnet blushed, still unaccustomed to the Vam Pŷr's praises and adoration even after all these years. She curled into her dark mistress's form and asked how she had met the Moroccan stranger.

"He was part of a trade emissary's delegation from the N'um Vala'Shiya J'in and I slipped him a note." The Persian woman chuckled in remembrance. "I had to run clear across the other end of the castle, out over the turrets as the sun rose. The stones were so cold on my bare feet." She paused and breathed a sigh of relief as Linnet imagined a frantic Fizza sprinting through the opened air. "He found a way to meet with me before his departure and together we devised a plan to free the Vam of the Tien Däm Mu J'in.

But Ornn found Ramielle in my chambers one night when he intended to come to my bed, nearly upsetting all of my plans." Linnet gasped. "By this time she had her strength, and in truth I was just hanging onto her because I did not know what else to do. I'd grown accustomed to her face. I liked having her around. And though I knew I had to find a way to plant her among the slave population I did not readily want her to leave.

Ornn returned from a trip one evening and thought I was privy to his arrival and had left the woman there for him, as a repast to nourish himself after his long journey. When I entered my chambers I found him supping at her neck. Instantly, I knew that my loneliness had cost me my one and only chance in three hundred years of escape. I was sure he would drain her to appease his rank hunger." Dominique huffed and smirked, a devilish grin. "Luckily, it was not blood that he craved that evening and Ramielle was spared.

After I calmed his passions and we lay together I asked him if he'd consent to have Ramielle enter the Ja Rů Tộk. He declined and chastised me for keeping her around to feed my own dark need for blood, saying that it would draw unwarranted attention, that it was undignified for a Vam to retain a consort as I had done."

"So he suspected nothing?"

"No. Humans were nothing more than meat to the Omjadda. The Vam were set apart, raised only slightly by their symbiotic condition. Though mere slaves, we carry the sacred vessel, the Jadaraa Soo. We, who are chosen, become property of the clan. By their blood they own us. Ornn did not find Ramielle worthy of such a distinction and bade me to return her from where I found her. He failed to see past my own symbiotic condition and see the human spirit that still dwelt within me. For all his gentle love and tenderness he failed to see who I was. I was nothing more than an instrument to satisfy his appetite and lust."

In Ornn's bed she plotted her exodus, thought Linnet.

"I knew that if I returned Ramielle as Ornn commanded that she would be dead in a matter of days. The cruelty of the guards was monstrous, but I had little choice. If Ornn found her in my chambers again he'd have killed her and I'd be punished. He would have no choice but to see it through. I was, after all, a Vam. The Lord of the Keep could not be seen showing favor to a lowly slave.

With less than a month before Joshua was to return with a militia to attack the Omjadda stronghold my hands were tied. So, I instructed the young woman to go willingly into the arms of the beasts, to feign billowing lust, and embrace their brutality to lure them in. When the moment was right, I told her that she needed to bite one of them on the neck, drawing their blood into her mouth and drink heavily of it.

I told her that if she did this she would become transformed like me and that the guards would have no recourse but to put her among the slave population in the mines to cover their own misdeeds. I explained to the poor woman what would happen to her if she did not do what I instructed. Ramielle understood and I shared with her the plans I'd made with Joshua. He was set to return on the moon's next rise with an armed contingent, and for his assault to succeed, we needed the might of the Vam to revolt. I instructed her to go among the slaves and unite them for the attack and await the first cannon shot to rise up.

It was a long, slow month waiting in the wings with no word from her or Joshua. I honestly did not know if it was going to work or not. But when the signal rang out and that first canon shot took out the wall of the south tower, I finally knew what hope tasted like. The Vam, lead by Ramielle, took up whatever tools they could muster and fought. They fought hard and mean. Many died, but they never gave up, never surrendered, and we won the day. I promised her that if life still thrived within me that I would come for her. And I did." Dominique paused, her breathing strong and heavy in a slow, metered way, as she exhaled her final phrase. "I came for her and we left that place."

Linnet recalled lying in the symbiont's loving arms after the tale, thinking. Most of the candles that were lit had burned down to the base. The room smelled of wick smoke and had grown dark like the sky before her now. The feelings of resting in Dominique's pale arms, as her son rested in his bed in the house above, warmed the vampire's agitated heart. Like her dark mistress those bygone days still ate at her, raw and sore. Even after all of this time and the pain that had supplanted their love Lin still felt something for her Persian beauty. She thought about how the woman's curves fit against her own and how her once human breath used to be the lap of the ocean to the beach on which their love resided.

It did not please the stubborn vampire that her final hours upon the earth were drenched in intimate thoughts of Dominique. She came to Ramielle to get away from her. The two old lovers were tearing each other apart. They were fighting constantly, years of arguing, and after the last row, and all that broken glass, Lin had split. Decades of off-again-on-again romance had left the young vampire bitter, but resolute to start again. The entire nineteenth century was wasted, waiting for Dominique to come back from one thing or another. There was little love left in Lin's bruised heart, and yet, here she was thinking of Dominique again as the wind beat against her small frame in the blinding blizzard.

She turned to Jordan. He was still beside her. A small comfort.

He buried his face in the crook of his arm to block the sand-strewn gusts. Ramielle coughed and spit up a glob of dirty phlegm into the wind behind her. Her Jadaraa Soo was taking in too much soil. Even with Lin's scarf wrapped around her face she was still swallowing dirt and it was hard to breathe. She didn't know how the others could do it and began thinking that pretty soon they'd begin falling off, one at a time. *Trees in the forest. One by One.* No one would hear them fall. *No one at all.* The sandstorm would bury them like they never existed. All her pain and years with the grand matriarch would finally be over.

Strange, that on the first time that Lin had actually met Ramielle she did not like her. It was 1822. Paris, France. The carriage took her to a little villa overlooking the center of the magnificent city. Gaslight ignited the town in gentle orange blooms, as evening set heavy. A swirl of rain clouds deepened the sky with promise. Linnet wasn't even sure that Dominique had gotten her letter, informing her that her protégé was going to stop by for a visit. There had been no reply and her trip abroad took her out of Africa sooner than she had expected. She couldn't stay in that desolate place any longer. The air was too hot and dry. The nights too cold, and all that was left of her son, William, lay beneath a mound of fresh earth, next to his father.

The letter she received from Ana Luzia, informing Linnet of William's passing, arrived once she was already onboard the frigate. William's death came to Linnet in a dream, waking her in a frightful state, sheets soaked in blood sweat. The vampire didn't hesitate and arranged her travel. This voyage would mark the first time that she had returned across the Atlantic since her initial passage with the Vam Pŷr and Laurel in 1775. She was pregnant with her son then and journeyed in company and comfort. Now, the death of her son placed her onboard another vessel, alone, and carried her, once more, over the sea – William's life complete. A circle of time defined by the swells and mood of the ocean, defined by the pull of Jaci.

At the gravesite, William lay beside his father, Nsia Bah, for eternity and Ana Luzia had become gray and bent with age. The wrinkled woman marveled at how youthful and pale Linnet looked after all these long years. She told the grieving Mother about her son's life. Most of which she already knew from Ana Luzia's many letters. The Portuguese woman had remained a true and faithful servant to Dominique and Linnet, bridging the gap with the vampire's son between the Children of Evensong and the lost African Tribe. William's life, his sacrifice of birth, had stayed the hand of war just as the Vam Pŷr knew it would. Though, hearing of her son's adventures among the tribe without her made the gulf of loneliness in Linnet's breasts all the more painful and she ached to see her dark mistress again.

It had been nearly twenty-one years since Linnet had last seen Dominique. The Vam Pŷr's pursuits abroad to create a Vampire Council and reign her Children of Evensong into a single cohesive unit had pulled them apart. In less than a decade after Linnet was transformed by the blood of Ornn Däm Mu in the cellar of Casa del Rio Dulce, Dominique was gone, traversing Europe and Asia to unite her hybrids. The two distant lovers survived on letters, their passions put on hold for the grand scheme.

They were reunited on the eve of the aeon. Dominique returned the casa and Linnet's reticent arms at the end of the revolutionary era to pick up the pieces from were they last fell. Even though Linnet relished and loved her moments with the Vam Pŷr she knew in her heart that it would not last. The freed blood slave was consumed by her passion for The Council and the home that they'd built together in Brazil felt like nothing more than a way station.

With yet another war brewing on the horizon of the nineteenth century, this time between the emerging North American empire and the Atlantic coastlands, Ramielle had sent word, in the manly shape and form of Deven St. Cloud, to extract Dominique from the tranquil, loving lands of the Engenho. The tributes paid by seafaring countries for safe passage through the Mediterranean Sea had grown wild since the days and nights when the two freed slaves fed upon pirate coffers. Now, mostly driven by the greed of avarice men, the tax levied by the Ottoman Moors of the Barbary States of Northern Africa was a continual thorn in the sides of the emerging world powers of England and the United States. As the defacto J'in Ankh of the Tien Däm Mu J'in, Dominique was a tributary to the course of affairs on the Barbary Coast. Though no communication had yet arrived from the ancient clan to the hybrid monarch, Ramielle urged Dominique to negotiate on behalf of the Omjadda J'in with the President of the United States, thereby cementing her dual roles as a leader among the ancient race and the newly forming Vampire Council. It was an opportunity that could not be missed.

"It is a test," Dominique explained to Linnet on the roof of the main house during a humid night. A damp thickness filled the jungle around them with floral scents. "The Omjaddas show very little interest in aligning themselves to a council erected by former slaves and our half-bred brood. The Dalam Kha'Shiya J'in has great influence in the

West. With the burgeoning power of the North Americans and French Revolutionaries giving the humans a greater foothold in their own stately affairs it is just a matter of time before they begin to challenge the validity of the old ways. You will understand this better after a few centuries have passed and you've witnessed the way of the world."

"But I do not want you to go," Linnet restated, crossing her arms over her chest. "You have barely been back a year."

"Then come with me." Dominique hurried through the distance between them and enveloped Linnet in her arms. "We'll go to the States together and– "

"You know I can not." Linnet moved away, angry. "Without my involvement *here* your interests in this hemisphere would soon dismantle."

Dominique exhaled a rude, exasperating sigh, feeling the sting of truth as Deven climbed the ladder, joining the two lovers on their nightly perch. He was Celtic born, had a strong, broad chest, faint hints of red in his dark auburn hair and beard, and thick hands of a workman. His fingertips still had calluses though his days of manual labor were long over. He'd first come to Casa del Rio Dulce after Sergeant Francisco da Sillva and his men attacked the Engenho and killed Laurel Davenport along with the entire house staff in 1776. He arrived with two other consorts then; Anna Luzia and Coralene de Brienne: all of them were fresh off the boat and became vital members of the Vam Pŷr's entourage.

"I've just received word," he imparted urgently. "The ship is set to sail two days hence."

Linnet's eyes flashed angry with him, a riled hornet's nest of need, breaking upon his physical presence for his intrusion and the delivery of such awful news.

"Political attitudes have changed with the century," explained Dominique again, trying to make the young vampire understand her mindset. "Our revolts have spilled wildly into the world over the past two hundred years. Sometimes, in awkward and strange ways. I have a responsibility…"

Linnet turned away from her dark mistress and stormed the length of the flat roof. The Vam Pŷr's earnest words hit her cold back. "…to intercede on behalf of our people." Dominique's face contorted in hurt as Linnet climbed down the ladder. "I will not be gone so long this time. I will be back before you know."

Linnet was gone. Her footfalls clamored through the house below. Deven stared at his feet, feeling unpleasant and cumbersome. Slowly, he crossed to his dark mistress.

"Give her time," he said, placing a hand to Dominique's shoulder. "She knows. She knows."

But Dominique did not return as promised. Ramielle's intercession and building The Council took the Vam Pŷr farther from home as one thing after another erupted, requiring her attention. The First Barbary War gave small freedoms to the world by clamping a boot on the extortion of commissioned piracy. It gave the fledgling United States a chance to prove itself since their revolution. It also gave The Council its first solid foothold as a diplomatic entity. Even the closed minds of the Dalam Kha'Shiya J'in were forced to take notice, having their machinations to supplant the American Colonies as a new ruling power in the region thwarted by the efforts of the former blood slaves. The price for this small victory was abject loneliness and a wedge driven between the two ardent lovers. At first the letters and apologies were frequent, but over time they waned as Dominique was taken further and further from home. Eventually, the young vampire in the Southern slope of Brazil stopped looking for her dark mistress to return at all.

In Paris, Linnet stepped out of the carriage and stared up at the face of the building. Wooden portico doors, flower pots, lines of fresh plaster over aged cracks, the scent of piss and shit filled the gutters, while the aroma of bread and wine escaped from the warm glows inside. The vampire felt tired after her long journey, muscles sore, body humming from the sway of the carriage. She needed to feed. Linnet was not even sure that the address she had was viable anymore. Her eyes cased the windows of the top floor. Shutters closed, candle light burning from within. *If Dominique is here then she's going to be on the top floor. Jaci always had an affinity for the extremes of everything. The basement and the roof. It was the middle path that always troubled her.*

Climbing up the steps little things began to feel out of place to the vampire. The lack of human voices in the large, multi level building, the absence of empty milk bottles and newspapers lining doorways, and the same scents on every floor. There was definitely something odd going on. Reaching the top floor, Linnet found out what.

A young handsome man answered the door, half dressed, shirt wide open. Chiseled features and short, dark hair framed deep-set lazy eyes. Upon seeing Linnet he turned to the room beyond the hallway and announced in the dialect of the city that she was here. Linnet followed him in and the young Adonis left her in a large room without saying a word. Other men, also loosely attired, casual and languid on couches were spread throughout the darkly lit, opulent expanse. Bits of half-eaten food sat molding on dirty plates. It was their scents that Linnet had detected on her way up the stairs. Stacks of papers lined the walls under a massive chart with the names of various men and addresses written on it. Linnet felt their eyes on her pale form and one of them, a blond chap, sat up and winked at her…*as if to solicit me?*

The vampire heard footsteps in the other room coming her way. She turned and was introduced, without fanfare or acknowledgement, to the distinguished specter of Ramielle Eirinhas. The woman strode across the floor purposely with huge steps, welcoming Linnet to Paris. She was tall. Gorgeous. Linnet instantly felt dwarfed by her beauty. As she clasped Linnet's unready hand, explaining how she'd heard so much about her from Dominique, Linnet instantly decided that she hated her. Not just for all of the obvious reasons of being dazzling and sequestered away, for years on end, with the love her life. But that it was her fault that Dominique was taken from São Paulo in the first place.

Ramielle enveloped Linnet in her arms and led her to the balcony. She saw more men strewn throughout the place, some of whom had fresh bite marks about their person. They passed rooms filled with maps and tables piled with letters and documents. The domicile was a flurry of paperwork and social recluse. All the while, Ramielle talked in her ear like a sister, effervescent, leading her to the familiar form and face of her dark mistress.

"Oh, my gentle spirit," breathed the Vam Pŷr on a French tongue, rising. Her flesh was piqued from a fresh feeding and greeted Linnet on both cheeks in the continental tradition, hugging her tightly. Upon gently releasing her, Dominique stared within her marbled eyes. Linnet knew the look. She wanted to kiss her. She wanted to claim dominance in her soul once more, purchase the land of her flesh with her soft, pliable lips. The vampire pulled away.

"Have you already made arrangements for lodgings within the city?" inquired Ramielle.

"Yes. The Opéra Caravelle," Linnet lied. She'd come straight to the villa and made no such arrangements.

"Nonsense." Ramielle waved her hand through the air pushing the idea out of time and space. "You must stay here with us. We have plenty of room. And we shall not have it any other way."

Linnet looked from the tall, Spanish beauty to Dominique. The Vam Pŷr's demeanor was dour, eyes cautious to look upon her. Time itself was standing on the balcony between them.

"Yes, of course," she said, forcing a smile. "My things are still in the carriage."

"Excellent," bubbled the Vam Däm Mu. "I'll send André down to fetch them."

The woman momentarily disappeared leaving the old lovers alone on the balcony to stew in their awkward behavior.

"Your letter," began Dominique, "from Africa. It had only just arrived. You gave no news."

"He's dead."

Dominique's back stiffened and she folded her hands across her belly and walked lightly to the railing of the balcony. She overlooked the garden in the center of the city. "I am sorry."

"He lived a good life."

"Yes. I am sure he did."

The flat roofs of Paris stared up at the two estranged lovers as the last moments of a cloudy dusk buried itself in the horizon of a spinning Earth. Ramielle joined them on the outside landing feeling their quiet, heavy and clumsy, as small breezes carried the odor of the city across their deck. For a long while she said nothing, merely accompanying them in presence until she inquired if Linnet had taken a repast this evening.

"No," the vampire acknowledged. "I am traveling alone."

"Then I will send for Clèf," she announced. "What do you think?"

"Yes," Dominique agreed. "I think he would do nicely for her."

"Very well."

The Vam Däm Mu was off again, a bluster of activity, and returned with a young man in his mid twenties. His hair was long, past his shoulders, dark brown, and he had a lean face. He smiled at Linnet warmly.

"How would you prefer me?" the young man asked. "Here or should we retreat to some place private?"

Linnet found Clèf's manners cute. "Your Consort is very well behaved."

"Oh. He is not our consort," Ramielle informed. "He is a Prêteur de Sang. One of many actually. In fact, all of the men that you have seen here this night are blood lenders. They are in our employ."

"You pay them?" Linnet was a bit shocked at the notion. "Like prostitutes?"

"You did not tell her," Ramielle turned to Dominique.

"I have not had the time."

"Tell me what?"

As Ramielle explained, the two had hit upon the idea of providing a service to their kind wherein they would have no need to hunt for blood among the human populace. This Service, she outlined, would send Sanglants to the abodes of vampires for a small fee, thereby cutting down the problems that many of their kind had experienced in the past, risking exposure to human authorities. Ramielle detailed how they started it in Paris and how it had become highly successful. Murders in the capitol city had dropped since Ramielle and Dominique began providing blood lenders for hire. Now they were beginning to branch out in two other cities, London and Beijing.

"Even the Qamar Däm J'in have expressed their interest to partake of The Service," clarified Ramielle.

"It is the first real advance from an Omjadda J'in to take our efforts with The Council seriously," Dominique added.

"But I thought the N'um Vala'Shiya had already recognized The Council," inquired Linnet.

"They have," Dominique affirmed. "But they are isolated from the other six clans and had forsaken the use of humans as sustenance thousands of years ago. The Qämar Däm's interest in our Service is the first real tier in establishing ourselves."

Linnet shook her head passionately, disagreeing. "Why do you even pander to the Omjadda or care if they recognize your Council or not? I thought the whole reason you wanted a single governing body was so that our kind had some form of structure and balance within the world."

"It is," Dominique voiced, vividly animated. "And we've made great strides in achieving that balance. But to ignore the power and authority of the Omjadda, at this stage in our development, would be foolish. The humans, for all of their little power plays and wars, are still largely controlled by the influence of the old ones."

Ramielle burst out laughing. "I see now what you see in her, Fizza. Such passion and intellect. It is a shame that she has not been with us all this time."

Linnet withdrew internally. For all the Vam Däm Mu's good intentions her comment set a nail against the bone of her chest plate and drove the small iron stake through her heart. The past twenty-one years had been a long, lonely time, isolated in South America. There was much bitterness and sorrow in Linnet. She did not have the stomach at this moment to inform either of them that she would not be staying long in Paris, that she'd already arranged to do some business on the docks and return home.

Over the past few years Linnet had become an anonymous supporter of the Brazilian rebels, working to dismantle the African slave trade. In her dark mistress's absence, she picked up Dominique's passion against slavery and had taken to funding and supplying arms to the Quilombos that dotted the dense countryside. She came to Europe, in part, to solicit support for her cause in the great country. Brazil had finally gained its own independence from Portugal, but the new government was following in the footsteps of their northerly neighbor by ignoring the issue of slavery. It was the vile way of the world to build paragons of earthly achievement on the backs of the abused. Linnet was here to buy guns and take them home. So to ignore remarks now that would later have to spill, Linnet excused herself from the conversation, taking her Prêteur de Sang to a room so that she might nourish her thrumming and hungry Jadaraa Soo.

Ramielle coughed up another globule of soiled phlegm, pulling Lin from her memories.

The storm was thick and rancid, stinging their ears with shrill cries, never-ending. Impenetrable, the spirals of dust moved in such a way around them that it tormented Lin's balance if she stared directly into it. So she kept her head down, watching her feet trudge on.

The second time she met the Vam Däm Mu was in 1895. Linnet was traveling the rustic West with Dominique. They were on again, and Lin had joined the council member as she engaged in meetings with an emissary from the Dalam Kha'Shiya to further talks on the J'in's involvement with the vampire council. It had been exactly fifty-seven years since Ramielle and Dominique had formerly announced The Council's emergence and released their first bylaws, and the last Omjadda J'in was still on the fence. Though by now, the Dalam Kha'Shiya had relaxed enough to allow Vam, and the brood of Vam, to enter the northern district of the United States and Canada. Access was carefully monitored. The numbers of vampires admitted in America and places they could go were strictly limited and painstakingly supervised. It would be another twenty-five years before the Dalam Kha'Shiya J'in formerly recognized The Council and endorsed trade between their species.

Ramielle awaited them in the arid city of Los Angeles. They were heading out of Colorado, coming down from the Rockies where the Omjadda kept a fort. It had been quite some time since Ramielle and Dominique had seen one another on Council business. Lin had encouraged her dark mistress to go to California even though she had no desire to see the woman again. She tired of politics and fake enthusiasm quickly. Dominique's life, as a council member, was full of it, entertaining one dignitary after the other, quelling political fires. It was not to Linnet's taste and the quiet nights among the stars, as they had lived in Brazil, were gone. To Lin, America was vastly under-developed. The mountain air was cold. She longed for warmer climates, and found that she and Dominique got along better when they were on the road.

There were twelve ruling members that sat on The Council. Dominique and Ramielle were the first onboard, followed by Deven St. Cloud and Coralene de Brienne. Twice, Linnet was asked to join The Council. Once, when she had visited the furious business ladies in Paris and again in 1836, two years before the declaration of The Council's first regulations. Linnet declined both invitations, and for awhile it became a point of contention between her and Dominique. The Vam Pŷr felt slighted. It was, after all, Linnet who had helped her to birth the idea of the governing body in order to stave off war with the Tribe. Linnet felt that she had paid that debt of peace with her flesh, sacrificing her son to the warriors. So each time the raven haired beauty spurned Dominique's gift of office it left the debt unpaid.

It had taken Dominique a remarkable fifty-seven years to build the dream of her council. The flesh of Linnet and Nsia's seed had not lived that long. Building the framework between each party had taken the Vam Pŷr across the globe, many times. She left Linnet alone in a foreign land. She became obsessed with its creation, driven to see her race achieve what no other had in *all* of history: a single governing body, a unified band. Since declaring The Council in 1838, the gilded twelve maintained influence on the nightly activities of their species. Working in secret, they had their fingers in the development of many industries. The Council provided The Service, which labored toward the salvation of their race and the Omjaddas. The Service allowed the night creatures to retreat from interacting with human civilization altogether, and their existence quickly became myth.

It was a success that Linnet refused to share with her dark mistress. Too much time stood between them like a broken river. Only now, at the twilight years of the nineteenth century was Jaci finally able to return to her Arci. But there was nothing left to mend between them. One hundred and fourteen years had passed. The bloom of their love was ancient history. Even the ironic symmetry of adjoining fifty-seven years was lost on them as they crossed the great Southwest. When in each other's company they spoke very little about the past. It was what it was – *Gone.*

Ramielle greeted them on the open veranda of her L.A. home's courtyard. A voluptuous moon showered them in soft blue light and the lush flowers of the garden filled them both with a sense of ease and home. The former blood slaves quickly fell into conversation about council matters and Lin took to wandering the grounds of the high desert keep.

"So…" the voice entreated from behind, hours later. "Dominique tells me that you've finally met one." Lin turned to see Ramielle in a cascading blue dress joining her for a bit of night air. "Were they what you had expected?"

"I don't know." Numbness pervaded her assessment. "Not sure what I expected. I had heard so much about them from Dominique and Nsia that…" her thoughts drifted off. "They were taller than I thought they would be."

"That they are."

"Just hard to place, you know. How they were the same ones that had enslaved you and Dominique."

"Different J'in."

"But still. You know what I mean, trying to picture it. At first, they don't strike you as being able to enslave a race of people. Let alone the likes of you two."

"But they did."

Linnet shook her head in agreement and chuckled. "They move so slow, and all the damn ceremony…"

"Don't let that fool you. They can be lightning quick if they need be."

"That's what Dominique said." She tightened her lip, thinking. "I guess I was expecting to see the veins." She looked at Ramielle and shook her head. "But they don't have them, do they? Their skin is as white and pristine as freshly fallen snow." She sighed. "They are actually quite beautiful."

"I know." Ramielle placed a hand to Linnet's shoulder. "That's the part that always gets me too. How could something so pure and innocent-looking be so cruel and vicious?"

"I am almost sorry that I've finally gotten the chance to meet them."

"Why?" She slipped her hand away.

Linnet stared at the desert floor before answering. "Nsia's people have been fighting them for millennia. They will eventually hunt them to extinction. They are all that's left of a dying race from when the world was new. Before mankind. Before the stories of Atlantis. Before us. And despite all that I know about them, I almost feel that they should be protected. Preserved. My son was a part of their genocide. I was proud of him for that. For as long as I can remember I believed them to be nothing more than an evil scourge upon the earth. And now…after meeting them and seeing with my own eyes…I don't know if that is true anymore."

Cicadas buzzed, hidden among the brush. A hawk soared overhead, spying a desert mouse.

"Time, out here, in America, has given me perspective,"

announced the Spanish widow. "One of the things that I have learned is that we are all given to great evil and great good. It depends on what path we choose that elicits that good and evil within us. The Rom Pŷr, Tien Däm Mu, and Dalam Kha'Shiya are merely the shades of the N'um Vala'Shiya, Fedah Layal, and Qamar Däm. Each J'in chose their path when they migrated across the Earth. In our pursuits toward freedom and independence, we have done the same. The vanity of absolute good and absolute evil is foolhardy. We are, at all times, both. It is the choices we make in the conflict of our decisions that define us."

Linnet nodded her head in agreement.

"Try not to judge what has been." The Vam Däm Mu spread her hand out across the starry sky. "The universe has a way of balancing it out."

For two months Linnet and Dominique stayed in Ramielle's delicate care as the Omjadda emissary deliberated with his J'in Ankh. Linnet grew favorable toward the former blood slave, setting her tired jealousies down. She began to look anew at Ramielle. She found her affect amicable, liking the woman's strong will, learned wisdom, and delicious sense of humor.

So, it was little wonder that in 1934 once her sordid romance with the Vam Pŷr had finally run aground in a violent shudder of pain and agony that the sensitive form of Linnet Pevensey wound up on Ramielle's doorstep, heart in hand, crying blood. The poor girl decreed that the final nail in the coffin of their love was struck and she just didn't know what to do or where to go. Ramielle took pity on her and invited Linnet to stay with her until she found her feet again. The young vampire needed someone who understood her ravishing ex as intimately as she did and the only one that fit that bill was the kidnapped bride of the Tien Däm Mu J'in.

Lin accompanied Ramielle and her entourage on her business to the East Coast and was with her for little less than a month when they had found the deviled storm. Thinking it grand to drive, the vampires were returning to Los Angeles. High ideals and merriment always seemed to precede the worst disasters, doom birthed off the lips of smiles, screams waited in the dark loll of laughter. The Titanic sunk while a quartet played, it's patrons partying, rubbing elbows with the iceberg. The Hindenberg ignited on the triumphant wills of arrogant philanthropists. The jubilation that went up at the discovery of Tutankhaten's tomb was followed by a deadly curse. The Stock Market crashed on the heels of the

Charleston's giddy delight. Decadence always danced with the damned.

Now, the sky was a buzz saw because drought hugged the vast prairies, an unforeseen result of feeding a war machine mired in the foxholes and trenches of Europe. The way of it was unfair and to Lin it just didn't matter anymore. The universe was balancing itself out. All of her heartache and years spent pining for Dominique was wasted. *I could have been with her.* All of her petty jealousies, hiding in the jungle wars of men! *I could have been with her.* Dawn neared and was going to rear its bright, ugly head. The storm was going to wane. The sky would clear and each of them, in their own private hell, was going to find a lonely, fiery death. Lin wished that her last words to Dominique were not harsh, as they had been. In the deep bosom of her breasts she ached with a powerful need to tell Dominique that she was sorry.

But through the dense canvas of swirling brown death Lin saw a faint flicker. At first she thought she imagined it until it came again, pushing its thin weight through the blizzard. It bounced behind the storm, off to her right. Could it be?

A light.

Yes. A light pierced the thick maw. Lean and tiny in the distance, Lin saw a yellow speck. Jordan saw it too, and together the three nocturnal travelers gravitated toward it like wayward moths on a sinking ship following the moon. The closer they got to the light the louder Prophet's calls swelled. Marching onward, they suddenly found themselves upon their excited comrade. An oil lamp held aloft in his hand, the flame struggling to survive against the beating winds. It looked as if he was adrift in a dark sea with an alien object that he had not had when he'd run off.

He pounded on the swirling sky with a metal pot. It created a thudding, wooden racket. Suddenly, there birthed a crack of light, angular and tall, and the wall of dirt broke open. Hidden in the blinding blizzard was a door.

The four travelers entered the light.

Shaking the solid, heavenly firmament from their coats, their hair, and their eyes it was awhile before the Vam Däm Mu and the lost vampires could take in their new surroundings. It was a spacious room, lit by candlelight. It smelled of earth, roasted pinion, and beans. The warmth of a fire raged in a Kiva and could be felt from across the room. Thick, brown adobe walls, a thatch roof, and wooden floor planks creaked under the pounding winds and movements of the villagers that had gathered in the great house to weather the storm. It appeared the whole town was walled up into this one dwelling, families nestled together, waiting it out.

Ramielle pulled the hood of her cloak down, exposing a gorgeous face, an exotic beauty that had weathered time, Omjaddas, pirates, and Ottoman Moors to stand before them. Dark red burgundy veins crisscrossed under her pale thin skin, as did all of the mysterious travelers. The Vam Däm Mu looked at the humbled farmers, their families, and her eyes blazed, not from the glint of the fire's light but from something else.

"You are welcome to stay with us until the storm passes," spoke an elderly man in a gentle Spanish.

"Gracias, Señor," she said with a wicked smile. "But I fear the storm has gotten worse…much, much worse."

All around Lin, death bloomed like a rose. Fragrant blood coursed through thirty frightened souls, and here she was, out of the storm that she was so certain would take her life; flung into the raging center between the hybrid killers and a waiting feast. She could feel the tension rising in the air. It was palpable. She didn't know how long the sky would rant against them. Maybe it would end soon? Maybe, in an hour? Maybe, come tomorrow. All Lin knew was that the storm wasn't going to end soon enough. They were thieves, the whole lot of them, trapped in a treasure trove and all the villagers had that was precious to them was the crimson fluid that fed their lives. It was the jeweled Ip at the center of the monstrous tower…and Prophet had found it.

Lin's gaze swept across the vicious grins of her companions, and instinctively she knew that the people gathered in this place did not have long to wait before something more horrible than God's wrath would begin tearing the flesh off their bones, like the beasts from which they were descended. She scanned the raw crowd. They were bound, just like the Chaya, to one another through faith, proximity, and family. There was no need for marinated leather straps. Entombed in a mud house, in the middle of nowhere, in the center of a spiraling doom, it was already too late. In the madness of the heartland, cannibals had found villagers.

Brina was on stage dancing, chest bared to the wall. Strobe lights fell on her soft, tanned skin, cattle eyes drifted from liquid sockets, buried in drinks when Sarah entered late. She was overly dolled up, too tired, and tried covering it with makeup. She knew she was running long when she hadn't woke from the alarm clock thrilling through her head like a spaceship. She got dressed for the club at home and rode the bus like a hooker. Eyes heavy, on her the whole time. It made her queasy.

Sarah tried to avoid Eddie, moving through the club, purposeful, knowing. He was sitting on his ole metal stool, large carcass spilling over. But she didn't have much luck. His cigar smoke hit her from across the bar. He was puffing away, a gigantic locomotive sitting in the back of the room, the gatekeeper from the stage to the dressing room.

"Hey Missy," he prodded like a knife. "You think I don't see you?"

Caught and nowhere to go, Sarah stopped, sighed, and turned around. "Hi Eddie."

"Is your watch broke? I don't remember a schedule change." He pointed at the Rolex strapped to his meaty arm.

Why yes it is, you fat bastard. And fuck you for noticing! Sarah didn't respond and started to inch away.

"Listen," he said, changing his pitch. "I talked it over with Tone."

"Yeah? What's that?" Sarah stopped again, caught in the orbit of his belly, forced to draw closer and see how his deodorant wasn't working. All she wanted to do was go home. She didn't care what he had to say. It didn't matter one way or the other and the anxiety caused her leg to shake.

"We don't want you to fail your classes an' shit. Just don't make sense. Why'd we want that? That's no good. A bad investment. So here's what we gonna do." He leaned into her and it was obvious that he'd been sweating for most of the day, sitting on his ass watching the girls' work. "You get us a schedule and nights you got tests or whatnot an' you can work a single. Weekends you work doubles and pick up a Monday or Tuesday running drinks, 'kay?"

Fuck! He just overloaded my week. Son of a bitch! Sarah just stood in his orbit, drooping her moon face like breezeless bed sheets left outside to dry.

"Okay?" he asked again, irritated that she didn't respond. It snapped her from her daze.

"Yeah. Sure. Thanks." With that she turned and marched toward the dressing room.

"You don't have to be grateful or nothin'," hollered Eddie at her retreating back. "Little shit. Not like we doin' you a fava!"

He jabbed the stub of his cigar into the pit of his mouth and watched the end of Becky's show. Sarah was awake now. Loud and storming, hating life, feeling the heavy press between a rock and a hard place restricting the airflow in her chest. She felt like she was on the verge of a panic attack. She was barely keeping up with the pace she had. Finally, far enough away, she spoke her mind. It was a single syllable, almost inaudible with the crash of music and meager applause from the scant crowd.

"Prick!"

She felt the sting too. Just as if it were the sharpened points of tendril fangs uncoiling in her throat, or the vile rape of her delicate system, Sarah felt the hard prick. The last gasp of her ignorant innocence was gone. Slap! Bam! A tattooed fist that read: *I love You.* She was being fed upon by everything around her. It was tearing her down. Consuming her soul bit by painful bit. Her dreams were impossible mountains to climb, wicked and thorny, she felt every sting. She felt every single little prick.

Lightning danced in the stratosphere, punctuating tight, short bursts within darkened clouds, making the night between each electric flare darker. The lights from the convenience store spilled out across the street, garish and mean, surrounded by empty desert and a highway that was a quarter of a mile away.

Kate Mauldune crossed the bare street to the unmarked police cruiser. They'd parked on the other side of the road beneath a Foothill Palo Verde that had planted roots more than fifteen years ago. The small leaf tree was the only cover available. The wind smelled like rain, tinged with acid. Mauldune opened the passenger side door, with loud clanks and sucking oxygen, and passed Wallace the cardboard container that housed three stirrers, two coffees, seven tiny milks, and five sugars. In the sealed cab of the cruiser the scent of a midnight roast filled the air as its heat condensed, beading up the edges of the windshield.

Wallace thanked the Lieutenant, removing his dark charred brew from the carrier and held it close to his face, inhaling the raw, watery bean. Mauldune set the container in her lap, opening hers up and operated on the caffeine solution, dumping sugars and milk and two stirrers into it.

"Different owner. Said she'd put the flyer up."

Wallace nodded, bobbing his head, and sipped the hot, bitter liquid, his face a scowl.

"So, ah…" the female detective started slowly. "You call Sally yet?"

Wallace turned and stared at her like it was none of her business. She got the message, sipping her sugary roast. Silence ate her ears. She'd only been on the Phoenix beat for a couple of months, transferring out of Chandler, AZ. She and the Chief decided it'd be best if she rode around with the seasoned grumbler. She had advanced in rank quickly during her years on the force, a big fish in a small pond, and the Chief wanted to make sure that she had the chops in the field before he put her behind a desk barking orders. Kate Mauldune just wanted the thrall of a big city under her belt. Needed it in fact, if she was ever going to make Captain. So, Phoenix it was.

The big lug wasn't that bad to hang around with as she got her feet wet. He took her extra stripe in stride and was a damn good cop. So she forgave him his verbal skills. He tried. The files that the detective collected over the years on all the arsons and murders were solid work. He'd made connections that other departments had missed and he was ready to throw it all on the line to prove his theory. She admired that, even if it did scare the living hell out of her.

"So, ah…" her eyes stayed glued on the hot lights of the convenience store as, off in the distance, lightning danced above its flat roof. "What's this one? Cashier and a customer. '93?

"Two Clerks. One Customer. '96," corrected Wallace. "Fire department caught the blaze early. Left most of the store intact. Charred the remains, though." His thoughts drifted in the quiet lull. "Accelerant, localized to the bodies. From the store."

"Hhmmm," she thought loudly, her coffee warm and robust. Even with all the sugars and cream it still tasted like it'd been left in the pot too long. "You think they'll return to the same spot?"

Headlights dotted the outlying horizon.

"Don't know."

Here she was joining him on what had to be the most absurd moment in what was yet, a shining career, and he didn't know. *Did. Not. Know.* Her stomach prepared for the Olympic Games, pole-vaulting. Unease rode her flesh. Nervously, she shifted her weight in her clothes and turned back to the concrete box of loud white lights. There was a rumble in the sky, miles away and moving.

"Well…" she added to steady her resolve, "It sure beats dancing for a living."

Kate wasn't fond of stakeouts, but it was par for the course. *Getting into the role, into the landscape.* Without turning around she egged Wallace's human side again, "You should really give Sally a call."

Muffled thunderclaps heralded the oncoming rain. Drops fell on the road first, between the cruiser and the convenience store, leaving both objects islands from the cloudburst. Then, lazily the water found them, tapping out bad rhythms on the metal roof. Thick, fat droplets, and then a steady pour, making everything wet. The windshield was murky, streaking a greasy sideshow carnival ride, and Wallace turned on the wipers.

"That's conspicuous."

Rubber thudded a constant grating tempo. The more seasoned, but lower ranked detective gave her a look and flipped them off. "Better?"

Mauldune laughed. She'd asked for it. Visibility through the wet-streaked glass was nil. "I guess. Well…maybe not."

Wallace turned the wipers back on and started the car. While idling in the dark, under the pitted yellow canopy of the Cercidium Microphyllum, Lin's great big baby blue Caddy rolled by, sloshing down the road, followed by Jake and Darryl in their pickup truck. Both vehicles were obviously speeding. None of it was the detectives' concerns. Speeders were local fodder. They had bigger fish to fry.

Kate hated the traffic beat, back in the day; trolling through Chandler, it made her feel like a useless shark. Lying in wait for the little fishes to scurry past so she could fill a quota and fund the next Policeman's Ball. It was busy work – *plain and simple: a money plan.* She sipped her coffee and was thankful that she wasn't out there chasing assholes, like the ones that just screamed by.

"You know, it's not gonna last that long," she commented on the rain, feeling the edge of something else.

"Never does," agreed Wallace, eyeing the all-night joint with cold intent.

The motel was tucked into a group of trees, off the road, family owned. Lin paid for two rooms using a fake ID and money from the cash register that she'd taken the other night. Laughing and pulling from a fifth of Jack, the raven haired beauty and Darryl fell through the door of number eight, leaving Z alone with her tall, lanky cowboy in room seven.

Jake turned on one of the lamps near the bed and looked around. Off white plaster walls, Southwestern art prints stuck in average looking frames, a wall heater, vent to a swamp cooler, a faded brown dresser, bland carpeting, and a bible tucked somewhere in one of the bedside table drawers. Jake hadn't ever been to a motel with a strange girl before. Z turned out the light behind him and ran her hand along his back.

He had loosened up over a few games of pool, several beers, and nonstop teasing. The girls whooped up on them, dominating the table in a way that made the young men's inhibitions manifest at the smoky bar. Beneath the lingering scents of alcohol, the pool bar, and Jake's dying cologne Z could smell the man, a down home rustic flavor that vaguely reminded her of riding horses in Alabama with Simon Ray in 1929. She sensed that he was nervous, standing there in the dark letting her touch him, letting her make the moves. Z pushed him onto the bed and laughed.

The springs on the covered double sleeper moaned and wheezed, bouncing Jake to a teasing stop. Lying on his back he took the skinny punk in, room spinning, the hum of his alcoholic blood settled with his laughter. Z was backlit by moonlight busting through thin, opened curtains. Jake liked her outline and the way she laughed. It was a bubble factory. The silhouette removed her jacket and shirt and then climbed on top of him.

"You should've taken the bet," Z said as she kissed him.

"Why?" he asked, his lip wet with spit, as she began to unbutton his shirt. "Here we are anyway."

Z cocked a crooked grin. "Yeah. Here we are anyway."

The room smelled of mothballs and Ajax. She planted kisses on his chest, not wanting to talk. Talking made him more human, more real. She pulled on both sides of his opened shirt, snapping the little buttons out of their holes. They shot around the room like shrapnel. They both giggled and looked into one another's eyes through the dark. His belt buckle dug into the meat of Z's thigh and she scooted back.

"You still should have taken the bet," she urged, wanting him to understand that he had a chance, but didn't take it. "Would've worked out better for you...in the end."

Above the slap of leather and the clinking rattle of unbuckling his pants, Jake asked her what she meant. But the cocky female just smiled a knowing grin and pushed him back down on the bed and pulled his dungarees off his hip and down his legs. He fiddled with his boots, sliding out of them with practiced ease as Z threw his jeans in a corner of the room.

Jake's tighty-whities were crisp and clean and the bulge under the soft cotton fabric seemed promising. With lithe fingers, delicate and sure, she removed the man's underwear.

"Ooooh," Z smiled as her eyes popped. "Who's a happy girl?"

She drank the luscious man up with her eyes, all spread out, naked and gorgeous, a waiting buffet for all her desires. Her hand went to his member, which under her fine touch, grew harder.

"Yeah. That's it." She groaned, giddy as a Catholic School Girl. "My little meat hammer." Her Jadaraa Soo thrummed and panged, anxious and wet with appetite. His hard rod filled her eyes, her fingers; Z lowered her head and opened her mouth.

She's a gaddamned porn star. Wet and holy, working him good, Jake was reminded of the last adult movie he'd seen and imagined the blond girl from the low-budget film as he felt Z stroking his fat cock. Her head bobbed up and down. He groaned in pleasure, the alcohol in his system sent the joy back again, humming and vibrant, in waves of Oh Yeah.

Z sucked in a breath, rising. "That's it...get all of that blood pumping...nice and fat." She slapped the little meat hammer with the flat of her fingers and whispered, "All that gorgeous blood." Slap! Slap!

Sounding clinical and insane, her tongue danced on the engorged head of his penis. The scent of testosterone and blood was thick in the air, a righteous cocktail. Head swooning, excitement rode her bones as she took him whole in her mouth again, pounding his balls with her face.

Jake panted hard in delight as she stroked a hand across his chest, down along his ribs, cupped his lower back, and grabbed his ass. She definitely wasn't from around here. *Had to be a city chick. Just had to be.* Z broke her maddening pace just when he felt like he couldn't take it much longer. The hardened meat hammer was large in her hands. She lifted up and started stroking him slowly.

"You like that, don'tchya?"

Jake moaned, deep and rueful, "Yeah."

Panting heavily, his chest rose and fell like an oil drill. Z looked up his elongated form. *Beautiful.* He was a well-cooked meal. A crazy good time. Had strong thighs that were flush and red. She played with the hair along his happy trail and fondled his nipples with her fingertips. Z was in love. For just this brief moment, this expanded stretch of time, the vampire silently appreciated the craftsmanship of the man.

"Tease me with your tongue again," he asked. "That was...that was..."

Z did. Flicking her deviled flesh against his reddened joy, she started to sing. *Oh, I'll tease you alright, and then I'mma gonna get some da na, hey, hey hey...*

Z hummed the song, Satisfaction, as she descended her battered mouth over his cock again. She was absolutely sure that it wasn't the first time that somebody, somewhere in the world, had gotten head while humming the Rolling Stones.

Jake's hand found Z's soft, dyed red hair and pulled. Through quaking eyes he watched the punk. Pretty as a porno in the darkened room. Each tug against her red tufts made Z grin and she pulled her teeth across his tender, taught skin.

"You feel...you feel sooo..."

Z stopped, a wide smile, panting softly. "Yeah? How do I feel?" *Cutesy. I'm a little tea cup.*

"Real good baby. Real..." and he lost the train of thought as it pulled into her hot, wet mouth.

He was getting close. She could smell it and taste his pre-cum as he pulsated against her lips. Jake didn't want to explode in her mouth, but he didn't want her to stop, either. He wanted to be inside of her, but he was *so* close. He tried to think of something else, of anything else to calm his excitement. His toes clenched and his breath increased as he begged her not to stop, arching his back, ready for the release. But Z did stop, lifting her wet grin. Drool connected her bottom lip to his hardened tip. She stroked him slow and lovingly with one hand. Jake's eyes battered shut like landmines, buried deep.

"Oh, we're not stoppin', baby," Z breathed in a huff. "We're just gettin' started."

Jake's pending orgasm relaxed into Z's slow, knowing hand. She tilted her head back, feeling his engorged man meat throb to the pulse of her Jadaraa Soo. Her entire rhythm swayed to the vibration of his dick. She opened her mouth wide, fangs extended to gleaming, sharp points, the veiny parasite coiling tighter across her cheekbones, and fell into his lap, one more time, with sudden, stark ferocity. Unexpected pain ripped violently through Jake, causing the landmines in his eyes to explode as he shot up, screaming bloody murder!

⸗×※◉※×⸗

Filtering through the poorly constructed wall of the motel room, Jake's screaming shattered the serenity of the live thing in Lin's arms.

"What was that?" Darryl broke the long, groping kiss, and moving forward, sat perched on the bed.

Lin surrounded his back, running her hands over his bare chest, her nails drawing thin white lines on his hot pink flesh. "Oh, that's just Z havin' a good time."

"That don't sound like a good time to me." He listened. Lin encircled him, straddling his lap, and picked his cowboy hat from off the bed and placed it on her head. "Maybe I should go see if they're alright."

"They're fine," Lin urged and kissed him.

Reluctantly, he fell back into the tender gyrations of the tattooed woman's tongue. Lin scooped her arms around his neck as Darryl's hands traversed under her shirt. That is, until the tumbling knocks and the crash of a lamp in the room next door pulled his attention away from the girl in his lap.

"That don't sound right," he said with far away eyes, itching to know what was happening in the other room.

"I said they're fine," Lin commanded, getting tired of the distractions when she'd finally found some interest in all of the fondling.

Darryl just looked at her, his passion abating. "Get off me."

He tried to shimmy out from under the vampire. Lin sat like a lead brick, legs crossed, holding him in as all the fun drained away to the dismal routine of feeding. Blank joyless mood slid into the air between them.

"I said, get off me," he urged with a grunt and this time Lin let him move her.

She rolled to the side of the bed as he got up and grabbed his shirt. She wasn't ready for the nasty bit. It had come too quickly. She was getting into the hot groping, breathy pants, and was actively contemplating sex with the young stud when he'd gone all Nosey-Nancy on her and ruined the moment. She stared at the pattern on the bedspread as cold depression slunk in and filled her pores with nothing brilliant or memorable; a bad mood, a bland seething.

"I'm gonna go see if everything's okay," announced Darryl like it meant two shits.

Lin turned hard. *If that's the way he wants it.* "Get that ass back in bed. We ain't done yet."

Darryl's small brown eyes went wide, hearing what he thought he heard. "Oh, yes we are."

He moved to the door like he was leaving - *conversation effectively closed!* But when he looked up Lin was standing in front of him. His mind did a double take. She *was* sitting on the bed, a lax position. *Now,* she was upright and blocking his path. "What? How'd you…"

Lin didn't answer him. She'd lost her joy. The fun had become as dull as the motel room's carpet. Now, it was all down to brass tacks and the same ole, same ole. She palm pressed him, letting her Jadaraa Soo do all the work; her arm was a jack hammered spring. Darryl flew through the air with the greatest of ease and slammed hard against the far wall, sliding down it to the ugly brownish-gray floor.

His chest stung. His breath hiccuped in his throat. Air gasping, raspy and thin, Darryl looked up to the biker dyke with her short cropped raven hair as she removed his hat and tossed it over to him. It landed on his sprawled out legs.

"You aren't going anywhere...*Cowboy*."

There was no excited thrill in Lin's voice, no aforementioned joy that she had experienced up to this moment. She didn't delight in the death dance the way that Z did. Her raucous fury in the next room still bled through the walls, tumbles and knock-a-bouts. Lin stared down at her meal, helpless and legs akimbo, as she released the hold she had on her Jadaraa Soo. Darryl held his chest and watched in horror as a thousand tiny dark, squiggly lines became visible under the pale glamour of the woman's exposed flesh.

Yeah, murder is contagious. Easy.

She had turned into a fine killer. Yet, year after year, decade after decade, centuries blending into the menagerie of common faces, out-of-touch places, and eons of dark, bitter nights staring down at her with consummate judgement it also became boring as hell. Darryl's screams rose up to the roof of the motel as Lin attacked him and disappeared into the blue-black sheen of the night. It hung on thin, leafless branches as Layal's brilliant orb stared down. Listening to the sour, ruthless killings, a crow flitted from a tree.

Fluorescent lighting, white and pasty, spread out like a disease making the club look rancid. Dank, wet liquor sweat, ripe like an athlete's sock drawer, filled the drab expanse. Just like a carnival ride, a midnight rodeo, everything looked cheap in the light. Even the girls. Especially the girls. All dolled up, tired and haggard, faces showing signs of wear, skin tight and sticky. They gathered around the bar. Counted tips. Rallied around the money. It was all for the money, anyway. No one even noticed the smells anymore. Senses dulled over time. Spirits dwindling from bad music, grinding crotches; sucked through a straw of machine lust.

Eddie waddled up to the bar just as the bartender slid the girls their share. He made it his rite to educate the girls on the finer points of working at the club, and there was one girl in particular that was having trouble fitting in, and he was sure that she was getting too much special treatment. He aimed to curb that.

"What I tell you 'bout showin' up late?"

Her head turning, Eddie pulled the largest bills out of Sarah's share of the bar.

"C'mon Eddie," pleaded Brina. "The poor girl's takin' the bus for Christ sakes. Give her a break."

Several eyeliner eyes, gloomy and bent, stared at the young, cherry-blonde bombshell. Their tongues remained dormant in their mouths. Their wills battered and caged. They all had felt the hefty pull of Eddie's education at one time or another. *Why should she be any different? Just because she's studying to be a doctor, don't mean shit. She ain't better than the rest of us.*

"Don't make it a habit," chimed Eddie as Sarah glared at her dwindling stack. "I'm watching you."

Brina huffed as the beefy bouncer moved to the end of the bar. Tone came into view with two super model babes under each arm and an unlit cigar in his mouth. Her eyes were hot as she followed the fat man, watching him talk quietly with the boss. The saucy Latino cultivated no love for either man.

"Here. Take this," ordered Brina as she passed half her tips to the young girl.

"No. I can't," asserted Sarah in a curt whisper.

The elder woman's eyes begged to differ. She rolled up the rest of her money and stuffed it in her purse, saying nothing.

"Bri? What about Ricky?" urged Sarah in bright, hushed tones. "What about your son? You need this more than I do."

The angered Hispanic was resolute. Nothing else could sway her. It was done. As Tone pulled out of Eddie's ear she silently cursed them both, hating but needing her job, and wished that the two skinny bouffant super models would give the club owner a good case of the clap. As the proud man left for the night, his wanderlust under each arm, the only person he said goodbye to was the janitor. Yet even then, the old cleaner didn't hear him because his headphones were pumping out a soulful mix of classic Motown.

Tick Tock. The rain lasted longer than either detective had guessed, but it was thinning. Wallace moved his shirtsleeve back over his watch. Morning bristled with black coffee, orange juice, buttered toast, jam, and eggs – sunny side up – less than two hours away.

In the small hours of night the desert air bred a chill. Lieutenant Mauldune was snuggled in her coat, asleep. Wallace started the cruiser and the jolt from the engine woke her.

"What?" she piped, half awake. "We rolling?" She curled into the hard comfort of the door handle.

"Yeah," Wallace groaned, flicking on the lights and jamming the car into gear. "Gonna get you to a proper bed while there's still a few minutes of night left."

Mauldune stretched and switched sides, yawning. "We'll get 'em tomorrow."

"It is tomorrow," he mentioned as he pulled onto the road.

"See," Mauldune oozed, "we're getting closer."

Wallace smirked as he fed the engine some gas. *A "can do" attitude even with a bucket seat for a sleeper. The kid is ok.* He wasn't tired a bit. Too keyed up, thinking about his nephew Stephen, and how his sister had never really recovered from his murder. *Hell, ain't even spoke with her in about a year.*

She moved up to Tempe awhile back for some new job that Nathan got, and the embittered detective made a mental note to give her a call once he had bagged and tagged the assholes that took their bright-eyed boy away. He also made a note to call Sally tomorrow. He knew she wasn't worried. They had an ease to their relationship that he liked. It was much better than the nagging shrew that was his ex-wife. For that sole reason, and because he loved her, he knew he'd never marry her. *Why ruin a good thing?*

"What a bastard," said one of the dancers now that they were outside the club.

"He didn't have to do that in front of everyone," another chimed in. "We work hard enough as it is."

Brina rolled her eyes. She didn't hear anything from any one of them inside nor did they cough up any of *their* tips to smooth it out. No.

They just sat there on their fat asses, letting it happen. And now, outside away from Eddie's earshot, they all had something to say. *Pathetic.*

"Ahh," the Latino birthed. "You smell that?"

"Bullshit in the morning?" replied another dancer through an ugly grin, getting a chuckle from the waitress.

The chicks were slinging it thick, acting like they cared. *Each and every one of 'em, skanks.* Brina didn't need to think on it anymore. Her shift was over. Dawn's long eyelashes were poking through the night.

"Freedom," she said to Sarah, pushing the haters out of her mind.

"I heard that," voiced the drink girl, tassels still stuck to her tits under a buttoned-up jacket. "Gonna run me a hot bath, a little Cristal..." her grin finished the row.

The chatty dancer at the waitress's right laid out her woes as if anybody gave a shit. Brina tuned her out as the hypocrites dispersed to their cars. She turned to Sarah. "You want a lift?"

"Nah," Sarah stroked, thinking on it. "I'm gonna walk a bit, catch the bus."

"You sure?"

"Yeah." She slipped her hands into her coat pocket. "I need to unwind."

"True 'nough," commented Brina, fishing her keys out of her purse, a little jingle addition to her tapping heels. "Well, you be safe."

"Yeah. Thanks."

"Don't mention it," Brina warned, heading to her car. "Free health care, remember?"

Sarah smiled, nodded, and yawned moving off toward the bus stop. The sky brightened over the Sandia Mountains. Pink in the evenings, blue-gray at dawn, the edges of the peaks jutted into a pale sky. Brina honked and waved as she drove past. *The girl's amazing.* She'd been a rock for Sarah ever since she started working at the club.

All alone with the quiet of Albuquerque, a sleeping tortoise in the gulch of a desert - Sarah liked it best this way. Alone. A cool breeze pulled at her nickers, but she didn't mind the wait. The tranquil dawn was a soothing antiseptic to the infectious glue of the club. Real air blew from the West and filled her lungs. Wet sage and damp concrete. Out here, in the twilight before the waking, when most everyone was asleep, Sarah could let go, and find meaning in the shape of alighting clouds.

The sky cracked above her with an arid sulk pulling at the remnants of last night's rain from the ground. A hazy firmament carried birds as, blocks away, vacant streets came to life with a deep engine whine. Closer. Moving at a lazy pace, a tiny blue speck gaining miles, whitewall tires spinning, the Cadillac rolled across the horizon.

Sarah heard the car before she saw it. Turning, she watched the classic car approach, because it was the only thing on the street, because its dual headlights looked interesting between the chrome grill. Closer. Nearing her now, her heart beat a steady nonevent as seconds slid away. The face in the driver's seat stared at her with wide eyes and an open mouth – *Beautiful.* Pale. White. Raven hair cut short and dainty, it trimmed the driver's face like a picture, framed in the moving gallery of the driver's side window. Sarah couldn't remove her eyes from the girl inside the cruising machine. She was caught in the magnetism of the stranger's ashen stare, singed with red, burning into her soul. Everything slowed. Her heart beat, echoing and distant, buoyant on her cool breath. It was wondrous.

Moments glowed as the Caddy crested the hill, gliding past her. Feeling the separation pull a string in her chest, Sarah careened her neck to continue looking at the enigmatic woman. The driver turned around to face her. Sarah smiled and blushed, her heart skipped. She was panting. It was kinetic. The tendril fingers of fate messaged her pumping organ. The girl in the Cadillac had moved on, but Sarah still felt connected. She wanted the driver to stop.

Who was that? Sarah exhaled, her hand balled, pressing against the cleft between her breasts. She never realized that the bus had pulled up until the driver called to her, snapping the dancer out of her daze.

It took the vampires awhile to clean up from the cowboy affair. Stuffing the boys in the trunk of the Caddy with bloody bed sheets, broken furniture, and a busted lamp, Lin followed Z as she drove Darryl's pickup truck to a remote location and dumped it. She tucked the keys in her back pocket after she locked the vehicle and deposited them in the ramshackle backseat of the Cadillac when they began to dig uncomfortably into her rear. They fell to the floor with a dull thud.

The violent punk was exceptionally excited, full of spitfire. As she told it, Jake put up a good ole fight, thrashing about, trying to knock her off his nether region. But the vampire's bite was strong. Z found the scuffle exhilarating, all pumping fury and Nat Geo. The vampire was literally bounding in the front seat of the baby blue auto once they tore back down the road, a constant conversation of verbs and hard consonants. That is, until she fell asleep. Mid sentence and the quiet dropped. It had been blissful ever since.

Lin felt the pull of the road, body humming to the purring engine. Her fling had not been so exciting as Z's. Lin wanted to drive. She wanted miles away from the pit in her belly so they hadn't buried tonight's entertainment. She needed a skyline of stars and taillights, not hours spent digging a hole. The dead boys rocked quietly in the dark lull of the trunk. Just driving, catching as many yellow dotted lines as she could in the on again, off again rain, she could finally let go. Nearing Albuquerque, Lin veered into the city. It had been a long time since she had passed through the dusty old town. It always reminded her of a gigantic truck stop. She figured it was as good a place as any to crash for the day.

But she kept driving.

Streetlights, dark rectangle shapes, business signs, and garish neon, pulling onto the occasional odd street, Lin wandered off the beaten path. Her fingers wound tightly around her silver locket. She was rubbing it like Aladdin's lamp. Spiraling in, she snaked through the city, eating time with her exhaust, until the sky began to brighten, transforming into a cold hue that differed from the dry hot air. Lin kept swimming around adobe structures, modern architecture, warehouses, and Nob Hill. Absentmindedly she drove, fate's sticky fingers up her ass. She was the puppet master's puppet's puppet and nothing prepared her for what she was about to see.

Standing alone on the side of the street, a cardboard cutout against the pedestrian sky, was the most beautiful girl that Lin had ever seen. She wore a face that had been with her for nearly seventy-five years. *The gauge of her penetrating eyes, the bend of her cheek, the luster of her hair, the svelte curve of her neckline* – were all set in the vampire's memory. Lin had seen her before, but not here…not now. The apparition on the street corner, this wonderful flesh statue, looked at her with new eyes. Lin's fingers let the silver albatross plummet to her quiet chest as both hands gripped the wheel and pulled.

Time seemed to stop.

A collusion of brief and mere chances, Lin's mind suddenly flashed back. To the madness of the desert, to the frightened, huddled bodies pressed against the exposed adobe brick wall – near the back of the room – *that same face*! She had stared at the vampire as a light from the burning fire in the Kiva glinted off the freshly polished locket that dangled around her neck.. It sparkled in Lin's eyes, calling the weary, starved night creature. It bade her awaken and take sustenance. It caused her to crawl across the sand-strewn floor on her hands and knees. *That face!* Blessed and reposed, eyes wide in terror, Lin tore her throat out. Not a sound escaped her lips. The woman went to her death knowingly, quietly – *still*.

The momentum of the wind pounding against the earthen structure and the black hearts of her traveling companions were a freight train through Lin's soul. The slippery, tendril grasp of fate took that exquisite creature from Lin's gaze way back then and placed her here, for her now.

Such rancid cold conspiracy.

Jordan starved himself to death. Ramielle, butchered and burned. Juliana taken by the black blizzard. Prophet had found God in the face of the sun, and Lin was locked into an unending journey, there and back again...*there and back again.* Her heart was crushed in the ruin of all those lives. So long ago and haunted, every second of every day – torment meted out in hours – imagining it over and over and over again!

All that blood. All that blood...

Bruised flesh and broken bones, over the crass, grotesque smile of Prophet's misshapen teeth, and here now, the vision of loveliness stole the breath from Lin's Jadaraa Soo. The vampire couldn't pull herself away from the woman. The momentum of the Caddy's whitewalls rolled on, cresting the hill, and still their eyes locked. Weightless. Held aloft in such an extraordinary capacity to love. The girl was gorgeous. She was...*alive!*

Passing her – *she wasn't a mirage!* The girl turned in the direction of the Cadillac. She followed Lin with her eyes and her cheeks bloomed red. Lin looked at her diminishing form in the rearview mirror until Rah's brightly lit rays stole in through the open crevice of the clear glass windshield and Z burst from her deathly slumber, a frightened maid greeting the magnificence of the sun.

"What the fuck, Lin?! Are you trying to fry our ass or what?!"

A shrill shattering of senses, broken beautiful, upset serenity, the scream from just beside her was reeking fear. A loud violation and unholy clatter. Befuddled, Lin turned to Z and leaned to the side to avoid Rah's glorious touch.

"Why're you still on the road?!" Z hollered crouching down in the seat, lost in time and scared. *How did I get here?* "For Christ's sake, get off the road, Lin!" *Where's the night?* "Get off the road! I'm not one of those frickin' Bittaras, ya know. I prefer my skin the way it is to a darker shade of charred."

The driver remained calm, falling down a hill into shadow, slipping out of the sun's grasp. No drama. Easy. Pushed by the momentum of spinning gears. Through the hollering the girl from the locket was on Lin's mind.

"Bithtarans," corrected Lin with a steady voice. "They're called Bithtarans. Not Bittaras."

"I don't give a fuck what they're called!" Z was flabbergasted! "Get off the gaddamned road!" The panicking vampire was crammed between the dashboard and the seat, concealing her precious dead afterlife from the encroaching dawn. Her mind was a broken jigsaw puzzle where none of the pieces fit together. One minute she was sucking Jake dry, dumping the boys' truck, talking to Lin about the poor kid's vim and vigor, and the next they were God knows where with light screaming through the windshield and Lin driving oblivious to one of their most basic survival instincts, which is bright light causes severe boo-boos! Z knew she'd been experiencing blank spots in her memory and she hadn't thought too much of it until now. But seconds away from a witch's grave, it was all crashing in on her with a constant torrent of questioning syllables. "Jesus Christ!" the broken vampire exclaimed.

"Oh. Now, you find religion."

Lin tried to lighten the sudden gravity of mood. Z made a disturbed face at the smarmy remark. *Why is she still driving?*

"We'll be fine," assured Lin. "I'll just stick to the shadows. Keep *you* out of the sun and find a place to waste the day."

The raven haired lunatic sounded overly confident to Z's ears. She even looked calm despite the golden eye creeping over the mountain.

Lin took a sharp turn and Z banged her head against the hard rubber of the door. She was about to complain when another turn sent her flailing in the opposite direction.

The sun was taking over the street. Lin kept dodging patches of light, turning this way and that, down one road and then another, to avoid driving into the sun. Brilliant illumination was closing in, the suburban rows of houses and streets weren't going to lead her to the splendid dark. She had to find a place to hide. She had to get off the road. Her easy options were shrinking fast.

Ahead of her, Rah was claiming another street. Nearly half of it was gone to the fiery god. Thinning dark, the road t-boned. Lin depressed the gas petal. It was a race for space and the ancient god was winning. She was going to have to time this well or she'd send them both careening into the effulgent god's not-so-tender mercy.

"Hold on."

Lin pulled the wheel hard to the right and leaned down in the seat. No vision, only the sight of the classic car's silent stereo. If another vehicle were on the road it wouldn't have mattered anymore. She would die in the crash, well and whole, having seen the lovely from the locket, re-birthed by God, walking upon the earth. She wasn't a corpse in Lin's memory anymore. She wasn't a statistic of the evil that vampires do. Though Lin knew that if, in this stunning half circle of screeching tires, it was Z's time to go that the vibrant vamp would fight, tooth and claw, for a dark hole. *She had an unceasing will to survive and yet she is dying.* Lin didn't care and she was allowed to carry on. *It isn't fair. Fate is a fickle bitch!*

Sunlight glazed the metal side of the great big luxury car as it hooked around the T. Lin bobbed back up, into the driver's seat, and saw an alley up ahead covered in cool shadow. She took the turn fast. The Caddy bottomed out, bouncing up and down on the rutted dirt road. Z's head was a drumstick, clanging like a Neil Pert solo. It wasn't a rush!

"Oh! You are *so* dead," Z affirmed, trying to stabilize her position.

"Duuuh!" Lin coached.

The mouth of the alley at the other end was all glistening and awake. There was no more dim road to run. Backyard walls and garbage can niches bordered the narrow lane. Spotted behind every house, sitting behind low cinderblock and/or adobe walls were garages. Locked and fenced in, some were guarded by dogs. It was useless until Lin passed a garage that spilled out into the alley. She jammed on the brakes and the Cadillac ground to a noisy halt. Z banged her head again against the dash.

Shifting into reverse, Lin backed up as the sun crept down the narrow alley. She stopped just past the leaning wooden entrance. The thing looked as old as she was, and in far worse shape. They were running out of time. Lin hopped out of the vehicle and crossed to the locked double doors. Z panicked, watching her go. But a couple whacks with the heel of her boot and the little metal lock popped, falling into the dust.

Through the window of the opened driver's side door, Z timidly lifted her head to see what was going on. Lin was opening a battered door that lead to a dark hole. Inside were some hanging bikes, a rusty old ladder, a pile of pungent carpeting, and plenty of space to fit the Caddy. Lin climbed back into the driver's seat. Z was unexpectedly quiet, eyeing the sun as it moved down the lane, as the vampire pulled into the dark abyss of the estranged garage.

Sunlight tagged the rear end of the baby blue vehicle as it disappeared. Lin turned off the laboring ride and quickly climbed out and closed the doors, encasing them both in the not so perfect dark.

"There ya go..." Lin announced, walking slowly away from the secured entrance. "Still pretty."

Long
Day
Between
Nights

Hot water cascaded down Sarah's sudsy contour, flowing down the drain. It spilled into the Rio Grande, passing through a series of pipes and tubes; filtration systems, old and rusty, smelling rank, working below the radar of the city. Her sex was piqued. She'd been in the shower a lot longer than usual. She was too keyed up to sleep. The face of the driver kept tugging at her rambling soul. Sarah felt as if she'd seen her someplace before, like it should matter. Déjà vu and nothing but confusion over a stranger's glance; it was foreboding.

Out of the shower and dressed for bed, daylight crashed through the windows. Her apartment stunk. The trash needed to go out, dishes filled in the sink, and dust was throwing a party everywhere. There were only a few hours before she needed to leave for school. Beneath the fervent pulse of her excitement her body longed for sleep. Work was going to kick her ass tonight if she didn't relax and get some shuteye. But she was humming, body electric, rattling as she tried to calm her nerves.

Who is she?

The question spiraled through her mind like water through plumbing. Sarah wanted to know. In the deep pit, in the quiet expanse of her soul, she tingled. Thrushing on a needle's point, she didn't understand why — *all this agitation over the glance of a stranger?* People gawked at her everyday. *What's new, what's different?* Alone, her mind was unceasing. The young girl was never going to get any rest. It was going to be a very long day.

Out of bed and washing dishes in the kitchen, weeks old food got caught in the trap. Cleaning wasn't making her feel like taking a nap either. It only depressed her. So, she decided to leave it and buy a new set of dishes at Walmart next week when her check came. It was easier, and then she'd at least have a set that matched. The same for the trash too, piled high with Take Out cartons, Sarah decided it would be less of a hassle if she just ate out. *Simplify. Simplify. Who is she?*

Then it occurred to her that if she ate out she wouldn't need a set of matching dishware, and that cinched it. *Toss the cruddy things away, forget the trip to Walmart, and let someone else do the cooking and cleaning.* It was brilliant! No more living in a rat's den, forced to smell a rancid dump fuming out of the tiny kitchen. She could spend all of her extra time studying. Sarah laughed aloud at the thought…like she ever had "extra" time. That was like having "extra" money. It just didn't happen.

With all the housework bottled up in a Hefty bag and placed outside in the bin, Sarah cracked open one of the massive tomes she got from the university and began reading. Words, sharp staples stuck to her brain, flitted past her nose until the alarm clock sang an old blues melody from the air-conditioned archives of KUNM's sound library. Sarah lifted her groggy head out of the book, and out of her drool. She had finally found a sleeping pill that worked: a school book.

Moving through class like a zombie, Sarah's mind kept tossing back to the morning. She couldn't forget the face. It floated in front of her like a dream. She sat in the dark, distracted. Slipping through the white noise of her being, the teacher lectured at the head of the class showing slides. Some were grotesque, some clinical, some average and boring as hell - all on the human circulatory system. The heart pumped, a massive sewage plant pushing red globules through a series of tiny pipes and tubes, dumping in artery rivers, it was a self-contained aquifer. The mechanics of the flesh vessel, sloshing through its wet current was just as much loaded in Sarah's mind, as was her apartment's plumbing, where all her dead skin cells sunk to the bottom of the Rio Grande.

Opting out of the test that the teacher had badgered the kids about all week, the slide show breezed by at a stunning pace. Operation pics melded into the background of hand drawn diagrams, chests cracked open, clamps holding the skin back, ribs spread wide in a bloody oval, it gave the aspiring physicians something to think about. It was the teacher's way of stimulating the class to reevaluate their career choices. He did it every semester with the new recruits to weed out the weaklings. Get them up close and personal with the filthy, mortal business of human plumbing. Let them know right off that they were going to get their hands dirty.

Native America Calling blasted through the tiny speakers of the alarm clock radio as the LCD churned red, digital numbers to 12:05pm. Buried under old clothes, pizza containers, unwashed sheets, and empty beer cans, Chris Templeton barely heard his clock radio talking. But Mathias heard it. In the kitchen, scraping a pad of butter across a hot fresh piece of toast, wafting up good and delicious: the jam jar sat open. Raspberry. He spooned some of it out and laid it on the buttery bread, looking out the kitchen window, across the backyard, to the old wooden garage that sat on a lean.

Mathias Greene was going for a bike ride today. Dressed in tight colorful spandex, a Fanny Pack about his waist and his sunglasses hanging around his neck, he'd been planning the ride through the Bosque all week. His water bottle sat filled on the kitchen counter, condensing in the brisk, arid air.

Outside in the garage, Lin and Z wasted the day in the almost darkened interior. Cracks in the wood, bends in the spaces from how the boards aligned, let in sultry shafts of sunlight, glorious and unbecoming. Though roughly quiet now, Z had been pestering Lin all morning as to why she drove into the dawn. Getting nowhere, she sat stretched out in the back of the Cadillac, all the windows rolled down. Lin sat outside of the vehicle, her back against the passenger side metal. A pile of carpet was smashed against the front bumper and smelled like vomit and piss. The heat hovered three foot off the dirt floor. Time churned slowly for the two nocturnal creatures, a long day between nights.

Lin's palm held open the silver locket. She'd been staring at the picture, confirming what she already knew. The girl from this morning was the photographic vision in the locket. There was no mistaking it: Time had birthed her all over again.

How many times, in how many forms does life imitate itself over its great gulf?

Who did I cheat out of my face when I drank the Omjadda blood?

A nest of bees, furious through her cerebral cortex, collected the honeyed thoughts. It was now more obvious then ever; the violent wench sitting in the back seat of the Cadillac should not have joined her on this trip. The locket confirmed it. The girl was waiting on the side of the road for Lin. But she drove on with the maniac asleep in the seat beside her, dying.

What could have been? What should have been?

Skin fetid, unable to sweat. *Z should've stayed home in LA and taken care of Ryan's corpse.* Lin should have seen it through, all on her own. *I'm such a coward.* She'd known since Vegas. It was as clear as a striking bell. *A Zia Jean Bell.* The fabulous Mrs. Boyd wasn't supposed to be here. Lin craved a cigarette, gnashing her canine teeth, having smoked her last one several hours ago. She titled her head against the car door and sighed.

Closing her eyes, she saw the tempest: *Deviled winds pulling earth into the sky. A black sea. Suffocating. No escape. Screaming and blood splattered adobe brick. A fire crackles, faces cackling, murmurs of Christian prayers, sobbing, and chattering teeth –* Lin opened her eyes.

"So, are you ready to tell me yet what you were thinking or you just gonna stare at that gaddamn thing all day?"

Lin exhaled. "I told you. I just felt like going for a drive, is all."

Z shook her head against the side panel of the car's interior, arms crossed, face scrunched up. "Bullshit." She knew Lin was lying.

Lin grew angry. Days and weeks of lingering frustrations took sudden shape. She turned to face the opened car windows and stared into Z's distant feet – Converse All Stars decorated with scribbles and bad art. "Do you even remember this morning?"

"What the fuck does that mean?" Z shot up with matched hostility, feeling attacked. "Of course I remember this morning. You nearly got us killed and I'd like to know why."

"I mean before that. What's the last thing you recall…"

"Fuck that Lin, you're trying to change the subject. You went AWOL! You had your head in the clouds or stuffed in that gaddamn necklace of yours. I mean what the fuck is the big deal, anyway? Coming all the way out here, for what?

"No one made come along. You could have stayed in LA…"

"To lament some poor saps that got axed almost a hundred years ago. Gimmie a break!"

"But No!"

"I keep expecting you to snap out of it, but you don't. You don't!"

"You didn't want to deal with Ryan, so you stuffed him in the elevator shaft, destroying any possible hope!"

"You'd rather stay locked in your own head instead of letting the past go, just like all the other ancient fucks!"

Hard eyes. Staring violently and locked, Lin hated saying it the second it slipped out. "Yeah, and how many things can't you remember these days? A head full of black holes?"

Z's face dropped, belying the target of truth. Now, the dead elephant in the room was put on notice. But before Z could ask what she meant the garage door wheezed with a loud clank. Daylight spilled into the darkened crevice and fell across the front end of the classic car. Z, cursing, scrunched up behind the limp protection of the front seat. Light found the locket in Lin's hand and her Jadaraa Soo dived into the dark interior of the vampire's arm, killing motor function and sending the silver jewel to the dirt floor.

"Shut the damn door!" Lin yelled, scooting away.

Startled, Mathias quickly bottled the garage back up and stood there a moment, holding the lock and chain not sure as to what just happened.

"You ever heard of knocking when entering a room?" came Z's voice through the blank stare of decaying wood.

Mathias was dumbstruck, "Aaaaaah…Sorry."

Wallace harassed the young man with his eyes. Over the checkout counter, silent, the wanted flyer lay there like a stick. Mauldune lingered outside on her cell, having gotten a call from the Chief again. The register jockey waited for the cop to say something.

Wallace wanted to save the boy's life or the life of the person on the next shift. Unseen, slack-jawed yokels with bad acne, too much youth, and gallons of time left in their meters, he wanted to save them all. But all the cop had in his arsenal of personal protection was a six-shooter, a piece of paper, and a flat warning with a phone number attached. It was pretty weak by his account. It wouldn't have saved his nephew. So, it probably won't save this local either.

"Pack of Winstons."

Death is convenient, hand held, it comes with a slim purchase of a lighter or free with a pack of matches. It'd been two years since he quit smoking and the flavor still clung to the roof of his mouth like peanut butter. He could always tell when Kate talked to the Chief. Her shoulders bunched. Words got caught in her throat and had no where to land.

Forced to listen to bad advice, held quiet by rank, she paced a tight cage. Wallace knew the Chief wouldn't call him. That was pointless. A man didn't get to that kind of a position, comfortable behind a desk, by being a dummy. The Chief knew Wallace shut his phone off the second his officer had left Phoenix, and that Mauldune would scour the earth for an extra battery pack to keep her cell phone powered and charged until the cockroaches took control.

He knew the only reason the Chief even allowed this little expedition to happen was so that he could get rid of Wallace's cantankerous ass. As long as Kate kept the lifeline flowing, the Sergeant knew he could stretch the leash. At least for a little while, anyway. There was no love between him and the commanding officer and he knew he was betting his pension on this foray. Wallace knew he was lining up his own rear end for the Chief to kick off the force. It was either do or die time. He needed to show results or turn over his badge. *So, fuck it! Winstons and a free-pack-of-matches chaser!* Death was convenient. It came hand held. It fit into pockets. It loved you a long time.

"It's only been a few days," crunched Mauldune through the cell's tiny speaker. "You have to give us time."

"I don't have to give you shit," came the warm response. "Don't hijack one of my cruisers and tell me I have to do anything. Is that clear, Lieutenant?"

"Yes Sir."

"Now, how do you really see this thing panning out?"

"By the book, Sir. We're in their known target zone and all they have to do is raise their heads, even the slightest, and we're on them. A better response time means saving lives, and bringing them in.

"Bullshit. But I'm gonna let it fly." The Chief drew in a breath. "How's Wallace?"

"He's fine, Sir. Tense. But we both are."

"And your gonna tell me that you think he's gonna play it by the book?"

"Yes, Sir, I do. He's—"

"Then you've got a lot to learn, Lieutenant, and I suggest that you keep your eyes and ears open."

Click. The line went dead just as Kate felt the unmarked cruiser pull up behind her. She boiled in her skin. Not from the heat. The sun was brilliant, yes. The concrete was a cooker today, but the line was dead…and she could feel Wallace's eyes on her.

"No, Sir. That's right," she said into the dead receiver, straightening her stance. "Thank you, I will. Goodbye."

She closed her phone and walked back to the car. She didn't know why she lied, put on the little show. She just did it. Climbing in the cruiser, Wallace didn't ask what the Chief had to say, so Kate didn't tell him. She noticed he was smoking. *Finally gave in.* Kate didn't ride him about it. Her Grandmother was a smoker. Killed her at seventy. *Disgusting habit.* Just as long as he kept the car clean, Kate thought she could live with it.

The old man sucked up the last bits of cancerous goodness, like mopping up gravy with a piece of bread, and chucked the butt to the asphalt. In the blur of spinning wheels, Kate Mauldune let her shoulders unwind and Wallace fished out another cigarette.

Mathias stood in Chris's doorway. The room smelled bad. Like a garbage disposal unit married a gym locker and moved into a Bangladesh kitchen. But he'd gotten so used to it that he hardly even noticed it anymore.

"Dude? There's chicks in the garage," he stated, staring at the large mound of junk on the bed. "Dude? DUDE!"

The junky mound moved and Mathias saw Chris's head pop up between a pair of week old pants and a pizza box.

"Huh?" Chris's eyes stung, half open.

"Why are there chicks in the garage?"

"Wha…" It was too early too think.

"Dude, why're there chicks in the garage?"

Chris turned to face Mathias wanting nothing more than to sleep. "Oh, yeah man it's…It's cool. They're just…you know…"

It was futile. Slowly, as the young man spoke his head descended onto his rugby jersey, delicately down, tackled to dreams. Mathias gave up and walked back to the garage.

Z was freaking out.

"This is so fucked. So fucked! You know he's coming back, don't you? What if he's calling the cops right now?! Did you think of that? Did you—"

"He's not," offered Lin weakly. "Relax."

"He's going to come back, open that door, and fry our ass to crispy critters; that's what he's going to do!"

"No. He's not."

"I've seen it, Lin! I've fuckin' seen it! So, don't tell me he's not coming back. 'Cause you don't know...You Don't Fuckin' Know! I've watched vamps fry, Lin. It's not fuckin' pretty. I can tell you that. Charred like a burnt piece of bacon, like a fuckin' potato chip; you wanna be a gaddamn potato chip, Lin? JESUS! What were you thinking?!"

The elder vampire held her locket tightly in her hand. Its silver pushed the Jadaraa Soo to the backside of her fist making the flat side of her hand gnarled and extremely veiny. What had recently only been a few nagging misgivings, to have Z along for the ride, was now full-blown regret.

In LA, Lin spoke to Z about calling it quits before one of them said or did something that was going to irrevocably damage their friendship. Now, she was sure that line was about to be crossed. She felt Z's damage pressing on her shoulders, breaking her quiet down.

Back in LA, Z didn't hear that conversation because she had fallen asleep. Her Jadaraa Soo was decaying into its death cycle, so the vampish punk just trotted along with all the same pistons firing. It wasn't working for her anymore. Being clueless about her own condition just wasn't a good enough excuse any longer, and Lin now knew it with a moral certainty. Their time together was over and every second that she stayed tethered to the punk just dragged her down.

There was a knock on the garage doors. "Hello? Huh...I'm gonna come in now and get my bike?"

"Be nice," Lin whispered harshly to Z so that the bloke beyond the door wouldn't hear.

"Fuck that! I'm not gonna burn for you," the murderous wench fired back in the same harsh whisper.

"Hello?"

Mathias waited as the two nocturnal combatants stared each other down, silently debating the young man's fate.

"Oh, yeah," Lin chimed like a ditzy blonde, polite and inviting. "Come on in."

The door creaked open again and light fell across the same

worn path. Mathias entered his garage and the tension in the room was palpable. Or was it the rank carpet from the party last month? Mathias couldn't tell.

"Hey." He lifted his arm in a universal, friendly greeting.

"Hey," mimicked Lin from behind the protection of her Caddy.

"Sorry about earlier. Didn't know you all were in here."

"It's cool."

He passed the opened windows of the Cadillac, spying the brightly haired goth punk stretched out in the backseat, and his balls tingled. Mathias wasn't sure if it was because his bike shorts were too tight, or if he found the exotic girl a beauty, or if she scared the hell out of him. It was probably all three. He lifted his bike off the hook, set it down with a rubber thud and jangle from the chain, and placed his water bottle into the holder.

"You guys hangin' with Chris last night, huh? He's still passed out. Must've been a good one."

"Yeah," affirmed Lin, flowing with the young man's assumptions. "We were pretty ripped."

"That's cool."

With the sprocket clicking, he walked the bike out. Passing the tall, lanky punk in the car made him nervous and he wasn't sure why. So, he waved. And, Z waved back.

"You know, you guys don't have to hang in the garage. You can hang in the house. Chris'll be up in awhile."

"That's cool," said the scary thing in the backseat, trying to play it up too.

"Yeah. Thanks," said Lin, doing a better job at being normal. "We're good for now. Sun's just a bit bright."

"Yeah, it's a cherry day," Mathias said with a grin, looking up to the clear, blue New Mexican sky. "Goin' for a ride down the Bosque'. So, ah...maybe I'll catch ya later."

"Yeah. Later."

The young man closed the garage door, boxing the vampires back up, and peddled away. Z rose from the back seat with a wide grin dancing on her face. Utter disbelief washed over her like a Baptism.

"That was...surreal. That was *so* totally surreal."

Lin smirked, not wanting to give up her tension, but not wanting to get back into either. "I know."

Then the same thing happened that usually happens for the two raunchy, loudmouthed, and opinionated vampires – one of them started laughing. Murder was contagious. But even more contagious was Z's laughter. The buxom beauty bubbled up a wellspring of mirth and infectious giggles. Lin couldn't keep herself contained. Sandwiched between the hot dry air, the hard dusty floor, and the broiling day, the two slow-decayers laughed it up.

Chris wandered to the back porch in a pair of boxer shorts, sporting the University of New Mexico logo. He slid his hand under the soft band of the All-Cotton briefs and scratched an itch. Then he yawned and stretched, feeling the effects of last night's bender. The sun bore down on him and he felt like a vampire – like one of those nocturnal bloodsuckers from a dozen cheap horror films. So he went back inside, into the gorgeous dark, and found himself a nearly unused section of his bed. There he lay down to slumber as if he were curling into a coffin.

May 9, 1934.

Four months and two days since Flash Gordon first appeared in a Sunday Comic Strip, along a five hundred mile span of prairie and steppe that stretched from Mexico all the way to Canada, through the central United States, where Buffalo once freely roamed, the sky churned the heavens with topsoil. Two months and twenty days before Public Enemy No. 1, John Dillinger, would be gunned down outside of Chicago's Biograph Theatre, the winds ate the screams of all those who suffered inside the large adobe house. They'd become statistics of the Dustbowl. Lost, unchallenged, assumed dead and buried, or migrated to California during the two-day-long storm that had only just begun.

Union County, New Mexico, off Springer Highway, just south of Clayton, past the railroad tracks, twenty-one days before Clyde Burrow and Bonnie Parker would meet their fateful end, the vampires found the tiny village. Hitler planned The Night of the Long Knives. Vlado Chernozemski and the IMRO planned the assassination of King

Alexander. The Soviet Union and Afghanistan governments debated joining the League of Nations, Cole Porter edited his musical, Anything Goes, and Linnet Pevensey wondered how events had transpired so horribly wrong that she was stranded in the desert with no place to go, trapped by devil winds, murderous grins, and about sixty staring eyes boring into her soul with rank fear.

The Council was created with peaceful intentions. Meant to unite those that had been blood slaves under the yoke of the Omjadda or made new by Omjadda blood after the Eras of Slavery, it took fifty-seven years to establish the nocturnal governing body. By 1838 there were small pockets of hybrids throughout the whole of the world. Infecting themselves upon the provinces of men, they dug in deep, living half-lives, leeching off what others had created. Until then the freed slaves of the Kula Malaika, Shaytan Khalid and their brood had no governing system to direct interactions with themselves, the humans, or Omjadda peoples. These isolated pockets survived by their own codes, scavenging. They'd become parasites that fed off the fringes of the societies in which they resided.

For a while it looked like these unwanted, crossbred Children of Evensong were destined for genocide at the hands of an ancient African tribe that had been at war with the cannibal angels since the dawn of time. The creation of The Council helped to alter this fate. It stabilized the different vampire fractions, providing common shelter and wealth. It defined a social structure that was sorely needed and they began to flourish among the world of men and beasts.

The first edicts handed down by the twelve ruling members of The Council were concerned with murder. The taking of an Omjadda life was strictly forbidden. It was punishable by extermination through sunlight. No Omjadda J'in would even agree to deal with the vampire council unless it recognized the power and authority of the ancient race. It was a point of contention that withheld the Council's formation for many long years.

Animosities between former slaves and masters ran deep. There were many that wanted The Council as a rallying point to take up arms against the Omjadda and join the African Tribe to wipe them from the face of the Earth. The primeval species knew this and so they bartered for asylum in exchange for recognizing the symbionts' sovereignty. It was a clever move.

To murder one's own kind was also strictly forbidden. The Council sought unification and harmony among all the members of its caste, so killing one's own was sacrilege. Their numbers were closely guarded, kept pure, and untainted. To ensure the protection of the hybrid species, a set of rigid guidelines were enacted on the creation of progeny. These laws were put in place to ensure the purity of their race, only allowing members to join their illicit fraternity once they had proven themselves, and even then, they had to be voted in by ruling council members after an inquisition. By this, The Council thought to deter any contention among their kind, thereby making their furtive society a utopia.

In theory it sounded good. It was a grand scheme. Like the Soviet Communist Party or Roosevelt's New Deal, where war waited six years in the future and a bullet waited 206 days for Politburo member, Sergei Kirov, in Leningrad. Throughout history, grand schemes always ended the same, dependent on the purity of their architects and members. The symbiont race was spawned from the secular world, drawing down the elixir of the gods to disperse among vermin. Utopia came on blood rivers, ready-made with hairline cracks and waiting fissures. The Council thought by judging who would join their ranks they could breed out their weaknesses. It was just more grand schemes in a delusional state that they never saw.

When it came to framing legislation on the murder of humans the twelve council members found themselves in a quandary. Freed Vams and Children of Evensong had been using humans as their chief source of sustenance for centuries. How could they revert to something other than human blood to sustain themselves? How could they deny themselves the sweetest fruit?

The fact was…they couldn't. So, they didn't. When The Council crafted their laws on the treatment of human beings and the regulations of feeding they avoided the issue of murdering humans altogether, opting out to establish a vast network of feeding stations, known simply as The Service. The Service quickly grew into a global conglomerate under the direct protection and authority of The Council and provided its clientele with willing blood lenders, known as Sanglants, and regular shipments of cold, packaged goods.

Over time, with the advancement of technology, The Service perfected its procedures and branched out into other the realms, providing fantasy entertainment, where by a client could order a game. A game was based on the vampire's desires. Sanglants acted out the details of the game much in the same way that a prostitute played a role that led to sex. Though, instead of sex being the object and conclusion of the treatise, in a game produced by The Service the end goal was always feeding – the transfer of blood.

The use of Sanglants was highly governed by its own set of rules and regulations and the killing of a Sanglant was strictly forbidden. Huge fines or extermination were only some of the punishments for the mistreatment of blood lenders. They were a closely guarded commodity. But the murder of regular humans, outside of the hidden world of the vampires was left nondescript. Instead, symbionts were encouraged to use The Service for all their wants and needs. Thereby, allowing the dream of utopia to march gloriously in the forefront, much in the same way that the Chinese Communist would begin their Long March, five months and fourteen days after the horror in Union, New Mexico left its stain upon the Earth.

It was generally agreed among The Council that killing humans in the township or city where one resided was forbidden. It was punishable by banishment or death. This was due to the fact that it simply drew too much attention to the existence of a symbiont race. In the formative days of The Council, political leaders in the secular, human realm were not as clever as the Omjadda. They did not barter for the lives of their people, only for the lives of their ruling families. The people of any given country were always considered expendable at the hands of the Monarchy in which they were subjugated. The populace at large was seen as labor, militia, and fodder for the Captains of Industry. So why should the crossbred species, that was birthed from them and fed off them, look at the people of the world any differently? They didn't, and by proxy The Council left great big holes in their laws.

In their pride, council members thought to solve all of their problems by institutionalizing their species' feeding habits. But by not addressing certain inalienable truths about their own dark natures, the twelve governing members silently gave a nod to alternate feeding styles. Though it is generally frowned upon in all circles of vampire society to murder human beings, it is not forbidden. So, it was through these delicate loopholes of history, three months and thirteen days after the Apollo Theater opened in Harlem, New York, that the farmers in Union, New Mexico found themselves face to face with death.

The vampires went for the ones that looked to be the most trouble first. Breaking legs, snapping an arm, Jordan and Prophet made an example of the two largest, able-bodied men in the room. Then they tore into the poor fools that advanced on them. Tearing into them with their teeth, ripping out the front of their throats or the side of their faces, slashing them with razor sharp fingernails, both vampires dispatched the three assailants rather quickly, leaving their dead bodies to bleed out on the dirty, wooden floor for all to see. After this show of brutal force, amid cries of pain and fear from the broken men, the villagers were sheep, docile and controlled. Ramielle moved in to feed. As the eldest in the room and queen of the Coven she had first pick.

Jordan was the youngest of the surviving vampires, having been turned in the summer of 1880. Ramielle found him among the Ludar Gypsies. A violinist and knife thrower, she saw him perform in Bucharest with his family. She took to the young man instantly, seducing him into her fold, where his blood could warm her cold flesh in the great expanse of her bed. His ascension by Council decree was quick, unlike Prophet's, who labored under The Council's inquisition for more than four years.

Born Joseph Brahe in 1818, snow clung to dank, black rocks along Karlin and the sky was a drab gray on the morning that Prophet was born. By age eleven he was an orphan, surviving on the streets of Prague, pick pocketing, mostly. A little killing, some theft, he gained a nasty reputation. By nineteen he was arrested for the murder of a merchantman and sentenced to hang by the neck until dead. But the fickle fingers of fate were not yet done with him, throwing the young man a lucky, but peculiar break.

An urchin drunk, stumbling and singing mountain songs from his Ukrainian homeland had also been arrested. He had extremely pale skin and a veiny complexion, and went by the name of Dimitar Svenslovski. Mr. Svenslovski had been dead since 1721. He stank. Not from his death, but from the liquor and dirt that adorned his attire. He lay dormant, in a mumbling fit for about an hour and a half before he woke, ready to leave. Coming out of his drunken trance, Dimitar simply decided that he had some other place he wanted to be. So he left, and in so doing, he tore through half of the Constable's office to regain his freedom. Inadvertently, the drunk paved the way for the young Mr. Brahe to escape.

Leaving his homeland, Prophet followed the odd looking Ukrainian into the countryside. Dimitar only traveled at night and during the day he rested in a cave or darkened enclave in the forest, drinking whatever alcohol the little thief could procure for them. The crazy Ukraine weaved endless yarns about his youth and travels, telling Joseph things that he never thought were possible or true. Tales about bone white monsters that lived under the earth or where secluded high in mountain castles that had taken his life, thinking to enslave him. He described past wars with such vivid detail that one would instantly assume that he'd fought on their front lines if it were not for his apparent age. A steady thirty-three and holding; Joseph never believed him, but he listened with a prodigious ear.

When they had crossed Bulgaria and reached the Black Sea the odd afflicted man delivered Joseph into the more capable hands of Ramielle Eirinhas. In her care the student of the crazy Ukrainian learned that every word that was spilled by him, over the light of a burning fire and the repast of a drink, was true. The Coven queen was impressed by the fact that Dimitar traveled with the young man for nearly a month without ever feeding from him. When she pressed Dimitar as to how such a thing could happen, he simply replied that the boy was a good listener. It was for this reason and this reason alone that the Vam Däm Mu kept Joseph Brahe alive.

For two years Ramielle debated on whether or not she would let him live. There was something about him that she liked and something about him she feared. So, she kept the young man close, never feeding off him either. It was an odd arrangement. He stole for her, bringing her jewels and precious documents. He bartered with local townsmen on the behalf of his Lady's interests and when negotiations failed he improvised more apt solutions to achieve her goals. These usually involved the sharp tip of a knife or scaling a castle wall with rope.

When Joseph Brahe was first declined ascension into her realm Ramielle felt slighted by her other Council members. He was one of the first candidates to be recommended to the newly formed government, and she'd come to think of her dark haired protégé as a shoe-in. But the vote was 3 to 9 against. Her biggest disappointment came from Dominique De'Paul. Ramielle had helped her to build The Council and through all their years and lives together she had never asked the Vam Pŷr for a single thing. The first time she did, however, she was denied. From then on it became a personal vendetta to see the young Mr. Brahe enter their fold.

She took him under her wing, training him on the finer points that would sway The Council. And through all of their time together she never fed from him, not once, not a single drop. He'd seen her eat many times and though he lavished in the Spanish woman's affection, he was never invited to her bed. For some estranged reason that he never fathomed she kept him at arms length when moments turned intimate. They held personal conversations, he made her laugh, and she kept virtually nothing from him, except the key to her inner sanctum. He only asked her about it once. Ramielle's answer was quite clear.

"If you wish to remain among the living you will never ask that of me again."

Of course, he never did.

It was during Joseph's second inquisition that Ramielle petitioned on his behalf, stating that her young Kulak would become a prophet to their race, one of the enlightened that would lead them all one day. It was a moving speech even though she was the only one in the room that felt it. Mr. Brahe's thieving skills and past deeds were again arrayed against him, but Ramielle already knew the cast of the votes before they were taken. She had spent months prior to his inquisition meeting behind closed doors with fellow council members to negotiate his inclusion into their fold.

The only council member that Ramielle did not meet with privately was the Lady De'Paul. Her passionate speech on her man's behalf was for the benefit of the reigning Vam Pŷr. Though she felt Dominique owed it to her, Ramielle was again shunned by her eldest associate with an 11 to 1 split. The arrogant shade had again cast her vote against Ramielle's protégé, and in so doing, had slapped her other cheek. Joseph's win was bittersweet.

So moved was he by Ramielle's impassioned words that he adopted the name Prophet to remind himself of what he needed to live up too. Now, only nine years shy of a full century as a bloodsucker, Prophet was far from becoming an enlightened hybrid of anything. His eyes were gorged black on blood, his teeth held little bits of flesh stuck in them, and he was going through the villagers like a fat man at a buffet.

Lin was horrified.

She'd taken human life before. She had passed people under the cruelty of her teeth. Though never for sport, never to just feed in a wild heathen frenzy. Never for the fun of it. She had only taken human life for her protection. Her most violent days were when she was a soft, fleshy human being living in São Paulo, Brazil as a consort and lover to Dominique. Yet, even then it was in defense of her home, her family – *her lover and son*. When she fought in the Brazilian slave uprisings of the nineteenth century she found no pleasure in killing. Death was merely a symptom of war, a means to an end.

It had been eighty-two years, five months, and twenty-nine days since Lin last murdered a man with her teeth. It was over some property documents and forged birth certificates that she had filed with an office clerk named Emil Herdade. Emil figured out that the heir to the Casa del

Rio Dulce's fortune was a fake. He thought to profit from it, blackmailing Lin, who was posing as the new entitled benefactor of her own estates. For Emil, it was a short-lived mistake.

Lin was taught to survive off the blood of consorts during her days as a willing blood lender to Dominique. Later she became dependent on The Service for her survival needs. She saw the cruelty of men. She lived with savage war. She toiled the earth in barbarous lands. But nothing, nothing at all, prepared her for the immoral wickedness that descended upon these families, trapped in huddled masses during the murderous storm.

Ramielle pulled her bloody face out of the gash of a helpless victim, panting with exhilarated lust. She drew a raspy breath. The air smelled of dry burnt copper. Prophet kicked a man in the gut. Lin heard two ribs snap all because the poor sod had reached out to hold the hand of his dying wife as the vampire drank her life away. Madness burned in Prophet's eyes, bright and constant, twinkling like the Star of David.

"You can have her back now," he boasted. "I'm all done with her."

Prophet threw the corpse of the woman at the man and they both crashed to floor. The frightened man's weeping blended into the din of screaming that lit the clanging of the black blizzard. As the dark haired bohemian pulled another girl from the pile of scared villagers, the humans held onto one another. Sweat-soaked and crying, they clung to each other's limbs, intertwined like a life raft floating in a furious sea of sharks. It was only a matter of time before the knell of the raging storm sealed their dubious fate.

It'd been two days since Lin last took sustenance. Thinking nothing of it, she figured she'd eat once they reached Albuquerque. But they never made it. The storm had swallowed them whole. Now, blood and violence assaulted her deprived senses and her Jadaraa Soo wanted nothing more than to enter the fray. The pain produced by her parasite was unique. Nothing short of having all her flesh put on fire and her organs ripped out to a musical ballet of an out of tuned orchestra. It was unending. Convulsing dry heaves, curled up in a corner of the large house, Lin tried to put the whole nasty business out of her mind. Neither the vampires nor the screaming victims nor the gaddamn parasite would leave her alone long enough so that she could get the shaking under control.

"What's the matter?" Jordan asked the crippled vampire after stopping a few of the farmers from running out of the door into the turbulent winds. "Not feeling social?"

Lin didn't respond. His question was in bad taste, his mirth ill-placed and if Lin could vomit she would have. Chunky spasms would have been a release to her festering soul. Teeth chattering, the noisy orchestra playing in her head, winds rustled like exploding turbines, no, she didn't feel sociable. She felt wretched, regretting each one of the one hundred and eighty years that she had walked the earth, and in just two hundred and six days from now a bullet waited for Sergei Kirov. Thinking himself invincible John Dillinger was about to be killed – it waited two months and twenty-one days away. Polish-born Chemist and Nobel Prize recipient Marie Curie had fifty-six days left before death paid her a visit; and it was still fourteen years before Lin would meet the Chicago night-born vampire that would empower her to begin a healing process that would amass its own body count.

All those days and night in between, waiting, wedged among the pit and pendulum of fear, time wore down the thin fabric of cold existence, and there was nothing Lin could do to stop the juggernaut pulsating through her decaying veins. It screamed to join in the merriment that Ramielle and her crew made. It accosted Lin of its vast, unceasing hunger, and reminded her that she was nothing more than a shell, a host, its puppet on a string.

"r u on campus?" read the text message with a Marimba chime.

"leaving," Sarah wrote back.

"c u at frontier."

Sarah chuckled, putting her phone away and headed up the block to the restaurant. Sunlight warmed her crown, massaged her shoulders, and filled the air around her with hot, searing goodness. The Frontier was a vault of air conditioning, crowded booths, brown tile floors, and four rooms of wall-to-wall southwestern art. The balmy flour scent of baking tortillas, hashbrowns, and green chili salsa was a pleasant medley. Sarah wandered through the adjoining rooms until she found Jimmy. He sat at a table with two other guys under the paintings of John Wayne and a Navajo woman wearing a decorative blanket standing in a pueblo.

Jimmy introduced Sarah to his two buddies as she flopped into the natural wood-finished Formica booth. Small talk, pleasant – *quaint*. He had copies of his class notes in his bookbag and was happy that the green-eyed, auburn beauty had joined him. His friends didn't seem to mind either.

Staring at the half eaten plates of food, breathing the lush mix of the twenty-four hour menu, Sarah went to get something to eat. The line was long. But it moved fast. Giving her order to just another unidentifiable employee in a bandana, blue smock, and company logo, it was nearly two in the afternoon and she ordered breakfast. After a pit stop at the salsa station the #4 went down hot and delicious. Steady, Sarah listened to the conversation the guys were having, dreamily floating around the events from this morning.

Leaving the turnstile booth, the four of them wandered through the parking lot to Gary's, or was it Carl? Maybe neither. She walked with them to some guy's car where he produced a wrinkled joint. Casually, they lit up – old hat for the student ghetto. Dirt weed. Probably smuggled from Mexico in some bean's gas tank. It was a mellow after-lunch-breakfast mint.

Jimmy joined his friends leaving and handed Sarah the promised pages. Sarah caught the bus out front of the yellow and white rustic eatery. During the ride she cradled her textbook, distracted, looking more to the street than to the words on the page. Her thoughts were stuck on the girl in the Cadillac. She never actually opened the book.

Stop after stop, along Central Avenue, people pooled in, climbed out, and Sarah settled on her street corner high with a full belly. Drowsy, she unlocked her front door, opened the windows to draw afternoon breezes through her apartment, and laid her head to sleep.

Daylight screamed through the screened windows, neighborhood traffic hummed, and a drop of water beaded in the empty sink. Lazily happening, permanent, Sarah's lasts few hours of normalcy slipped away as her laptop collected dust. Her REI book bag slumped against the wall, clothes hung, mostly unused, in the opened closet, and the swamp cooler leaked on the roof. Leaves rustled unheard and geckos slithered under rocks of pristine Xerascaping. Everyday occurrences, miniscule and non-threatening, vanished like buffalo.

⋈ ✕ ✖ ◉ ✖ ✕ ⋊

Beaten lethargic by the scorching sun hitting the tin roof of the garage, wedged in a shack of planks, the vampires waited for evening. Lin had spat it out there like a loogie and it clung to the fat molecules of air, baking with them. With slow breezes, thickening shadows, and the arid pressure taken off, they started to move and Z asked about it.

"Whuddya mean?"

147

Lin wanted to ball up, crawl under a rock, feign ignorance, do anything else instead of answer the simple question put to her. She wanted Zia to figure it out all by herself so she wouldn't be the one to break the bad news and tell her that her Jadaraa Soo was dying. But there was nobody else around. The garage felt cramped and the vampire's honey-brown eyes just stared at her, waiting.

"You've started sleeping."

Heavy, it was understood, "Huh."

The rest of the day was quiet. Lonely, Z sat in the Caddy. Lin felt a nag to console her, to say something to make her feel better, but what do you say to someone that's on a downward spiral for the last time, circling the drain, and looking out the bowl like the weather's fine? *Nice knowing ya. So long and thanks for the memories.* It was weak, pathetic. Trite. So, she just kept a tight lip and let the heat wear her thin. It wasn't like Z would be dead and gone in a few hours or days. It wasn't a damn soap opera. They had time to work out the little things. They'd been together for over sixty years. Z wasn't rushing off.

Summer of '46, just outside of Spokane, Washington, rain was coming down as if it was freshly invented. Thick and pounding, it was a marching band. While driving to Alberta, Canada Lin hydroplaned off the road and kissed a tree with sliding metal.

World War II had just ended, the trials in Nuremberg were everyday ink, American Industry was on an upswing, and the Boston Red Sox looked like a shoe-in for the World Series. With all the traffic on the road earlier, Lin was surprised that she hadn't seen anyone in hours. Waiting in the car for a spell, she thought the rain would let up. But it kept coming down in sheets. Headlights broken, glaring oblong into the forest pit, her '41 Packard was curled around a tree like the twenty-first letter in the alphabet. She took a couple hard knocks and reasoned that if she'd been a normal gal, driving alone on the highway at night, she'd be dead.

Walking, soaked through to the bone like a drowned rat, feeling the road with her sloshing feet, it was awhile before headlights dented the thick pitch. A newly minted Nash Sedan, one of those family models, four doors and long that resembled an upside down bathtub on wheels, pulled past Lin to the side of the road and stopped. Its red taillights took a beating, rain pummeling down. Lin was thankful.

Nearing the super Sedan she saw a single person through the muted windows. Motionless, staring out the windshield into the steady night, the driver didn't even turn toward her as she approached the car. Lin opened the door and got in as quickly as she could to avoid bringing the weather with her. The vehicle was a cold bubble. Rain drummed on the bowl roof and windows, the six-cylinder engine churned and purred. It still had that fresh car scent, and something else.

"Thanks," the wet rat obliged. "I've been out here awhile."

"No problem."

Keeping straight, the driver's sandy brown hair covered her face. She didn't turn to even recognize the new passenger. She just shifted gears and pulled back onto the road. Lin noted that the lone woman was skinny, like a beanstalk sitting in a tub. She looked out of place and it was obvious that she'd been caught out in the rain too. Though, it was much earlier. She had that dry wrinkled look, pressed into the huge bucket seat. Lin pulled her wet hair back with her fingers and knew immediately that the out of place woman was one of her own kind. It was probably why she didn't look directly at Lin when she got in the car. *Didn't want me to see the veins.*

Lin had pulled her Jadaraa Soo deeper into the cavity of her body as she approached the car so as to appear right-regular and normal. Spying the quiet driver's white knuckle grip on the steering wheel the tiny burgundy veins were visible twisting out from a decorative sleeve. Lin also noted that the driver didn't ask where she was going. She chuckled to herself, *probably had that one all figured out: A lone stranger on the side of the road, a dark night, lots of wide open spaces, off the beaten path...Yup! Food. Must be a newbie.*

"So, where you heading?" asked Lin, striking a conversation.

"Seattle."

"Is that where your family is from?"

It took the driver a minute to answer and Lin smirked.

"No."

"Just going for the sights then?"

"Something like that."

Lin eased off and looked around the vehicle as that 'something else' began to take shape in her nostrils. *Blood.* Hours old and roughly cleaned by the look of it. But that papery copper scent still clung to the newly minted leather interior. Lin knew that if she searched hard enough she would find specks of it in the creases of the bucket seats. This wasn't the vampire's car and had been recently acquired.

"So, ah…" Lin started, "this is one of those new Nash Sedans?"

The driver's eyes titled around, peering out from underneath her hair. She moved her head in a small cage, avoiding to place her face directly at the passenger. "Yeah."

"You like the gas mileage? It's a big car."

"It's alright, I guess."

"Still got that new car smell." Lin sucked in a breath. "I'm surprised your husband even lets you drive it out of the driveway."

Lin noted a twitch in the driver's shoulders. She was too busy trying to hide to notice that Lin was messing with her. The wet vampire almost laughed.

"I'm not married," spat the driver with a tinge of rancor edging her gums.

Lin waited a few beats. "I know." The driver's head jolted toward her, ever so slightly, as her eyes careened to the side of her face. *Almost had you. Now, the Coup de Gracé!* "Did you kill the owner of the Sedan or the whole family?"

That did it. The driver's neck snapped toward her violently. Dead eyes with those unmistakable coursing red veins glared out from under strands of soft brunette hair. Lin laughed and the driver slammed on the breaks.

For a huge boat the vehicle didn't swim. Its back wheels whipped around and they slid down the night-born road broadside. Lin was sure she was about to wind up in another car accident. It hadn't been her decade. She was about to swear off the mad metal machines forever when the vampire compensated, easing up on the break, twisting the wheel around to bring the tub to rest with a small lurch in the center of the narrow two lane stretch of highway.

"Who are you?" the driver commanded in the still-shaking seconds after.

Lin's laugh was a full belly yowl and the tips of her fangs came into view. It was evident. The driver's whole body sighed as the need for pretense vanished.

"Jesus, I thought..." The vampire shook her head. "Of all the places."

"Yes," Lin responded. "Pretty astronomical odds."

"Wha, what are you doing out here?"

"My car slid of the road a few miles back. I was walking for sometime before you picked me up."

"Do you need to get back to it?"

"No, I have everything I need. Could do with a change of clothes, though."

The driver thought on it first. "I think there's some luggage in the trunk."

Before Lin could pit an argument against it the vampire was already out of the car, rummaging in the trunk. A few minutes later, she returned with a thick suitcase, tossed it onto the back seat and climbed back in, closing the door with a wet thud. Now, she was soaked too. Though, she didn't seem to mind.

"Thanks, but you didn't have—"

'There's bound to be something in there that will fit you. No sense it going to waste."

Lin climbed into the back seat, where the blood leather scent was more prevalent, and riffled through the suitcase. The luggage was monogrammed: R. J. Wilkens, Jr. Mr. Wilkens was a solid fellow when he was alive, portly. His Oxford button down shirt hung like a dress over Lin's lithe, curvy frame.

Back on the road, it turned out that the driver was a closet conversationalist. Her name was Zia Jean, but everyone called her Z. She was out of Chicago. Lin had heard about the Chicago Coven from Dominique and was a little shocked to meet someone from there, as they were considered a rogue bunch, never ones to align themselves with The Council. Lin had always pictured them as rebels against the great vampire machine living out their wretched afterlife in Rosehill Cemetery on their own terms. Her imaginings were cavalier and American Western, but listening to Z, curled warmly in the passenger seat, in R.J.'s huge shirt, she got a different impression.

As it turned out, Z was a newbie who had been turned by the Chicago Coven leader, a crazy Civil War cracker from Virginia named Franklin Cross. He was a Lieutenant with the fighting 7th during the War Between the States under Turner Ashby. Lin had heard a little about him from Dominique. Her dark mistress bore no love for the man and it appeared that neither did Z. She was running away from him. For thirteen years she had been a prisoner of the wild bunch, living under the cemetery within its huge catacombs, surviving off Chicago vermin: criminals, degenerates, and homeless mostly, but some rats too. Cross had taken a peculiar like to Z after she and her husband, Simon Ray, encountered him and a couple of his cronies back in '33. The Lieutenant considered the woman his own personal property after he'd forced Z to murder her husband. The whole time that she had spent with the Confederate instigator Z wanted nothing more than to escape. She'd tried before, but he always found her. Now, she had hit the bricks for good, commandeering the freshly plucked Sedan.

Lin told Z how she came from England in the eighteenth century and about the Vam Pŷr, Dominique De'Paul. How she'd spent most of her life in São Paulo, Brazil before she took to her own form of a walkabout, traveling to Asia and back through Europe before coming to the States. She explained how she was on her way to Alberta to meet with the leader of The Council and a few of its members.

It was amazing to the runaway vampire to come upon someone who was so well connected to other covens and the history of her race. Z had been kept in the dark, surviving on the fringes of the vampire society for so long that she'd forgotten that the real world was out there. She yearned for it. But it was always out of reach through the cemetery gates. Night after delirious night, a bustling Chicago beckoned the young rascal to come play, but she was hardly ever allowed to wander far from Cross's side. The world had changed; growing around her while she remained locked in the catacombs under the graves. The raven haired woman was a blessing and breath of fresh air, and for the first time, in a very long while, Z felt like she might actually have a shot at leaving Cross forever.

Lin invited her to go to Canada, promising to help her gain asylum from the Confederate soldier. The young vampire could not have been more excited at the prospect. The way she told it, she never wanted to go to the windy city in the first place. It was all part of some cockamamie plot of her late husband's to join the Chicago Outfit, and she'd been stuck there ever since.

The two vampires didn't drive through the rest of the night. Lin knew of a safe house just north of Spokane, deep in the woods, where they could spend the day together before returning to the road again at dusk. The safe house, she told Z, belonged to a quiet pair of bloodsucking freaks named Michelin and Oasim, who were one of the first hybrid couples to settle in North America when the Dalam Kha'Shiya J'in had lifted the ban. Lin and Z rested with them during the day, talking, enjoying each other's company. They became fast friends until the young vampire went suddenly missing.

Z was only left alone in the house for a half-hour. But it was just enough time for her to vanish. Though they searched, neither one of them could find her. It was a head-scratcher that upset Lin terribly, and she was forced to abandon the search in order to make it to Alberta in time. She arrived late to the gathering using Z's stolen car. She begged Dominique to intervene in the matter and negotiate with the Chicago Coven for her release. But her former lover would not lift a finger, claiming that the coven existed outside of The Council's jurisdiction, so there was simply nothing she could do. The other council members confirmed this ridiculous stance, but Lin knew it was bullshit. They could do what ever they wanted; and without The Council's help there was little she could do alone.

It deepened the wedge between the old estranged lovers, becoming a point of contention and aggravation. But slowly, as time crept back into familiar molds, Lin learned to let go of the wayward traveler that she had met on that cold, rainy night. The mystery of her disappearance remained unsolved, settling into the rest of the hurt that sloshed around Lin's abused soul. Meeting the runaway brunette was the first time in eons that the woman from Abingdon had felt connected to another soul.

The twentieth century was too strange and loud for Lin. It moved around her too fast. Living was becoming increasingly unbearable, plagued by ravenous memories of an insane sandstorm, the vampire found it difficult to deal with what she and the others had done. Finding Z along the highway that night felt purposeful. Her plight held meaning for Lin. But discovering her gone the next day felt like a piece of her was knifed out and stolen. It was insidious and had wormed Lin back to her flat, condemning existence.

So by the time Z found Lin in Los Angeles in the summer of '48, the English maid, though engaged in some construction projects, building a few high-rises downtown, was close to committing suicide by sunlight.

Lin had lost all hope of ever seeing her again, but the vampire had sought her out. They hit it off just as if there had never been an interruption in their friendship and Lin finally learned what had happened back in Spokane.

As Z told it, Michelin turned her in, sneaking away to call a confidant. She detailed how Cross had boasted, saying how he had people all over the globe that owed him and there was no where for her to run. For two months he kept her tied to a wall with a twenty-foot length of hard cast-iron chain as punishment. He wanted Z to understand that she was his and he wouldn't release her until she promised to be his completely. Lin was so enraged at the couple that she never spoke to either Oasim or Michelin ever again.

"I had to kill him," confessed Z one evening as they made plans to go out on the town. "He wouldn't let me go. He started hitting me again and I finally had enough."

"How?" Lin asked, shaking her head. She understood the vampire's side of things, but she also knew Council edicts and feared a reprisal.

"I lured him with sex. Got on top and clamped down on the son-of-a-bitch with all my might and drained the bastard dry. As he weakened I grabbed a knife that I'd positioned under the mattress and began stabbing him. But that didn't kill the him either. So, I tied him up and dragged him to the cemetery and threw him outside." Z paused for a second. She was shaking and looked at Lin as if she were afraid. "I watched him fry from the shadows of a crypt."

Lin crossed to her and held her until she stopped shaking. "It was the only way," Z kept saying, over and over again. "It was the only way."

"I know," replied Lin. "I know."

To murder one's own kind, even the likes of Franklin Cross, was forbidden by The Council. As she held the battered and distraught vampire she knew the soldier's death was going to come back one day, looking for Z. So, it was with little surprise three months later when The Council came calling on the brutal killer, demanding an inquisition.

Lin assisted Z through the tribunal, acting as her Directorate. She knew The Council had their moment back in '46 to avoid the whole nasty business and blew it. In Canada, they had been firm to Lin about their limitations, saying that they could take no stance in the matter because the

Chicago Coven was not a registered entity. The political stink to finally round the northern brood into The Council's alliance was all over the proceedings. Members from Chicago demanded the widow's head. They called her a rogue, an outcast, claiming that she needed to be destroyed. Whatever promises passed between thin lips, behind closed doors, could not change the fact that when Cross kidnapped Z she was outside of Council jurisdiction. So they could not act. When she killed the vampire to gain her freedom The Council still held no Jurisdiction over the coven, so they could not judge anything that transpired there. It was a great big gorgeous loophole which the prideful Council either had to forget about or admit to.

Z's actions in the Windy City were free and clear from The Council's judgment and there was nothing they could do about it. Lin was boastful; sticking to Council edicts, as the Chicago brood got nothing they bartered for and lost all of their independence. The vampire flagrantly waved the facts in the faces of the twelve ruling members and there was little cause between the old lovers to commemorate any pleasant visitation. From the cold, dispassionate eyes of Lin's former love and mentor the verdict that cleared Zia Jean Bell was delivered, cementing a bitter dislike between the Vam Pŷr and the rogue. After this small victory, Lin made sure that nothing else was going to happen to the frank and spirited symbiont ever again. She wasn't letting her out of her sight.

"Thought you said you were gonna dump these guys," said Z as she opened the trunk of the Caddy "It was your turn."

In a breathy scoff Lin reminded her. "Dumping Ryan in the garage doesn't count as a turn, Z."

"Well, that was different. He just showed up."

Lin glowered at her and shook her head as the delusional fiend picked up a piece of clothing from under a stiff, naked butt and put it to her nose.

"Aw man! There's dead guy all over my stuff."

For over sixty years they'd been together, like a platonic married couple, sharing a turbulent ride of corpses, good times, random acts of wonton delirium, and festering hostilities. Being sandwiched in a cinderblock and wood plank shack with two huge slanting doors and evening blowing a cool breeze through the crack in the planks was par for the course. They had shared a lifetime together. It was longer than what some human couples had, and it was ending. The writing was on the wall.

As Z rummaged around the dark belly of the Cadillac, searching for something to wear under the lifeless bodies of Jake and Darryl smashing her luggage, Lin grabbed her cosmetics bag and a change of clothing from the floor of the back seat with every intention of a shower before she went in search of the mysterious woman from the locket. Dead eyes, colorless and glassy, stared up at the runaway vampire as she lifted a pair of slacks through cold crammed interlocking limbs.

Frothy, cobalt skies hung over Albuquerque, slowly darkening. Garish neon came to life along Route 66, Sandia Mountain washed away in a murky pink, and the vampires crawled out of their hovels. Inside the house, Chris Templeton and Bernard Macavoe were killing digital aliens, throttling their joysticks to the bombastic explosions, recorded grunts, and the sterile jams of the video game. They were locked in a struggle to the death and didn't hear the back door open and close. However, they did see the gorgeous women when they entered the room. Slinking slowly, licentious smiles splayed across their fish belly faces. They giggled and the boys couldn't stop staring. Z waved hello with oscillating fingers and Lin got to the point.

"Which way to the shower, Chris?"

He tried to place them, like his mind was a CD stack, going through the alphabet; he pointed to the door at the other end of the hall. The girls followed his finger. Z tuned up the sex appeal, casting a big net, as she walked across their game. It kept them distracted, eyes on her, as they watched her perfect little ass like tools. Once they'd disappeared into the bathroom Bernie jabbed Chris in the ribs.

"Dude, you didn't tell me you had hot chicks staying with you."

"Guess, it slipped my mind."

Bernie stared at him as the game continued on its own. "You let them slip your mind? You need to lay off the weed, my friend."

Just then, secret Alien attack, and his avatar bit the dust, one life down. It jogged Bernie back into the game. Though his player aspirations of being interviewed on the G4 Network were irrevocably altered when laughter spilled into the living room from behind the bathroom door that the girls had conveniently left open.

Both men silently looked at each other. They felt the air was thick with sexy and put the game on pause. Chris was the first to get off the couch. It was his house, after all. Steam started billowing from the opened door and the timbre of hot water cascading down the sensuous curves of two tattoo-clad harlots sounded inviting. The bathroom was a thick, muggy mask of fog. He stuck his face in.

"You girls find everything okay?"

Z's laughter emanated from the hot shower. "Almost. I think we need your help."

"Aw Dude!" Bernie silently mouthed, getting an erection just thinking about the possibilities.

They disappeared into the cottony white steam. Loosing their clothes, finding willing limbs and soft fleshy bits, Chris and Bernie entered the shower. It started out like a Dear Penthouse Letter, but it never climaxed. Somewhere along the second paragraph, in the ramp up to the gorgeous nasty part, they both felt sharp pricks along the base of their necks and soon found themselves unconsciousness.

They would wake up in a few hours once Mathias returned home from his awesome bicycle ride along the Bosque. He'd find them both, intertwined and naked, with the water running cold, and in each other's hands was the other's private parts.

Lin was firm. They discussed it before they entered the house. It wasn't much of an argument. They were not killing them. Z could tease them if she wanted, and they could feed from them just as long as, come tomorrow, breath still gathered in their lungs just like it did before they encroached upon their lives. Lin was calling it quits to all of the "unnecessary" killing. The prospect of the face in the locket, out there and whole, walking around, clothed in flesh again brought with it the terrible consciousness of her previous actions.

She needed to change if she was going to connect with the mysterious woman. Her life of wonton destruction standing shoulder to shoulder with the violent vampire was over. So, she fed from the geeky college boys. She enlivened her pallor and made sure that no one got hurt. Sure, the boys would wake up with a little bruising above the collarbone, fading puncture marks, and the indentation of teeth. But they would also be too embarrassed at being found fondling one another's junk to even talk about it. Dominique taught her how to survive through the eons of forever night without ever taking a life to sustain her greedy veins. For so long now, since that disaster in the desert, back in '34, Lin had been spiraling down toward an all-consuming death, lost without a parachute and clinging to the only soul she could find who never judged her.

But the world was changing. It never held firm. Her time with Z was ending. Lin felt that. It was natural and they just hadn't said goodbye yet. Lin had held on because she loved the crazy vampire from Chicago. Z entered her life at a time when she needed her most, but those days were long gone. It had been obvious for years, but she wasn't paying attention. She deluded herself and when she found out that Z's Jadaraa Soo was dying, well…she deluded herself some more. It was easy. *Denial isn't just a river in Egypt.*

Now it was crystal clear. The woman from the locket had been reincarnated. She was out there and Lin was meant to find her. She had to change her ways. She had to! She had a shot at redemption. Life held the door ajar. Lin thought about Ryan Silva, bleeding out on the concrete, his eyes asking a thousand whys. *Z had her shot at redemption, the beginning of a new chapter, and she threw it away, slicing his neck with a switchblade as if he were a loaf of moldy bread.* Lin wasn't going to let that happen. She wasn't going to fuck it up. The girl in the locket was her last, best hope at forgiving herself for all of the death she'd caused over the span of her life, and for the pain and anguish that she made others endure. The souls of the dead clamored around her heart, plagued her festering mind with jolting visions, and they could only be put to rest at the feet of the girl she saw on the side of the road. Lin felt this with unwavering certainty.

She had to find her again. Just had to! *There was a purpose to this life after all, unfolding from the unknown.* Lin felt focused. She had to find the mysterious girl from the locket. There would be no more killing along her path. Those days were over. Her karma was wrecked enough. Retribution was alive and kicking in the bodice and beating heart of the girl!

Two
Bodies
Of
Water

November 1992. Hobbs, New Mexico.

Katarina's ballet shoes were missing, the new ones that she had just gotten for school and her tutu. Through the course brown curtains, Sarah watched her mom, Eva, talking with Mrs. Greigos by the clothesline. Her mother's back was stiff. Her dirty blonde hair fell on her bare shoulders and down her smock in a ragged waterfall. She'd barely gotten home from work and had stepped outside for a drink and a smoke when Katty's Mom came out to collect the laundry. Now Eva Somers held her beer, but she didn't drink from it. Her cigarette butt lay stomped under the foot of her work shoes as she stood there listening with her arms crossed.

The air outside was motionless. Cooling, as evening tackled the hot day. Sarah jumped down from the couch and sat back on the floor, pretending to watch cartoons as her mother entered the trailer. The screen door flapped in its jamb, and without turning away from the 20" TV screen, Sarah heard Eva set the beer down on the kitchen counter and light another cigarette. Sulfur and mints. Sarah waited for it.

After a minute or two, her mother closed the trailer door and stormed down the hall. Her cigarette dangled from pursed lips. Sarah could tell that the knocking about and banging were coming from her room, and then it arrived, swiftly, on wings of fury.

"Gaddamn it Sarah, where is it?" Her mom appeared in a hail of smoke, a locomotive at the foot of the hall. "Where'd you put the damn thing?"

Sarah looked up from the TV. "Put what Momma?"

"Don'tchyu lie to me." She yanked Sarah off the floor by the arm, a yelp of sudden altitude, and dragged her to her room. "I know you have it. It's just like the one you wanted for your birthday and Katty got hers. Hell, she was wearing it Saturday out in the yard. I saw the look on your face." She tossed the child into her room. "Now, where is it?"

Eva Somers took the cigarette out of her mouth and ash fell onto the spotty old carpet. Sarah was shaking, looking up at her mother – *angry again.*

"Honestly, I don't know what you're talking about."

"That's how you wanna play it?" She jabbed the cigarette between her lips again and crossed to Sarah's dresser. "Fine."

Eva opened each drawer. Grabbing a handful of clothes, she tossed them onto the bed and floor. Some of the items hit Sarah in the face. Her mother was pissed, moving rapidly, a frenzy of scraping wood and bright colors flaying softly through the room.

"You think you own any of this shit? I feed you. Clothe you. And you wanna lie to *me*? Worst yet, you're gonna steal in *my house*! I work hard for what little we got, Sarah, and all I get for it is constant bullshit. I've had enough of your antics, young lady; what I'd ever do to deserve someone like you who don't appreciate shit, I'll never know."

The dresser drawers hung open and jagged like Frankenstein. Her mother huffed like a monster, staring at the child who looked down at the floor, fidgeting with her fingers and the hem of her shirt.

"All this crap is trash. You got that," she informed the girl, taking the cigarette from her lips; it had burned down to the filter and gone out. "And I ain't buying you anything else. You can go to school naked for all I care. Now, where is it?"

Quietly, Sarah's eyes swept the tiny room. Her clothes were strewn as if from an explosion and the TV blared crazy cartoon sound effects and hyper-happy music in the other room. It cut against the gravity. Sarah didn't want to give it up. She had always wanted one. Her mom said that she could have one for her birthday, but she turned seven last month and it never came. Eva was always saying things that never happened.

Sarah started to cry and reluctantly went to the closet. She didn't mean to steal Katty's ballerina outfit. She just wanted one for herself. As far back as she could remember she desired to be a dancer. That was all she ever wanted to do when she grew up. How was she supposed to dance for a New York Ballet Company now? Her momma couldn't even afford the classes. *At least she could have gotten me the dress!*

The child pulled an average-looking box from behind a mess of shoes and stuffed animals. Lifting her crayons and coloring books from the top of the box, she unfolded the pink tutu and ballet shoes. She handed them to her mother, thinking that Katty was going to be mad at her just as soon as she found out that Sarah had taken her stuff.

Ms. Somers stared down at her daughter, clutching the little, soft items. Sarah's eyes were wet: big and innocent. *How could they look so gaddamn innocent?* She slapped the young girl across the face.

"You don't steal."

Leaving the child whimpering, a red handprint tattooed on her jaw, Eva crossed to the kitchen. Sarah peered out from the opened doorway and saw her momma toss Katarina's tutu and ballet shoes in the trashcan. Then the woman turned, picked up her beer, and started drinking. Sarah met her mother's eyes over the rim of the can and Sarah ducked back into the ramshackle catastrophe of her bedroom. Hearing the stomps of her mother coming down the length of the trailer, echoing under the wheel carriage, the little girl started shaking.

"You don't breathe a word of this to anybody," Eva said in a stiff voice, framing herself in the doorway. "You never saw that gaddamn thing, you hear me?"

"Yes, Momma." Sarah shook her head, frightened.

A scowl wrinkled Eva's face. The child looked like a buoy in a clothing sea of disaster.

"Now, clean up this mess!"

ϗΛϡ

Turning off the lights around the mirror at her station, Sarah headed for the stage. She actually got a decent amount of rest today and felt good. The joint helped too. Sometimes she didn't mind the dancing. She'd always liked to dance. As far back as she could remember it was what she wanted to be. Though, back then this wasn't exactly the kind of dancing she had in mind. Adolescent dreams of New York City, a handsome choreographer, roses, and adoring fans – *it'd all been pretty simple.*

Dancing at the club wasn't that bad. Even stripping could be fun when she just focused on the moves. The only thing that sucked about it was the men. Though ironically, if it weren't for them and God's green eye to make them all horn-dogs, she'd be out of a job. Probably slinging hash like her momma. Sarah's track started pumping from the house speakers and she set the rhythm through her toes. From back stage she could tell that it was a large crowd tonight. Large crowds were always better. Easy to look out and not recognize anybody's face. Better money.

Moving sexy wasn't hard either. Her hips became a cartoon character and America loved a nice pair of tits. Jesus Christ alive on a stick had seen to her endowments. She'd always been a looker; took after her momma on that, developed early. Dragging the wooden chair, she strutted across the stage and slammed it down near the platform's edge, just out of reach from grabby hands.

Swaggering away from it, abandoned, an object of curiosity to set their teeth on edge, Sarah took to the pole. Once around and a pelvic thrust, she spread her legs and glared through them, a mass of blank upside down faces silhouetted by bright stage lights. Controlled, she slid down, grabbing onto the cold metal. *It takes a lot of muscle to do that.* No one ever considers the amount of grace it takes to work the pole when they come to the club. It's all nipples and tassels, bare ass and what's-on-tap, the dancers work hard for a living. *Like to see some construction dude come in here and do what I do.*

Gravity is my bitch. Sarah rolled along her spine at the base of the pole giving everyone in the room a wide glance at her crotch, shorts so light they're practically invisible. Then, she rolled forward on her belly, flat and hard like a damn super model. The stage floor smelled of booze and Mop-n-Glo. Her hands compressed her bosom. *Now, stare wantonly, open the mouth just a bit, and let them think I want 'em.*

Easy. Sarah kicked her legs back and stood. She bent over and pushed her ass to the entrance. The door opened and closed – *more money coming in.* Sarah moved her torso like a wave, syncopating the rhythm of the song in a sensual tease as she rubbed her hands all over herself. Becoming the voyeur's dream, she fondled her hair, messing it up like bed sheets after. She did a split down to the floor and arched her back, falling onto her hands and pressed her crotch up to God, pumping the ceiling like a Catholic girl after school. Then a handstand with both legs tumbling over in a pinwheel, and she stared into their blank, you-could-be-my-daddy faces. Thick hands, stubby fingers, shot out at her, galvanizing thanks and approval with little green paper certificates.

Love me. Sarah let them stick the dollar bills, *looks there's a five*, into the band of her short-shorts and the curving lip of her red, white, and blue brazier. She's an all-American gal who went for the flag costume tonight. It was always a crowd-pleaser. *Patriotic in a time of War.* It's not so much that she sells the audience sex as much as she convinces them that she's enjoying her own body. That just by being who she is, she's a creature of sexual prowess and unattainable desire. That's what gets them rowdy. That's what gets them off.

The heightened point of hands, an affection of commerce, Sarah moved away from the front of the stage and tore the tight, bright shorts off the luscious mounds of her well-rounded bottom. The crisp commitment of cash, so delicately placed in the hip huggers just seconds ago, eager for a grab, but careful not to peek the eye of the bouncer or offend the dancer, went crashing to the stage floor with the panties. The thong she wore underneath kept her jewel hidden, but gave the horny onlookers a surprise. *All American!* Sarah flashed the packed crowd her star.

It was just a glimpse, a reward to the men who spent their hard-earned pay. Sarah worked her waist, gyrating, keeping the show moving, feeling the song inside. *It's playing just for you. I'm here for you, baby. No one else. I'm all yours. I'm your little fantasy girl. The candy striper, prom queen, wife who wont go down, the friendly doctor that's out of reach, and the girl next door that never gave it up. Touch me with your eyes. Love me. Caress my flesh. I'm yours, baby. All yours.*

May 1995. Hobbs, New Mexico.

It was another night her Eva worked late. Crunching dried dirt under the soles of her shoes Sarah got off the school bus at the corner of Morales Ave and N. Llewelyn St. and walked the wide, gravel road to the trailer. A few years back they moved up to the Country Mobile Home Park and Sarah got stuck with a longer bus ride to school.

Hobbs wasn't much of a place, a small drop in the New Mexican desert on the border of Texas, but to be stuck in the ass end of that small drop, surrounded by flat lands, a few dried up arroyos, and nothing but sky was even worse. Sarah didn't complain about it though because she always figured it was her fault that they moved away from the Chaparral Mobile Home Park. She just assumed her momma didn't want to live next to the Greigos' anymore because of what she'd done.

After school Sarah turned on the TV. She put it on Oprah and fixed a sandwich. She watched the end of the episode and ate the rest of the ham, mayo, lettuce, and cheese on white bread while sitting on the Delarosa's swing. The Delarosas where an elderly couple that lavished everything on their grandkids when they came to visit. The kids had a swing set, wading pool, and tons of toys. They visited on the weekends, and during the summer they stayed for about a month. When the kids were around Mr. Delarosa would play with them in the yard and Mrs. Delarosa would fix all sorts of goodies: cakes, cookies, and brownies. She was like the old woman that lived in the gingerbread shoe, always baking, and there was plenty to go around. The Delarosas' sort of looked in on Sarah when her mother worked late, which was all the time, since they moved up to Country.

Sarah came back in when the winds picked up. One thing

about spring in the desert that completely sucked was all the damned wind. It would drive you mad if you let it, knocking you about, covering everything in fine brown silt. It was like living in the belly of a hurricane all the time. The wind liked to kick up dust devils. They danced their way across the mesa, spinning like tiny tornadoes. They were beautiful. The desert's natural Dervishes. Sarah liked to watch them when they were in the arroyos. Caged beauty, carefully gliding over the terrain, a constant pirouette, rising and dissipating with the direction of unyielding winds.

By nightfall, homework done, after watching Married with Children and The Simpson's, Sarah went to bed. The air kept kicking up. It howled like wolves lived in the rain gutters. *There'll be nothing but trash in the yard come morning. Probably blew in from Kansas.*

Sarah woke up from the banging. The wind knocked hard and was moaning. It roused the young girl from her bed and she went to see if her momma was home yet and to get a drink of water. Her mouth was parched, bland, and sticky. Even when she was inside the trailer the desert still sucked all the moisture from the air. Sometimes it got so bad that you considered crying a luxury. Sarah padded softly down the hall, bare feet, rubbing gobs of encrusted sleep out of her eyes. She saw lamplight spilling out of her mother's room. The door was opened a crack. Sarah peered in and slowly it formed in her little pubescent head that it wasn't the wind making such a terrible racket, it was her mother.

Through the thin sliver of light between the wooden door and the jamb she saw a man. He was naked, propped up on his knees behind her momma. She was naked too and on all fours. The bed sheets were tussled, falling onto the floor. Her mother's face was scrunched up and sweaty. She moaned and sighed in great breathy hisses, a shrill octave, as the bed squeaked and hit the wall. The man was pushing himself into her from behind. The hair on his chest was damp and matted. His hands held tightly to Eva's hips as giant snaking veins trailed up his arms to a tattoo of a lion's head. It roared. His lion's paw grabbed her momma's hair, white knuckled, and she reached out for him, scraping his thigh with her fingernails. Sarah saw the word, Love, tattooed across his fingers in a money script, curling around dirty blond locks. He looked like a cowboy riding out across the plains. Her momma was his horse.

They both began shouting and groaning louder, screaming up to God and Jesus – who was coming. They both wanted it harder and then they fell silent and meek. He collapsed on Eva's back and she fell onto the bed. She kissed him, reaching around for the man. *She wanted him?* They mumbled something to one another as he climbed off her.

Slapping her on the bottom, he headed for the door. Sarah didn't move. She didn't know how to move. She wasn't sure what she even saw. They were wrestling...*sort of.* The naked man opened the small trailer door and almost ran into the girl standing absently in the hall.

"Well, looky here," he said, turning to Eva.

He stank, sickly sweet. Eva, limbs weak, trembling from orgasmic aftershocks, peered around Derrick's svelte, taught ass and saw her daughter.

"Aw shit Sarah, what you doin'?" Eva quickly sat up, feeling her joy drip out of her toes like it was ink, and pulled the fallen bed sheet around her. "Get some clothes on. That's my daughter."

Derrick didn't move to get dress. "No shit," he replied, crouching down to eye level with the child. "Hiya doing? My name's Derrick. I'm a friend of your Mother's."

Sarah didn't say anything. She just looked at the man. He was grinning. Had blue eyes.

"Sarah come here. Get outta the doorway."

Derrick stood up. "Cute."

Sarah watched the naked man as he walked down the hall, turned on the kitchen light, and disappeared. She could hear him rustling about in the refrigerator and she looked at her momma with her shoulders all bunched up to her ears.

"C'mere honey."

She went to her mother. "Are you okay?"

The young girl was worried that the man might have hurt her. She hugged Eva about the neck. She smelled sweaty. Eva smiled, feeling bad, and combed her daughter's hair with her fingers.

"I'm fine. We was just playin' is all. How 'bout you got back to bed?"

"Okay."

Derrick swaggered back into the room drinking a beer and flung himself onto the bed.

"Would you put some clothes on," suggested Eva with strong

emphasis through her eyes.

"We ain't done yet," announced the Texan, strong and confident.

He took a swig from the fermented hops as Eva tossed a sheet over his exposed mid section, wrapped a sheet around herself, and got up. "I'll be back in a minute."

She took Sarah's hand.

"Don't think I can wait."

He smiled crooked, looking up at Eva, and Sarah noticed that he made her momma grin. Blushing and wide. Sarah couldn't remember the last time that she saw her momma smile. It had been awhile. Before Chaparral. Before Hobbs.

"Nighty-night," Derrick said to Sarah and she quietly waved goodnight as her mother led her back to her room.

In bed with a glass of water Sarah listened to them talking for a bit before she fell asleep. Their voices were buried under the wind whistling outside and she couldn't make out what they said. Every now and then, drifting off to sleep, she thought she heard her mother moan.

Come morning Sarah didn't remember her dreams and Derrick was still there. He was dressed in a tee shirt, jeans, and scuffed work boots. He sat at the kitchen table smoking a cigarette with the word "Hate" tattooed across his other knuckles. Sarah stared at the way the smoke from the tobacco stick curled around the letters. Eva was busy cooking breakfast – bacon and eggs; buttered toast. It had been awhile since Sarah had anything other than a bowl of cereal. The kitchen smelled nice, but felt weird, with the stranger so easy and smiling at the table. Everything felt oddly normal, like he'd been there forever. They were quiet. The wind was quiet. All the noise came from Saturday morning cartoons.

After breakfast her momma sent Sarah outside to play and she got a look at Derrick's faded, midnight blue El Camino. It had Texas plates and had seen some miles. There were a couple of primered square patches around the wheel wells where Derrick had done some bodywork to the old car. She traced their gray edges with her fingers. Toolboxes were in the back of the flatbed along with some jugs that were tied up with rope. Derrick and her mother spent most of that first day in her bedroom, behind closed doors, and Sarah avoided the trailer altogether.

Opting to walk along the dusty arroyo, she picked stones out of the dirt and pitched them into the desert. When she got bored with that she visited Mr. and Mrs. Delarosa and they let her watch TV.

Later that evening the three of them piled into the single seat of the El Camino and drove twenty miles up to Lovington and back so her momma could go to Walmart. Sarah sat by the door, looking out of the window at the desolate landscape, blurring by all the same; she did her best to ignore them. They were talking and laughing about stuff she didn't care about. Dry wind, cooling with the setting sun, moved by the might of the metal, whipped her hair and thundered loudly in her ears. For the whole ride Sarah couldn't get the sight of Derrick, naked, out of her head.

Sarah slid to the front of the stage and rubbed her fingers along the thin lone star printed to the strip of cloth that ran between her legs. Men thanked her with money. In the midst of her caressing moves, the face of the woman driving past this morning flashed through Sarah's mind, filling the empty silhouettes with pale skin, dark hair, and eyes that burned into her soul. The dancer shuddered as a moistened bloom erupted under the bail of her fingers.

Sarah arched her back and released her breasts from the patriotic bra, flinging it into the crowd. Some one was gonna go home with it. Covering each one of her nipples was a star spangled pasty. *Love, American Style - gimmie your money.* Cocks at salute, cheering and pumping their fists in the air, club patrons praised her with more cash – tucking the bills between sweaty flesh and the soft, cotton thong or tossing them onto the stage floor, like flowers.

Admittedly, at first, Sarah never got it. She didn't understand the attraction of the club and why anybody would want to spend their hard-earned money on any women they weren't screwing. But then again, she didn't have to understand it to be a dancer. She just had to work the numbers, work the corners of the stage, and let social etiquette, peer excitement, nature, and selling the fantasy do *all* the rest. It was ingrained in the human psyche. Tone explained it to her when she started working at the club.

"It's like milking a cow," he had said with his chocolatey voice. "Though, instead of getting your hands dirty on some greasy udder all you have to do is flash 'em your tits and smile. God takes care of the rest."

Eventually, Sarah got it. She saw the mechanics at work and focused on her dancing. Blindly staring into the stage lights, she reached out into the writhing mass, testosterone thick in her nostrils, and grabbed the nearest guy, planting his face in her freshly freed bosom. He loved it. The crowd loved it. Everybody wanted some. She was the carnival ride. But she wasn't easy. Tossing the man back into the obscurity of his seat Sarah strutted away. The lights pulsed, flashing in time with the throb of the song, and she worked the pole.

🐕🐎🐕

September 1997. Hobbs, New Mexico.

Derrick likes the red lipstick. Eva did her hair, put on her make up, was ready to leave, and Sarah wasn't even dressed yet.

"Don't make me late young lady. I've had enough of your shit. We're walkin' out that door in five minutes."

Sarah grumbled, looking out the window. The sky was just lighting up. It was too damn early. School had started a week ago and every day she was forced to get up early. It was Saturday. She wanted to sleep.

"I don't wanna go," argued Sarah. "Can't I just stay here?"

She flopped down on the couch. The cushions hiked her pajama top up. Eva stepped out of the bathroom with a stern look under the freshly applied doll face.

"You're going and that's that."

"But I don't wanna go," the girl whined in a mad gruff, stomping off to her room to get dressed, as Eva sighed a second away from throttling her own seed.

Sarah didn't see any point to it, driving all that way to Forth Worth, TX just see Derrick in jail for about half an hour. All she did was sit on the bench anyway. *Another fucking Saturday wasted.*

Derrick and her momma had become a regular thing. He moved in before he got pinched on an outstanding warrant in Texas. Some petty bullshit that she couldn't even recall. If truth be told, Sarah was actually glad that things had shifted back to just her and her mother, though she'd never say it out loud. Ever since that first night, Derrick was always around. Always gawkin' at her as her breasts grew in, making some off comment, or worse yet, trying to be her Dad.

The proceeding months before he was arrested Sarah started to fill out. This past summer she even got her first visit from Auntie Flow, as her momma called it, and last spring Sarah's moods where a roller coaster ride through a twister. She couldn't seem to find any clothes baggy enough to hide under. Even the dweebs at school were taking notice, grinning at her all the time with their metal mouths and acne. All Sarah wanted to do was stay home. *What's wrong with that?* Now she had to endure a six-hour car ride, up and back, with her mother being frantic, and then mournful, only to be paraded around a meat slammer to a bunch of degenerates and perverts. It was awful.

Sarah hated the prison. It stank of stale air and sweat with the occasional waft of vomit or blood as you entered from one section to another. The Guards always looked at her. She tried crossing her arms over her chest but that didn't keep them from staring. They brought Derrick out in an orange jumpsuit and he had a cut lip. Eva lamented about it and he played it off tough. He was only on a three-year stretch and his state's appointed attorney was trying to get him moved to a smaller facility up in Lubbock. Sarah sat at the little round table hunched over, ready to leave. She couldn't fathom why her momma would even want to see him in a place like this.

"How's school?" Derrick asked her.

Sarah shrugged.

Eva pushed on her shoulders. "Sit up. Don't slouch. Answer the question."

"You know..." she shrugged again.

"She's just tired is all. Cranky." Eva hugely sighed.

Derrick smiled. "Well I tell ya what, I've got to be the luckiest son-of-bitch in here 'cause I've got two of the finest women visitin' me. Comin' all this way from New Mexico. It does these old eyes good, I tell you."

Eva blushed and Sarah thought he was being an asshole. But deep down in the small pit of her belly she liked the comment, even though she'd never admit it. Eva reached out and took his hands, cradling his volatile love and hate in faded blue serif letters. His metal bracelet clanked on the table and Sarah watched as Eva ran a finger along its hard edge.

"You got your birthday coming up, how old you gonna be?"

"Twelve."

"My you growin' up." His eyes danced on her. "Takin' after your mom you are."

Eva cut in. "Any word from Dawson on getting you outta here?"

"Not yet. Should hear something by the end of the month. I'll call ya and let you know. But you don't have to keep comin' out here all the time…"

"I miss ya, baby."

"I miss you too." He stared at her until her eyes began to well up. "But I'll be out soon enough." He turned to Sarah as Eva delicately wiped her eyes so that her make up wouldn't smear. "Whatchyu gonna do for your birthday?"

"Nothing much I suppose."

"She's only turning twelve," informed Eva, dotting her eyes with a napkin. "Sixteen's the big one, baby."

"Well, even still. You should do something nice." He turned to Eva. "Why don't you take her out? Use some of that money we put aside last spring and buy her a dress and take her out on the town. Just look at her, she's becoming a woman after all."

"Thought we were saving that money for a trip to Hawaii when you got out?"

"All I'm saying is, you should treat her nice for her birthday. Time's too short as it is."

Eva curled her fingers tight around the dampened napkin. "Sarah? Why don'tchyu wait for me over there?"

Told ya, the bench. Sarah got up and walked to the far wall. The visiting cell was sparse today, only a few convicts enjoying social calls. Fencing lined the rectangular room to the corridor where inmates were led to the convict corral. Beyond that was another fenced in lane, where two guards beat a worn path, and beyond them was a huge, steel door. *So much metal.* Even in the short time that Sarah was here it beat her down. She leaned against the cold brick wall and tucked one leg under her, for support, and glared at her momma and Derrick as they got their "*alone time*". *So alone that everybody's watching!*

In the car ride home Sarah noted that Eva was quieter than normal. All those rustling thoughts battering around in her blond head with nowhere to go. She kept her lip tight and just drove. By the time they neared Sweetwater, before the turn off to 84 in Roscoe, Sarah got the carrot she wanted.

"You're right," said her mother, keeping her eyes on the road. "You should stay home. You don't have to visit him no more."

For the rest of the drive Eva returned to her brooding silence and Sarah stared out the window.

⚓

Sarah sashayed to the chair and began dancing around it. Falling to the floor, she grabbed handfuls of crisp dollar bills and rubbed them on her body. The crowd went wild, releasing more cash for her to spread along her hot pink flesh. Her writhing figure, the compacted heat, pounding bass, and bobbing lights connected to the crowd's lust. She and her audience became one motion, one panting breath. One.

Tone looked up from behind his station at the bar, saw her working the men, and smiled. Sarah was seventeen when she started working for him. He kept her as a bar-back until she turned legal tender and then he put her on stage. He had her dancing early shows until she found her groove and since then she'd been a great earner. One that Tone took great pride in cultivating. That was the main reason why he chose to help her out with school.

Knocking back and forth through getting her GED at the community college and starting medical school at UNM, Sarah's path had been fairly focused. Tone knew she was going to go off and do her own thing one day. The girl had too much spitfire and attitude to stay grounded to his club. Working for him was time-stamped. It had an expiration date. So when the girl came to him, shortly after her twenty-first birthday, and asked him for the loan for school he didn't really have to think about it. Though he acted like he did, making her wait for about a week before he sat down with her and worked out the conditions. At least that way he could keep her on the floor a bit longer before she hit the bricks.

Tone returned his attention to the day's receipts and continued counting. The front door opened and closed and he quickly scanned the two pale women who stood in the entranceway. He liked the whole Gay and Lesbian Movement, how it kept getting wider attention and more national focus. It increased his consumer base. Tone smirked at the ashen, tattoo-clad wenches. *A couple of dykes.* He glanced back to Sarah at the foot of the stage and nodded his head in time to a couple beats of the song. He always enjoyed her shows. She really knew how to dance.

ᛏᛉᛏ

February 1999. Lovington, New Mexico.

Light busted through the trailer windows like police officers, shinning and heavy, hazing across the TV screen. Sarah entered flush from the sun, perspiration dotting her skin. The screen door slammed loudly in the frame.

"Sarah? Get me another beer, would ya?"

She crossed the fading linoleum, opened the icebox, basked in its brief cool, retrieved a cold brew, and handed it to Derrick. "Here ya go," she said, walking off to her room.

"Would you do something about that blind? It's ruinin' the game."

Sarah exhaled loudly and walked over to the couch. Climbing on it, Derrick watched her fine, slim curves and piqued flesh as she bent over and fooled with the curtains. Lazily, his finger lingered in the metal beer tab, pausing to opening it, when Eva came back inside, gently closing the screen door.

She carried an empty laundry basket and saw him staring at her daughter again. He'd been out almost three months, just before Christmas, and they'd all been happy. She thought nothing of it at first. He was away for two years. Sarah had grown in that time, any man would look if blood still pumped through his veins. It's just their nature. Though more and more, Eva had noticed how his eyes were wandering to her child.

"Could really do with that dryer being fixed," she announced for the second time today.

"I'll get to it right after the game." Derrick turned to her. "Promise."

Sarah stepped off the couch. "How's that? Any better?"

"Yeah. It's fine."

He popped the top of the beer can as his eyes darted to her and away. Her tank-top was stained with sweat, accentuating the soft round victuals of her breasts. The young girl walked the long distance to her room. Staring at the back of his head, Eva knew his eyes were on Sarah instead of the game and she felt old, tired, and dirty. Time chipped away at her like a bad statue and she didn't have anything left that compared with the young emerging woman. Sarah was the new model. The better her. The girl's gawking youth was nothing short of cruel. Eva set the laundry basket down. It carried within it, after all, nothing but emptiness and regret.

"Hey baby..." she said running her fingers through Derrick's hair, coming around to the front of him. "Let's you and me take a shower?"

"Game's almost done." He took a sip of his beer.

Eva curled in his lap and whispered in his ear. "You'd rather watch TV than go get wet with me?"

She pulled her face in front of his, big eyes and pleading.

"It's almost done," he emphasized.

Squeezing her ass, he changed the angle of her pitch in his lap so he could see the TV better and she nestled against his chest, dejected. Hollow, she listened to his heart. Steady. Drumming. Just hearing it soothed her worry.

Two plays later and the score unchanged, Sarah crossed the living room. Eva got up from Derrick's lap and crossed to her purse. "Go down to the market and pick up some milk and butter."

"Can't I go a little later? It's hot out."

Eva shot a quick glance at Derrick, stretched out in the reclining chair. "Do it now. I need it for dinner."

She put the money in her daughter's hand. Grumbling, Sarah left the screen door rocking in its jamb. The Cherokee Village Trailer Park sat at the crossroads of West Avenue Q, McAllister Drive, and Main Street. The little store was only a mile up Main Street, but during the middle of the day, even in winter, it was a scorcher.

When Sarah got back the front door to the trailer was locked and the hum of the swamp cooler beat as loudly against her as the sun on the front porch. Inside, through the thin tin and wood walls, she could hear the shower running and the faint grunts of them doing it.

Sarah felt the sweat dripping down the backside of her arms. It collected in the band of her shorts. The air was stolid. The butter was melting. Every now and then a car passed, kicking up dust, and it was at least an hour before the front door unlocked. When it did, Sarah wanted nothing more than to take a shower, wash the grime and stink away, but just the thought of the two of them in it, minutes before, made her feel icky all over. She'd rather wear the dirt and perspiration then grab a shower just now. In her room, Sarah wiped down with a towel and picked up reading her book from where she had left off.

It was two days before the dryer was fixed. Her momma was at work and Derrick had finished replacing the tumbler. After dinner, Sarah did her homework while listening to music and the ex-con watched television. She cleaned up the dishes and took a shower after Derrick had had his. They both moved like blocks in the long rectangular box. Having him back wasn't as bad as she imagined it would be, and for all her insecurities and petty jealousies Sarah actually liked the guy. He was decent to her momma, had a job, and brought money in. But neither had too much to say to the other. School was fine. Work was fine. Friends were fine. Everything else was bullshit.

Just before nightfall it rained, dropping the temperature of the already cold night. Derrick sat on the front porch and polished off the last beer once the sky water had passed and Sarah gabbed on the telephone. One of her friends from school, he figured, as the light muffles of the high-pitched conversation filtered outside from the opened windows. The girl sat alone in her room, connected. The ex-con held down the porch.

Sarah left a plate of dinner for her mother wrapped up in the fridge and by the time she lay down to sleep Derrick had driven off to the liquor store so Eva wouldn't come home to a barren rack. Sarah was still awake when Derrick returned. Lying there in bed, she looked up at the ceiling, unable to sleep. Getting up, she threw on her robe and went out to the living room to watch TV, joining Derrick on the couch.

It wasn't too long before the dulled beats of reruns and the low flickering light caused them to stretch out. She laid her bare legs across Derrick's lap, and fell asleep. Under the girl's soft weight, he couldn't help but notice – *a full woman.* Eyeing the curve of her thigh as it disappeared

Headlights screamed across the darkened windows through the blinds, piercing his eyes.

"Shit! Your Mother's home."

Sarah spasmed and shocked, eyes crashing like glass as she bound off the couch. Pulling her robe tight around herself, she ran to her room. Derrick slowed his breathing, looked at his glistening fingers, and wiped Sarah's vaginal juice onto the backside of his jeans. He heard Eva's car door open and close. Keys rustled. He took a frantic sip of beer, calming, and waited for the front door to open staring at the mouth of the hallway that led to Sarah's room.

The adolescent girl lay curled in bed. Eyes a crime scene, peering through the dark, listening. The stain between her thighs was sticky and moist. She had fantasized about him touching her and now he'd gone and done it. Slowly, Sarah pulled into herself, a fetal position, as she heard her momma come home. The front door opened and closed gently. *Gently?* Muffled conversations. *Food in the fridge. Worked late, tired. Sarah get her homework done? Wanna beer?*

It was hours before she fell asleep.

Lin noticed the black man behind the bar glaring at them. He was dressed nice, groomed, and held a fist full of cash. She took him for the owner. When his eyes fell off her she noticed the girl on the stage. It was the same one from this morning. It seemed like years had passed since then. She was on her knees to a barking throng rubbing money all over herself. Her star pasties twinkled in the oscillating lights. Z stood next to Lin casing the joint in a glance: exits, body count, assessing the level of threat, and PVP *(Possible Vital Prospects)*. It was all old hat. Easy. The two vampires crossed the room to an empty table.

Salty sweat, cigarettes, and liquor permeated the blood rank air. Lin didn't take her eyes off the dancer. Pulling a man from the crowd by his tie like a dog on a leash the beautiful thing led him to the chair just as she and Z sat.

The precocious vamp drummed on the table and sang out of time to the beat of the song that pounded through the house speakers so loudly that it ensured that the listeners would have the rhythm's echo reverberating through their heads for weeks to come. "Wanna get wasted. Wanna get fucked. Wanna bay-bee shit outta luck."

Seductively, Sarah writhed in front of the seated patron on stage. He was a willing pawn in her show and he quickly became the spectacle and object of jealousy to the men pressed at the rostrum. His buddies egged him on, shouting at him. He was now the Viking of their raging libidos, nervous and horny, he wanted the dancer too, but was afraid to do anything about it.

Sarah's contorting body was a siren's call that swelled Lin's ears and trapped her eyes. Her mere presence, dancing, juxtaposed against the gaudy carnival attraction of the club made the vampire realize, yet again, just how ugly a sense of humor the universe possessed. It teased her viciously. Here was the vision from the locket, the reincarnated soul: a stripper, a side show meat display. It smacked Lin across the face, hard and wanting. *The bounty of flesh is appetite.*

Z was talking at her, but Lin wasn't listening. The table between them, the expanse of the room, Lin felt so close to the girl on stage that she could taste her scent just as if she could recall the flavor of her life gushing through her veins from the Jadaraa Soo, oh so long ago. Yet seeing her now, reformed in all her naked splendor, a capsule of clanging regret, through a haze of cigarette smoke, pitted darkness, and bright garish lights beating on her relentlessly made the symbiont feel that it was impossible to reach her, as if the illusion on the stage would always remain a photograph in a piece of jewelry. Lin felt vaguely out of time and out of touch.

"Whudooya want?" the waitress chimed, tray in hand, high heels and a golden thong.

Z spun the tassel on one of the woman's breasts. The waitress was taken aback and raised her eyebrows.

"It's like a propeller. Hey, Lin we should get some of these."

Z spun it again.

"Yeah, yeah. Vroom, vroom," the waitress muttered flatly. "Sumtin' ta drink?"

Z was having too much fun, spinning both tassels repeatedly. "Pilot to Co-Pilot. Prepare for take off! Pilot to Bombardier…"

Z whistled as she flicked the tassels with hard fingernails, dropping the bomb, and the drink-tender just gawked at the imprudent wench. Lin glared at the dancer, oblivious, and the vulgar punk, laughing, delighted in herself. The entire atmosphere of the club matched the harking, garish smiles of Prophet and Jordan from that horrible night. Life had come alive with peculiar revenge and only Lin could see it. Everyone else seemed in sync with the world. Fate dangled her above it, forcing the reincarnated soul to dance. To dance for her, blatantly, in open submission, a mad perverted nightmare giggling at her squeamish hunger.

"Gimmie a whiskey aanndd…" Z banged out a snare drum roll on the table, "another whiskey."

The waitress turned to the dyke with the short-cropped hair. "And you?" She waited to no avail. "Hello, Miss? What can I get for you tonight?"

Impervious, Lin stared on.

"Lin? Lin?!" shouted Z, snapping her out of it.

"Huh?"

Z pointed to the waitress, bare bones, curvy hips and all, tassels at the end of her titties staring her in the face. Lin felt her fleshy presence, and Z calling her name was nothing more than an annoyance.

"A beer's fine."

She shifted her attention back to the dancer, ignoring everybody else. Z stared at her for a minute, noticing how she'd locked eyes with the action on the stage and vanished. Z slowly turned around and looked at the dancer. *Another Betty with a tight ass and Lin's gone baby gone.* Eyes tattooed on the skinny bitch's thighs. Her tongue pressed against the hard palette of the dancer's back. The vampire might as well have been drooling. Z cocked her head. *Lin's been a silent cunt all day. First this morning, now this.*

"So I…uh, was thinking I'd dye my hair green again, and stick a spike through my neck, file down my teeth and become a belly dancer in Tangier. What do *you* think?"

"Uh huh."

Lin's lips barely parted, grunting syllables, eyes glued to nothing but the stage. The wild hellcat truly felt neglected. Nonexistent, a speck of dust on a gnat's ass, floating in a dandelion storm, somewhere off Cape Hatteras. The nocuous din of the club and all her vacant memories, holes as big as bicycle tires, clamored about and Z grew hot.

"Un-fuckin-believable."

Z slammed the edge of the table with her palms and sent it tilting into Lin's gut. That snapped the ditzy broad out of her narcissistic muse.

"What the fuck?"

Lin was awake now, but Z was already up and moving away. Lin called after the punk, curious as to why she jabbed her in the belly. But Z kept cruising. Sarah did a leg split, twirled around the pole, and slid up from between the crotch of her boy-toy in the chair as her song concluded in a tremolo shake.

Lin missed it. Applause rippled her attention back to the front of the room and she turned in time to see Sarah grab the last flakes of cash off the grimy stage floor as she headed backstage, out of sight. Lin turned back to where she last saw Z walking away from, but she was gone too. In the thick press of bodies standing, wanting an encore, Lin was buried behind the loud gloom of the club. Stage lights tipped on mechanized rotators across a sea of blank, scruffy faces – *A gallery of men*. She was alone.

June 2001. Lovington, New Mexico.

Eva held the panties in a tight fist, starring at nothing: her blank reflection in a window, the brown livingroom beyond the glass, hours of birth pangs, her water breaking, the feel of him inside of her in the backseat of the car, the sound of dreams crumbling when she told her momma that she was pregnant, the smell of freshly waxed linoleum and cat litter, and the feel of Derrick lying in bed next to her.

His scent was all over Sarah's dirty underwear. Eva's face was a stone scowl and she swore to it. She knew Derrick's musk anywhere. *And motor grease!* His smudged fingerprints, so small on the colorful striped band of the soft cotton briefs was unmistakable. He was guilty. *He's a man, how could he not be anything other?*

Eva chained smoked.

The air was thick and choking. Her fingers smelled like tar and nicotine as she waited for Sarah to get home. A breeze blew across the flat gray landscape and a flap on the construction plastic buckled. It pulled Eva's eyes to the addition that Derrick had been working on. The trailer was getting an upgrade. He'd started it a month ago. For Her! *Finally, after all these gaddamned years an extra room!* Eva exhaled bitter, rancid smoke.

Her trailer felt like a coffin, doublewide and mobile. Her heart was sinking. She'd known it for some time, but didn't want to admit it. Like if she did, all her smiles would hide and never come back, that by admitting the awful truth she'd somehow become the wreck of a woman that she always imagined herself to be. *Gaddaman it. There's a hole in my fucking trailer!* The addition was only half way done. Derrick had been working on it during the weekends. Sometimes at night after work too. He was building it for her.

For me, gaddamn it!

When Sarah came home Eva was sitting in a chair in the livingroom, smoke trailed up between her fingers. The ashtray was full. Laundry still sat in the basket on top of the dryer where she had left it. Sarah went straight to her room and never noticed her mother's eyes following her. After a few seconds Sarah's stereo disrupted the intense hush. Eva sucked another gulp of ash into her lungs and ground the stick out, knocking butts onto the little round table where the ashtray rested. She rose from the chair, nostrils flaring smoke.

Sarah's door was partially open. The cat squeezed through, rubbing his side up against it, stepping into the hall. Eva pushed the door back. Her daughter sat on the bed, hunched over, looking at a magazine. Eva threw her spoiled undies onto the page. Sarah turned toward her, picking them up.

"Go ahead, smell 'em."

Sarah just stared at her momma, the light cotton briefs resting delicately between guilty fingers. "Momma I–"

"Can't even imagine the indignity in my own house?" Her face was reddened. Tears welled in her eyes. "You can't be fit with some boy your own age to whore around with you gotta go sleepin' with mine."

A lump lodged in Sarah's throat and it felt like it had moved in forever. The knot in her belly untightened and she was glad it was finally out in the open. "Momma, I'm so–"

"Don't you dare say it. Don't you dare." Her eyes spilled over. "I want you out of here."

Eva turned and walked away, leaving a wide girth of silent space where she once stood. It was a gigantic empty wound that ate Sarah alive. The teenager sat looking at her panties. She remembered the night well. It was only a week ago, the last time they'd done it. She didn't really want to; wasn't really in the mood, but he was. Sarah was in the kitchen, getting a bellyache just thinking about what they'd been doing for the past two years, slowly coming to the conclusion that she didn't want to do it anymore. Yet, there he was playfully chasing her around the trailer, and she let him. They fucked in the bathroom and the metal of the sink left an indentation in the small of her back until the following morning.

"Don't you even care that your boyfriend has been fucking your own daughter behind your back?" Sarah fired at the absent space that her mother had left.

"Don't you dare," came violently from the livingroom on storming feet. "Don't you fucking dare speak to me about what the fuck I care about! You don't know a thing about it!"

"I was thirteen when he—"

"You're always parading yourself around here half dressed all the damn time. He's a man gaddaman it! What d'yu think would happen?"

"You think I wanted this!?"

Eva drew up hard and silent, mouth a compactor. "I've seen the way you look at him."

"Momma?"

She tossed her hands into the air. "I don't want to hear it."

"Momma?" Sarah pleaded, crying, following her down the hall.

"You think I like this?" fired Eva in a crushing ball of tears. "You think I want any of this bullshit here? You have no idea what it's like trying to find a decent man in the world today when everyone around you is younger and prettier than you are. After awhile they stop looking, Honey. You're gonna find that out some day. You think..." and she wiggled her hand at her daughter's extremities, "all this is gonna last. Huh! You're sadly mistaken. Think you can float by on that ass of yours alone? Well, I got another thing for ya if ya think I'm gonna stand by and let you take what little else I got. I done did my part, you hear? That's enough. You hear me…that's enough!"

Shaking, Eva exited the trailer. The screen door rocketed loudly in the frame. Sarah just stood there, alone, with the balled underpants tightly held in a clenched fist. She was shaking and the doublewide was closing in. After awhile when the trailer door didn't open and the angry vestige of her mother hadn't returned, Sarah entered her room and threw the soft-striped-smoking-gun onto her bed. It landed softly, eating the atmosphere of the room with its large significance. She grabbed her backpack, dumped out its stored contents, and started packing.

That night she stayed at Angie's place. Angie was a girlfriend from school and her parents had always been pretty kind to Sarah. The young girl figured she would couch surf until she came up with a plan.

A week later, Sarah and Angie rode by the trailer park, borrowing Angie's brothers' bike, so the two of them could peddle the distance. Sarah didn't know what to expect when she went back inside of the doublewide, but the place looked the same. Derrick's busted El Camino was still in the back yard. The tarp was still stretched across the rear of it. The enclosed deck had a few new beams added to it, a flank of plywood, and more wiring. Other than that, it was mostly the same. Her momma and Derrick's room was still a mess and there were a few leftovers in the fridge next to a stack of beer. Everything looked right regular and normal, and for some reason this bothered Sarah the most.

She grabbed what little stuff she wanted from her room and she and Angie rode away. It was the last time she saw the trailer. Angie had family in Albuquerque and the girls finagled a ride from some older kids who were going there one night. Angie stayed with Sarah for three days before she went back to Lovington, leaving the orphaned girl alone at her cousin Jimmy's house.

Sarah stayed with Jimmy and his family for a couple of days before taking off. His right regular, nuclear family smacked Sarah of everything she never had. It was too much for her. So, she wound up crashing with some people that she had met at the Blue Dragon. Within a week, Sarah had found a shit job making shit pay and started to think that everything was going to be okay.

"Hold it there, Missy." A hand grabbed Lin by the arm stopping her in her tracks.

She looked down at the meaty digits, pudgy arm, and the fat man it was attached too. She couldn't remember the last time someone had grabbed her or even touched her without her first wanting them to. He had a squishy face. A cigar stub poked out from his round cheeks and his eyes were glassy and mean. "Where'd ya think you're goin?"

He was amusing. A guard dog, barking. A lone sentry. Lin's eyes poked holes in him until he let go. She jabbed her head toward the backstage dressing rooms, indicating her direction.

"I don't think so," Eddie informed curtly, pulling the unlit stub from his jowls. "No one gets back there unless they're shakin' their ass on that stage. And you don't look like you're shakin your ass."

Lin regarded him as the barking dog he was – *yapping, just yapping* – a stiff face, blank eyes.

"What?" He inquired like he'd offended the girl's soft sensibilities. "You gots a problem with that? Panties all in a bunch 'cause you can't git your girl freak on." He laughed and it made him look even uglier than he was.

"No," Lin assured him. "I have no problem with that."

"Then what the fuck you still hangin 'round for?" He jabbed his cigar butt back into his greasy mouth and eased back onto the metal stool. It was a sure sign that the conversation was done and that she should now go. But when the Lesbo didn't budge he figured she just needed a bit more prodding. "Beat it sweet checks before I have ta get rough."

"Oooooohhh," Lin eased through her gums like a windmill, acting stupid and sexy at the same time. "A tough guy. I *like* that."

Eddie stared at her for a bit. Her level was off. "Crazy bitch. Now, ya gone an' made me git outta my chair."

Slowly, he inched his bulk forward until Lin stepped into him and gently placed a finger to his chest, allowing the compressed, springy dexterity of her Jadaraa Soo to push him back down. The stool squeaked like rusty pipes under the strain of the bouncer's weight. Lin cocked a sideways smile with a hint of fang glinting off stage lights. "Now, we wouldn't want you to go to all that trouble, would we?"

Eddie pressed against the girlie's lone finger, but he couldn't budge it. *It don't make no sense!* He grabbed her arm with both hands and tried pulling as he pushed, but that only wore him out. He couldn't move her. For all his size and muscle he could not bend a simple finger. *She's like a block of damned cement!* His squat face wrinkled with worry. Sweat matted his hairline. His eyes were diminutive among his large, awkwardly balanced cheeks, and when finally the fear set in Lin could tell he was open to negotiation.

"Here's what we're gonna do..." She pulled a wad of folded bills out of her pocket with her free hand. Hundreds mostly, Eddie's eyes darted to the hefty bulk of cash. He was panting, loud and raspy. His cigar butt was close to falling out of his mouth. She removed her finger and the fat man came crashing back on all four legs of the stool with a creaking thud.

She tore a large portion from the stack and slapped the cash down hard onto Eddie's round belly, and returned the rest to her pocket. He felt the sting all the way around the world to his bottom. She kept her hand on the money, feeling him breathing, labored and slow.

"There's over two thousand dollars here," said Lin, leaning in close. "And what I'm buying with it fat boy is an excuse *not* to kill you... drain *aaallll* of that delicious blood in that gross body of yours and leave you in a ditch somewhere where nobody will give a damn that you're missing." She paused to let him think on that tasty tidbit and brought her free hand up to his round face and began stroking him gently. "Now, I'm going to go and talk to one of your dancers and you're gonna sit here, count your money like blessings, and mind your own fucking business from now on." Eddie tried to remove his face from her touch. So, she pinched his cheek. "Are we clear?"

He nodded his head and his whole body shook. Meaty hands pulled at the cash, but Lin wouldn't let it go. "Like crystal," he muttered as fear-sweat beaded his brow.

Lin chuckled in the dark of her throat, carving a figure eight with the tip of her finger on the pile of money on his belly. She had fed earlier, but it wasn't enough. Inhaling his rank pulp of fear, he was a large bucket of blood squirming under her that the Jadaraa Soo wanted. *Just a gallon or two from his ample supply.* She bared the gleaming points of her fangs and slapped the bouncer on the side of his portly cheeks a couple of times to let the threat sink in. "Good."

Removing her finger, the fat man sighed. She left his large orbit as a few hundred dollar bills slipped through his ham-hocks, lightly parachuting to the floor. Eddie was unsure of what really took place. His eyes darted to the back of the brunette as she walked away, his face a crashed cable-car of disbelief. He felt scared and was sweating as if he were in a sauna. His shirt stuck to him in odd places and he was *really* thankful to still be sucking down air. He'd never felt anything like it before. The girl had actually put the fear of God in him, and he prayed. Eddie climbed down from his stool, picked up the fallen green printed scraps of paper off the backstage floor, and prayed. Prayer was the cup of loneliness that begged to be fulfilled.

Scantily clad women passed Lin, blathering about something or other. Each step she took down the hall felt languid and huge. Her feet were gummy bears. Lin looked for the dressing room. *Starlets. Starlets.* Everyone's a starlet, twinkling from sequin memory when she was last backstage: *Cats. New York City. Looking for Z. Sometime in the Eighties.* The symbiont had wandered off and Lin found her backstage sucking down a performer. It was a good thing that she'd discovered her in the prop room or the show would have lost its first cat to the cruel intentions of the night creature.

Z celebrated her likes in blood. She mourned her sadness in blood. She even soothed her ache in blood. In blood, Lin recalled the taste of the girl from the locket and her tummy tilted. This backstage area was a labyrinth of numbered doors and special rooms, a mop closet, and bare ass. Lin heard Sarah's voice before she found her. The air was a buzz-saw of anticipation that hovered two inches above Lin's dying skin.

"…No. They have me waitressing on Monday nights. Back on the floor Wednesday."

"Well, either way Lonzo said he'd watch Ricky. So, just let me know which night you wanna switch."

"That'll be great, Bri. Thanks."

Lin eased into the dressing room, spying the dancer through a clothing rack. She sat at a long table with another girl in front of a lighted mirror like a Hollywood movie star. She combed her hair and in the pure white light Lin could see now that it was much lighter than she had first thought, more auburn with a touch of red than a true brunette. It made the girl's green eyes pop.

"Oh-kay," Brina said to the image of herself in the mirror, wiping the lipstick at the edges of her mouth. "See ya on the floor."

"Yeah."

The saucy Latino passed Lin in the doorway and the vampire avoided making eye contact with her, stepping further into the room. Lin looked out of place, like she'd wandered in from a Heavy Metal concert or a car show. Though, Brina didn't have time to think about the out-of-place girl. She needed to hit her mark or Eddie would dock her. That fat fucker was always trying to find ways to pinch the dancers' cash. He called it a lesson, but it was nothing short of stealing and everybody knew it.

Lin looked down the length of the lighted table. There was only one other dancer in the room with the girl from the locket. The symbiont felt nervous. She couldn't think of anything to say. Numbly, she watched Sarah from the hidden comfort of a clothing rack. Beautiful outfits, loud colors, Lin tried to recall the face of the woman from that horrible night, decades ago: *gleaming metal from behind a ring of frightened faces tucked into the greedy hands of shadow.* The resemblance to her then was uncanny, even though Lin was sure that the woman in the sandstorm was older. *This is ridiculous.* Silently, Lin stepped further into the room. She looked down at her feet, busting to say something...anything.

"I uh...saw you..." mumbled Lin as Sarah paused at the quiet voice and her eyes flicked up. Through the mirror, she glimpsed the driver from earlier this morning standing behind her in the dressing room. "...Up on the...It was ah, a really great show."

"Thanks." Sarah smiled.

Viewed between the dangling locks of Lin's raven's nest the dancer's cute smile sent a jittery river through Lin's arms and fingertips. "You're a wonderful dancer."

Sarah returned to brushing her hair. Long, slow strokes. She watched the curious woman in the mirror. "Well, something's got to pay for school."

Lin stepped closer. "So, you're in school?"

"Medical Student."

"Wow." Lin was impressed, feeling life's bitter joke slap her on the shoulder.

"I saw you too." Sarah paused for effect. "This morning."

"You did?" Lin smiled wide and nervous like it was weird for her to be in her skin. It was a new sensation. It beat oddly against the thrushing Jadaraa Soo that wiggled deep in her body, pulled down by the vampire's conscious energy before she even entered the club.

"Yeah," said Sarah, setting the hairbrush down. "As you drove by. You were looking at me."

The vampire blushed, "Yeah. I was." Absentmindedly, her fingers began fidgeting with the silver locket. "It's just that...you were, well, you are...so radiant."

Sarah blushed. "You sure that just wasn't the sun?"

Lin softly chuckled. "Yeah. I'm sure."

An awkward silence descended between them and Lin sat down at Brina's station. She pulled the chair out and it grated across the floor like a zipper. She straddled it with its flat back between her legs. Sarah turned to the hard luck woman who had tattoos spilling out of her clothing. Her skin was slightly pale, eyes sunken, and hair as black as night itself. Both wanted to speak, to uncurl the jumbled feelings, but neither knew how.

"Do you like dancing?" Lin asked after a time, poking around the makeup at Becky's station.

Sarah thought about it. "No. Not really." She was surprised by her answer, having spent years clinging to childhood dreams. "The money's good. But I get sick of feeling like a piece of meat in a freezer, you know."

"Yeah," Lin did know, though she felt more like the butcher than the lamb as a sharp sensation to hide kneed her in the ribs. "So, ah...You wanna get outta here? Go some place better and talk or something?"

By the time Lin rolled the question past her lips and gazed into the live girl's smile her jittery, uncomfortable energy was fleeing through her boots. She thought that by simply connecting with the dancer, she would instantly know what karma had in store for her, that by merely placing herself in the woman's presence again she would have an answer as to her decades of journeying, her obsession with the past, and the lingering press of guilt that rode her old bones like a carnival. But that didn't happen and the magnetic press of the enclosed dressing room and all its giddy brightness suddenly became too much for the vampire to handle.

"I'd like that," Sarah coached. "But I'm expected on the floor." Sarah rose to leave. "Gotta work." Looking down at the mysterious driver, it never occurred to her to even ask the woman's name.

"No, um...it's ok. I..." blathered Lin.

"Not that I wouldn't," Sarah quickly added. "It's that I have to work."

"Sure. Yeah," Lin piped, rising too. "But, I ah...spoke with, with the fat guy. He..."

"Eddie?"

"Yeah. Eddie." Lin didn't bother to ask him his name when she was threatening his life. "Spoke with him before; said it was ok."

"Eddie said that?"

"Yeah."

"Eddie?" Sarah squinted. It was hard to believe. She leaned against the long counter that spanned the entire room.

"Yeah. He just...I spoke with him just before coming in here."

"Huh." Sarah's eyebrows were raised. Heightened disbelief in a magical realm; curious questions zipped through her head. Lin leaned against the station counter too, smiling, and looked up at Sarah.

"So. If you wanted...you could."

"Yeah?" She searched the stranger's face, deeply.

"That is if you want to," Lin pressured slightly. "You could go out...with me."

Sarah thought on it and muttered, "I could use a night off."

She didn't want to be here and was deathly curious about the woman. First this morning and now this. Coincidences never fell into Sarah's lap. Life was a jagged staircase ever winding upwards. Eddie was a tight miser and held onto every little thing he could get his grubby hands onto. So, it was hard to swallow that she could be so close to running out of this place with a decent purse full of cash. She turned to the vampire. "I'll be right back. Wait."

Sarah exited the dressing room, leaving Lin alone to stare awkwardly at the empty room. *What am I doing?* Reason crept in. *I shouldn't here. I shouldn't be doing this. I should just go.* In the sparse absence of the girl, doubt began to play the symbiont like a fiddle. But before Lin could devise any logic to remove herself Sarah entered with a curious look on her face.

"Not sure how you did it, but he definitely remembered speaking to you, and you're right." Sarah gazed strangely at the girl. "What did you say to him?"

Lin shrugged and grinned, lips tight over her protruding canines. "You'd be surprised what a smile can do."

Sarah chuckled, "Lemme get dressed and we'll..."

"Cool. I'll wait over..."

"Yeah; then..."

It felt weird like a dream and Lin could not stop grinning, "Oh-kay."

"Okay."

They stared at each other for a moment, smiling like fools, awkward instruments, strumming their own internal symphonies.

"Well, I'll just..."

Sarah nodded toward the wardrobe rack and Lin leaned against the counter as the dancer disappeared behind a row of stage clothes. Calm euphoria sprang through the vampire's alien system. She was treading new territory, felt possibility again creeping across her skin, old and rusted, its gentle mechanics creaked in her ears. Her Jadaraa Soo quivered, squeezing her heart with rapid palpitations. Not just for blood, but for the anticipatory yang of the girl's charms. Lin felt as if she was stepping outside of her glide and the impossible nightmare of bygone years finally began to feel like a story in a book that had happened to somebody else. Its clutching hold appeared to be slipping, its days long over. Finally, it could become unfamiliar, like all that pain and death could be cleansed. With eyes cast downward, hair dangling in her face, Lin read the floor like subtitles. She beamed, a wide, welcoming smirk that made her face glow. Silently, Lin mouthed the word, *yes.*

Sergeant Wallace pressed a pin into Apache Junction. Then he stuck Brenda. Salomé. And Phoenix twice. He picked a different color tack and stabbed Holbrook. Silver City. Deming. And Las Cruces. Choosing yet another color, Wallace speared Happy. Amarillo. Abernathy. Lubbock. Lamesa. Pecos. And Del Rio. He stepped back and looked at the map.

Truth or Consequences, Pueblo, Green River, and Hurricane were the only southwest cities stuck with white tacks. Everything else was a rainbow of destruction. From the plum borders of California as high up as Salt Lake City, stretching across to Boise City in the panhandle, trailing down to Mexico, decades of multi-colored lines lead *there* and away.

Wickenburg. Quartzsite. Tucson. And Wilcox. Stafford. Flagstaff. Reno. And St. George. Elko. Clifton. Montrose. And the newest peg in Mohave Valley dotted the map. The motel room's furniture was displaced. Rearranged. The map was taped to the motel wall. Files littered the bed, open and not sleeping. A police scanner squawked intermittently burying Wallace's coarse breathing with possible leads. Though mostly it crackled noise.

His arms were crossed. Then he pulled them to his sides. His hands rested on his hips. He pulled in close, studied the print on the map like it meant something. Deciphering codes. Wallace stepped back and took the map in as a whole. He crossed his arms again. Rested his hands on his hips. Grunted. Each pin was a step…that led…*there*? It was somewhere. *There* was in the chaos. The only trouble was Wallace didn't know where *there* was just yet. It was somewhere. *But where?*

Keys clanging in the lock and clothes rustling beyond the door alerted him that Mauldune had returned with food. He could smell it the second she stepped into the room. He was starving and it felt like she'd been gone the entire afternoon.

Kate cleared a spot on the table and set the bags of fast food down. Checking out the map on the wall with heavy eyes, she tossed the car keys between the upright portals of grub. Wallace dug in, stopping only to listen to the scanner when it talked. He gobbled a few bites before he excitedly told her about the map.

"Blue ones indicate where we've been. White are possible hits, though, I'm not sure of the dates, still waiting on information. Green are from the 1950's. Yellow the 60's. Red the 70's. The clear ones are the 80's. Purple, the 90's. The metal ones are current." He took a bite of his sandwich.

"All these confirmed?" Mauldune scrutinized his display.

He swallowed hard. "Not really."

She stepped over to the bed, glancing at the opened files. There were more here than what he had shown her earlier. She picked one up. "Some of these are just arson cases…" The bewildered expression on her face said it all.

"You've got to step out of the box on this one. They've been at–"

Mauldune cut him off, stepping toward the Piñata-gorged map. "You've got Colorado, Nevada, and Texas up here for Christ's sake. None of this was in your earlier reports. What makes you think any of these are even connected?" Kate exhaled. "That would make our would-be assailants at least sixty or seventy years old by now." She glared at him. "C'mon, John?"

Indignantly, she closed the file in her hands, tossed it back onto the bed, crossed to the cluttered table, and hid in the bags of fast food, finding nothing that she really wanted to eat.

"If you follow each decade there is a consistent pattern. A path." Wallace picked a color and followed it with his finger, jabbing an oily digit in a blank spot in the northeastern tip of New Mexico. "It's always the same. Each incident report outlines almost the exact circumstances of every occurrence. Coincidence?"

He removed his finger from the map, leaving a greasy mark over Clayton, NM, and took another bite of his unhappy meal.

"But over fifty years?" The sag in her voice said it all.

"That's why I only gave you the files as far back as the eighties."

The straw sticking out of the plastic drink cup squeaked and he slurped loudly, sucking down a hefty portion of the large soda. Kate set down her unopened sandwich and walked over to the map again. Wallace's little oily mark over Clayton shimmered in the room's bad light. She sighed heavily.

"I…" she wrestled with it. All afternoon she'd been wrestling with it. *Now was as good a time as any.* "I can see where you're going with it.

It's an interesting theory. And if it's even remotely close to the truth, then it's more obvious than ever. We should head back."

In the numb silence that followed Wallace stared at the back of her head. He was sure of what she'd said, but it still took him a little off guard that she'd gone and said it. He'd gotten used to her. *Mistake.*

"We need to regroup," she continued, turning to him. "If this thing even remotely resembles what you've put up here on this map than we need the help of other agencies. Perhaps get the U.S. Marshall's Office involved or the Feds. We need to widen our search parameters. You and I just don't have the resources to sustain such an in-depth manhunt."

Wallace set down his nearly empty drink cup in a small pool of condensation. "No one asked you to come along. You can go back any time you like."

Kate rubbed her eyes, pitched her body. This was exactly the kind of thing she was hoping to avoid. "Being obsessed about this is not going to bring Stephen back, John. Okay?"

"Hmmrrm." *And there it was.* "Sounds more like the Chief talking. Not you."

"Dammit John! I am trying to help you here."

"Help?" His nostrils flared and teeth grated on edge. "Is that what you call it? Judging me with somebody else's words? Yeah... Stephen's dead. He was seventeen with a scholarship to Arizona State and these Sonna-bitches tore his throat out and burned him alive. Like he was *nothing.* I will never forget that." Hate bristled in his eyes. "That was over ten years ago. He's gone...and so are all the others that came before him and after him." He tossed an instructional arm toward his most recent motel room decoration. "This here's a ritual. There is something along this route that keeps them to it. Something that they are compelled to do that ties them to this place." He turned and walked over to the map in two large, brisk steps. "You see it, don't you?"

"That's not the point."

"But it is. They're out there, right now. They've started the pattern all over again and it's just the same as last time with only one difference." He drew closer to the Lieutenant. "Me." His eyes were fire and coal. "Over fifty years of brutal murder, unchecked, under the radar. But this time...*This time*, I'm not stopping at any border. There is no jurisdictional red tape for people like them. They kill at random. Whenever and whomever they please. Destroying lives. And I'm not going to let them get away with it any longer."

Kate folded her arms and glared at her partner. "Sounds more like vigilante justice instead of police work, John."

"It does, huh?"

"You even listening to yourself? 'I'm not going to let them get away with it'." Her mouth hung open, trying to reach him, as she imitated him. "Revenge is not the answer."

"Hhrrmmm." He shook his head and glared at her. "If that's what you think I'm about then why'd you tag along in the first place?"

"To tell you the truth, John, I..." His eyes felt like spears through her soul. "I don't know what to think. You're a good cop. A good man." She paced and stammered, unsure of how to answer him. "I don't know why I came, actually. I guess...I guess... Look it doesn't matter why I did what I did. We're here now and all I'm saying is I'm not so sure that what we're doing is the best way to bring 'em in." She paused and crumbled into her body, feeling her forehead like it was hot. "Either does the Chief." She looked at him with sad eyes. "He thinks you've lost it."

"What do you think?"

The question felt like his hands were squeezing her spine. "I don't know," she exhaled loudly. "It's all beginning to feel a lot like the tail end of a spiral."

"Huh."

His lone grunt was accusing. It stuck her to the wall, next to the map. Pinned her like just another murder, a crime scene of her own good intentions. They stood alone in the room, two bodies of water, drowning on their ideals, egos, and predilections of duty. He glared at her. Kate crossed her arms over her chest, feeling a bit on display.

"They're out there tonight. And, they're close." Wallace took a step toward her and she wanted him to stop, to just stop. "Closer than we've ever been before...and you wanna just pack up, go home, tail between our legs so they can do it again?"

His hard features hovered in the air before her, immeasurable beats of her quickened heart, and then he turned and left the motel room. The compressed hinges on the door wheezed softly as it slowly closed, letting in a cool breeze from the Burque night. Kate imagined that if Wallace could have slammed the door he would have. She heard it in her mind.

She sighed long and painful, standing in his room as the police scanner squawked and screeched annoyingly. Her eyes followed the rainbow colors on the map, all leading to the greasy spot. They swept across the mountain of unpacked files littering his bed, years of solid police work – *even if it was just speculation,* and they fell, like tired mules, onto the bags of cold fast food. The air was rank from the congealing fat and her stomach was dropping like a lead balloon.

Wallace said they were out there. He was confident in a way that she knew she could never be. Confident in a way that she knew she never was. It was one of the things that she admired about him since the first day they partnered up. His conviction was all around her, glorified on the wall, on the bed, and he'd left her to choke on it.

Why did I come along? Kate shook her head from side to side, a tight cage of her own musings. *Why the hell am I here?*

The night screamed bloody murder, raucously loud, all around them. Flashing lights. Stars a minefield on display as the departing plane roared into the sky. Lin and Sarah lay on their backs in a patch of dry grass just outside of the Albuquerque Sunport. An opened bottle of wine rested between them and the air wafted down smelling of high-octane diesel. They laughed, feeling the massive engines in their bellies.

"It still always amazes me," Lin lassoed her words to the tail end of the plane, "throwing oneself through the air in a tin can." Her eyes were big, challenging the moon. "Incredible."

"Really, you've never flown?" Sarah rested on her arm, staring up at the night sky.

"Not even once."

"But I thought you said you've been overseas a few times?"

Sarah turned to her companion. They'd been out here for awhile, talking. Drinking wine. Lin told her about some of the places that she'd seen. Europe. Asia. South America. Sarah's gone nowhere. She had lived in New Mexico her whole life and just assumed that Lin flew. Everybody flew. Even terrorists.

"I took a boat."

Sarah smiled, trying to picture it. "That's hard to imagine."

"What?" Lin chuckled. "Me never flying?"

"No," Sarah blurted out and tapped the woman against the leg. "All that water. I've seen pictures of the ocean. Seen it in movies; on TV, but I've never really seen it, you know. Never looked out and all there was, was just water."

Sarah pictured herself on a boat, rolling along gigantic waves, sea spray kissing her face. It had the impossibility of dreams. Lin turned to the indelible girl and watched her as she stared up at the heavens.

"It's beautiful." Lin meant the girl instead of her sea voyages, but she couldn't tell her that. She couldn't tell her how being next to her made her feel. And Lin felt. By the gods, she felt! Thrushing with life – *it had been ages*. "I could take you to see the ocean if you want."

In this moment Lin wanted nothing more than to climb into the Cadillac and drive to the Pacific. Retrace roadways to give the girl her dream. Race across days and nights of highway just to show her the sea, let her hear its wet music. Sarah turned to her and smirked.

"That'd be great." But the vampire saw it in her eyes, heard it in the lilt of her voice, before she turned back to the sky. Staring upwards, they were the same stars as over Hobbs, over Lovington, over Albuquerque. Everything was the same. Everything was always the same. Time dripped languid in the desert, slow and unrolling. Sarah's been feeling it her whole life, boxed in the Four Corners, going nowhere. "Though, with school and working the club I don't think I'll get the chance anytime soon." The night was quiet without a plane. "Thanks."

The dancer's hand lingered on Lin's thigh for an immeasurable instant. Warm and wanting, just there. Lin wished that she would never move it, feeling emptiness once she did. The symbiont sat up and rested her head on her knees and gazed at the dancer.

"The whole world is waiting for you. It may not seem that way. But it is." Lin grabbed her locket and instantly thought about opening it. Showing Sarah the picture inside and asking her if she ever dreamed her before this night, if she remembered Lin killing her, oh so long ago. But time and experience tempered the vampire's consistent yearnings. It was a slow drip, never ceasing, perpetually remolding and reshaping itself; life crawled by in slow increments of time dulling the desire to even breathe. Fate's tendril fingers, wiggling up the backside, never left. They grew dormant, yes, but never disappeared. "Things can be whatever you want them to be."

Sarah chuckled, trying not to be insulting. "I wish it was that easy, but it's not. It never is."

Lin's fingers grated over the worn silver, thinking how the girl was too young to be so hard. Her Jadaraa Soo curled around her bones and begged its host for a little bleeding, for a little taste – *Just a gallon or two.*

"You'd be surprised."

Sarah sat up and folded her arms around her knees and stared out across the mesa. Lin watched her for the longest time. She couldn't remember ever being around somebody for so long whom she just met, vampire or human, where she just enjoyed the presence of their company, not feeling pressured to fill the silence with inane blather. She and Z had reached a point of quiet acceptance, though it took time. They lived together. They shared space. It was expected. This was altogether different and the only person that flashed through her mind, with whom she had ever felt an inkling of this quiet comfort, was Dominique.

"Have you ever wanted something so badly," said the bright-eyed girl. "But you didn't really know what it was that you actually wanted? You just wanted something..." Sarah rattled her head from side to side trying to find the right phrase and turned to the woman beside her. "Different?"

Lin smirked, knowing exactly what she meant. "Yeah."

"What was it?"

Your green eyes, such bright strokes of light seeping through the gorgeous confection of your lips. Lin's quiet bones stirred and she felt her heart skip a beat. The veiny beast squeezed her old cuddle-muscle. A few pulses, starting – *It loves her too* – and then it grew rapid.

Sarah pulled from the wine bottle, a rich Pinot Noir. The wine's scent mingled in Lin's nostrils with the flavor of Sarah's saliva. It made the dancer's wet lips glisten from the trash of airport lights. And Lin ached to kiss her. It'd been so long since she felt desire for another person.

"Well," said Sarah, turning to her, "you gonna tell me what it was?"

Lin smirked. "At first, I thought it was this girl." Lin struggled naming her, conjuring her shape with the word, "Dominique. She showed me things. Opened the world to me in a way that was both frightening and exhilarating at the same time. And the more she revealed to me the more I thought I loved her. For the longest time I thought that was what I truly wanted. To be with her in her world; make her proud of me, but…"

Sarah thought of her mother and Lin shook the Vam Pŷr from her hair. "It wasn't." Lin locked eyes with the dancer. "Chasing her only left me alone and wound up taking me farther away from what I was truly looking for in the first place."

"What was *that*?" Sarah accentuated the question by raising her eyebrows and devilishly smiled.

Embarrassed, Lin grinned, rubbing her locket between forefinger and thumb. "A perfect connection?" She shrugged, letting her jeweled albatross go. "If that even exists."

"It's like its always there, but just out of reach. You're searching for it. But it eludes you." Sarah turned and caught the mysterious woman looking at her intently. She blushed, embarrassed by her summation, and an odd feeling came rushing through her. "I know. I sound like a complete dork." Sarah grimaced and tried to hide her face. Picking up the wine bottle, she took a swig.

"No. Not at all."

Lin's words held gravity and Sarah passed her the bottle. The vampire accepted it and supped its weak red mixture.

"When you talk, there's this deep sadness or something," reported Sarah. "Did she hurt you?"

Lin wiped the wine off her lips. "No. I hurt her."

"Oh," Sarah raised her brows and gently pulled the bottle back to her corner.

She gulped a healthy bit and passed it back to Lin. Their fingers brushed, electric, and the live girl's eyes darted up to the raven haired beauty. A shudder ripped through the symbiont and she let her gaze drop. Burying her face in the bottle of wine, the alcohol passed between her gums and her fangs receded, just a bit, falling like rot to her gut from the bitter taste.

Sarah watched Lin breathe out slowly. "It's like you revel in the simplest of pleasures."

The thought was automatic. Instant, watching how the bottle touched Lin's pale lips. Sarah wasn't even surprised that she said it. The urge wasn't sudden. It had been creeping. Though, it was strange. *Definitely, strange.*

"You have no idea," diffused Lin with humor and set the bottle down between them. Its round base crushed the dry, brittle grass.

"Then show me."

Lin's neck snapped sideways upon hearing the dare as Sarah raised a single brow accentuating her comment. Then the girl leaned in and kissed her. The dancer's warm mouth on Lin's was startling at first. Unexpected. *Wanted.* Definitely wanted. It took a few beats of her lazy heart to pump before Lin fell into the kiss. All a flutter, she felt Sarah's hand on her face. Her mouth, groping and moist; the vampire survived on the live girl's oxygen alone. From her lips Lin could feel Sarah's heartbeat. Pounding. Her Jadaraa Soo grew through her fangs wanting to pierce the woman's active tongue. Lin had to focus to pull it back. It was like holding the reigns on a team of wild horses. Straining. *Is this what it was like for you, Dominique? All those years ago – I, a live girl, and you a blood slave, craving?*

Both creatures of desire panted, hungrily, pulling one another closer. Chests heaved up and down exhilarated in their union. Lin and Sarah never even heard the plane arriving, crashing through their ears, an elephant in a china shop in a silent movie. Sarah lifted her leg to craddle Lin, knocking over the Pinot Noir. Red liquid spilled out of the bottle from the little round portal. It seeped into the parched hungry earth, and slowly, they eased away from each other with eyes closed. Lin was spinning around Sarah's orbit, slightly trembling.

"You're dangerous," she whispered.

Sarah wiped spittle off her lower lip and smirked, "I know."

Their eyes met over the lapping wine, quenching the hard ground, and they laughed. Whole and hearty, they laughed together, as overhead another plane descended for a landing.

The metal railing cut into his elbows. Smoking. Overlooking a flat landscape of lights, planes descended in the distant horizon, Wallace's mind was frozen jelly. Stuck, Kate's words battered back and forth like a badminton birdie. He remembered the look of his sister at Stephen's funeral, grim. Proper, all in black, thinking how he'd never really been in the boy's life all that much. Never really been in Helen's life all that much either. The whole sky was a finger pressing down on her and Nathan.

He didn't make any promises then, over that gaping wound in the earth just staring up at everybody, hungry for whatever was left of the child. Last he'd remembered Stephen was seven and they were fishing. *Damn, life happens too fast.* Flicking the cigarette butt into the concrete air, Wallace knew he wasn't doing this out of some misplaced sense of vengeance. He wasn't doing it out of loss. He simply didn't want the bastards to keep doing it, and getting away with it.

How's that so hard to believe? It was what he was paid to do. He became a cop to lock up bad guys. He did his job, worked the angles, played it straight, and all it had ever gotten him was grief. He had no illusions – *a gold-plated watch and a shitty pension when he retired, dying slowly in a rusty cop bar.* There was something different about this case, though. He had always felt it. Unable to stretch it out, he just kept moving, just kept following the breadcrumbs, and asked *simple* questions. *So, it had legs fifty years deep. Who fucking cares?!* It took him nearly eight years to compile all of the intel that he possessed. Didn't believe half of it himself when he first started connecting the dots, leaving who knows how many more pieces to the overall puzzle still missing. Spreading his arms wide across the thick painted banister, rough and choppy, the world's a sick place. *A cop ain't nothing more than a slack-jawed agent of karma.*

His eyes swept the level field of lights. Sandia Mountain was an ink spot. *That's where they do all of that government shit.* Bombs. Secret tech. Nano-bullshit. Wallace didn't like Albuquerque. It was a glorified truck stop smack-dab in the middle of a Petri dish. *Would be glad to see the last of it.* He sighed and returned to his room.

Mauldune was gone and the map stared him in the face, tauntingly. The room was a trash compactor, smelled like greasy shoes. He closed the files and cleared them off the bed. Like it or not, morning came early, and he intended to roll with it. *How the fuck she ever worked her flat-chested ass to outrank me in that little hick town I'll never know. She doesn't understand how to work a line. How to follow it no matter how crooked it looks. Kate is smart, all right. Book smart. She has to get her head out of the game if she wants to play, live by her gut. That's how a cop makes the collar. Follow the gut. Follow the rancid, sick feeling, falling off the universe to some inevitable splat, gut.* Wallace wandered over to the map, staring at the greasy spot. Each colored pin was a highway that led right to it.

"Hhrrmm," he grunted, cocked his head, and slowly began removing the tacks.

Sarah lay in bed, jittery, replaying the evening. She couldn't believe she had kissed the girl. *And more than once!* So few lovers in her short life, she could count them on one hand, and she never would have guessed this. All so sudden, Lin was there. Sarah turned to the darkened windows of her apartment, shades undrawn, dawn threatening to come crashing through like soldiers any minute now. She needed to get some sleep.

Closing her eyes, she saw Lin's face. Something about that girl, the taste of her was still on her lips. Sarah wished that Lin hadn't brought her home. She was content on the mesa, wanted to share the sunrise. She wanted her here, now, in her bed. *Oh my god! Did I just think that!* Sarah bit her lower lip, a soft smile curling the edges of her mouth as she drifted off to sleep.

Her last thoughts were of the ocean, vast and forever wide, and Lin taking her there. Flying over the sea they didn't need a boat. They were ephemeral angels. Sea spray reached out for them, delicate and refreshing; they were gilded birds. Below, dolphins followed them, rolling with the waves. Wet dunes soaring, heaved like panting breasts, and they made love in mid air. Slowly, always touching. Whale song filled the air around them. Clouds departed, their nakedness was set against an iridescent sky. Sarah dreamed blue.

A jackrabbit scurried under sagebrush. It watched the lone woman in the shot of headlights making a hole in the desert floor. She smelled wrong, a pile of dead things. The rabbit nibbled the dry brush, ears twitching – *a coyote lingered over the dunes.* The sky was immaculate, clouds rolled behind the earth.

Lin tossed the shovel to the ground and stepped out of the hole. It was deep enough. All nightlong she kept thinking that Sarah was gonna ask what that smell was coming from the back seat. She knew she needed to get rid of Jake and Darryl. Popping the trunk, their rank deaths hit her in the face.

"C'mon," she said, pulling Jake's naked body up by the arms. "Last dance."

She hefted him to the hole and in a cloud of dust dropped him in. A blunt thump reverberated throughout his still, unbeating chest. She gave Darryl the same ceremony. They looked lonely in the ground, two bodies of water, supped and drained for an evening's entertainment. Lin wondered where Z had run off too. She didn't miss her, was just curious. Knowing that devil, she'd pop up when she felt like it.

Each weight of each shovelful, filling the pit, buried Z just as much as it covered the decomposing corpses. Lin had half a mind to take all of Z's crap in the trunk, all of that junk in the backseat, and bury it here with the last hurrah. If it wasn't for the need of keeping an extremely low profile at a future crime scene Lin knew she would have left it all behind —*especially that crap in the back seat.*

Lin chided herself for not getting out of the relationship before all of the bad feelings had crept in. *How many decades now am I going to have to put up with uncomfortable silences?* Avoiding the dead, on this small rock, was a chore. *God! What am I going to do with the condo in LA?*

There were too many thoughts to worry about now – knee deep in a dumpsite. *Fuck it. Z can have the building. I need to move anyway. Time to get out of America. Been here too long.* In her musings Lin imagined taking Sarah to Europe, back to her old stomping grounds. Just travel the world. Keep moving. Thinking of the girl made her smile. She was something all right. *And that kiss?* She had surprised Lin, and that, in and of itself, was pretty hard.

Lin tossed the shovel back into the trunk of the Caddy and closed the lid. She walked to the driver's side door and looked to the clean sky. Any minute now and the horizon would pop. She had time to find a motel, though. Before she climbed into the trusty old Cadillac she removed her necklace, opened it, and stared at the picture inside, one more time. A cool breeze blew across the desert, flitting under the vampire's armpits, and she could smell three coyotes waiting for her to leave. She'd left them breakfast.

Climbing in, she hung the silver locket on the rearview mirror. She turned the key. The smiley face that hung on the metal collection jangled happily as the Caddy roared to life in the dwindling night. Sarah might have surprised her earlier, but Lin held all the aces. The locket swiveled back and forth as she bounced along the canyon road and Lin knew she had to tell her. She just had to. She couldn't put it off another night. Best to get all those nasty revelations out of the way and get down to the aftermath. That's where all the work or fun began – *it just depends on how you trip it.* Sarah was gonna show herself. In that, Lin was sure. Tell a gal you're a vampire and killed her in a past life, show her the object, just to be proof-positive – *it's all normal stuff, really. Should go over like a lead balloon. Easy.*

Lin sighed, feeling dread ride her shoulders as fate pushed its tendril fingers up her tail. All she could hope for was that Sarah wouldn't freak out too much. That by revealing herself to the girl all those wonderful possibilities they felt together tonight wouldn't be trampled. Life dangled the dancer in front of her like the pendulum motion of her locket. *Back and forth, there and away.* It could be crushed by the dancer's marching feet out the door when Lin lifted her mask and exposed the young woman to her veins. She shrugged. *Maybe now was just the right time to keep driving. Leave New Mexico and let the girl live her life.*

"Arhhhr!" Lin gritted her misshapen teeth. *Decisions, decisions, decisions?*

Circumstance
Of
Time

Bible thumping on the door, annoyingly loud and wouldn't go away; Sarah dragged herself, entangled in a bed sheet, to make the racket stop. Eyes burning. Mouth spiky and fat, all her muscles were in mutiny at movement. Sunlight smacked her across the face. Fading into Sarah's not so distant vision as she opened the door was Jimmy beaming like a Lotto winner.

Sarah grumbled and he apologized as his cousin Angie popped out from behind him like he'd suddenly grown another person. Angie was loud like a parade, yelling surprise or some other expletive, and Sarah was ecstatic to see her again, though it came out like stale soda. It had been at least four years. They hugged and barged into the apartment. Jimmy told her that she made him bring her, knowing full well how cranky Sarah could be on so little sleep.

Scuffling to her closet, trailing the bed sheet behind her like a royal dress, a single butt cheek poked out of the folds to Jimmy's happy surprise. Sarah got dressed, pulling the clothes across alien limbs, slowly waking up; the fabrics were abrasive. The livingroom area of her apartment was small. About big enough for a throw rug, a futon, and a single picture to hang on the wall. Except, Sarah didn't have a picture hanging on the wall. She had two stolen milk crates against the blank, plaster surface, covered in a scarf that she'd picked up at a thrift store. She used it like an end table/bookshelf/dust collector.

"So what brings you up to Burque?" Sarah asked as she curled up on the futon with a pillow, lying down.

The chestnut-haired girl beamed, a bit pudgier than Sarah remembered. "I'm getting married."

"No shit?"

Angie's smile smashed her face. Nodding her head up and down, she was excited. "And I want you to be my bridesmaid."

Syllables tumbled through Sarah's mouth like the three eyes of a slot machine, spinning to an inevitable acceptance. Her enthusiasm was only tempered by her worn out body. Her friend's exhilaration made her forget, if even for a little while, about her crushing schedule of school and work. Mundane, all so mundane, Angie's news was extraordinary. Dancing on the heels of her evening with Lin, rekindled and awakened, Sarah's own fire began shining forth like a golden light. Or was it the morning sun streaming through her windows cascading across her almond hair?

Jimmy couldn't tell. He watched her and his cousin as they went girlie, pushing him ringside. But it was good for the three of them to be together again. It felt right. He smiled.

"Are you pregnant?" Sarah asked when they broke from their hug.

Angie gasped and hung her mouth open to dry, "No!"

Sarah shrugged. "Had to ask."

Jimmy stifled a laugh.

"So, tell me about the lucky SOB. Who is he?"

Angie commenced to tell Sarah all about him. She referenced a few emails and pictures that she'd sent a while back, but the dancer didn't remember them and curled into the cushions of the couch, listening.

Being the only boy in the room, Jimmy felt a little like an outsider. Everything was slightly out of touch, like he was wearing cellophane gloves, peeping through a glory hole to the other side. The girls conversed and made plans together about the upcoming wedding. Angie wrote things down in her little date book as ideas took shape in the room between them. Excited, life coursed through Sarah's veins and she wasn't concerned about the practicalities. She swore that she would make time for the ceremony. Angie made Jimmy swear that he'd keep her to it – *like I held her leash.* It made him a part of the thing and kept him close to Sarah, which he liked. Him, spiraling around her orbit, a geeky satellite.

Eventually, they went out for breakfast. Coming to the stunning conclusion that Sarah didn't possess any cutlery, plates, or a stocked fridge, it was the only logical choice. Over the meal, in a crowded diner, conversations drifted away from the impending nuptials and Jimmy was inserted into the normal gum flap of la-la-land. The three of them, together again, it always felt like old times. Comfortable. Good shoes. Half the day gone and still vanishing, they picked up a bottle of wine on their way back to her place. Walking along the sidewalk, shadows of trees waved at them, but they were talking too deliriously to even notice.

Hours breezed by and through it all, in the unpacked compartment of her mind, Sarah still thought about the girl – *her bleached complexion and how she spoke sounded like forever.* When Angie asked about whom Sarah was seeing nowadays she lied, saying no one. But in the folds of her chest, in those silent parts of her soul, she felt Lin's touch. When Angie joked about Jimmy having a crush on Sarah, since his tenth grade year, egging him about it right in front of her, his face all a blush, Sarah recalled Lin's kiss. As the afternoon wore on like a coat of paint it made her wonder if she would see the girl at the club tonight. They didn't make any plans when Lin dropped her off. Sarah simply didn't know if she'd ever see her again, like the woman was nothing more than vapor – *A drive-by love affair!*

Angie laughed and needled Sarah about coming to the club that night. She wanted to watch her dance. But the green-eyed gal ground through a hail of sad excuses, trying to dissuade them from ever visiting that place. Even if it weren't for the dark-haired woman with the strange, doughy eyes Sarah didn't want Angie or Jimmy to see her there. Something about that just felt wrong. They were in her world, her *real world*. The club was a lie, the bullshit – *the daily grind*. Sarah didn't want them anywhere near it. Like if they did it'd be a quantum explosion, opposite universes colliding – *everything would turn to dust.*

Night fell with all the wine gone. The clock was a bastard. Angie helped Sarah get dressed, and they made a mess of her closet, of her bed, of the whole apartment. They didn't care. Jimmy thumbed through her CD stack and played DJ. Against Sarah's whining protests they drove her to the club. It was all she could do to keep them from coming in. Finally there, with two worlds on the verge, she told them both, straight up. "I don't want you to see me like this."

Angie got it. Jimmy got it, but he didn't like it. And Lin's Cadillac pulled into the parking lot. Three worlds on a spinning axis now, Sarah felt like she was the center of a collision that was about to happen. Seconds away. She followed the baby blue boat with her eyes as it rolled into a faded line spot. Her ears drummed from Angie's voice. Saying long good-byes, her friends hung on. Not letting her go and too polite to just walk away, Sarah desperately wanted them to leave. She wasn't ready for her wildness to be so exposed. Tiptoeing in the same sex pool was one thing. Throwing the door wide open and wearing a rainbow colored top hat was another.

Lin was heading her way – *a cute smile, hair bobbing with each step.* "I was hoping I'd catch you before you got inside," she said as she stepped around the rear of Jimmy's car.

Hanging out of the door, Angie wrinkled her nose like the newcomer smelled bad. Goosebumps rose on her arms as the short-haired stranger saddled next to Sarah. Instantly, Angie disliked her. Not sure why, her glare was scrutinizing lasers.

Lin saw the people in the car looking at her. She nodded and said, "Hello."

Jimmy nodded back, suddenly intimidated and not sure why.

"Look, I've got to get inside," said Sarah. "My shift is starting and they don't like it when I'm late."

The dancer shifted on her feet, from side to side. Lin watched. She was a ball of nerves, holding herself with one arm clutching the other. Lin felt like she'd just intruded.

"Gimmie a call tomorrow and we'll hook up," added Angie as she hugged her one last time and climbed back into Jimmy's little Caprice.

"I'll do that."

Eyeing Lin, Angie's apprehension crinkled her brow. She took Sarah's hand, "Call me."

"I will."

"You better."

Jimmy started to drive off slowly. The vampire watched as Sarah and Angie's hands separated, their fingers clutching until the last second. Her own digits wandered to her favorite piece of jewelry, but it wasn't around her neck. She'd left it in the Caddy, hanging on the rearview mirror to give to Sarah when she told her everything. Now, watching her standing meekly in the parking lot of the club with her friends passing her the evil eye, Lin felt like a shipwreck waiting to happen. Nerves suddenly up after centuries, old and rusty, told her to walk away. *Let it be and drive. Find tomorrow night some place else.*

Yet in the red glow of taillights, Sarah's eyes were two pitchers of starry night and Lin could no more walk away than she could sky dive into the sun. She couldn't let it be. She was *so* close, spiraling in the girl's atmosphere. Lin was snared, wrapped up in the live girl's gorgeous green eyes; she was melting. Lin imagined that all around her the universe was screaming, "Yeah!"

Both Jimmy and Angie watched the two women standing there in the lot as they drove away, disappearing into cosmic dots. Sarah's good friends silently railed against unknown feelings that clashed about their insides wearing goulashes. All wooly and glass, tumbling, Angie couldn't look away, like if she did, Sarah would vanish forever. She wanted to tell her cousin to stop driving, to back up and ferry Sarah into the car for a getaway. But the young gal chalked it up to the wine, the good time they had been having, and her own fears of stepping up to the alter. Change, as she knew, was a hard thing to swallow sometimes. It was a mixture of blank possibility slipping into new shoes as the momentum of time walked away with you in tow.

"Came to watch me work, huh?"

Lin shook her head. "No."

The dancer turned on a fidgeting heel. "Well, you wanna come in anyway? I've got to start my shift."

She started walking toward the club's entrance.

Let her walk away. Let her walk away. "Listen, I just came by tonight to tell you something."

"What is it?" Sarah stopped, hands folded.

Lin crossed the short expanse to her. "It'd be better if I showed you."

Sarah's whole body sighed, sagging. "I gotta work."

"I know," said Lin gravely, stepping into her gravitational pull. "And I'm not trying to mess up anything you have here, but I've already cleared it with the fat man." She paused for effect. "The night's ours if you want it."

Sarah tilted her head back, groaned, and noisily sucked in a breath, considering the enigma of Lin. She wanted to run off with the girl. She didn't want to be dancing to a bunch of sweaty vampires groping her thighs as they wedged dollar bills into her panties. She wanted to burn the place to the ground and tap dance on the ashes. But that wasn't going to get her what she ultimately wanted.

"Don't get me wrong," started the dancer, lowering her head in a breathy exhale. "I want to. I *really* do." She stepped closer to Lin. "But…" her finger began tracing Lin's collarbone. "If I keep running away with you I'm never going to be able to afford school, and if I don't go to school I'm just gonna end up like my momma, livin' in a dive trailer park. And as much as I like you…" her eyes flicked upward at Lin's small specks poking out from the jagged wisps of coal black hair. "And I do. I don't wanna live in a trailer park."

"It's ok, I understand." Lin lied.

"Really?"

Lin shook her head, yes, but she mouthed the opposite, "No."

It made Sarah laugh. Exasperated, she scoffed and kicked a pebble across the lot. It dinged the rear fender of somebody's Pontiac. *God!* She irked, wanting nothing more than to run away. *Run far, far away.* "You're trouble," the winsome girl lovingly uttered.

"Nothing but bad."

Sarah's eyes searched the woman who tugged at her soul in a way that she'd never felt before and kissed her. Keeping it brief, she pulled away, bringing a hand to her mouth.

"Ow! Something sharp in there."

Lin smirked, enjoying the taste of the girl. "Just the dark side of bliss, baby."

Sarah sighed again and stepped back. The air between them was a hard valley.

"What if I said I'd—"

But Sarah pressed a finger against Lin's lips and held it there. The look on her face said that it wouldn't matter if Lin spoke or not. The girl was a conflux of unease and her mind was trying to hammer it out. *Should have walked away. Should have...*Silently, mouth held fixed, Lin decided that she'd give her all the money she needed to do her school thing. It was wrong for her to even think to use it as a bargaining chip so she could spill her soul to her out in the desert. Instantly, the ancient woman was thankful for the girl's decent heart and for shutting her up. She would have made a fool of herself had she'd been allowed to speak. It made Lin love her even more. It made her pine for her own humanity, lost all those centuries ago in a blinding desire to love forever. *Foolish!*

Sarah released her hold on Lin's chiseled mouth and the vampire thought it best to just keep it closed. *Safer that way...*for them both. The look on Sarah's face told Lin all she really needed to know. It wasn't happening tonight and it may never happen again.

"C'mon," Sarah said after a heartbeat or two looking grim. "Let's go."

A reflex to the words made Lin's smile flatten her face and beam like a lighthouse. She hadn't expected it, so she picked the girl up, kissed her hard, and set her down on planet earth, spinning. Shocked and unsteady, Sarah looked around to see if there was anyone about who might have seen them. She laughed and grabbed Lin's hand, pulling the vampire to her out-of-date-but-very-cool car.

Kate woke early. She kept the curtains on the motel window open with a clear view of the car insight as she washed up and got dressed. She wanted to make sure that Wallace didn't leave without her. The thought crossed her mind last night to take the keys. They were right there on the crowded table, between the fast food bags. It would have been easy and ensured that he wasn't going anywhere that she didn't want him to.

Kate knew women who were manipulative like that. She marveled at their abilities to get men to dance like trained monkeys. It just wasn't her cup of tea and it never worked for her even when she tried. Men, she learned, were just immune to the Mauldune method.

Snagging two cups of coffee, she waited in the car. During her brief interim in the motel lobby she noticed John had started loading things into the trunk, packing all his files neatly away. The map and a box of multi-colored tacks rested next to an extra pair of clothes that he'd purchased once they hit the road. All so organized, Mauldune found a place to stuff the small travel bag that she'd bought. As she rounded the rear of the cruiser she noticed the police scanner sitting in the back seat. He'd left the car doors unlocked and the door to his motel room was ajar. Kate watched the dark abyss of his room like it was a stakeout.

Inhaling the bitter roast, she tore open packs of sugar and dumped them in. She liked a little coffee with her sweetener. A plastic stirrer held between two taught fingers clanged inaudibly against the Styrofoam cup. With the concoction ready to abuse her system she lifted it to her face and allowed its small warmth to kiss her cheeks. The morning was bright, cold, and annoyingly slow. The coffee smelled bad. Sipping it, it tasted bad – *shit in my mouth*. The door just hung there, an open sore in the building's façade. *Was he ever coming out?*

Half a cup down, rotting the lining of her stomach, finally, the man emerged. He looked grim, like a chewed up piece of leather. But then again, he always looked like that. John was exactly the kind of cop she always dreamed about becoming when she was at the academy. Hard as nails. Monosyllabic. Ruled by instinct alone and honest to a fault. He crossed the lot and tossed a bag in the trunk.

"Thought you left," he grumbled as he climbed in and fastened the seat belt.

"No. I'm still here," she paused, listening to the car warm up. "For now."

"Hhrrmm," he groaned, teeth on edge.

Hitting the road, he headed for the highway.

"Thought we were gonna canvas the city some more?"

"Albuquerque's bunk," the detective announced as he finished the coffee that Mauldune had picked up for him. "Heading north instead."

Kate peered at him, wondering what was turning in that caveman brain of his. "Any place in particular?"

He turned to her to make a show of it. "Yup."

"Care to enlighten me?"

He just tossed her an eye and cocked his brow. Kate sighed. *It's too early for his pandering bullshit.* "Can we at least stop for breakfast? Sort of missed out on dinner last night."

"In Santa Fe. Gotta get gas. Might as well."

Mauldune sipped the rest of her bad coffee, "Gee John, mighty kind of you." Annoyed, she shook her head. *Bastard!*

"Hhrrmm."

A country breakfast. Flapjacks. Eggs. Grilled meat. The table between them was a tomb. Nothing passed their lips besides food. Whatever it was, wherever he was taking her, he wasn't budging. *Must be a decent lead. He always keeps it close until he knows for sure. Yet another fine charm of his dazzling personality.*

Three hours later and a road to nowhere, miles of desert and short blooms of green life, sparse and prickly, dotted the landscape. Even with the radio statically singing, Kate felt like clicking her heels together three times, spinning in a circle and calling for Auntie Em so that the magical Witch Glenda would take her home. Her legs felt cramped all the way up to her hips. Sockets and joints rebelling, breathing recycled air conditioning, she needed to walk.

Entering Union County, gaining altitude, volcanic rock and sandstone bluffs poked out of the grasslands. Miles off, two flat topped mountains watched them for the longest time, not shrinking, not increasing in size, always visible on the horizon like they were painted there. Named after an Indian chief, the Rabbit Ear Mountains were a perfect spot for scouts to watch the slow approach of westbound wagon trains. With three to four days notice the natives had plenty of time to plan ambushes as caravans crossed the Corrumpa or Seneca Creeks.

Over a century ago, the Mexican Governor of the Spanish colony in Santa Fe sent a Cavalry to deal with the Cheyenne Chief, and his bunch of savage heathens. He feared reprisals from the emerging Untied States Federal Government for killing so many heartland homesteaders. The natives were interfering with the flow of trade throughout the Cimarron Cutoff. If something hadn't been done about it, it would have led to an earlier occupation of American troops and shifted the desert tides of the Southwest.

The Spanish Cavalry found the Indian village at the base of the mountains. Situated between the two flat peaks, the natives had lived there for many long years, surviving as they had always done until the intrusions of the Spanish and English threatened to choke them out. The Cavalry surprised the Indians at dawn and by midday only the women and children were left to sing the death song. The mountains were named after the spilt blood of the chief and commerce along the Santa Fe Trail in this region became safe again. Though, despite this relative safety the U.S. Federal Government still moved in and swallowed as much of the Mexican Empire as they could grab.

Neither detective knew anything about the bloodshed that once milked the land. Seeing only a flat, barren landscape where the wind faintly smelled of Yucca and sagebrush, it in no way reminded them of their homes in Arizona, even though the terrain was close enough to the random observer. Driving through the one-story structures of Clayton, Wallace searched for the town's library. A Dairy Queen and Subway were the only recognized beacons of established order. They were so close to the Texas border they could smell cattle shit.

"What the fuck are we doing here, John?" Kate exited the car, finally stretching vertical, all those hours of quiet welling up in her voice.

The town smelled like cedar and dry brick. Back stiff, legs sore, Sergeant Wallace just stared at her. After a heartbeat or two, he walked inside the little building, leaving Kate little choice but to follow him. Speaking with a wrinkly blue-haired woman, Wallace was led to the library's periodical section. As the Librarian explained, they hadn't completely made the technological jump to computers. They were still in the middle of data transfers. So, many of the older newspapers were available only on Microfilm.

Alone in a little wooden terminal Wallace whipped out his notepad and pen and set them down next to the archaic viewfinder. He searched for the power button. Mauldune just glared at him, waiting. Finding the button, Wallace pressed it, and the machine hummed. Kate felt her tolerance rapidly evaporating. She was close to loosing her cool.

"Enough of this horseshit," Kate barked, noticing the eyes of old Librarian casing her. She lowered her tone. "Tell me what you're looking for."

"Anything."

"What do you mean anything?"

Wallace reoriented his seat to face her. "I mean that I don't know what I'm looking for. I'm just hoping I'll recognize it when I see it."

His sudden attack of brilliant honesty numbed Mauldune's mind. Stunned, her mouth hung agape and her eyes just poked a wild stare. "That's your amazing plan?" her voice was a coarse whisper as her stupor wore off. "To rummage through old newspapers at the ass end of nowhere and *hope* that something jumps out and grabs you?"

"Yeah." Wallace thought on. It had seemed pretty simple. "Basically."

"That's it," Mauldune spasmed. "I'm calling the Chief. We're done here."

The Lieutenant started to leave, cell phone in hand, but Wallace grabbed her arm. "Look," he grumbled low, eyes darting to the old maid that ran the place and then back at Kate.

"We know they've been using this road. We know they've been circling this area for at least fifty years now, maybe more. This could be a family thing. Generational. But like it or not, something happened here."

The look on his face was deadly serious. *He believes it.*

"Or very close to here," he surmised. "And it had to be compelling enough to keep them bound to make it a ritual. Something like that has to be big enough to be newsworthy." He gestured to the microfilm viewfinder and the computer. "Maybe it got ink, maybe it didn't. All I'm asking is that you try. Just give it a whirl and see what we get. If it's bunk we can go back." He paused and removed his arm, feeling pressured by Kate's scowl. "Two days. Just two is all I'm asking." He leaned back to give her some space to think on it. "Because you're right, we could cover more ground by bringing in other divisions to coordinate our efforts. But, I'm tellin' you. There's something here. I feel it."

Kate breathed, long and slow, thinking. She leaned against the empty, wooden portal next to the one Wallace occupied. She was tired of the road, of washing her socks in a sink. She missed her bed, but he had made a strong argument. In less than twenty-four hours she'd heard more out of the man than she had heard all year and it was either genius or uncomfortably sad. Though, watching him grovel to simply do his job was like spying on two quadriplegics wrestling. Kate hated being the one that held his leash. It was a long shot, digging through a haystack not knowing what you were looking for in particular, yet she had to admit it, they hadn't really come up with much else.

"*Give it a whirl?*" she teased finally, and slowly tossed him a grin. "Ok. Two days. But that's it." She pulled her coat off and sat down at the computer terminal next him, laying out her pad and pen. "Now, let's see the big, bad, and the nasty…*whatever it may be.*"

Wallace looked at her, chewing the inside of his lower lip. "Thank you," he said after a time.

Hot damn! That's a first. Kate was floored and didn't know what to say. Hard to even imagine hearing those words tumble out of his sequestered mouth, let alone have it smashed to actual sympathy. If he didn't stop soon she was gonna start thinking he was a real human. "Let's get busy," she ordered and grabbed the computer's mouse.

Hours later and even more sitting, the library was about to close. They'd combed through eighty years of northeastern New Mexican history and came up with a practical timeline for a group of familial personalities to develop and begin ritualistic habits. It was a rough sketch, a plausible theory.

Thinking loose, but generational, they each filled a few pages in their notebooks. Murders mostly, that took place in the region that had bigger ties than your average local boys drinking it up and knocking off one another over some lying wife. There were a few political land grabs that had upset some ranchers over the years. They looked interesting and seemed to have long family trees with deep roots. Some of the ranchers had moved away, some had stayed in the area. Overall, nothing jumped off the page like the Sergeant was hoping for.

They learned all they cared to about the local arts and airplane clubs, camping at the State Lake Park, and the dinosaur track. The oddest bit of news that either one of them came across was the disappearance of a small settlement, just south of Clayton.

As the story spun it, the village was nearly plowed under during a two day sandstorm back in the early thirties. All the villagers were reported missing. They were either believed to have been lost, buried in the violent winds and dirt of the storm, or had moved out because of the storm. No bodies were ever recovered. So, local speculation teetered more to the inhabitants abandoning the village for California as many people were doing back then.

It wasn't even a major article. Just a three-inch blurb a couple weeks after the storm had passed. A neighbor, ten miles away, dropped by and noticed that every one was gone. It had the earmarks of something the History Channel would exploit during one of their documentaries, pointing out how bad it was along the Great Plains in the mid 1930's. But it didn't sound any alarms in either of the detectives.

Craving food, they found a quaint diner and joined the local patter. It was a slow southwestern town just like the one where Kate had grown up. *Good people, salt of the earth. Hard to imagine anything happening in or around this town that would lead to ritualistic killings along several stretches of highway leading to and from this place.* Throughout dinner both of them felt gnawing failure biting their guts, but neither gave it a voice.

Kate was surprised at how quickly Wallace's smoking had become a naturally accepted thing, like he'd been doing it all along. Standing in the diner's parking lot, night dropping with the temperature, she debated calling the Chief. She didn't know if she could stand up to his digging comments and questions right now. She felt shaky. Even though she'd already agreed to the two days, she felt like they were at the end, like there just wasn't any other place to go. It wasn't that the trail was cold, it was positively abstract.

Wallace flicked his cigarette butt to the tarmac and the wind picked up. Breezes carried the little stub to the thistle of some brush. The soft, stroking fingers of air felt good after the long day. He exhaled, removing a weight in his chest. He stood there letting the air wash over him. He knew he was onto something. Even after the mediocre news bits had filtered through his system. It still tugged at his gut: *This is the place*. He just didn't know why. The wind circled around his neck and he listened to how it howled, watching it push tumbleweed up the street. The cop focused on letting his mind go and dropping all the hoo-ha that he had poured through at the library.

Possibilities and time frames. Words eked out through light and were chased like an invisible rabbit down a hole that he didn't know the size and shape of. He had walked out on a pretty fine limb, balancing on some awfully thin bullshit. Something had to give. Something had to crawl through the cracks in the ether and point him in a damn direction. Time was looking bleak and he'd sold himself out for all the minutes he could spare.

Kate watched the graying cop as he stood there with his eyes closed feeling the breeze. She was absolutely sure that he'd finally tipped. She shook her head and steeled herself against a gale that blew dirt and debris their way. It stung her eyes and she thought about how blinding it must have been for those settlers all those years ago, during that two day sandstorm. Just this little rise and prick of dust made her dream of California too.

"C'mon," Wallace said as the wind died down, barreling to the car.

Renewed with energy, he opened the backdoor and pulled out the scanner, carrying it with him as he climbed behind the steering wheel. Plugging the adapter in the cigarette lighter, he placed it on the seat between them and closed the door. It squeaked to life as he turned the key. He flipped the dial until they heard chatter from a local signal. He looked up and noticed the odd expression on Mauldune's face.

"What?" He half expected some blighting comment.

"Nothing." She gently threw her hands up.

"Hhrrmm."

Wallace pulled the column shift into gear and took off down the road with a direction from the wind.

May 10th, 1934.

Bodies were piling up. The screaming eyes of the dead stared at loved ones and murderers. Blood-drunk and staggering, eyes black, parasitic veins flat and ruddy, the vampires were growing lazy with their cattle. A few villagers decided to fight back. They rushed the door. Prophet and Jordan were barely able to push them back this time. Ramielle cackled. The humans were too weak from a lack of food and water, hammered by fear. They trembled in their sweaty clothing. The place reeked of rotting flesh and dread.

The dark coven leader kicked at the pile of corpses. "Get rid of this." She turned and skulked the line of whimpering faces. "Now, you know hell. Now, you see what I have seen and live as I have lived."

Crammed in the corner, Lin watched Ramielle pace back and forth from half-closed lids. Her parasite gnawed her own decaying flesh and screamed in her ears to feed. She was delirious and gaunt as muscles atrophied. She'd become like so much furniture in the large adobe house and they began to ignore her. Delirious in their own way, floating on the protein, capillaries, and glucose of their hosts, the vampires were punch drunk.

The crushing din of the storm buried the terrified screams of the villagers as Prophet and Jordan began carting the dead to the door. Ramielle grabbed the face of a middle-aged man and jerked him forward. His eyes were dreaming on the wind that whipped through the crack of the opened door.

"Do you believe in God?" The man stared at her, eyes swollen red and blazing. Ramielle's hold left wet, crimson fingerprints on his unshaven jowl. She slapped him. "I asked you a question?" She searched his terrified eyes. "Do you believe in God?"

The villager breathed hard and erratic. "Yes."

"Good. Good," she said, stroking the slapped side of his face. He trembled under her perilous black gaze and touch. "Faith is a powerful thing. I used to believe…long ago. But let me ask you this. If God truly loved you then why would he allow you to suffer so?"

Confusion twisted the man's sweat-soaked brow into furrowing knots. Hard to imagine any of these creatures ever believing in God, attending a church, *they are sacrilegious spawns of Satan!* He was struck dumb at how to answer the wretched beast. "I don't know," he muttered softly.

"Of course you don't." She stood, mind reeling backwards like a spool of yarn. "I didn't either."

Ramielle turned to her boys as they tossed the withered husks of family members outside for the storm to lovingly shelter with its maddening dirt. The winds howled through the large house, covering the floor with heavy silt. It blew across the emaciated vampire in the corner. The air, rising up through the flue whistled eerily, and made the fire dance. The ancient woman stood at the head of the frightened mass. Blood streamed down her gown, dark and viscous, her shadow buried a quarter of the hapless victims who were still left alive, still clinging to their last few seconds of time like greedy robbers.

The Vam Däm Mu witch reached out suddenly, grabbing the hair of the woman that sat next to the man whom she was just conversing with. The poor woman yelped as Ramielle threw her at Lin. She crashed between the revenant's legs, shaky and weak, breathing a panicky noise.

"Indiscriminately," she whispered at the man. "God loves indiscriminately."

Prophet pushed hard on the door to close it as Jordan stepped away from the dusty blasts.

"Make that bitch eat," Ramielle ordered as she loosed the tattered clump of hair that was collected and smashed between her fingers. "Her mood disturbs me."

She extended a blood-caked palm to the man, holding it out for him, to help him stand. He looked up at death. Death did not smile. She stared down at him with eyes as pitch as the deepest night and he started to cry.

"Come," said Death as he took her hand gently. She would help him to face the inevitable. He followed the terrifying woman to the far side of the adobe structure, where he had seen her kill at least four people that he knew. His whole body shook. Each step was galvanized in his soul. "Let's you and I talk about love," Death said as she sat and the wooden chair creaked.

The man stood in front of her as she ran her hands along his abdomen and chest. "I too was used like you are now." She looked at his rough, heavily creased face and could tell he worked in the sun. "They killed my husband and daughter right in front of me and I asked God why?" She began undressing him. His musk was palpable. Dirt was lodged under his fingernails and he quivered, fluttering timorous breathes every time her fingers made contact with his skin. "They raped me repeatedly and I begged God to save me. I begged God to kill me. Everybody I knew was dead, their homes set ablaze, and I prayed for deliverance from the hell I endured at the hands of the white demons."

She motioned for the man to kneel down between her legs and he squat, following her gentle tug. His worn clothing was piled on the floor around him. "Do you know what God did through all of those incredible horrors?"

The man's face twisted in fearful pain, "No."

"Nothing."

Ramielle delicately kissed the man on the lips. His salty tears flavored his skin, pouring down his face. "Ppplleeeaasssee," he begged, whimpering.

"Shhhh. Shhhh." Ramielle stroked the side of his face with the back of her hand. "It's alright. I know. I know."

His body spasmed and quaked. His breathing jumped out of his mouth and ran away. So tenderly...tenderly she cooed her meat. Calming him, she leaned in close and whispered.

"Take comfort in knowing that in what time you have left that I will love you more than God has ever loved you your entire life." She pulled back from him and cradled his face with her stare. "This is going to prick at first."

She was gentle. Floating on the high of so much fresh blood, her Jadaraa Soo humming all the while, insatiable and fulfilled, she eased the man's head to the side and bit him at the base of the neck, cradling him in her loving arms. His warm life pumped into her as if she were an empty sponge.

With the scent of a pulsating blood-sack so near, Lin felt her body jolt toward the woman as she arrived in her orbit. Lin was catapulted not by her will, but by the beast that dwelled within her. It craved sustenance and racked the vampire's body with pain and terrible visions. Lin forced herself to turn away. The woman was crouched on all fours between Lin's splayed legs, reeking of so much goodness. She breathed hot, dry air all over Lin, trembling and whispering prayers of salvation. Jordan wrestled the woman into his mighty grip.

"Eat, you stupid bitch." He pressed her against Lin's face. "Get off your high horse and feed. Your attitude is deplorable."

"Leave her be," advised Prophet.

"But, Rami said—"

"She is busy. Let her be."

Prophet wandered to the huddled corner. The surviving villagers writhed against the maniac's approach. Prayers and pleading rose up with fervor as whimpering and stifled hate ate his shoes. The mass of flesh pressed tightly against the wall, but it was of little use. Jordan jerked the panicky wench out of Lin's face.

"You think you are *so* special and unique," he berated. "Just because the one that made you thought you deserved this gift does not mean that you do. You've got to earn the right to be one of us."

In one fluid gesture of his head Jordan tore a gapping hole in the front of the woman's throat with razor sharp fingernails. Blood sprayed across Lin's inert face. It gurgled profusely from the wound, serous down the front of the vampire's dress, and fell, splat, onto the floor between Lin's legs.

Dimming eyes of the dying witnessed Lin's beast rise up against the roof of her skin. The blood parasite was anxious for the rush of a billion tiny cells through its calabash system. It sucked greedily the warm liquid down through the pores of Lin's flesh. The opened wound in the woman's throat was more than enticing. It was a chain that yanked Lin's spine froward. Yet, the obstinate host gritted her teeth against the parasite so hard that cracks formed in the enamel of her flat teeth, and she turned away.

"You have to *earn* the right," Jordan reminded.

He tore into the wound on the woman's throat and suckled. His lapping tongue was vile and loud, and Lin could hear how his Jadaraa Soo unwound from his canine shaped teeth and snaked through the dying woman's vascular network. Lin's Jadaraa Soo was jealous. She trembled so violently that it shook the dirt off her that had gathered in the folds of her clothing while the door was ajar.

Quietly, in abject desperation, the parasite pushed and prodded against the walls of Lin's pale sticky flesh. It ached mad and hungry, threatening to burst from its prison for the blood that was only inches away. It curled tightly around the bones of its stubborn host, locked in a grievous struggle, the puppet master felt the ire rebellion of the puppet.

Headlights danced across the adobe ruins, igniting dark places and hidden secrets. The Cadillac came to a stop. Sarah had quit asking questions about where they were going two hours ago. Choosing to discover the ramshackle backseat of the luxury car, she became a subdued substitute for the regular, brightly colored, tattooed Minister of Funk, choosing scratched CDs to put into the player.

Mostly, their ride was quiet. Some conversation. It was just so nice to get out of the city that Sarah enjoyed the ride. Every now and then her eyes fell on the swinging pendulum of the silver locket, hanging from the rearview mirror, but she didn't ask about it. Turning off US-412 onto the dirt road Sarah's curiosity peaked to a titillating point. Though, when the car came to rest at the broken mouth of dirt colored walls her enthusiasm was less than ciphered.

"Not exactly what I was expecting." She climbed out of the front seat. "Dancin' at a club maybe, a swank hotel with room service, midnight boat cruise, even a rave. But this..."

She wandered to the front of the vehicle, searching the dark. A thick scent of earth and engine oil filled the air. Lin removed the locket from its perch and unpacked from the driver's seat.

"This way," she coached with a nod.

Sarah followed her. Under the shimmer of a pregnant moon, four structures poked jaggedly out of the ground. Time had worn the plaster walls away to the crumbling adobe bricks. All the roofs were gone, support beams vanished; each decrepit house stared up at the naked sky, open. Bits of rusting metal jutted out of the sand between the cracking frameworks, unrecognizable as to what they once were.

They entered through the outline of a door at the first house. The room looked like it was once a large rectangle, spacious; now it was a ruin of decaying bricks. Sand tapered each end of the walls like a dress. Lin crossed to a point in the dirt just off center, near the back wall, and held her hand out.

"I found this here a long time ago."

"Found what?"

Lin loosened her fist and the locket dangled from a crooked finger. "Take it."

Sarah had seen the thing in the car earlier and it was about Lin's neck yesterday when they went out. She didn't understand why Lin would drive all the way out here to give something she'd already seen. She cupped the jewel in her palm and ran a finger over its decorative engraving. She hadn't noticed the artistry of the object when it was dangling from the rearview mirror or when it was around Lin's neck. But now bathed in moon-glow in the bowl of her hand it glimmered and the craftsmanship of the locket struck her sensibilities.

"It's beautiful."

"Open it."

The dancer pressed her thumbs to the tiny halves of the locket's latch, squeezed, and pulled it apart. It was shaped like a clamshell and unlocked like angel wings. Inside there was an antique photograph. Sarah stared at the picture, recognizing the face.

"What?" her mind instantly rejected the sight, "where'd you get this?" Her brow wrinkled, eyes scrunched up. Her whole body was a question mark. "Did you make it?"

"I told you," Lin replied. "I found it here. A long time ago. In this very room."

"But, it..." She ran a pulsating fingers over the image, unsure.

"Looks exactly like you," finished Lin.

Sarah stared at the vestige of the woman for the longest time, trying to gauge the item that portrayed her in a Victorian dress with her hair put up, detailed in black and white. Her breathing picked up a notch and she grew flush. "You're fuckin' with me, right?" *It's the only logical conclusion.* "You made this on a computer."

Lin silently held her ground. Bloodstained and invisible, the echoes of screams drifted through her head. Her quiet oozed into Sarah like bleach. The dancer's gaze fell to the aged image again and she whispered, mind reeling, "How's it even possible?"

Lin took a step forward and lightly grabbed her shoulders. "Do you trust me?"

"Huh?" Sarah looked up, mesmerized. Lin had a serious face.

"Do you trust me?"

Too many thoughts collided across Sarah's cranium. Questions were beginning to blossom. What Lin was asking her for seemed alien, so she shook her head, "Yeah."

The raven haired beauty let her hands drop from Sarah's shoulders as she stepped back, nervously, cradling her fingers. "The storms were pretty rough that year. The whole Midwest was getting thrown up; something about the irrigation and wheat farms left over from World War I. We thought we could drive right through. It never even occurred to us that we had anything to fear. But we did. Though, it wasn't the storms. There were five us when we started out: Me, Jordan, Prophet, Ramielle, and Juliana. We were going back to LA and thought to make a journey of it when the sandstorm hit. Our car choked on dirt and we were stranded.

We started walking. In less than an hour we lost Juliana. She just vanished. The wind was so ferocious and the sand was so thick that I literally couldn't see two feet in front of me. It was a brown wall. A few steps in the wrong direction, and she was simply…gone." Lin's voice disappeared for a moment and she was still. Her eyes were immeasurable valleys, watching the girl.

The locket pulled at Sarah's hands as the woman spoke. She wanted to ask her what she was talking about, but suddenly Lin blurted out, "I thought for sure I was going to die right then and there. If not by the sand then definitely when the sun rose that morning."

Nervously, her eyes flicked to the live girl. "I watched Prophet scout ahead and disappear into the swirling death and I was sure we'd never see him again. But he found this place." She gestured with her eyes and the tight movements of her head to the room around them. "The people here gave us shelter and for two days we were alone with them as the storm raged. They...They...They let us into their homes and we…" Lin's heart pounded, her Jadaraa Soo was furious in a nervous cage. She felt fear ebb her bones at saying the horrible truth. "There was a young woman that lived here. I…I never even saw her face until…until it was too late." In two strides she crossed to Sarah and placed a hand over the locket that rested in the dancer's palm. "This was her locket. I took it off her corpse and kept it with me all these years, because some how, I knew I'd find her again." Lin stared into Sarah's eyes. She was frantic. Her gaze was a drill. "That I'd find you."

Two bodies of emotional water stood facing each other. Lin haphazardly tried to impart the circumstance of time, but was lost amid a turbulent sea of bitter emotions. Her thoughts became jagged symbols expressing no clear picture. All she had to do was speak it now, plain and simple. The groundwork had been laid. The pretext was in position. *What am I waiting for?* But it was a different voice that cracked the silent tension.

"Did she neglect to tell you that her and her little band of freaks murdered everyone that lived here?" Z stepped out from a pitched black shadow. "Oops. Lemme guess. You were *just* getting to that part."

"Stay out of it Z," Lin flared, feeling the grind of the bad penny digging into her heels as her hands fell away to her side. "This doesn't concern you."

Z threw up her arms. "My bad. Do continue..."

Sarah watched the newcomer with worried eyes as the punk motioned the floor back to the dark-haired storyteller. The intruder took a couple backward steps and leaned against the exposed dirt bricks and watched them fumbling through the awkward moment. Lin's face wore an angry scowl.

What the fuck did she have to be angry about! Not, like I abandoned her for some stripper floozy. "I mean," voiced Z, peeling herself off the wall, "I've only been with you for the past sixty odd years and this is the first time I've heard this side of this little gem and I've been dragged to this dump more than a dozen times since then. So please, by all means, *continue.*" She waved her hand at Lin, egging her on and leaned back against the adobe brick. "Tell Ms. Thing your big, bad terrible secret and let's blow this Popsicle Stand."

The air suddenly grew frigid and rancid to where only a single heartbeat thudded between the three of them. "What secret? What is she talking about?" asked Sarah, trying to grasp the logistic of time being tossed about. She was confused by the intrusion of the loudmouthed punk.

Z parted from the wall again with a hurtful grin crushing her face just as Lin was about to say something. "I gotta tell you honey, this whole soft, tender side of you is boring the hell right outta me." She crossed to Lin. "So, what d'yu say...let's kill the bitch and hit the road."

A blur of movement! Quicker than Sarah could have ever thought possible, Lin held Z around the throat and slammed her into the broken bricks of the adobe wall.

"I'm warning you Z, stay outta this," spit Lin through gritted teeth.

Z laughed. Sarah jolted in her shoes, but was more shocked at the intruder's steady stream of laughter than the sudden violent outburst. It bubbled like brittle light, cracking around the edges of everything holy. Sarah wasn't sure what Lin was going to do next.

"What does she mean sixty years?"

Sarah's probing question, put off by Lin's youthful glamour and the punk's comment, made Z's malicious grin grow wider, more devil-may-care, and Lin released her. Panting tight in her chest, Lin's Jadaraa Soo was flush to the surface of her skin. She glared at Z, eyes two bails of hateful rocketships. This wasn't the way she'd intended for Sarah to find out about her dark condition. *Z, as usual, is putting her brutal spin on things and fucking it up.* Lin didn't turn around with the parasite up. She had to focus hard to get the veins to recede deeper under her flesh.

"My…" cooed the brightly tatted punk. "You are rather touchy about this one."

"Just stay out of it."

"Look," interrupted Sarah, "I don't know what's going on here. But obviously, you two have something that needs to be worked out. *Seriously.* So, I'm just gonna go."

To Z, the look on the girl's face was hilarious and she almost burst out laughing again. The live doll turned to leave and the vampire found it cute.

"Oh, where are my manners…" voiced the intruder, crossing to Sarah with her hand extended.

"Stop it Z," squeezed Lin through clenched teeth.

"I'm just tryin' to play nice." The vamp smiled – all white teeth and fangs.

Feverishly uncomfortable, eyes darting to Lin, Sarah reluctantly took the outstretched hand, palming the necklace into a freed limb.

"Hi. My name is Zia. But most folks jus' call me Z. And oh yeah, by the way…" She pulled the dancer in close. Off her feet and tumbling, Sarah fell into the stranger. "I'm a vampire." Z roared and flashed sharp teeth. Her Jadaraa Soo flexed and pulsated, horrifically.

Sarah stumbled back, frightened, as Lin rushed to her. But Z kept egging it on doing a bad Bela Lugosi impersonation. "I wanna drink your blood. Blah, blah, blah…"

"Cut it out Z!" Lin shouted as she neared the girl.

"Suck you dry like a lemon tree." Z grunted loudly, smirking, "Oh Yeah!"

Scrambling to her feet, Sarah turned and looked at them both: A nasty pair stuck between the shoulders of night. The punk rollicked, holding her belly, guffawing at her fear. Lin's face was crushed in worry and pity. Sarah ran from the ruins into the caliginous desert.

Lin's shoulders sagged. She saw the face that she feared on the girl. The vampire called after her, but Sarah kept going. Z's prattling bursts, sick like a Hyena, ran up Lin's spine as hot razors. She wanted to smack that smile off Z's face and cram it down her chortling throat.

"Nice one," Lin uttered, glaring at the destroyer of souls. The last shreds of her fondness for the vampire were trampled under her own feet as she followed after the live girl. "Sarah wait…"

"Don't worry," informed Z through ruckus chuckles. "She won't get far."

Stepping through the decrepit doorway of the large house, breaking from both the bonds of memory and a chiseled want to expose herself in the right way, Lin climbed up the dune and rounded the corner of the moonlit structure. She was about to call out for Sarah again when she spied the girl, docile and mute, in the grubby hands of someone she hadn't seen in over a hundred years. "Dimitar?"

Too quickly were events spiraling out of control. Now, Sarah was bound in the languid grasp of the dirty Ukrainian. Sarah's eyes bulged above his thin snaking fingers with black sharp nails pressing against her tender, pink flesh, screaming at Lin for understanding, for get-me-the-hell-out-of-here! Lin had seen that look on Sarah's face before, not so long ago, on these same hallowed grounds. Vicious fear, without reproach, unyielding, soul damaging and it seemed to be happening all over again.

"Hey Boo," the rusty Ukrainian greeted. "Lose something?"

"No, she's…" flustered, Lin redirected. "Would you *mind* letting her go?"

"Sure. Just holding onto her for you." He did not release her. "Didn't think you wanted to lose such a pretty thing."

He bent his nose into the crux of her neck and inhaled Sarah's fear-soaked flesh. She wiggled against his spindly, but taught arms, as he growled in the back of his throat.

"Dimitar, please," urged Lin.

Abruptly, he let go and she crashed to the ground. Lin rushed toward her.

"Don't!" Sarah warned from the hard pillow of earth. "Don't touch me. Just stay away from me."

Lin inched forward, hands out and open – *wanting*. Empty for all but the air that fluttered through them.

"Stay away," the dancer promoted, and turning, walked into the clear, dark glade of the desert.

Standing abject amid the ruin of crimes past, the present collided with all haste to the destruction of her will; Lin was galvanized to the spot. A breeze flitted around them, the desert wheezing, and spun a tiny dust devil on the horizon. It smacked of winds past. A mocking tempest to the storm that raged during those two days of hell, and never in all her unnatural life did Lin ever feel so inadequate, so incomplete, and inconsolable that blackness was all that she could muster in her spirit. Watching Sarah walk away destroyed her.

Ryan Silva's corpse flashed through her mind: Bleeding out on the concrete floor of the garage before she and Z left on their journey. This moment and his death were a symmetrical wheel. Lin felt that same pooling dread gathering about her knees that she had felt back in LA. She was drowning on dry land. Z sliced his throat with a switchblade without batting an eyelash. *Now, she's gone and done it again, killing my hope, destroying my last chance at redemption.*

A fire rushed up in Lin, strong as west Georgia lightning, and threatened her to violent action, that was, until the unsettled words of the woman she longed for blasted her disdain.

"I don't know what fucking game you're playing at or who the fuck all these people are. But I'm not some silly pawn for any of you to fuck with." With trembling hands Sarah opened the locket and glared at the facsimile of herself, gazing out of the oval. "What is this?"

"No one's gonna hurt you," said Lin moving toward her. "You're safe. You are safe here with me."

Z wandered from the adobe ruins and listened to Lin grovel and coo. It was deplorable. She spied worry and fear, flush and evident, on Sarah's features. A frailty that framed her composure, she talked big, but she looked small. *So very, very small.* Tears streamed down the girl's ruddy cheeks and the devilish vamp grinned.

"I don't know what you want from me." Sarah threw the necklace back at its owner.

It bounced off Lin and landed in the gritty dirt at the vampire's feet. The face of the dead woman in the photograph stared up at her killer. Sarah strode away. The whole night was pressing down. She stopped at the edge of some dry grass and held herself.

Lin looked down at the locket. *Should have left. Should have...* Eventually, she bent down and picked it up. Sand shifted through her fingers. Awkward glances passed from her to those that she'd known forever. She felt exposed. *This isn't the way it was supposed to happen.*

Dimitar pulled along side Z. "Thought you said there'd be a party out here?"

Z shrugged defensively, "So, I was wrong. Sue me."

Lin walked over to Sarah. The slow crunch of her shoes in the soil was the only sound she heard. Each step sent her back; memories colliding with the Now. She stopped a few feet from the dancer and stared at her crumbling shoulders. Sarah did not turn around.

"Is she really a...a..." blankly, she'd asked, finding the end of the sentence hard to say.

"Yes."

Lin's quiet response was deafening. Sarah's world shattered and she began to shake. "Are you...like them?"

Lin exhaled loudly and whispered, "This is not how I wanted to do this."

The vampire reached a hand out to Sarah's frigid back, but the girl turned around.

"Are you going to kill me?" fear crushed her face.

"No!" blurted Lin. "I'd never let anything happen you. Ever." She stepped to her and gently grabbed her shoulders. "You're perfect just the way you are. I'd never sacrifice that."

Bowing her head to think, tresses of almond hair fell across Sarah's face. Lin delicately moved the locks away, searching for the dancer's green eyes. "I'm sorry you found out like this. I was going to tell you. There's more to it than just..." The cable car of Lin's words jammed in her throat as she looked upon Sarah's wrinkled brow. All of a sudden Lin's excuses and reasons didn't seem to matter. "I'm sorry."

The smile on Z's face vanished and formed a jealous scowl. *Such open intimacy!* Years of unlavished affection and holes as huge as bicycle tires spun in her head. Z sneered, crushing a desire to communicate to her sable haired friend. Now she understood how the passengers of the Titanic felt watching the boat slip under the murky, cold ocean.

"She's under my protection," Lin announced to the unwelcome crowd. "No one touches her. Not even a hair." Her eyes darted to Z. "You got that?"

"What's a little blood between old friends, eh?" agreed Dimitar. Always one for amicable alliances, he shrugged and scratched the back of his neck, at the base of the skull.

Z propped a two-cent smile across her gums and didn't say a word. She started strolling around the cute couple, a wide girth anchored to the gravity of the Ukrainian madman, and watched the sudden newbie *now under the glorious protection of the Vam Pÿr's bitch.* Hate bristle in the cuticles of Z's fingers.

"No one's going to hurt you," Lin softly reported to Sarah. "Z was just trying to scare you, is all. I'd never let anything happen to you." She pulled in close. "Not ever."

Sarah's heavy eyes searched Lin's face. She wanted to believe. She wanted to be sure. She wanted to be safe. She wanted to trust Lin, but she didn't know how.

"She's losing it," Z commented to herself, choking on an urge to vomit.

"Who are you?" Sarah's green eyes pierced with quiet fortitude. "Really?"

It wasn't the vampire standing in her oxygen that answered her. It was the smelly brute with the leering grasp, ears so sharp in hearing that each one of Sarah's Alveoli filling with breath grated in his head like a crank. "Me? I'm a Pisces. I think Z's a Gemini..." He turned to her.

She flipped him off, presenting a parade of her middle finger.

"Definitely, a Gemini," He asserted with a smirk.

"Do you all mind?!" quibbled Lin.

Her hyper thoughts, ticking on how she'd just gotten the girl back into some semblance of confidence was threatened again by the lewd opinions of uninvited guests. Lin glowered hatefully at the annoying punk and the hapless victim of circumstance that she'd obviously conned into a ride. Ironic, that Lin drove all this way from Albuquerque, hours by the clock, for solitude and isolation with the dancer, only to wind up in the midst of a sad excerpt from some estranged reality TV show. Her lost efforts bordered regret.

"You know I get the distinct impression she doesn't want us here," Dimitar said to the pent-up punk.

"She's lost it," stroked the dyed red vampire through thin lips. Her eyes were fixed rods on the two ladies at the edge of the field.

"C'mere." Lin grabbed Sarah's hand and started walking with her to the far rear of the desolate village.

"You know," Dimitar retorted to the punk. "I just came to dance. Not interested in the freak show. What's everybody so down for? It's a beautiful night."

Z ignored the crazy Ukrainian. Public Image Limited thrummed through her head as she watched Lin and Sarah heading off toward a rusty swing set. *"This is what you want. This is what you get. This is what you want. This is what you get. This is what you want. This is what you get."* It twirled and reverberated on an unceasing loop in Johnny Rotten's wicked tongue. "Better than a ride on a flat dirigible," she finally answered.

Dimitar chuckled, deeply in the back of his throat. "You owe me *big*, Pinky."

She hated being called that. He always called her that. "Bite me," she replied.

"Don't tempt me," he warned, teeth edging in her direction. "You dragged me out here for nothing. No liquor. No tunes. I thought we were gonna dance. Have a party. Light a fire. Gotta get my jollies somewhere."

Z rolled her eyes and exhaled, "Alright, sure." She shook her head. "But this time I'm on top."

The dirty, skinny brute laughed. It filled the iridescent night, wafting on Lin and Sarah's heels as they strode away, trying to create a little pocket of space. Along the way they passed Dimitar's motorcycle hidden behind a crumbly wall of earthen bricks and finally came to rest at an ancient swing set. It leaned at an odd angle and was rusted to a dull red. Only one seat remained tethered to the frail metal. Sarah wandered over to it, tested its strength by pulling on it, and sat.

She was tired and worn out, feeling like an empty apartment. What had turned out to be an evening of lovely possibilities quickly evaporated into a seething mess. For the longest time, neither one of them spoke. Lin gave the girl space to sort it out. Sarah didn't know where to begin. Creaking, badly in need of oil, Sarah rocked back and forth in the lone seat.

"Here," Lin extended the necklace to her. "I want you to have it."

Soundlessly, Sarah accepted it and set it in her lap. She looked down at it and thumbed the engraving slowly. "Is it true? Did you kill the people that lived here?"

Lin sighed. *There's just no way to spin it.* "Yes."

The swing creaked throughout the long silence that followed.

"Because, you're a…" Sarah tried to ask, but she still couldn't say it.

"Vampire?" Lin cocked an eyebrow. "The word doesn't bite, you know."

Sarah cracked a smile and turned to Lin. The girl's grin was infectious and the symbiont felt warm in her glow. The dancer's gaze transported Lin and absolved her of her previous sin. To the bloodsucker, Sarah was an angel, a gift of light and time – *circumstances of fate convalescing into a shining point.*

"Tell me what happened?"

The girl's request was sincere and simple. Lin was glad to hear it. She'd imagine telling Sarah the whole horrible truth since the second her eyes fell upon her in the street. It was what she had come here to do in the first place. All those trips, throughout all those years, Lin was mending generations of loss through her endless journeys, waiting for this soul, this perfect gleaming soul, to reemerge from the ether. From that first drop of blood that the vampires spilt during those horrid nights of demon winds they had set this moment in motion. Each death brutally canonized on this once prime real estate, now strewn in tatters around them, was the cadence of Lin and Sarah's eventual meeting. The circumstance of time was upon them.

"Okay," Lin said, and started at the beginning.

May 10th, 1934.

Ramielle listened to the timbre of the storm. Its rude clanging had changed. Between her legs, the skirt of her dress was gathered up, and folded against it was the half-dead body of a man. He leaned against one of her blood stained thighs waiting for death. Slowly, the Vam Däm Mu poured over him, sapping his fluids. Hours were spent together in the cruel witch's embrace as the other two monsters tore into his group, dwindling the villagers down. So few of them were left now. So few.

The man's frame was shrunken and gaunt. Beady eyes stared at the creature in the corner. Lin had not moved for hours and panted like a rabid, wild dog. Feverishly. The man wondered what was wrong with her, why she did not join her fellow creatures in their horrific merriment. He wanted to ask her, but his lips were too dry. His mouth felt burnt and his jowls were too weak to move. He inched closer to the light beyond the veil. He wanted it. Flesh was cruel. Painful. He accepted death now and wondered if the thing in the corner did as well.

"Dominique said you were a strong one," boasted the coven leader to Lin. "But all I see is weakness. Pathetic. Human. Weakness. How could she get it so wrong, I wonder?"

Prophet joined in. "Perhaps she meant stubborn."

The progenitor cackled like a braying horse. Her hellish merrymakers joined her laughter and Lin's head rolled to the side weakly gazing at them. "You are the weak ones."

Her voice barely scratched out, but it cut a harsh path of silence in the room – All but the storm, banging its incessant drum in their ears. The dying man smiled. Ramielle pushed the living corpse off her and rose.

"You conceded whore," Jordan indignantly flared. "Damn you and your high-placed morals. It'll be all too soon when I see the backside of you."

Ramielle crossed the room. She laid a calming hand on the shoulder of her blond-haired brood. Jordan huffed and quieted down. She slunk. Slowly. The storm beat like lazy trees against the roof of the large adobe house. The hem of her soiled gown swished silently on the sandy, bloodstained floor. Prophet rose and stepped over to the tired huddled mass of terrified flesh, and choosing, he separated a mother from her daughter. The related humans cried as Ramielle neared the silent creature in the corner. They pleaded for their lives and begged to be spared, clutching onto one another as if they had a choice. It was useless. Prophet pulled from the grieving flesh, separating bonds by breaking hearts. Weeping, the child fell to the floor. The mother's only consolation was that she did not have long to grieve.

Ramielle crouched down in front of Lin and spoke softly. "Do you hear that?"

Lin tried to listen. She tried to push past the sobbing and prayers to God, pass Jordan clicking his teeth, and Prophet draining yet another victim. She pushed past her own head rocking explosions and the painful singing whine of her parasite. It was hard to focus on anything. Yet, she heard the storm.

"The winds are slowing," Ramielle explained. "By nightfall we'll be able to move. But look at you." Her black engorged eyes splayed across Lin's shrunken carcass. "You've starved yourself, and for what? Thinking yourself the better of us?" She scoffed. "I tell you now that I will walk out of here."

Ramielle swiped a smattering of fresh blood from her lips and smeared it roughly on Lin's mouth. The vampire's starved Jadaraa Soo yearned hungrily for it. The parasitic veins that formed Lin's fangs greedily unwound and writhed for the small smudge of blood on her lips. It was sad to watch.

"Oh, the pain must be exquisite," noted the coven leader. "Yeah, that's it. Yearn for it my sweet. Yearn for it." She egged the veiny beast on. "Teach her truth." Ramielle grabbed Lin by the jaw and spoke slowly. "I will leave you here to rot with all the corpses. Do not think for one instant that I won't." She released her roughly and poked her in the forehead, jabbing a dot of blood on her like a Hindu. "Come nightfall, we leave." The freed Vam Däm Mu rose. "The choice is yours. Feed and live. Or, stay here and die."

The poignant master returned to her meal and put him quickly out of his misery. His flesh shrunk against atrophied muscles and heavy bones. She sucked every drop of life out of him to show the judgmental bitch just how easy things could be. Ramielle's words volleyed through Lin's head. Drained, in a drug-like stupor, she could hear the change in the tempest too. She knew Ramielle and the others would leave her. That much was assured. They'd no more show compassion for her than they did for the villagers that opened their home to them, offering sanctuary from the storm. *Kindness unpaid!* Lin could imagine it now, how they'd tell anyone that asked – *Poor Linnet Pevensey was lost to the bastard winds.* Just like Juliana she vanished from sight. Lost forever. Dominique would never know the truth of what really happened to her Araci.

Lin rolled her head to the other side and peered at the small remaining group in the far corner of the large adobe house. Something metal glinted in her eye off the fire's light in the tight packed flock. It shone like a tiny star. Instantly, Lin knew what she had to do if she wanted to survive. It wasn't even a question that she should have presupposed here in this barren waste. She was what she was. She made her choice long ago with the Persian woman, under the Casa Grande in São Paulo, Brazil. She did not have to gorge herself like her fellow travelers had done. She was not a lady tethered to extremes! She did not have to enjoy the slaughter of innocence. She did not have to die. Here in this god-forsaken country she still had the choice of mind - *to live or to die.* By her will. Not the beast's.

Weakly, Lin pulled herself to the small, frightened mass. Crawling on her belly like a snake, inching toward the five remaining villagers, the vampires watched her. She became spectacle. Taunts and jeers erupted around her from her fellow travelers, but she blocked them out. Their mockery and ridicule became a wall of noise blending into the din of the sandstorm. Her Jadaraa Soo began to pang loudly against the walls of its prison, giving her groaning muscles strength. The meager villagers scuttled away from the crawling beast. They clamored brutally for release, for sanctuary, and for God's tender mercy. The vampire inched closer. Her springy adversary pulled the corpse of its host to the delicious, screaming feast.

Once Lin was enraptured in the realm of the villagers' warm flesh her body reacted and her will vanished to that of her constant companion. She was unaware of the primal savagery with which her vestige performed. Violent cheers rose up from her cohorts. Lin's actions were cruel and quick, tearing into anything that moved. Biting and slashing!

Her Jadaraa Soo deformed her features to liken the spawn of hell itself. Thrushing, a whirling blade, she massacred the remaining villagers and her merry cohorts joined in the bloodlust frenzy. Fat and bloated already, they did not care. They still felt aching hunger in their own bottomless pits. Outside, the storm died above their red-covered heads and the large adobe lodge truly became nothing more than a slaughterhouse.

"There really wasn't anything I could do," explained Lin, wrapping up her tale. "Ramielle was right. I was suffering. I'd already made the choice a long time ago. I feed; I live. I don't and I die. Simple." She watched her words roll over Sarah and added. "Blood consumes blood. That's how it works."

Sarah sat in the swing, motionless and silent. The terrible relic from this place rested in her palms. The silver chain was curled around her fingers. She held the locket up for the vampire to see. "And what about this?"

Lin watched the item dangle in Sarah's hand and a grave expression framed her face. It was not easy for her to share as much as she had. She gazed upon the locket and recalled scooping it out of the hand of a corpse. Yet, the guilt that was usually attached to the memory was missing. *Damn that Prophet. Must he always be right!* Lin parted from the rusted iron of the child's device where she'd been leaning and crossed to Sarah.

"I've done things I'm not proud of. Been around long enough to make plenty of mistakes. Life sometimes becomes easy to take for granted. We have so much of it. That's not to say that I excuse the abuse of what we did. It was wrong. And we each have paid for it in our own way." Lin gently tugged the necklace out of Sarah's hand, unclasped the chain, and placed it around the girl's neck.

"I did not leave with Ramielle and the others. I stayed behind and buried the bodies. In the palm of a dead woman I found this." She backed away from Sarah to admire the necklace around her neck. The albatross was now dead and buried by Lin's truth, sharing her pain with time's beautiful muse. "It is yours now. It always has been."

Sarah wasn't sure what she meant by that last part. Though, just knowing how she acquired the locket made it creepy. It was twisted, to have it around her neck, but she didn't mind it being there. *Everything has history. Every place is a graveyard.* Everyone's a suitcase of instances and the circumstance of time. She held the locket and thought of Derrick and her momma. *What's important is not what a thing was, but what it could be.* Sarah saw real possibility in Lin. She recognized the woman's pursuit to change her existence, become her own gal, and make amends for what wrongs she had done. In that, they were kindred spirits.

"What's it like…Being a vampire?"

Lin softly laughed at finally hearing Sarah say the word. "Imagine a one hundred thirteen pound mosquito that won't age, is hard to kill, and has an affinity for a fatal suntan."

"Seriously," Sarah poked. "What's it like?"

Lin became sober again. "You don't wanna know. And I don't want you to know." The vampire picked the woman's hand up and placed it to her chest, instructing her Jadaraa Soo to cease all work at the bio-factory. "What do you feel?"

Sarah felt lots of things. Before this night she'd never even suspected that real flesh and blood vampires roamed the streets and brothels of Albuquerque. She'd just been given a piece of early twentieth century jewelry and told a real life ghost tale. She'd had her life threatened by a brightly tattooed punk vampire and had a run in with another grubby suspect. Everything was kind of happening pretty fast for Sarah, and on top of it, to add the little cherry to the crème of her ice cream cake, she'd learned that her best friend was getting married and she'd agreed to be her bridesmaid when school and work were crushing her soul. Lin's question was not only a little vague, but interstellarly inarticulate. So Sarah, when faced with a mountain of confusing feelings that clashed about in the unfathomable abyss of her soul, answered the only way that she knew how and said, "Nothing."

"Exactly," Lin affirmed, letting Sarah's hand go.

Slowly, Sarah removed it off Lin's chest, not exactly sure if she understood the woman's point.

"It's the slowest form of suicide you can think of. Without it ever ending." Lin paused for effect. "You don't want this."

Sarah creaked in the swing, gently moving back and forth. An ebb and flow, her tumblers turned. "But I want to know you." Her expression was sincere and it was the first real glimpse that the girl still cared for Lin. "I can at least try to understand. Maybe, there's a way to reverse it or fix it, or something; I don't know. Medical science has accomplished a lot over the past–"

Lin's laughter stole Sarah's word and she felt small. The vampire reached down and picked up the locket. "I got this in 1934. I am two hundred and fifty-six years old. There is no going back. This is what I am."

Lin's curt explanation hit Sarah like a ton of bricks, falling over her in a hot wave. She'd never even considered how old Lin was. In everything that was going on she'd forgot to ask. The woman looked the same age as herself. So, she just assumed.

As the two clandestine creatures unspooled themselves from the tangled skein that drew them together, Dimitar caught a delicious scent on the wind. He inhaled deeply its rich aroma and was instantly transported to when he was just a boy growing up on his parent's farm in Kursk.

"Do you smell that?" He turned to Z.

Z plied her nose to the air, but could not detect what the elder vamp had sniffed out. There appeared nothing enticing in the air at all.

"Sorry, ladies," he politely voiced with a nod. "Don't wanna buzz-kill. But it looks like you've got your own shits to stew in."

With that he took his leave, bounding away into the dark desert in three large leaps. The sight of the strange man crossing so much distance in such a short time, with so few strokes and little effort mesmerized Sarah to stunned silence. She was overwhelmed. Lin took her hand and they began quietly walking back to the car. Turning to Z as they saddled up, Lin half expected more attitude, but the raucous vamp's face was forlornly agape.

"Shit," the punk exhaled. "There goes my ride."

The night wasn't working out the way she'd planned either. Z figured that she and Lin would at least be on their merry little way by now, finding some sort of misadventure to get into to. But here they were, still stuck out in the desert. It felt like an old fashioned nipple twist, smarting for lack of any real amusement. Z turned her nose to the air again to suss out what had caught Dimitar's fancy. She couldn't smell anything alluring, just a hint of home-cooked raisin bread and dirt. The air was boring. There was no taste of blood on the breeze, no threat of violence dancing in the wind. The air was calm and normal. Z hated normal. *Normal sucks!*

"Things just couldn't get any weirder," stated Sarah, shaking her head as she walked to the car.

Z cocked a hard smirk and darted a look at the annoying newbie. "Things can always get weirder, sweetheart."

"Yeah?" the live thing asked, annoyed.

Z started walking over to her and Lin, "Yeah."

Lin knew Z's tactics and could quickly see where this was going. "Give it a rest."

"She's a big girl."

"It's ok," Sarah informed her protector with soft eyes and dangerous hips. "I wanna know."

"No, you don't," urged Lin – *belly sinking like a ship.*

Z chuckled. "Well, Ms. Polly Pure Thighs..." she grinned triumphantly. "You ready to get weird?"

"Sure," replied Sarah, accepting the vampire's unspoken challenge. "Whatchyu got?"

Stealing
The
Thunder

What I thought would fulfill me only left me bereft.

Dominique rose shortly after Lin departed Chateau le Rouge Mort, though she did not leave her chambers for some time. She met with Prophet. Caged within the hurt, pain clutching and pulling at all the soft places inside. Hope was the first sacrifice. It was also the needle that the Bithtaran Priest used to sew the crushed woman back together again.

Hope? It worked its own charm. Not so easily dismissed, Dominique unburdened her heart. The old lovers' brief and awkward union was nothing short of the final nail in the coffin of their slow-to-die romance. That was obvious now. It had been clear for decades, but the Vam Pŷr desperately clung to falsities, drawing the inevitable out of the wound of love as if it were snake venom.

"I thought she would open up to me like she used to." Dominique's face formed a bitter scowl. "She could not even look me in the eye." Her cheeks were stained red by blood.

"You must give her time," counseled the Priest. "She has a hard soul. The ground has only been tilled. The seed merely planted."

Dominique forced a smile through the hurt, recalling. "We used to be each others' everything." *Inseparable. The moon and the dawn – united.* "Linnet crossed the great expanse for *me*." Tears leapt from her lashes. "She entered night so that we could be together. Forever."

"You of all people should know the deception of that."

Her face twisted into a harsh vision again. "I left her to build my Council." She paused, flung her head back, exhaled, and drew against the wall of her circular room. "I am doomed to know this."

Prophet slowly rose from where he sat on Dominique's large round bed and crossed to her. "You are only doomed if you allow it to fester. You have done remarkable things." He placed his hands upon her shoulders. "You are a remarkable woman." Dominique touched his hand. "Purifying yourself in the bright eye of god will only make you stronger."

The Vam Pŷr looked up. His jaw line was rugged. His eyes were glassy and deep. His skin was fine. There were no visible scars from his ordeal in the sun. Slowly, she calmed. "I will consider all that you have said."

Prophet shook his head, understanding.

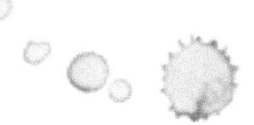

"Now, if you'll excuse me," said Dominique movin away. "I'd like to take a bath."

"Of course."

He left her chambers and a day later she emerged, lonely, from her tomb as the tide of the three-day festivities at the Chateau waned. Dominique retired to her Atrium to walk through her garden and dine. Her mood was heavy, her thoughts tangled and intertwined, unable to let go of the highborn lady from the Opera.

The Atrium was a hollowed out bowl under the earth, massive in size and stroke, one of the prizes of Chateau le Rouge Mort. It was built to emulate a South American jungle and had taken Dominique thirty-five years to cultivate after initial construction. Recessed lighting was designed to imitate both day and night, and those twilight places between. Sprinklers provided rain and mist. It was climate controlled. She stocked her jungle with a half dozen primates, two large cats, various rodents, some snakes, and several species of birds and insects.

The creatures filled her tiny landscape with life. An engineering marvel, it was her own personal habitat. On most days, it was a great comfort to the symbiont monarch, though tonight, it was not. She was alone, rattling through her calabash system, feeling venom wash her soul.

The Vam Pŷr partook breakfast on the observatory, a high tunneled out balcony that over looked the expansive forest. Her chef had prepared freshly crushed pineapple sprinkled with refreshing mint over a fluffy cheese soufflé and waves of bacon. Three mangos had been skinned and cut and garnished a scrumptious dish of Dal Poories. White Tapioca made with coconut milk and cardamom pods was surrounded by purple Thai rice pudding in a clear, chilled glass and topped with a single green mint leaf and one uncooked spice pod. There was caviar on hand-churned buttered dark bread with champagne and raw cashews over sliced bananas covered in melted chocolate, topped with cream. These delicious delicacies were the appetizers to a main course of Eggs Benedict with Salmon and Rosemary on toasted muffins smothered in Hollandaise Sauce.

Am I always doomed to love?

Dominique's food fetish had increased in recent years to such a point that she'd retained a personal cook. He saw to the preparations of all her unnecessary meals. She also retained a physician who assisted her with cleansing her bowels after each culinary adventure. Dominique was not as carefree or public about her D'oeuvre Fetish as other vamps and former blood slaves had been. Hers was a private affair relegated to the staff of her house, and though she chided herself about her obsession on occasion, she continually devised ways to explore her chef's mastery in the kitchen.

The unique constitution of the hybrids sometimes had unexpected results, causing allergic reactions. Her personal physician inspected every recipe for approval before her chef was even allowed to prepare it. Blueberries, as it turned out, were a deadly killer of the veiny blood parasite, as well as the Brazilian Açaí berry. These berries' rich antioxidants and amino acids caused immediate paralysis and death. High levels of caffeine, found in many espresso drinks and the Guaraná Fruit often caused seizures or the symbiont to sweat blood in jittery spasms. Garlic, a well known and written about deterrent for vampires, was not poisonous to the night creatures, as was described in novels and movies. Ingested, it was fine and rather tasty – a favorite delicacy among the obsessed brood. Though, the garlic bulb's aroma, in raw form, caused a gag reflex of the esophagus that closed the throat and restricted oxygen to the dark blood.

Many exotic foods that were poisonous to humans had been found not to be toxic in vampires. Luxury dishes made from Pufferfish, Xanthid Crabs, and Blue Ringed Octopus have become celebrated in small circles with certain chefs' reaching notoriety and prominence for their recipes of these platters. Eating live Electric Eels was popular among zealots. The pectoral fins of the Torpedo Ray and the tails of Scorpions have also been made into tasty soups.

Dominique did not promote her personal chef as other cuisine admirers did. He was for her comfort only. Though, ironically, in her sheer diligence to retain him in private he became infamous among the small fetish groups. The great mother of night, architect of The Council, and bloom of the Children of Evensong did not have much in the way of privacy. She was always the center of talk among the covens. So, she coveted what little intimacy she could, taking small solaces in her Atrium, her dining, grand parties, and her bastard love for the girl from Abingdon.

Though the place that had birthed her had long been gone, the girl remained – her darling Linnet. Her Araci – *the dawn from which Jaci fell.* Dominique's cravings for the unnecessary meals were only heightened by the hurt that the raven haired beauty always seemed to cause. The Vam Pŷr was a gaping wound that needed to be healed and it was no consolation prize to have gleaned that lesson, *yet again,* in Lin's dominant presence.

Two human consorts, Annabel and Gregori, briefly joined the council member for breakfast. They did not speak. They knew their dark mistress's mood and only stayed long enough to refresh their own appetites so that their bodies could handle the feedings later on that were sure to come. They were the Vam Pŷr's real delicacies, her true nutrients. The spread on the table before her was only solace. Comfort food. Consolation for love lost. Dominique's attention throughout her meal was chiefly given to Urubu, a cute spider monkey that often joined her on her retreats in the jungle paradise.

First climbing up to the balcony, the monkey, who was named after a Brazilian vulture, screeched his presence and climbed onto Dominique's shoulder as she fed him mango and banana. Clyde always seemed to find the Vam Pŷr in her garden with matters of business that could no longer go unattended when she least felt up to it. The cross-dressing secretary procured Dominique's signature on several documents and entreated Urubu to their customary greeting, as he sat on her neck and tried to comb mites out of the tribal tattoos that decorated her head. It was always amusing that the little primate mistook Clyde's ink for hair.

In her duties, Clyde was proficient, diligent, and had been a member of Dominique's entourage for nearly a century. It pleased the grand mother of night that her secretary liked to reinvent herself every ten to twenty-five years. It kept things fresh. Interesting. So easily their kind vanished into the dull march of time.

"The Prime Minister of Quebec is leaving and asked if there was anything else he could do toward the little matter that you and he discussed yesterday."

"Tell him that he will be contacted if there is any change. So, for now, continue as planned."

Dominique stroked Urubu's long, bushy tail as he climbed off Clyde's back and sat on the breakfast table.

"Very well. Also, Monsieur Delacroix's invitation to join him at the tournament has yet to be given a reply."

"When is it?" Dominique rubbed her temples.

"The tenth night from now."

The Persian woman sighed and looked out over her indoor forest as brightly colored Toucans flitted over the green canopy. "Tell Michele that I will attend. We'll take the full house, leave a provincial staff to care for the garden. I think we'll travel a bit after."

"Very good. I will inform him of your decision and begin preparations of the Chateau. Mr. Prophet requested your presence."

Dominique reflected, playing with the monkey. "Tell him that I will meet with him tomorrow and to make himself at home, if he has not done so already."

"Very good."

"Oh, and ask him if he'd like to join us on our trip."

"Yes, Ma'am."

Dominique handed Clyde the documents resting in front of her and pulled the Tapioca and Thai Rice Pudding dishes over to her sphere of orbit. She lifted her spoon. *It is time to begin enjoying life again instead of suffering the bondage that love bore.* The bald secretary excused herself and began walking away as the Vam Pŷr ate her desserts. The heels of Clyde's Italian leather shoes clanged in the huge underground dome.

"There is one other thing," Dominique recalled, wiping the corners of her mouth with a cloth napkin, as the soft matter slid delicately down her throat.

"Yes, Ma'am?" Clyde returned to the swampy smells of the table.

The secretary was not a practitioner of the food fetish. Her obsession was personality and identities. She did not have an opinion on her mistress's gourmet lifestyle. Dominique was a great lady in her eyes and the mother of their race. The one-time slave of the Omjadda could afford any luxury or appetite that was known across the globe and it would not dissuade Clyde's loyalty or interest to perform her duties with the utmost assiduity. The vampire respected her mistress and bore no judgements.

"That matter with the Agents I discussed with you a while back. Do you recall it?"

"Yes."

Dominique paused before uttering her decision. It would have irrevocable consequences. No reset button that could be pushed. "I initiate; with one addition."

"And that being?"

"My daughter's pet, Zia... She is not recoverable. Do I make myself clear?"

"Yes, Ma'am. Completely," nodded Clyde. "I will call them immediately." The secretary turned to leave, but paused. "Might I add, that I believe you are doing the right thing."

Dominique gazed up at the sharp dressed vampire. Her choice in the red tie matched the exquisite pattern that her Jadaraa Soo made under her pale, Armenian skin. Despite her acceptance to move forward with the personal plan, worry still wrinkled her brow. *There is no going back from such a bold step.* "Thank you. That will be all."

Clyde nodded and left her mistress to her meal and the company of Urubu. Mother Night's afflictions after her visits with Linnet were easily soothed in gluttony and solitude. Clyde had witnessed it often. On her way to make the most important call and copy and file the signed documents, she informed Dr. Gladys to prepare for the mistress's flushing colonic and bath. By the size of the meal that Chef André had prepared, and Dominique's cloudy mood, the secretary knew it was best to have the physician's services ready and waiting when he was called.

One of the attractions that most vampire food fetishists often claimed was that by enjoining the whole cycle of bingeing and purging it was reminiscent of living a human life. Dominique did not feel such nonsense. Her brief expanse as a fully live thing was mostly endured in the dark mines of the Rom Pŷr J'in. She'd known little of human existence or of earthly appetites having been captured and enslaved as a young child. Existing as a blood slave was all that she could ever truly remember. The dark light of being human was merely a dream of circumstance. Something she relied on prior to her becoming a hybrid more than a definite understanding of self. She was a night creature through and through. Her attraction and zeal for human food was in the taste, the enjoyment of brief repast. To sup from all forms of life and not just be limited to the red liquid. In her dead heart she craved life and sought to imbibe it fully.

When Dominique was a slave under the Omjadda's yoke she never tasted the pleasure of a grape or the simple delicate beauty of a

Honeysuckle or Rose Vinaigrette. During her courtship of the Abingdon girl she took to dining with her during the woman's meals. It pleased Linnet when they shared a table, some wine, and a block of cheese. Back then, digesting small amounts of food were easily evacuated by ingesting alcohol, which the parasite naturally purged from its system. Over the years, lush in the bloom of their love, food sometimes became a bed. They raised Lin's child, William, together until he was near the tender age of five. They conquered lands and adversaries and formed a lasting constitution for their kind while naked and in bed, surrounded by the smells of fruits from the jungle. When Lin was human, and their love constantly growing, luscious foods were abound. Their scents mingled with the sex of the English girl and her blood. She was in Dominique's veins. Dominique's love for Lin thrived there still – *love in vein and bleeding.* But it could no longer rule the tide of Jaci.

Though the lust for food was born with the love of the girl now gone, removed much like the place from which she was birthed, each were now clothed in a different name and face. Memories were all that the Vam Pŷr had left. Traveling through the modern world, Dominique was vexed by old recollections of streets and towns that had been paved over and buried. They bore no resemblance to bygone eras. It was a constant irritation to set one with directions. So too was her time again with Linnet. All that she had loved in the girl had vanished and in its place stood a dark shell.

Each bite of food could not bring back what was lost. The delicious flavors of the meal ground the Vam Pŷr to the Now. Too often she dwelt in the long arms of night, forever tinged by growing memories, locked within the knowledge of old, dead things. Humans were simple creatures. They had simple tastes. They were never meant to peer behind the veil of time, Dominique knew this. Her hybrid race, an amalgamation of Homo Sapiens and Omjadda, were stealing the thunder of the cosmos while envying that which was, and could never be again. Minds trapped by unceasing desires, tasting the blood of freedom often came shackled. Each bite of the delicious food freed Dominique of her afflicted love for Linnet and bound her to the hoses of Dr. Gladys.

I need you no more, my sweet. No More. No More.

Urubu climbed onto Dominique's sublime shoulders again and curled his tail around her jugular. He ate a piece of mango, dripping juice onto the Vam Pŷr's blouse. Every so often she fed him what she ate from her spoon, delighting in his simple company. One of the large jungle cats growled and Dominique made a mental note to have more elk delivered to the Chateau before they left for Michele's tournament.

Pressed into sweaty folds of dirty clothes, drinking piss warm liquor, cold beer, smoking like chimneys, Slim's regulars whittled hours away dotting the little hole in the wall like strewn pennies. The swamp cooler was on the fritz again. Windows, open in the front and the back, sucked cool mountain air across the slow drip of Country Music lazily pumping from the boombox behind the bar. A dusty Out Of Order sign leaned on the old jukebox in the back. Slim read the news. His patrons drank. The normal drool and hum of the tucked away bar was only interrupted by the rockity whirl and clank of headlights streaming through windows, stopping unfamiliarly in the parking lot. It grabbed attention.

"Would you lookie that," muttered Rita from behind her beer as the three girls finally stepped into the place.

Obvious out-of-towners, they took their time showing themselves after car doors clanged. Eyes cased them from across the room, except those of Slim, the owner. He was content to just read his paper. If they needed him they could see him. He was, after all, the only one behind the bar.

"This is not a good idea," Lin whispered to Z as they entered the smelly, dingy wooden drinking establishment. Unease held her back.

"What's the matter," Z glared, fixed like a compass, whispering harsh tones. "'Fraid precious won't like you in the morning once she's seen you get your teeth dirty?" The punk smiled maliciously and threw an arm around Sarah. "C'mon cream-cake, let's get us gals a drink."

Rooted, Lin watched them cross to the bar. Her eyes swept every face, temperatures dropping like lead in her belly. *These people don't need any of this. This is wrong.* She followed after them; needing to dissuade Z from the collision course she'd steered them toward.

The raucous punk drummed on the flat of the bar. It annoyed Ernie just as much as the girlie's tattoos and bright red hair. Everything about her was loud and abrasive. She made his eyes hurt, his ears clang. So, he moved over one seat to give himself some space. Z found this amusing and laughed. Lin saw the looks she garnered from the copper scented crowd. She had seen it before. Too many times, in fact.

Slim peaked over the top of his paper at the newbies. He took his time folding it up and setting it down before he climbed off the stool where he was parked. Walking with a limp, a surviving war relic before Sarah's time, he passed the freshly posted Wanted Flyer that two out of town cops had given him earlier that day.

"Yeah-up," he moseyed. "What do you want?"

"Something warm to wet my whistle." The hyper vamp smiled.

He checked them out. *City folks. Out and about.* He'd seen their kind before. Impatient. *Moving so fast they forget to live.* "We don't serve no fancy drinks here. Beers' on tap or in the bottle. Hard liquor is what ya see is what we got."

"Thank you," Z replied kindly.

Lin could've sworn that she had more time, but the crazy vampire got down to it. Grabbing the unsuspecting barkeep by his collar, Z pulled him over the faded wood of the bar and bit down hard. Blood misted into the air and hit Sarah's face. Normally, Lin would have followed through on Z's lead, picked a viable prospect, hunkered down and blocked the door, joining the fray. But Sarah was here. Lin pulled her back as a frightened gasp erupted from her surprised mouth.

Z was quick. She didn't move to feed. She moved to shock and disrupt. Her base disregard for human life reminded Lin of Prophet, from his younger days. *Shame they never met.* As Ernie jumped out of his seat, spilling his beer, Z's eyes tilted at him. *Jackpot!* She threw Slim back over his bar, blood splattering across it. Teeth agile, face dripping wet red, the violent wench reached out and plucked Ernie up as easily as if she was picking a flower.

A huge construction guy was heading their way. Behind him the whole room rose in a sea of enticing pheromones, sweat, and fear. Panic and alarm sent everyone in motion. Instinct and muscle memory kicked in and instead of running away, like she wanted to do, Lin stepped between the beefy man and her endearing flatmate.

"Get out of my way, Bitch!" He intended harm.

Thinking that he was easily going to pick the dark-haired woman up and toss her aside and reach Ernie, he put his hands on Lin. But she was faster than he could have believed. The vampire cold cocked him with one solid punch and he went down like Dolph Lundgren in Rocky IV – *a hulking mass bouncing on the mat.* Suddenly, there was a shotgun blast!

Silence ate the room after the loud burst with panicked calm. Bright white rippling pain hit Z in the side of the face. She stumbled back, parasite bleeding. Ernie hit the floor during the echo of the blast. Legs limp, he wasn't moving.

"You Mother Fucker!" Z was shocked. Pissed. It'd been seventy-four years since she was last shot.

Slim didn't know why she didn't go down with both ends of Betty and he rightly didn't care. Bleeding profusely down the front of his ruined shirt he popped the noisemaker, emptied the two spent shells, and got busy reloading. The look in the bitch's eyes wasn't good.

Sarah was afraid. It was all happening fast. Everything turning wrong side gray, she wanted to get out of there. Lin moved toward her as another unfriendly hand was put upon her shoulder. She snapped outward, body reacting, and twisted the meaty palm, turning, and nearly broke the man's arm. She kicked the guy as he went down. The knife in his other hand clanged on the scuffed wood floor.

BLAM!

Z stumbled back. Both ends of Betty again, square in the chest, pain lit her up like a pinball machine, all wins, bells and whistles! She could feel her Jadaraa Soo jittery and crawling. That last hit hurt a lot. Though, she wasn't gonna show it. "Now, I'm really getting' mad! That was my favorite bra."

Z gritted her teeth as Lin grabbed Sarah's hand, trying to pull her away from the spot at the bar. The violent punk saw Lin's mouth moving, but couldn't make out what she was saying. Her head was a flushing whine, a static complaint from the parasite, screaming in agony. Everything moved in slow motion. Lin was moving away. Z advanced on the idiot with the shotgun and she moved...*away?*

BLAM!

Everything went black! Both Sarah and Lin jumped as the blast rocked the impending silence that followed. You could have heard a pin drop. Two hot smoking barrels emptied and their effect was on the floor.

"You gotta get outta here," Lin told Sarah, recovering quickly.

She stared down at Z. The punk wasn't moving. Everything felt as if it were incased in silicon gel. A moment in time. Z was bleeding out. Her face was mangled Swiss cheese. Adrenaline pumping, shock was setting in and Sarah was vaguely aware of Lin pulling her towards the door. The vampire's gaze swept the angry crowd. There was more than enough of them to over take her and Sarah. She heard the barkeep reloading his weapon.

"Sarah, move it! C'MON!"

The vampire pulled her to the door as the locals of the dingy bar pressed against them. *BLAM!* Another shot rang out. It barely missed Sarah and hit the wall. Real fear crept into Lin's pores and it was highly likely that she was going loose the girl too if she didn't step up her game and get her the hell out of here!

Lin pushed the dancer roughly through the door, thinking more about her longevity than her piqued sensitivity, just as another blast exploded the wooden jamb where her head had been. Lin threw herself through the door too as sharp splintering pieces of wood imbedded in the side of her face.

"Jesus, Slim!" One of the locals yelled. "You nearly took my ear off with that thing! Watch where yer aimin'!

Rita ran over to Ernie. He wasn't looking that good. He was bleeding out from a half-dollar-sized hole in the side of his throat and a dozen or so pockmarks along the side of his face where Slim had clipped him. He was convulsing. Rita yelled for somebody to call 911 as the lot of them rushed the door. She heard the rockity engine of the car that the strangers came in on and its screeching wheels as they high-tailed it out of there. Slim sagged against the bar and set Betty down. Its muzzle was hot, smoking like a cigarette. He was feeling woozy, loosing blood, and this evening had started out quiet enough, all right.

The call came through, a sizzling ham sandwich on the grill. Tired and about to pack it in, but the 211 seemed interesting. Shots fired. People down. An ambulance had been dispatched. It was an address they visited earlier that day. The silent look shared between them said it all.

Wallace whipped the wheel around, pulled a smoking half circle, no other traffic, street dark and open, he punched it and headed for the oncoming rain. Thunderheads rumbled, fulgurating in the distance, and miles down the road it began to drizzle. The sky made an awful fuss for too little water. The desert, happy, drank all the H2O up before billowy mountainous clouds could reproduce.

Kate pulled out the map. *Sure enough*, there was a big red circle and the address written in ballpoint ink. It was the first place they'd hit when the Sergeant got a wild hair up his butt to canvas the area after dinner. It was pretty far out. Tucked away, secluded. John had called it a prime target, and at the time, Mauldune didn't believe him. He'd been off the range all day, *chasing invisible rabbits down dark bunny holes.* If this panned out she knew she wouldn't be surprised, just concerned that her partner was a practitioner of voodoo. He had that sense, that damned operational sense; *shame his attitude kept him down.* He surfed the glass ceiling of rank and they both knew he'd never bust beyond Sergeant. Even if he did deserve it.

A Chicken. I could get him a chicken. It'd go well with his smug ass after this is over.

Finally, they were on the verge. She couldn't wait to call the Chief and gloat, tell him that they'd bagged 'em and tagged 'em, and were coming in. *Wait a minute! Don't get ahead of yourself. It's only an attempted robbery. Might not even be them. This could still all be a Snipe Hunt.* Time and miles to burn, anxious, Kate loathed the passenger seat. She wanted the big chair. *Christ, I outrank him for god's sake.* She should have taken the keys when she had the chance. Kate Mauldune breathed. Somewhere, out in the cold night, rain teasing to fall in buckets, the criminals had made a massive mistake. It was just as John had said, *we're close and because of that, we're gonna get 'em; not let some imaginary border stop us.*

Giddy, like on Christmas, the Lieutenant wanted it to be them. More than anything, she wanted these past few crazy days to mean something more than jurisdictional breech. *It had to be them…just had to be.*

Sarah didn't speak. It was as if she'd forgotten how. Lin drove. She just drove. Tearing out of there at first, Sarah expected sirens and lights. Flashing badges and television high speed chases. But there was nothing like that. Silence. Fucking silence, crushing down, leaving you with nothing to do but think. Sarah felt cold. Frigid from the inside out, the hum of the road lapping against her body, she thought they were heading back towards Albuquerque, but wasn't sure. Places looked unfamiliar, everything was tinged with a gun powdery scent and images of blood. *Of teeth and blood!*

Lin was a vampire. *Dear God, what have I gotten myself into?*

Dawn was coming, a continual bastard – the earth on its axis, the sun in the sky, Z on the floor and blood oozing out of her head. Lin had seen vamps take a lot more punishment than that and still keep going. *What had happened? Did her ticket finally get punched?* Perhaps, her ailing Jadaraa Soo just couldn't handle anymore punishment and gave out. *Was she playing possum or suffering from another narcoleptic seizure? Fuck!* It was frustrating. Not knowing, moving on with no time to look back sandwiched between the rising sun, a frivolous death, and the disaster of the girl in the seat beside her.

Lin searched for a place to pull off the road. A motel perhaps, but mile after mile, trees and flat nothing, interspersed with not knowing, everything felt huge like she had balloon hands, tethered to yet another plot of earth in the far corner of the Great Plains. *Should have left her in Vegas? Should have left her at home? Should have left...*

Lin didn't want to be with Z anymore, that much was obvious, that much she knew. Though, she didn't want it to end like this. Not under these circumstances; *it isn't right!* It was messy and gross. A heart transplant abandoned half way through surgery. She thought about calling Dominique. The moon stared down at her from the sky, following her in the windshield, and she knew Jaci would at least want proper protocol followed. There was a symbiont body out there being touched by grubby human hands, quite possibly on its way to an autopsy. This was Lin's mess. The moon stared her in the face with guilt. She had let it happen. She was responsible. She needed to call Dominique, but all she could think of was how her former lover would relish Z's unfortunate passing. *Fuck! Fuckity Fuck, Fuck!*

Lin remembered. Not long after Z found her in Los Angeles, they were going out, almost every night. Familiar bars, nightclubs, and homes of other Children of Evensong, even then, Z never really liked hanging out with her own kind. Lin was her one exception. Z said they were all stuck up bastards, calling themselves by Dominique's cute little moniker: *Children of Evensong.* It sounded too clean and prestigious for people that whet their appetites on blood. She never liked being called that. Z preferred the term, *Vampire*, and dragged Lin out to see Bela Lugosi in Dracula during a Halloween screening. Z liked the fear that her kind bestowed. She loved the power.

It started with little things at first. Z told her that she could just take whatever she wanted and damn the consequence. Lin didn't have to pay for it. She was a vampire. She was above it. Everyone and everything existed solely to sustain her and her amusement. It was a hard sell after being with Dominique for so many years. Nearly two centuries in the thrall of the Vam Pŷr, Lin was trained to think and be like the Persian woman. Z helped her to see that. Z helped her to break out from the bondage with which the Vam Pŷr had ensnared. Lin didn't even realize it at first. She and Z bickered constantly in the beginning, though, not in a bad way. It was philosophical. Fun. They debated. Like a kid in a candy store, the first thing Lin ever took under Z's watchful tutelage was a few pints of blood and somebody else's car.

They were out cruising the strip and fed from a couple of sailors on leave, seducing them with the allure of sex, plying them with liquor all night. It wasn't a familiar consort or a blood delivery or a Sanglant from The Service. It was dirty and raw and good. Lin was nervous and it was exhilarating. Z called it *popping her vampire cherry*. Even though Lin had passed strangers under her teeth before or, worse yet, a few foes, Z had called her a virgin. The wild vamp claimed that all those people of whom Lin had partook during fights and skirmishes in Brazil while liberating slaves didn't count.

What Z compelled her to do was different. It was random and fun. Lin didn't have to feed off the sailor, but she wanted to. That was the whole difference: *The Want.* The choice that she could have anything and anyone at her will's command was intoxicating. Z told her that was how they did it in Chicago. It was the whole reason why The Council annexed them. The northern coven was free. Truly free to do what they damned well pleased and because of that The Council believed they were a threat. Z used to laugh at the irony of Lin working to free African and Indios slaves in Brazil while, with each bite and consumption of blood, she shackled herself to an invisible yoke. A yoke, Z pointed out, that was built, crafted, and conceived by a former slave. Lin was recycling Dominique's karma. In the heyday of their friendship, Z broke upon the symbiont like an epiphany.

When Lin took that sailor it was in a bathroom stall, at the back of a club. Big band music bopped and they made out in the Men's Room. It smelled of rancid piss and sweat and she'd bit him on the thigh. She left him there, passed out, pants down around his ankles stuffed in the corner between the toilet and graffiti. From that moment on she never looked back. Two blocks from the club they found a Chrysler that seemed appealing and drove away into the balmy night. Her memories hinged on the frailty edging through her fingertips, colliding with what had just happened. That sailor and all those years ago seemed farther away than they were. Behind her eyes, Lin felt cracking.

A faded motel sign dotted the distance between a row of trees. Lin pulled in and parked next to the all night Manager's Station. She left the Caddy running. Sarah waited in the car, arms across herself, balled up, staring straight ahead. Words felt like inappropriate things. The door chimed as Lin stepped into the low light of the little office. She set her hands on the black counter top and rang the bell.

The place smelled of pine and feet. After awhile a man rambled from behind a half opened door. He yawned and asked what he could do for her. He was younger than what Lin had expected, probably in his late thirties, and looked as if he'd been sleeping in the back.

"1 room. 2 nights."

Lin needed to get her head together. Find out what happened to Z before she called Dominique. The man turned and looked at Sarah sitting in the car. The copper scent of his blood pulsating through his pounding jugular vein thrummed through the vampire's Jadaraa Soo. She was hungry.

"Just the two of you then?"

"Yeah."

Lin pulled off two hundred dollars from the wad of cash in her front pocket and laid it on the countertop. The motel owner eyed the cash as he procured a guest card and pen, laying it out for her to sign. "I just need you to fill this out and then we can get you started."

Lin pulled another crisp hundred dollar bill from the roll and tucked it into the man's shirt pocket. "No questions."

He stared at her for a short bit, tossed another glance at the girl in the Cadillac, and chewed the underside of his bottom lip. *Three hundred dollars?* It had been a slow season. The post-Bush Economy was squeezing everybody these days. It was getting harder and harder to make ends meat. He slid the cash off the black countertop, lifted a room key from its hook, and passed it to her.

"Room 143. It's around the side."

Lin grabbed the key.

She parked the car at the south end of the one story building. It was a thin shaped 'L', two toned with a pitched roof. Turning the engine off, Lin still felt the road humming through her body and knew that Sarah felt it too. She opened her door and got out. Sarah just sat there fidgeting with the locket. Lin turned to her like she was about to say something, but when she saw the girl's fingers working the worn engraved silver like she used to do she remained silent. Lin left her there, sitting in the car, but she left the motel room door open for whenever Sarah wanted to join her. The vampire didn't push. She didn't rush her. The poor girl had enough unloaded onto her this evening.

Lin washed up in the sink. The water felt good. She craved a bath, a long, hot, sulking bath. The room only had a shower, no tub. Outside, dawn's greasy fingers slithered up from the backside of the Earth, wiggling light, silhouetting tree branches clawing heaven. Sarah still hadn't come in. Lin stood by the opened door for a spell as the world woke, standing in the center of the 'L-shaped building', thinking about the Letter that had changed her life. Z cut her with her presence and she cut her in her absence. The girl was damnable. She was a hoot. *And I left her there to rot.*

The bodies were unmoved by the time Wallace and Mauldune arrived. Someone had thrown a sheet over one of the corpses and the Medical Examiners were just about ready to load somebody else into a body bag. Deputy Barney Fife, at least that's what Wallace wanted to call him, he called himself Daniel Hodge, was the first officer on the scene. He'd called it a gruesome mess, walking the detectives through the setting, describing the details as he'd heard it from the gaggle of patrons that they had corralled near the back of the bar.

The detectives stopped over the body of the assailant, crouched down, and the young cop pulled the sheet back. Wallace stared into pale, pounded hamburger. He grimaced as Kate looked away, wishing she had stomached it better in front of the rookie.

"Yeah," he said after a spell. "That's her." Wallace rose. "Well, one of 'em at least."

Mauldune felt vindicated.

"Slim said he put 3 rounds into her before she went down," explained Officer Hodge, pointing at the bar's owner, who was holding his neck, being attended by a local EMT. "And he fired another two more at her friends as they high-tailed it outta here. Guess they didn't expect to rumble with a bunch of good ole boys, did they?"

Wallace's beady stare cut the smile off the young cop's face.

"The...the other one...Ernie," Hodge redirected sheepishly. "He's, he's over here."

The three police officers crossed to the other body as the Medical Examiners were loading it onto a gurney.

"They must've been on some serious shit, huh?" Hodge asked, pulling back the flap on the body bag. "To withstand three blasts from a double barrel." He turned to Mauldune who barely recognized him as a breathing life force standing next to her. He was just an annoying thing. *Buzz. Buzz. Buzz.* "What do you think, PCP? Crystal Meth? Real freaks, huh?"

"Hhrrmm," Wallace commented, having a better time ignoring the officer.

"Ernie MacWilliams," the cop finally said and Kate wrote it down in her little pad. "Local fella. Slim, that is, the Owner, claims that the girl...the dead one, was biting him on the neck when he first shot her. Like a vampire. Can you believe that? A vampire."

As the cop whispered the last part he leaned into the two detectives, not wanting to draw too much attention to what he'd just said. Like it would make him look bad. Wallace produced a pencil and rolled the deceased Mr. MacWilliam's head to the side. There was a half dollar sized hole in his throat that could be consistent with the diameter of a bite, but there was too much congealed blood and buckshot along his neck and the side of his face to accurately tell.

"Well, Slim," Officer Hodge belatedly informed. "He uh...he also clipped poor ole Ernie here when he shot the woman."

The cop hooked his thumbs into his belt and bobbed his head up and down and shared a few quiet breaths for the familiar dead man in front of him. Mauldune excused herself to talk with some of the witnesses. Wallace watched as the M.E.s took the body out. *Another one to add to the pile.* His eyes fell to the sheet-covered corpse. *One down. One more to go.*

Mauldune wasn't gone that long and looked a bit more animated than when she had left. "Got a partial license plate number, a weird one, out of California. Witnesses claimed there were 3 of them this time around; Saw two perps fleeing south in a beat up, baby blue Cadillac.

Vintage."

She smiled. Wallace hadn't seen her grin in a couple of days. It was nice to see her usual zing back in her step.

"Excuse Me!" An organized, intruding voice shouted from near the entrance. "May I have everyone's attention."

Both Wallace and Mauldune turned. Standing in the doorway were three FBI Agents, two males and one female. All of them were smartly dressed. Black suits. Slim ties. Average and anonymous, well-pressed and cleaned shoes, they looked like they had just popped out of a comicbook, wearing so much dark ink. The chatty one flashed his ID as he moved into the room.

"I'm Special Agent McCallister. These are Special Agents Davy and Gorman. Effective immediately we are taking over this crime scene. We'll need everyone's cooperation for processing. So nobody leaves; not even for coffee."

His team split up. McCallister ate up the center of the room as Gorman, a tall, dark haired, Native American woman, crossed to the witnesses and police at the back of the bar. Special Agent Davy looked as if he was crossing over to Deputy Fife, Mauldune, and Wallace.

"This is bullshit," Kate managed to squeeze out before the sharp dressed goon descended upon them.

"You two." He pointed at the detectives like they owed him money. "We'll need all the materials and evidence you've gathered so far for our continuing investigation."

Wallace stared at him like he didn't understand English and Kate waited for the old man to give it to the usurper. *Jurisdictional prudence, the Feds were crawling up our ass and now they want all the goodies that John has put his own sweat and shoulders into so they can call it theirs. No Way!* Kate palmed her notebook and filled the silence between them with a question. "Continuing? Did I hear you correctly?"

"That is what I said," Special Agent Davy dryly informed.

"What about this is continuing?" she inquired, quietly tearing out the pages of paper that she'd taken notes on since she'd arrived.

"That's classified," he blurted out like he had no neck, yet he turned toward her.

His eyes were too small for his face. He was a big man, taller than John, bulking in muscles under the black jacket, thin tie, and white shirt. The Lieutenant folded the pieces of torn paper into her sleeve and handed the federal goon her notepad. "Well, we wouldn't want to obstruct justice, now would we John?"

The Sergeant didn't say anything. He just glared at the *"Special"* agent, a breathing statue.

"Detective," the G-man cooed. "I will need access to the boxes of files in your car." He motioned for them to lead the way, "If you please."

"Hhhrrmm?"

Special Agent McCallister's cell phone rang and he answered it as the Arizona detectives, led by Special Agent Davy, went to their cruiser.

"It's them," McCallister said into the tiny receiver and listened. "No. Your daughter appears to have fled the scene with a familiar." He stepped off to the side, away from the earshot of locals. "Yes, we've got the scent; and it appears that Zia will no longer be a problem. She's—"

"She's Gone!" shouted Officer Hodge with a stupefied stutter.

"Hold on." The special agent turned toward the body that was there only a few moments ago.

All that was left was the bloodied sheet. Crumbled up, abandoned, just like the wet spot on the floor.

"The body..." Hodge looked for it, like it would suddenly pop out. "It was just here. But...but it's gone!"

A stern countenance washed over McCallister's face as he pulled the phone to his ear. "I'll have to call you back."

He closed his phone in the midst of Dominique speaking, and putting his nose to the air, sniffed.

Lin was battening down the windows, drawing the blinds and curtains when Sarah entered, closing the door. The girl's eyes wouldn't hold her. Looking away, she crossed to the bed and sat cocooned within her clothes.

"I had to get off the road," Lin informed. "But this should keep us 'til nightfall. After that..." She didn't want to say it, but it was the only way. "I'll take you back. And you can just...forget about all of this. Live your life. You'll see. In no time it'll all seem like some faraway dream, and none of it will matter anymore."

Sarah was looking at her. Now, it was Lin who couldn't hold her gaze. She was embarrassed. She'd almost gotten the dancer killed. "You won't have to worry about school. No more dancing at the club either. I'm gonna take care of it. I can afford it. I'll put you through medical school. You wont have to..."

Her words fell away as Sarah reached out and grabbed one of Lin's pale hands, pulling the vampire to her. It felt like there was nothing but charred ashes between them. The night was strewn in ruins, sacrificed with blood, a red dawn, and the simple touch from the girl brought everything crashing down. Lin trembled. She inched forward and cried. Blood tears streamed down her face. No matter what Z did, or who she was, or how bad things were in the end Lin had loved her. Sarah hugged the vampire's waist and for the longest time they remained there, holding onto one another, the sorrow of loss binding them as if they were adrift in a turbulent sea.

Slowly, Sarah looked up at her and Lin, feverishly, wiped away her tears. They left rusty stains running down her cheeks. Lin's Jadaraa Soo was visible. Weak and emotional, the vampire had relaxed her hold on the beast and now it was flush to the roof of her skin. Sarah examined the vampire's hand, tracing the veiny parasite with her fingers. Lin watched her. Her veins writhed against the girl's touch, sensing delicious warm blood above.

"Are all your veins like that, *so*..." It was a gross curiosity, an interesting quirk of the symbiont's condition..."Independent?"

"Yes," Lin replied, removing her hand out of Sarah's.

The girl stared. "You are not like me."

"No, I'm not. Haven't been for a long time."

Sarah thought about it. She wanted to know more, but no questions popped to the surface. Everything was a numb spiral.

"I've closed the windows and blinds," Lin instructed. "I'll need them that way. I am light sensitive. It can cause blindness and paralysis, and death with prolonged exposure. I am by no means keeping you here. Though, if you must go out during the height of the day please make sure I'm clear of the path of light when you open the door. Okay?"

Sarah nodded, not seeming too surprised by her request. *Movies. They have their advantages.* After a time, Sarah finally asked her. "Is she dead?"

"Not in the way you think."

The girl made a smarmy face. "You know what I mean."

Lin thought about it. With Z's condition it was just so hard to tell. "I don't know."

Sarah grabbed Lin's hand again and begged her toward her with a pull. Lin crouched down between Sarah's legs as the girl brushed her raven's nest out of her face. The vampire had to admit it, her touch felt good. *Soothing.* Beyond the incessant need of the epochal creature Sarah's tenderness was intoxicating.

"What's going to happen to her?"

"I'm not sure."

Staring into the vampire's eyes, the veiny parasite was even more visible. Sarah reached out and grabbed Lin's cheek. She had an urge to touch the milky white of Lin's pupil, but restrained herself. "It's everywhere." The live girl was intrigued.

Disappointed, feeling the retched thing under her skin claw across her shoulders, Lin turned away. She was beginning to feel like an ugly fiend, broken and grotesque, but Sarah wouldn't let her go. She turned Lin's face back toward her and kissed her softly. Her lips were surprising creatures, lightly touching, seeking moist flesh. Both of the live girl's hands were caressing Lin. Famished for her embrace the vampire returned the kiss vehemently, falling into the soft gyrations of the dancer's tongue. Lin pressed into Sarah's tender form and her Jadaraa Soo moved closer to the warmth of the girl's body heat.

Lin removed Sarah's shirt, breaking apart the dark tunnel of their connected mouths and looked at her. Hungrily, Sarah's eyes lured the vampire in. Lin tore off her jacket and removed her shirt and stood as Sarah scooted backwards on the bed. The dancer looked up Lin's gorgeous gait, imperfect and pale, to the winged heart tattooed above her breasts. It had a single latched lock and keyhole in the center of it. Her right arm was a continuation of the jungle scene on her back that Sarah could only see spilling along her ribs. Her upper left arm had a Celtic band; entangled knots in a lush weave that mirrored the inked ring on her finger. Poking out from the tops of her jeans was the visage of another decorative tat curling around her belly button. It formed the heads of two dragons facing one another. Sarah longed to see the design, full and flowered. Lin was a blanched canvas superimposed with a burgundy road map that lay just below the skin. Sarah unbuckled the woman's belt and began pushing her pants to the floor.

The vampire stepped out of her boots and the wrinkled dungarees. She stood naked before the girl in everything except her underwear. Seeing them, Sarah cracked a grin and cocked her eyes at the odd, toothy woman. Hello Kitty, soft and cute, Lin was stunning. Statuesque, resplendent and a cougar ran up her leg. Sarah trailed her fingertips gently over Lin's calves and thighs, grabbing her by the waist and kissed Lin on the abdomen delicately, just above the panty line, below the open roar of the two-facing dragons. Her face was warm against Lin's belly and the vampiric veins arched toward the heat.

Sarah eased back on the bed, making room for Lin, and took off her bra. The cougar climbed on the bed too, between Sarah's legs, one massive paw reaching out, claws extended, climbing up the symbiont's body as she bowed down toward the live girl's breasts. Lin planted kisses in the valley, curled Sarah into her form, kissed her neck, and climbed to Sarah's panting mouth. The dancer was beautiful, blood pounding, body soft, yet firm from her years on stage. Lin could feel her teeth ache and the parasite panged to be satiate. It wasn't Sarah's blood that Lin craved. It wasn't even the landscape of flesh that she longed to journey across. She simply wanted to love her then, full and deep, and as true as one person could ever love another. Lin felt the silver locket pressed between them and she wanted the girl so much it made her tremble.

Sarah began to crawl out of her pants as they kissed and Lin completed the chore. Traveling across her pink field, pressing her lips along the creme-white curves of her thighs. Sarah's heat and the bloom of her sex enraptured the vampire with delight. Dizzy, Lin raised up to get some air and felt the veins on her eyeballs pulsate. Slowly, she gazed down at the willing form underneath her as she came into focus.

"You are…" Lin began, but the words seemed flat in comparison, "so beautiful."

Sarah smiled and pulled Lin's face to her waiting breasts, arching her back into the vampire's gaping mouth. Lin suckled, never breaking the skin. The pleasure of the girl was agony. Her bodily force visibly rose off her in waves as they groped each other. Pulling at entwining limbs, ardent and fiery, Lin fell back into the nape of Sarah's neck with habit. It was cradled within the pull of her luscious shoulder, and she heard the girl whisper, "I want you too."

Lin pulled back, "No!"

Sarah panted, chest heaving, a sensual snake charmer, Lin hovered over Sarah's hot torso like a cobra.

"Bite me," she urged.

"I can't," Lin moaned.

"Bite me really hard," pressed Sarah through gritted teeth, pulling on her.

The vampire's fangs ached. Her Jadaraa Soo pined and vibrated for blood, smashing images of hunts and kills from her past and the past of Ornn Däm Mu violently fled across her mind.

"I can't," Lin complained, moving away.

Sarah quaked in the cold absence, a rush of air occupying the space where Lin had been.

"Don't," begged Sarah simply. "Don't pull away from me."

Lin's face was a frown. Juxtaposed, she wanted everything the girl was offering yet feared the worse within. Sarah enveloped Lin from behind, kissing the jungle on the woman's back. Her lips climbed to Lin's shoulders and the Southwestern girl bit the vampire hard on the nape of her neck, where she had seen it done in the movies. Exquisite pain burst forth from Sarah's teeth and the parasite wiggled under her clamp. Lin's body sighed and moaned as the live girl surrounded her. She cried in wanting.

"You don't understand..." and turned to face Sarah.

"Then make me," the dancer eagerly said, planting kisses on Lin' chest, trying to pick the lock on her tattooed heart. "Make me understand."

Sarah did not wait for Lin to respond. Her fingers climbed into the Hello Kitty undies and tore them off her waist as she moved down her body. Lin spasmed with pleasure, her Jadaraa Soo humming so loudly that she could barely hear her own groans of pleasure as they escaped her lips. Sarah paused, only momentarily, to enjoy the pelvic tattoo of a tribal ram's head with horns so large and snaking that it curled around the vampire's hips in one direction and traveled up her abdomen in the other forming the broken dragon heart that surrounded the jewel of her naval. Lin was a work of art, a two hundred and fifty-six year old antique in top shape, and writhing sexy. Sarah did not hold her in her hands like a relic, instead she made love to her like a woman.

Wallace was outside the convenience store when Kate pushed through the door carrying her To-Go cup, sugar packets, creams, and stirrers. It was a cold morning, brisk. The sky was a clear blue-gray and smelled fresh. They both had been up all night. She hadn't said anything yet, but Wallace knew she was pissed. Ever since the FBI guys took over the case she'd been a clam. Steaming. For as much as he sometimes wished she'd curb her yapping the Sergeant had to admit it, he missed her cheerful banter.

He watched as she tore open the sugar packets. *Violent.* Adding more white powder than normal, she fiercely dumped two creams into the hot dark brew. She stirred it angrily and it spilled over the side and onto her hand. Kate cursed loudly and suckled the burn. The spilled coffee ignited her rage.

"I can't believe you just gave them all of our stuff like that! You didn't even say a word. Just handed it right to him like it was…it was nothing. Thought the borders didn't matter, huh?" She mocked him by imitating his demeanor and voice. "Not gonna let them get away with it on my watch." She drew her face in a scowl. "Now, they're *going* to get away with it because of jurisdictional bullshit; can't believe I followed you all the way out here for nothing."

And there it is, the rub. He looked at her with that placid stare of his, impervious and intimidating. He knew she hated that mug, which was why he did it. "You done?" he said, gauging her breath.

Words flopped around Mauldune's mouth like a fish tumbling to a close for a few seconds. For all sense and purposes she was done, at least, for now. "Yes," she yapped, dreading the long ride back to Phoenix. She intended for him to sit in the sissy seat, no more following. Kate slowed her breathing not liking his smug demeanor.

Wallace tapped himself on the forehead, his mind a vault. "They're not getting away with anything, and I'm *not* off the case."

Mauldune smiled and her eyes lit up. That was what she wanted to hear! "Good. 'Cause I've got this." She produced the torn notebook page from her pocket and held it up.

"Origami?" he teased.

"License plate," she said, overly extending each word. "Well, half of it anyway and a description of the vehicle and the other two assailants."

Wallace smiled too, chuckling softly as he took another sip of his black coffee. "Heading South, right?"

"Yeah," Mauldune proclaimed, scooping up her To-Go cup from the trashcan's lid, "South."

They both started walking toward the cruiser with a renewed spring in their stride.

"What's the half, ya got?"

Kate opened the folded pages. "E.T.R.N.L.B." She shrugged

Wallace stopped near the driver's side door and laughed, shaking his head.

"What's so funny?" Kate wanted to know, feeling left out.

"Deputy Fife," he squeezed through his grin.

"You mean, Officer Hodge?"

"Yeah," he said, laughing. It was so obvious. The cup of Joe was warm in his grip. "He said they were vampires."

Kate didn't get it and her expression said so.

"Read it again," he encouraged.

The Lieutenant read the letters to the license plate again and shook her head with as much disdain and confusion as she had the first time around.

"Eternal," Wallace informed, saying the word slowly.

Kate grimaced, not liking his glee. "Okay, smart-ass what's the 'B' stand for?"

He chuckled. "Bitch," he said curtly, drinking a gulp of coffee. "Eternal Bitch."

Kate stood still at the front of the cruiser as Wallace opened the door with purpose and climbed in. She looked back down at the license plate letters that she'd written and didn't like what it was shaping into. She didn't believe in the Supernatural. She had a tough time accepting most religions, believing in God and all that stuff. Sure, she called herself a Catholic because most everyone else did. It helped her to fit in on the force, look regular at office parties.

"Vampires?" questioned the Lieutenant with frank disgust. "Now, we're chasing vampires?" *I didn't sign up for an episode of Ghost Hunters International!*

Wallace's buoyant expression didn't waver and he tapped his melon again. "Or people who *think* they're vampires."

Kate sighed a breath of relief as she packed herself into the seat. Insane, homicidal maniacs with a fetish-type delusion were a plausible enough realty to handle. *A vampire cult!* It had headlines written all over it. She joined the detective in the car and they took off down the road in search of a vintage Cadillac with fins, baby-blue in color that had a license plate that read: *Eternal Bitch.*

It sounded like something that shouldn't be too hard to find. It should stick out like a sore thumb, that is, if they hadn't dumped it already. Kate fired up the onboard computer and drank her sugary, milky brew. A special license plate was easier to track to a registered owner than a regular one. California would have the plate listed in their database. Despite the lack of sleep banging through her body, Kate felt invigorated. On the hunt, chasing clues, this was what it was all about and she felt it. She felt it in her gut. They were onto something. Kate silently vowed that they were gonna get them before the Feds. These sicko-vampire-cult-fucks were their collar. *Just bet!*

Lin watched Sarah sleep. Nestled against her bosom, eyes closed, rhythmic breathing lapping against her side, the vampire needed to feed. What she took from Chris in the shower yesterday wasn't meant to sustain her this long. She figured she could hold out until tonight, but being around Sarah so much, with all the physical activity, was aggravating her system.

Looking down at the girl curled under her arm, Lin knew that Sarah would let her feed from her. They spoke about it after they made love while she drifted off to sleep. Lin was just as resolute about it now as she was earlier in the morning. She didn't want to break Sarah's skin, pierce that delicate trust. It wasn't about desires, or need. It was about integrity. The symbiont was absolutely sure that Sarah's blood would be more tantalizing, more encapsulating and erotic than what they had just done to each other. And Lin needed to be able to walk away.

Sarah had a life. That was paramount to Lin. A full, natural cycle. It was one of the things that she'd learned to appreciate about her human origins that she had no affection for while alive – *To live a normal life cycle*. Though small, the span of a human life was magnificent in accomplishment. That cut off point, mortality, was an ingenious design. Lin didn't want to mess with that.

Vampires had no such motivations. They were decadent and flamboyant, throwing every whim into the wind, riding high in the gutter of forever. Longevity did not improve upon their ethics. It darkened them. Lin didn't even know how long the average life span was for her kind. It varied so widely, seeming to choose at random those that outlived others. She knew symbionts that were over two thousand years old and heard tell of others who had lived near as long. While still others couldn't even handle seventy-five years as a symbiont. Most of their kind wound up killing themselves after awhile, finding it difficult to live without loved ones or unable to bear the brutality of change. Environments crushing and loud, they walked into the sun. *Slow deaths for a cowardly race.* Silently, Lin knew Dominique's Children of Evensong were godless bastards...and she was chiefly among them.

Mother Night was over eight hundred years old and considered ancient among her people. Lin never thought she'd ever reach the impressive age that she had and yet Z was already dying. One hundred and five years old and the life of Z's Jadaraa Soo was fading. *She could already be dead.* Thinking of Z, Lin rustled her position on the bed and Sarah stirred, flapping her eyes open.

"Hey, Sleepy."

Sarah stretched, "Hmmmmorning."

"More like afternoon," corrected Lin.

She rose from her nestled perch, leaning on one arm. "Been awake long?"

Lin sat up. "I don't sleep."

"Ever?" Her whole face was a wrinkled question mark.

"Not ever."

"Hhmmm?" Sarah moaned and it turned into a yawn. Climbing out of bed, "Then, how do you dream?"

Lin chuckled at the thought as Sarah closed the bathroom door behind her. Dreams were another thing sacrificed to the Omjadda blood. *No sense dreaming about things when you are your own dream.* The door popped back open and the naked girl, all scrunched up in her delicious form, tumbled back to bed.

"Oooh, it's cold out," she uttered with a shiver and snuggled next to Lin, who wasn't feeling the slightest change in temperature. "Well, you're not exactly very heat producing are you?"

"Sorry," Lin said with a smirk. "But I can still make you hot."

Sarah kissed her. "Yes you can."

It was a short kiss as she gathered the covers tightly around them both and exhaled into Lin's curves.

"Who's William?" Sarah asked, having wanted to ever since she'd read his name tattooed in the small of the vampire's back.

"My son."

Sarah sat up and looked at her. "Is he like you?"

"No," she replied. "I had him just prior to the change. He was raised by his father in Africa."

"Africa?" she blurted, surprised. "His father's black?"

Lin chuckled and Sarah immediately felt embarrassed by her blunt question. It came off rude. "Yes," the vampire announced. "He was black."

Sarah felt dazed by Lin's terse response. William didn't sound like an African name and Lin was the whitest woman she'd ever laid eyes on. It didn't add up. "Well?" she cooed, scrunching her shoulders with enthusiasm. "What happened to your son? How'd you meet his father? Do tell…"

Sarah wanted the dirt. Sitting fully erect, she gathered the covers about her exposed pink flesh, staring at the vampire. Lin rolled her head in muted acceptance, never easy with her past, repositioned, and told her how William had become a vital member of his father's community. How he had taken a wife, had several children, and stayed in Africa until his death in 1821. In the telling of William's life, Lin avoided such details that framed her son and Nsia as members of an ancient warrior tribe that fought against a prehistoric humanoid race in a never-ending war since the dawn of time. Lin kept it simple, light-hearted, and it still intrigued the girl.

"And how did you meet William's father, Nsia?" prodded Sarah.

Lin smirked, recalling. "He tried to kill me."

"What?" Sarah's eyes bulged. "Look at you with the deep, dark past."

Sarah had said it jokingly, but the gravity of truth that it supported weighed heavily between them and it sullied the room. Lin looked away and Sarah thought of Z. The events of last night still hung in the air. The locket adorning Sarah's neckline was an obvious artifact. The face of the dancer was a ghost in Lin's memory. Everything smacked the symbiont across the cheek with deep, dark past. Lin sighed and Sarah deflected, attempting to keep the mood light-hearted.

"What's this mean?" she asked, touching the weave of the tattooed arm band.

"This was the first one I got." Lin looked at the interlocking Celtic knots. "I was with Z. 1948. It's a friendship ring. She has the same thing on her ankle. In fact, I got most of these with her."

In trying to avoid the fallen vampire she'd inadvertently stepped in it. Sarah thought about it before she asked. It had been nagging her. "Were you two ever…" She failed to finish the question, feeling intrusive. "You know…"

"No," Lin flatly answered. "We were just friends."

A blossom of relief bloomed in Sarah's gut next to the other nagging, little question. "That killed people?"

Out of the mouth of the face from the photograph came the truth of it. It drove the point home like a nail through Lin's breastplate. She felt a cold cracking behind her eyes and steeled herself against all her wrongs. In the presence of the girl, the amalgamation of destiny and time, there was no getting around it. It was as if the redheaded wildcat was in the room with them now, bright and loud, stealing the thunder again as she had last night.

"Sometimes," admitted Lin, feeling the eyes of so many dead.

Sarah's relief turned to fear. "Do you always have to kill to feed?"

"No," Lin uttered. "In fact, it's quite the opposite. Our Sanglants are treated very well. We own many blood banks and are connected to hospitals throughout the world. There is no real need to hunt in order to feed." She saw Z laughing inside her mind and was surprised at how much she looked like Prophet in the desert. "Which is why we do it."

Sarah stared at Lin, feeling dejected and detached, alone with a lioness. The woman's blunt honesty dimly washed over her. She hadn't known what to expect when she asked the question, but the answer left a flat aftertaste in her mouth. She wanted to know more, but didn't know where to begin. There simply wasn't a cheesy B-movie that had prepared her for this.

"At least," Lin added, "that's why I did it. Z?" The vampire paused to reflect. "Z was different. She got off on it, I think. She liked killing."

"What's a Sanglant?"

"Blood lenders. They are employed by The Service to furnish our needs."

"Do you take from them often?"

"On occasion." Lin chewed the inside of her lip. "I've grown fond of my solitude in recent years and tend to sustain myself without their use. They have their place, though. Drawing blood from a body, any body, has its price."

Sarah scooped up Lin's left hand and silently fondled the tattooed ring on her third finger. Lin was not surprised at her loquacious tongue.

Sarah's affect put her in a bubble. She didn't feel a need to hold anything back. The girl made her want to tell her everything. For so many years the face in the photograph had held Lin's awful secrets. Now birthed by God's will in divine flesh, Lin desired to confess.

"What's this one for?"

Lin looked down at Sarah holding her hand, playing with the tattoo on her finger. "It reminds me of who I am. Of where I came from."

"Dominique?" Sarah asked, not sure if that was the woman's name that Lin had told her about.

"Actually, it's my family's crest. Pevensey. I had it redesigned into the shape of a ring back in…" Lin had to really think. "62? No. When was the Beatles?"

Sarah shrugged. Her momma used to listen to them. Lin shook her head from side to side. "Sometime in the sixties. In upstate Washington."

"Pevensey," Sarah repeated. "That's an English name."

"Yes, it is."

Sarah laughed. "You don't sound English."

"Aahh," quoted Lin, raising an index finger. "That's because you Americans have bastardized the language. Been stuck around y'all for too long."

"So, it's my fault?"

Lin raised her brows. "Yes, it is."

They laughed, playful and quick, jostling one another, falling into amorous limbs. Sarah felt a nag of hunger, not wanting to go out and get anything to eat. She felt that if she left the island of the bed that she'd never have another moment like this with Lin ever again. It was a foolish thought. An odd, fleeting thing. So greedily, she ate up the vampire's company instead of soothing her belly.

"What's with the jungle along the side?" queried Sarah as their mirth faded.

Lin rolled over so that Sarah could see the tattoo better. The live girl sat up again to look at it, crossing Lin's mid section, and placed her hand to the vibrant image that encompassed half her back. The inked tapestry was a thick jungle. Brightly colored birds were perched and flew across pale flesh, they added depth to the scene that trailed down her right arm.

"It's only half done," explained Lin. "When I crown three hundred I'll finish it. Probably with a cityscape on the opposite side." She turned to face the woman in the bed.

Three hundred? Mused Sarah internally.

"I lived in São Paulo most of my life. I got used to the jungles out there and missed it when I left." Lin shrugged. "Now, I don't have too."

The pulse of Sarah's burning palm on Lin's hip beat through her entire body and the look between them crackled of sexual tension. The vampire was almost thankful when she lifted her hand, but Sarah soon laid it against Lin's chest as she rolled over. It made the symbiont's heart flutter as her Jadaraa Soo skipped a throbbing tremor.

"And this?" The curious cat examined Lin's locked, winged heart.

"Oh, that," Lin replied with a grin. "Saved the best for last, I see."

Sarah shook her head no, "That's not the best."

Slowly, she slid her hand down the vampire's smooth body, coming to rest at the two-headed dragon heart of the tribal ram horns.

Lin eyed Sarah's fingers on her belly. "You like that one the best?"

Sarah smiled wide, thinking about last night, and lazily rolled her head from side to side. "No," she chuckled. "Don't think I could shave the whole thing myself like you do. Itches just where I shave for the thongs at work. Yikes." Sarah squeezed her legs around her crotch, thinking about it.

"Hair grows slower and no razor burn," boasted the vampire.

"Lucky you."

Am now, thought Lin. "So which one's your favorite?"

Sarah rolled over and pulled the sheet off Lin's legs. "This one."

Her hands caressed the jungle cat as it clawed up Lin's left calf. The vampire stared at the enigma of the girl's lustrous back until she moved. Climbing over the covers, the woman pounced on Lin's legs, making her smile and snicker.

"I've always been a Wildcat," Sarah admitted, referencing her high school football team's mascot and growled in the back of her throat. "Stalking prey in the deep, dark jungle."

With a menacing scowl, she started climbing up Lin on all fours. The pale, tattooed lady could scarcely contain herself. Sarah roared like the inked Cougar and Lin hollered boisterously, tingling all over. "And what? Am I *your* prey?

"The jungle and the feast," the poignant, prowling cat explained.

The irony was too rich for the vampire's blood. "I don't think so."

With that, she tackled Sarah, overturning her on the wide double bed. Sheets akimbo, covers disheveled and twisting like whirlpools, the vampire leered over the girl. Falling on top of her Lin kissed her hard, passionate, and sweet. Upside down the painted feline crawled up Sarah's side as they intertwined. Groping hands, squeezing mounds of flesh, their love came alive, and across Sarah's belly she could feel the veins of Lin's parasite writhing against her, caressing her too in their embrace. She knew what it wanted, and it terrified her that some day soon she was gonna find out what it felt like to satiate its burning thirst.

The dancer groaned and quivered as Lin leapt from her lips and traversed down her torso. She was glad to learn that she wouldn't have to kill to be a vampire, that there were other means available to survive the strange thing lurking under the skin. In studying to become a doctor Sarah had already accepted the fact that she was most likely going to kill a few people throughout her career. That knowledge never really bothered her. It was par for the course for a surgeon. Death was a part of life, and...*Oh yeah, that's it.* Life? *Damn!*

Everything that Sarah had done: Medical school. All those years at the club. The loan from Tone and Eddie. It was all to change the quality of her life. She wasn't gonna live in a trailer park at the ass end of the dustbowl anymore, like her momma. Sarah promised herself that long ago. And last night, as she sat in the Cadillac, she thought about the unlimited possibilities that were attainable by her encounter with the vampire. She knew that Lin intended to take her home, leave her in Albuquerque where she had found her from some sick moral high ground. *Like that was even possible anymore.* Sarah's body spasmed with pleasure. *Like I don't even have a say in the matter!*

Their meeting wasn't a fluke or a disruption. *How could she even think that she can get rid of me so easily?* Sarah pressed her pelvic into Lin's face. *I could study to be a doctor in the next millenium if I wanted too.* Just imagining the leaps and bounds of medical science in the years to come boggled the live girl's mind. *Shit! That feels good.* Even the woman whom she embraced, that now lapped at her treasures, exploding her body with delight was the Shangri-fucking-La of medical science. How Lin ever thought that Sarah was going to let her walk away from her was beyond comprehension. *It was...it was...* "Ahng. Ahng." She panted heavily... *Stupid.*

Bad
Penny

1930. Chicago.

A moldy earthen stink, a rotting flesh and sewage stink assaulted the recently widowed Mrs. Boyd in the dark, damp tunnels. A roving triangle of three vampires led her through a winding passage under Rosehill Cemetery. She could barely see anything through the plush darkness surrounding them. Several times Zia almost lost her footing on the uneven bricks of the dank, cobblestone floor. With each scuff that nearly sent her crashing, the bloodied ghostly specter of Emily Rosenthal grinned and laughed, filling the eerie catacombs with a shrill twittering cackle.

Benjamin Douglas Raines flanked her on the right. He barely spoke, but she could feel his presence, a hulking mass. He was dressed casually in a worn, modern suit. The elbows of his jacket were threadbare. He had a deep voice, learned manners, and a politeness that belied his veiny, ashen complexion and sharp teeth. The crazy Southern-fried cracker led point. He still wore his coat of arms, the faded glory from the War Between the States, and claimed to be a Lieutenant with the fighting Virginia Seventh under Brigadier General Turner Ashby. Zia had fallen against the confederate man more than once due to the uneven passage.

The feel of his hands that kept her from hitting the ground was repulsive. Zia didn't want his help. She didn't want anything to do with him or his band of freaks. Slamming against the old, inlaid bricks, scraping a knee or two would at least allow her to feel something. Something other than this numb thickness that pounded against her.

Simon Ray's blood still dotted her face. The sound from the single shot that she sent ripping through his skull from his revolver echoed in her head. *He's dead.* It was all Zia Jean could think about. Simon Ray lying there on the dirty floor of the Grande Hotel with that lone bullet hole dotting his forehead. It reminded her of an article that she had recently read in the Indianapolis Star about some little Indian man who was marching to the ocean to make salt. There was a picture of him. He had a dot on his forehead too. But he was smiling. *How the fuck is he going to make salt from the ocean?* Simon Ray wasn't smiling when they left him there on the floor, blood pooling behind his head. The dot looked so tiny, so insignificant for the magnitude of change that it had caused.

He had made her kill him. The Lieutenant with his soft southern accent and devilish grin presented Zia Jean with a simple proposition: *kill your husband and you live, don't and you both shall die.* Nothing seemed to make any sense anymore. The world had turned topsy-turvy. Ghoulish fiends fed off the dead, claiming to live well past their years of apparent age, and had bleached faces with tiny veins running under their skins that moved of its own accord; a man making salt from the ocean was headline news, and Simon Ray was dead. The widow's senses had come undone.

Eventually, the odd party came to a large room, deep under the graves of the cemetery. Several massive brick arches reached up high into the darkened ceiling, relics left over from before the great fire. Candelabras hung down from pitch black, connected to rope pulleys that were tied off to hooks mounted somewhere in the walls. Other faces that the frightened former Mrs. Boyd had never seen before unfolded from the darkness – *white as angels wings, evil and damned.* Conversations and music swirled in the air around her. More candles were alight along the back walls and sloping floors. There were couches strewn about and tapestries tapered down from the invisible dark. She wasn't kept in that antique room long.

Lieutenant Cross led her away. Taking her gently by the arm, he coached her through another series of bending tunnels. His hand felt cold and callous, finally lifting when they came to a smaller, unlit room. Zia heard a door close behind her and the vampire began to light the room with candles. In the flickering light the widow saw a writing desk with papers strewn atop it and an inkwell with quills. A couple sofas, a wardrobe cabinet, bed, chairs, stacks of books, and an old riding saddle on a headless wooden horse furnished the room. Dust touched many places except for the damp, black bricks, dangling moss, and the polished leather saddle.

"Here," cooed his soothing voice, but she merely stared off into the blank distance. "Allow me to unburden you of your possession so that we might make ourselves more comfortable."

The southern gentleman tried to remove the leather satchel from Zia's grip. She'd been clutching it tightly to her chest since they left the ruins of the hotel. Her eyes flicked toward him, angry and full of hate. "This is mine."

"Of course it is," he cooed. "I am merely suggesting that you relieve yourself of it momentarily." He tugged on it again and begrudgingly she let it go.

"I am setting it here." He made a show of placing it on a stack of papers on his desk. "You may retrieve it at your leisure." He wandered over to her again and looked at her "My," he chuckled softly. "You are a mess."

Zia followed him with her eyes as he crossed to a cistern on a stand and poured water into it from a ceramic jug. "What's going to happen to my car?"

Franklin Cross smirked. His back was to the woman. He dipped a cloth in the water and rung it out several times. "One of my people will collect it and it will be sold or broken down into parts. It is the only way to insure that there is no connection between it and your late husband, I'm afraid."

Turning, he discerned the woman's expression: Face tight, eyes down, she was not happy with it.

"What of my things?" she eventually asked as he neared.

The Lieutenant paused. "I will have them delivered to you, here."

Zia stared at the man. He could have been handsome once. He had a nicely cut face, soulful eyes, a short crop of dark walnut hair, and sideburns that ran too long. His glance was blank and inspecting, as if he were looking at Zia under glass. It made her uncomfortable.

"Thanks," she quietly uttered because it felt like it was what he wanted her to say.

He smiled, toothlessly. "You are most welcomed. I want you to be comfortable here. This is your home now."

A shiver raced up Zia's spine. *This dank earthen tomb is to be my… what?* She ground her back teeth agitatedly and heard the gun going off in her memory. All was lost. Cross swiped the wet cloth across Zia's cheek and it took all she had of her limited control not to flinch, not to shake with utter disgust.

The vampire appeared delighted at cleaning Simon Ray's splattered blood spray off her face and told her how he'd come to Chicago with Benjamin Raines and a few others shortly after the great fire. How they'd found this place and made it their home. He told her that the coven numbered fourteen. Though he alluded to its size being more at another point in time. He spoke each of their fourteen names to her and claimed that they alone were the last known frontier of true freedom in the world; everything else had been consumed by governments, men, and something he called The Council.

He bid her to undress so that he could finish what he'd started. His request, though polite in tone, was indignant to the widow. He forced her hand to kill the man she loved. He wrecked both of their lives and now wanted her naked and bare for the glory of his eyes and hands so that he might wash her? Bloody water dripped into the cistern as Cross rung out the cloth. It echoed through the sparse room, bouncing off dark algae-coated bricks that fit like nasty teeth into the thick dirt wall.

Slowly, she began to undress.

Again, Zia Jean did not seem to have much of a choice in the matter. She was surrounded by revenant killers under a smelly cemetery and completely unsure as to how to navigate her way out of the place. For the time being, at least, she needed to rely on the confederate soldier and couldn't afford to upset him.

He did not stare unduly at the naked Mrs. Boyd. He found her attractive, beautiful even, but was utterly a gentleman as he slowly ran the wet cloth over her plum, pink flesh. Zia was cold under the earth. She followed his movements with her eyes and held firm, standing sublimely in the room. When he had finished, she bent to retrieve her clothing, but he suggested that she remain as she was.

Zia envisioned the rape that was to follow. Soiled in the blood of her husband, this polite beast meant to lay her down and claim her in such vile carnality. Her gut twisted, her heart sank to the floor, and she became even more accessible to the frigid air than she was before, so she wrapped her arms around herself. Franklin rinsed the cloth out, hung it on a small wooden rod on the cistern's stand and, turning, crossed to the frightened woman.

"Do not be afraid," he told her allowing his eyes to finally and fully drink her in.

Tall, svelte, ample breasts, and child baring hips. The woman had a gorgeous face and strong shoulders. He liked what he saw and how she smelled. Despite all her fears she still remained definite, yet willing before him. The juxtaposition titillated his unique senses.

"I am going to bite you." He explained as he crossed to her and laid his hand in the small of her back, embracing her nakedness.

Zia Jean was confused, trembling. His proximity repulsed her, but she held firm against his cold fingers.

"I am going to bite you…here." He touched her neck. "I will

drink of your blood and by so doing you will sustain me." He searched her terrified face for any hint of flight or violent reproach. "Other than a sharp prick when my teeth enter into you there shall be no other pain. You might even come to find pleasure in it.

"I discourage you to look upon this act as a disgrace to your person. I will not defile you. You are precious to me beyond measure, but you belong to me. This is how it will be for us for awhile." He paused for effect, leering deeply into the widow's honey brown eyes. "I will educate you on how to live among us and in time, you will *be* one of us."

Zia did not speak. She didn't know what to say. Words were just frail, inaccurate little things. Every muscle fired in her skin to runaway. To run far, far away, to punch the man and flee. She knew that was what he expected, probably wanted. She was terrified. But not of him. *Not of him!* Too many changes too fast, she couldn't keep up. She kept his eager stare and waited for his villainy to be done. Silently, she vowed to kill him one day and make him pay for what he'd done to Simon Ray and all that he was going to do to her.

The Lieutenant bent his head into the crux of Zia's throat and her neck swallowed him. She felt a sharp snap of skin and quivered in his arms. Her knees went weak, but she would not fall. *Damn you! I will not crumble at your feet.*

The vampire drank heavily of her vital, red life. Draining her to the point of unconsciousness, Zia fell into his waiting arms and he carried her to his bed. Gently laying her down, the eccentric soldier covered her up with the blankets on the cot. When he was sure she slept comfortably, chest rising in a soft, steady rhythm, he gathered up her sullied clothes, rich in the stench of her husband's death, and tossed them into one of the fires that were burning throughout the catacombs.

He felt warm and excited with the obstinate woman's blood coursing through his Jadaraa Soo. She aroused his spirit with rushing life, a kindness that he had not felt since his days in the Calvary. The woman was supreme. He held her scent close to him, bound with zeal, and simply could not wait for her to wake up so that he could begin her education and taste her once more. She was a rare flower of ethereal appeal sent by all the gods of war for his delight. *A kindred soul whose heart beats close to mine!*

The scent of fresh blood pumping through veins woke Z up.

Her instincts told her not to move. The sweat of a man, an older man. Cigarettes. Fast food. Motel soap. He was leaning over her. He was close. There were two others. One was a female and the other was a younger man, bad cologne, wore Doctor Scholl's shoe inserts that kept odor down and increased his height by a quarter of an inch. She could smell the gun oil and knew instantly that they were cops.

Slowly, the audio of the room came alive around her in a visual swell and hot searing pain. Her face was alight like fire and she couldn't remember why or how it would feel such a way. All she knew was that she had to remain still. People were everywhere, talking. It was a humus mixture of smells. She was in danger and hurt.

She felt them lay a cloth over her as they walked away. She opened her eyes and listened. She couldn't see anything through the darkened matter. Straining to isolate conversations so that she could figure out what was going on, she got a pretty clear picture of what had happened: Three of them came into the bar and she'd attacked two customers until some guy named Slim, Z guessed correctly that he was the owner of the bar, shot her a couple of times with a shotgun, and the other ones fled. *Other ones? Who could I have been with who would have…*

Lin?

The name surfaced from the mangled din of her pellet-shot memory. She instantly saw the woman's face and relived moments of their history together. *Lin left me behind?* That seemed incredible based on what she could recall. They seemed so close and had done so many outrageous things together.

Slowly, Z lifted the edge of the cloth and peered through the gap. Her vision was crap. Only one eye worked properly. Bizarre images of hunting and feasting ran through her head in a twisted, violent rush and it took the symbiont a few moments to remember that it was how the parasite communicated its needs. She wasn't normal. The word 'vampire' careened through her head on silky ephemeral fingers and it made sense that she was one. She had to get out of here and find something to eat. The pain was too intense to remain dormant and prone on the floor for much longer.

Then another voice rose above the clatter and everyone fell silent. Only his voice cut through the room. Z instantly hated his scent. It wasn't right and there were others with him that had the same irregular smell. Z was afraid of him and the people he was with. She didn't know why. She just knew that they were dangerous and the sooner she got out of there the better. For some reason she felt her abnormal life was in peril if she hung around.

Z waited for the others, who smelled like the loud man, to start moving through the room. They created a stir. They upset the awkward balance of the place, causing a distraction, and it seemed like this was her best and only chance. Though, just as she was about to flee from underneath the sheet and head toward the back of the bar to a door that she recalled being there, the loud man's cell phone rang and the voice on the other end of the line caught her attention. Z knew who it was. Despite the compression of the tiny cell phone speaker, the timbre of the voice pulled another name from the cold din of memory.

Dominique.

Automatically, Z remembered hating her. She pictured the face of the woman that went with the voice and bitter rancor bit her agony-strewn gut. Images of her and Lin laughing at the Persian specter passed across her mind, and she recalled Lin in the woman's arms. *Was that why she ran away and left me here?* More memories assaulted her: *Vast tracts of forest and running a wild beast down through a thicket of broad leaves; and engorging on the intestines of the captured animal's belly.* It was either now or never. The shuffling distraction was nearing its end.

Z slipped from under the sheet, a flicker of movement. She rounded the bar, went through a backroom and spilled out of the backdoor. She tossed a backward glance at the little dark shack, aglow with red and blue lights from police cars at the front of the building. She ran a few steps, then decided against fleeing into the darkened woods and crept around toward the front of the lonely bar, thinking to steal a vehicle or perhaps hideaway in one. Awkwardly, she caught that strange, familiar scent again and spied two more people milling about outside with the other regular humans. Then Z saw the loud man who had been talking on the phone to Dominique. He walked straight up to the strange smelling bunch. One was black, the other white, and they were all dressed in the same bland, standard business suits. No flare. Simple cuts. He called them both Johnson and Jonston.

"The package is gone," she heard the loud man say. "Get her scent and track her down. I want results."

So, am I the package?

Fear, gnarled and curling, pulled at every fiber of Z's muscles to get moving. Something about them scared her deeply and as far as she could remember, which was like staring through a block of Swiss Cheese, she didn't scare to easily. Car or not, she had to get the hell out of here!

As the plain dressed agents wandered back inside Z snuck across the moonlit road and disappeared into the forest. She smelled cider and pine, juniper and sage, and knew that she was heading up a sloping mountain. She walked until her instincts told her that it was safe for her to run, and then she ran. She ran hard and fast. A full, round moon beat down on her. She wasn't sure why she felt that she should be running. She didn't even have a clue as to where she was going. She just knew that she had to put as much distance between her and those strange smelling police as possible. Something about them wasn't right and she had no intention of finding out what it was. She had to find Lin. That much was clear.

Lin left me behind. I gotta know why.

1930. Chicago.

Zia woke. Disoriented at first, she forgot where she was and began to climb out of bed before she realized her nakedness. Pulling the unfamiliar bed sheets around her, she saw Cross sitting in a rocking chair reading a book. He turned to her as she stirred. Sparse candlelight lit the room and the man wore an antique set of bifocals. The woman regarded him momentarily, recalled his bite, and raised a hand to her throat to feel the wound where his teeth had punctured her. Zia could feel no marks.

"Our saliva," he said, closing the book in his lap, seeing the unasked question splayed across her face, "has regenerative qualities. The bite, though painful at first, only takes a day to heal."

Her expression continued to be disconcerted and wondering. "You've been asleep nearly three days."

Time washed over her and she looked about, avoiding his stare. "I'd like to get dressed."

"Of course," he said, removing his eyewear and setting them down. He stood and indicated her trunks from the car. "I've taken the liberty of having your possessions brought here. Until we can better accommodate you and get you acclimated to our procedures this room will act as your own." He stepped toward her and pointed at a folded stack of clothes by the bed. "I've laid out some things. But do dress how you see fit. Once you are attired we will dine."

"Do you mean to bite me again?"

The wily lieutenant grinned. "Not just yet. First you must eat. Replenish yourself. We all have sins of the flesh to attend too."

With that, he excused himself, closing the double wooden doors. Zia was alone. It was the first time in a long time that she could remember being alone. Before Chicago she was with Simon Ray and since blundering into the derelict hotel she'd been stuck with the crazy confederate soldier. She climbed out of bed and stood. The cobblestone floor was cold on her bare feet; the air brisk on her thighs. She flipped through the stack of clothes that Cross had chosen for her to wear. None of them were hers. Cute, but not hers.

She looked around, eyes tuning to the dark. More things stood out from her recollections of the other night. Spying a mirror, she went to it and pulled her hair back, surveying the curve of her neck where his mouth had been. But she could not see any sign that he'd bitten her and drank her blood. It was incredible to believe and she wondered if it was his bite that had caused her to sleep so long. Though, upon reflection with the bank job, the stress of the getaway, and Simon Ray's death, even without the sting of his teeth she knew that given half a chance she'd spend a week in bed sleeping.

Zia crossed to her trunks, pulled out some clothes, and got dressed. She checked the hidden compartments, but her guns were gone. Noticing a dust covered stack of newspapers she investigated and found them going as far back as 1888. The man was a collector. Books lined the floor, some were piled thigh high. She found a couple street signs thick with sooty dust. Zia sauntered to the rocker and picked up the hardbound edition he had been reading when she woke. *Ulysses*, by James Joyce. The double doors popped opened and Cross entered the room. Zia set the book back down.

"Good. I see you are dressed."

"Yes. Thank you for bringing my things."

He shut the doors with an arrogant smirk. "You must not thank me unless you mean it. I know you are upset and quite confused. But I would never ask you to act in any manner that is contrary to your disposition."

"Well, in that case," blurted the woman as she crossed her arms over her chest. "I'd like to get the hell outta here."

The man tipped his head as he moved through the room. "I am afraid that is the one thing that I can not allow just yet."

"Figured as much."

"You have seen us." His kindly smile belied the threat he sought to mask. "Therefore it is unwise to let you leave." He paused as he came to rest next to the rocking chair, close to the strumming heat and pumping heart of the live girl. "I have the welfare of my family to think of."

His presence made her uncomfortable and she moved away. He picked up the copy of Ulysses. "Have you read it?"

"I don't like to read."

"Deplorable," he judged. "Your generation so ripe with capital and industry appears to have abandoned self education for vain pursuits. A man's library is a measure of his mind." He held the book up as a symbol of his statement. "I first came across Joyce's stories in The Little Review in 1918 and consider it a great honor to revisit it in its singular bound form."

"Whooped-di-do." Zia flatly uttered with the shrug of her shoulders.

The cavalryman grinned wide, barring his sharp canine teeth. "There is the spark I remember." He slapped the back of the book against his hand, sending a loud echo through the room, and laid it back onto the seat of the rocker. With a zing in his step he crossed to a stack of books and began searching for one in particular. "If you are to be my guest—"

"Don't you mean prisoner?"

He stopped and looked at her, his expression blank and hard. He'd asked for the horns of the bull and Zia had every intention of sharpening their points.

"If you insist." He returned to his search in silence, and having found the book he crossed to the disgruntled girl.

"Anderson's Winesburg, Ohio. I think that is the best place to start. It is a collection of short stories. I found some of them most intriguing. Topics of loneliness and frustration and the repressed emotions of inarticulate people. I think it would suit you."

He held the book out for her, but she did not take it. She looked down at it and at the man holding it, and felt the raw gnaw of a stomach that had not eaten in three days. Finally, she snatched the book. "I'm not promisin' nothin'."

"Promises are but the vain utterances of the hopeful," he said charging away from her to the wide double doors. "And as you have so clearly illustrated, we here are without hope." He threw the doors open and said, "Come."

Zia stared down at the painted cover, a nighttime scene of an empty Ohio street. She'd seen many places like that on her travels across America. Some were more desolate than others, but they were all empty, all quiet save from the peerless spectrum of stars. The feel of the book in her hands and the smell of its musty pallor tugged at her rambling soul, and she hated the man even more because of it. *I've flipped speakeasies, fast cars, jazz, and fifty-cent gin for a dead Civil War lieutenant's long-winded speeches and dusty old books. God, please kill me now.*

She set the book down on the pile of clothes that her pale, bloodsucking host had laid out and followed him to where he had prepared a meal. It was noting fancy. Two stewed potatoes, a roasted flank, and some greens. Zia ate it all and afterwards he showed her where she could fix her own meals. It was nothing more than a hot plate on a wood stove and an old icebox in a small alcove. But it would do.

He encouraged her to eat healthily, as his bites would often leave her body wanting for nutrients while it healed, replenishing its vital stock. Cross joined her for every meal during those initial days, and Zia learned that he and his kind did not eat. It wasn't that they couldn't consume human food if they chose. There were ways of making it work. It was just that all they truly required to sustain themselves was a little blood.

The lair under Rosehill Cemetery was not set up with the modern conveniences that she'd become accustomed to. A bucket and tissues in a secluded wing of a North-East tunnel was left for Zia's privy duties, and Cross had to show her several times where to dispose of full buckets, as she often got lost in winding tunnels. In this regard, Zia envied the night creature. Never to suffer the humiliation of pooping in a bucket and wiping one's own bottom in the dark, or pissing like a racehorse and having it splash up one's thigh. *Ugh!* These were just a few human affinities that she could live without.

At first, Cross only allowed Zia to wander around the lair in his company. Though after some well-crafted nagging, he allowed her out of his sight for an hour or two a day and she did not come across any of the inhabitants of the coven. Zia found this rather odd. He'd introduced her to several members of his gang and she hadn't even found the other two vampires that had brought her here. *Perhaps the place is abandoned.* Cross assured her that everyone was still there, that they could see her even if she could not see them. She didn't like that. It made her nervous – eyes peering at her from the dark.

He told her that they were purposely avoiding her because she was his. Zia didn't like the sound of that. She was no man's property. Even her husband knew better than to think along such ignorant, masculine lines. She made a big show of it, yelling at the top of her lungs, storming on the conditions of women today, and demanded her independence or at least another room away from him. All this, of course, the southern lieutenant found humorous. His laughter only spurned Zia to even more fury and vocal indignation. Eventually, she calmed and he explained that it was not so much about her being his property, than it was that she possessed his scent. The widow did not understand.

"I have marked you," he spelled out. "Our senses are most acute. The saliva we produce does not just aid you in healing from the bite. It also produces a distinct marker that is unique to the carrier from which it came. My people know this and because I have not told them otherwise they have avoided you altogether."

"Then I'm to just remain down here with you forever, is that it? While you continue to stick me like a pig."

Zia was hot. Nostrils flaring, she was caged and unnerved from weeks without even a hint of the sun or another soul except the tenacious bastard who appeared at every dark turn of the tunnel. Zia fumed. He dined with her, but did not eat. He drank from her ceaselessly and made her kill her husband. He was everywhere and all she'd come to know since that unforgettable night. He was like a bad penny that popped up at all the wrong times. She couldn't get away from him. Cross stood, and placing a hand to his chest, bowed and apologized.

"Forgive me. I did not think about your isolation. I will move to correct it henceforth. We are naturally shy and avoid people." He moved his hand in an oval around his face. "Our countenance can sometimes be disturbing, so we keep to ourselves. I did not mean any harm. I only meant to keep you safe."

From a down-turned brow and a twisted up chin Zia regarded the gentleman. He tried so hard to please her, but she did not make it easy. Over the past weeks his politeness and frank demeanor ingratiated itself upon her and she found herself, on several occasions, thinking kindly about him. She hated that.

"Thank you," she softly uttered, and it was the first time that she actually meant it.

Zia looked down at her hands – fidgeting in the lap of her dress. An odd thought tugged at her mind. She sighed as her anger ebbed away, asking, "How come you wear glasses? I always see you with them on. If your senses are so much better than mine then why do you wear them?"

A sheepish grin bashfully swept his face. "That, I'm afraid, is one of my more obvious human ticks. There are others. But…I'd grown accustomed to wearing them in my life and well…" He looked at his shoes, almost ashamed. "I guess I've just grown used to having them on."

At times the man was like a boy, enthusiastic and discovering the world as if it was all brand new and spit-polished. Other times he seemed old and tired, worn so thin that Zia feared some hidden outburst. He'd made room for her in his damp little cell. It would be nice if it weren't for the fact that she was his prize, his pupil, and his blood sack. He kept her stowed away from the rest of Chicago, from the rest of his coven, and she felt cooped up, buried.

All those bright lights and beepop, motor cars, and factories danced above her head. She wanted to get out. She needed to get out; see the sights, feel the glow of a streetlight on her skin, at least. So, she began asking Cross with increased frequency about going above, but he only replied that she wasn't yet ready. Zia knew he thought she'd run and he was right, she would have. She'd run straight into the arms of a Copper if she thought it'd give her a single minute away from him. Her desire for freedom burned, but she could not be trusted, and thus sadly, withheld the key to her own freedom.

In her isolation she eventually picked up the book that Cross had given her. At first, Zia found it difficult to sit still and read. She was antsy and restless at being locked away from the rest of the world. Though, as each page described with wondrous detail that imaginary place between the lines, she was transported to where she could not yet go. Above ground. Outside. Cross called his little band the last true outpost of freedom. Yet, to Zia Jean it was simply a tomb that she could not break. Her only solace, her only escape, was now found in the passages of some else's pen.

A day or so after Cross's huge apology, time seemed displaced, an impractical invention under the cemetery, Zia went for a walk. She found a room, much in the same size and manner of the opening that she noticed on her first night. Though, she had yet to find that particular spacious hollow again. This room too had curving arches made of brick, candelabras, and hanging tapestries. There were more tree roots and moss visible hanging from the ceiling in this room than what she remembered in the other one. She also noticed the remnants of old, dirty caskets poking out of the ground, pushing the stacked bricks out of place around the worn paths and lived-in areas. It was all rather macabre.

Zia found the man with the baritone voice from her inaugural night at the hotel playing chess alone in the room. Upon seeing her, he stood and bowed, just as he did on their initial meeting and introduced himself again, though there was no need of it. She remembered him. She returned his greeting and introduced herself, having recalled never doing so before. Though, instead of providing the hulking vampire with her formal name she merely labeled herself with the letter Z. Benjamin Douglas Raines found her moniker amusing and assured the young woman that he would call her that from then on.

He invited her to sit with him and she did. After so long without any other face but Cross to stare at, any company seemed pleasing. As it turned out Benjamin was an educated man born in the hey-day of Chi-Town when it was the Midwest hub of transportation between the original states and the untamed territories of the West. His family had been one of prominence and political position on the city council. Because of a disagreement with his father over the young man joining the Union Army to fight in the war between the North and South, instead of staying at home to work the family business, he was disowned.

"Did you meet Cross in the war?"

The vampire chuckled with a fond smirk. "We had, on occasion, met several times during the Valley Campaigns." He moved his bishop across the board, taking out one of his rooks.

"You fought against one another?" the young widow interestedly asked.

The vampire pulled the side of his right ear down to show Z a missing half-moon piece of flesh. "It was his musket ball that nearly took my head off."

"Then how did you..." Z stared agog at him, failing to piece together the small string of events that had shaped two foes into friends.

"We shared a common enemy."

He moved the white queen into position as Z waited for him to continue his explanation. But he didn't. Instead, he moved the black knight and a white pawn and then a—

"What enemy is that?" she finally asked.

Benjamin Douglas Raines looked at her and smiled, a pleasant grin with a blank vault-like upturn of the cheeks, as he toppled the white queen. "Cross will tell when he is ready for you to know."
A small puff of anger flared in Zia – *so many questions, too many tight lips.* He was the only person, besides Cross that she'd seen in weeks and she still couldn't do anything more than scratch the surface of this strange abode. She tilted her head to vent her persisting irritation and noticed that they were being watched.
Sitting on one of the caskets, high up, toward the back of the room was a woman. She was dressed in a long dark green gown, pale skin so white that she practically glowed, and she had the blackest hair. She was staring at them, completely quiet, a fixture among the rotting brick, and Zia was absolutely sure that she was not there when she had sat down with the tall vampire. Benjamin Douglas Raines followed Z's eyesight to where it had stolen her attention.
"That my dear, is Selina. Selina Pillar." He moved another piece for the coupe de grace. "I would avoid her if I were you."

"Why?"

"Let's just say that she and Cross are...working things out." Checkmate. The vampire began re-staging the board and he pointed behind her. "That is Perceval Jones and I believe you've met Gavin Peshawal."

Z turned to the two vampires and they both greeted her with a nod as they passed her by. Zia returned the polite, slight bow of the head. She recalled Cross introducing her to Gavin a few days after she'd arrived.

He had seemed pleasant then, sandy blond hair with a mustache and the hint of a beard on his chin. He measured as tall as she did. The new face though was as pale as everyone else under this plot of earth, but looked as if it belonged to a black man. He had a broad, flat nose, big lips, and nappy hair. He glared at her and Z became uncomfortable.

"Do you play?" the refined vampire asked after putting the last piece in place.

Zia turned around and immediately was taken by two more coven members strolling, arm and arm, through the room. Weeks with nothing and nobody but Cross and suddenly they were everywhere. She recalled their names: *Tyler Delgado and Alayna Paige*. Cross pointed them out once from across a room during the first few days after she had arrived. They bid Benjamin and the live girl hello as they passed. Z and the tall man both replied politely. Her voice seemed soft and meek against the deep resonance that emanated from Benjamin's chest. "Do you play?"

"Huh?" uttered Z, whipping her head around after watching the departure of the two vampires.

"Chess." He pointed at the board between them. "Do you play?"

"Ahh? No."

"Great," he said, beaming with energy. "You shall learn."

Benjamin Douglas Raines explained the game to her and she did her best to comprehend it. But she was more concerned with the constant stare from Selina Pillar and found herself, many times, keeping her eye on her instead of the board. *So, she was Cross's lover.* Worry crept into the widow's brow and she felt exactly like she was – *The New Girl.* It didn't matter that she despised Cross and was here against her will. She was here and that was enough. His attention, whether Zia wanted it or not, was given to her and not to the vampire throwing daggers with her eyes.

Z noted how pretty she was from afar and was positive that the vampire was even more beautiful up close. Zia had no intention of finding out. She was, as Mr. Raines suggested, going to avoid her, at all costs. The last thing she wanted now was to get into a turf war over the asshole that had forced her to murder her husband.

"Where has everybody been?" Z asked once they'd started to play her first game of chess.

"Around," replied the tight-lipped gamer as he corrected Z's movement of the knight.

She remained there with Benjamin Douglas Raines learning the game until Cross came to collect her, and by that time, Selina was gone. From then on Zia meet with the old Union officer daily for the game of pieces. Zia never truly took to it, but found Benjamin's company incredibly enjoyable. Eventually, she loosened his tongue a little and learned a few things that only sparked greater interest.

He was the one that found their present location under the cemetery. He knew about it from early city planning maps that his father had prior to the great fire of 1871. When Z asked why he wasn't the leader of their little band of freaks, the gentleman simply replied that Cross outranked him. But he never stated his military badge of office. Z didn't press the matter. Having learned a little of the man she knew he would tell her when the mood struck and that, unlike the damnable Mr. Cross, Benjamin did not need to comfort himself in the vanity of his past.

She learned that he had also lost his entire family in the Chicago fire and would have returned sooner to his place of birth had he and Cross not otherwise been engaged in Charleston, South Carolina and New York City. Again, he did not provide the details of these engagements. Though, Zia did glean that Cross was only recently made the coven's leader. Another vampire, Armande Francis Bellecourt, was the original head honcho and that, until recently, their numbers toppled thirty.

Benjamin told her that when news reached other covens about how they had not joined with The Council many like-minded followers abandoned their old haunts, flocking to them. He explained to her what The Council was and Zia was shocked at how organized and vast the secret society was. When she questioned him as to what happened to the rest of their ilk and how the confederate man was put in charge, all the old Union soldier would tell her was that she should ask Cross. The Lieutenant, it seemed, kept a tight ship where all roads led back to him. His presence, even in his absence, was suffocating.

But despite the funneling of information to a single source, Z did ask Cross about how he came to his seat of power. At first she thought he wasn't going to tell her. He went quiet and pensive for the longest time before he opened up, and his explanation took several hours. When it was all said and done, she didn't believe it. She couldn't believe it. Despite everything that she had seen up to this point it was too farfetched, too extreme in the molds of the earth and the history she knew for her to grasp. So she went to Benjamin for confirmation of Cross's strange and sordid tale.

Benjamin not only confirmed what Cross had told her, he showed her proof as well. It was only a few years ago, the stain of the attack still permeated throughout the coven, when a group of creatures known as Omjaddas invaded the crypts. Z was overwhelmed to learn of their existence working behind the mantle of human history, and that they were the cause of the vampire affliction.

The Council, under an alliance with the ancient clan, Dalam Kha'Shiya, orchestrated a hit on the Chicago coven that killed most of their members, including their leader, and had propelled Cross to the unfortunate position of power. A young Omjadda named Kaleva Mir led the assault with two other kindred warriors, laying waste to the nocturnal horde. Benjamin recounted his fight with the swordsman and showed Z his scar, which spanned across the breadth of his chest.

"I thought y'all could heal?" stated the widow as a question as she pulled her hand away from the rough wound.

"He nearly splayed me in half," replied the decent hybrid. "I've been healing ever since."

The gravity of it pulled at Z's mind. To suffer for two years, broken and mangled. It was nightmarish to consider. "It's a miracle you survived."

"No miracle," he said casually, moving a pawn from the outside. "Just good tactical training. Cross devised an excellent defense and we pushed them back. Besides, I don't think they meant to exterminate everyone."

"What makes you say that?" Z asked, as she swept his pawn off the board.

"When I was down, trying to keep my guts together, I heard Kavela Mir tell his companions to thin us out. That we were growing like weeds."

"Jesus." Z stared at the vampire in awe. "There were only three of them?"

"Yes." He moved his queen across the board.

"And how many did they kill?"

"Eighteen of us. Would have been more had Cross not led the charge."

A shiver raced up the widow's spine. It was hard to imagine anyone being able to decimate so many vampires with so few. It occurred to Zia that while the coven was fighting for its life she and Simon Ray were robbing banks in Jacksonville Florida and getting pinched in Georgia for a petty grocery heist. It was disturbing to think about. So many lives spiraling through the void, though different than hers, were overturned by war and violence while the world moved on with its own concerns, none the wiser.

"What makes you think it was The Council instead of a lone attack?"

Benjamin Douglas Raines removed Z's bishop with his queen in a decisive action that she'd completely overlooked. "In all this time, there have been no other attacks on any other covens but our own. The Council has alliances with all Omjadda J'ins. The Dalam Kha'Shiya was the last to recognize their authority. Our persistence to retain sovereignty is a natural thorn in both of their sides. To the Shiya we are nothing but weeds growing unruly in their garden. To The Council we remain the last vestige of what they can not control."

Z stared down at the unfinished board, head swooning. She could not complete the game, so she excused herself, returning to the quarters she shared with the man that had saved his people. Cross was not in and she found solace in the book he'd given her. *So much to swallow, so much to take in.* She was numb. Nothing in the whole of the world was how she imagined it to be. *It's a strange frontier.* Her lust for fast times and cash seemed ridiculous and moronic under the wide glow of so many revelations.

Simon Ray used to bitch about the federal government all the time, how they never came clean in the elections, trying to steal all the ideals the country was founded on. But this was beyond all of that. This was…*huge.* The only way she could even begin to take what she was shown and make it a part of her was to get pissed at what The Council had done. Anger was an energy. It made her whole; it made her feel real again.

Even Cross did not appear so vain as she had supposed. He was a reluctant leader, doing the best he could in a world that shunned them all. A world that existed under the surface, between a more brutal truth, that if exposed would rain down death and destruction on the foolish machinations of her kind. Suddenly, Z felt softer to the crazy confederate. In an odd way she understood the vampires' resistance to

The Council at the cost of everything, willing to fight, tooth and claw, never surrendering to the capital machine. *Liberty bound in blood. Staking out a claim, in savage lands, on their own terms.* It was what she and Simon Ray had always done, why they robbed banks.

Zia sighed at her disillusionment undone and felt a strange thing indeed. Acceptance. It was quiet and small, something that she would give a different name to, but it was there all the same. She'd finally accepted her fate under the cemetery. Thinking it unwanted, she would've denied it if asked, but little Zia Jean had found a home.

Dawn was never far away. Every second of every day it was somebody's dusk, somebody's dawn, the whole world over, in constant rotation and Z felt the tug of its morning-creeper fingers scratching toward her scrawny ass. It wasn't visible in the sky yet. It was just a scent, but it was coming. Z slowed down, having reached the top of the mountain, and walked slowly through the trees.

Surveying the multiple holes in her gut, chest, and arm, the vampire was aghast at her current condition. Each tiny murder of skin wrought from the 10-Gauge, 2 ounce shells filled with large, double-odd buckshot still couldn't help Z remember exactly how she had gotten herself all shot up. Bits and pieces of memory floated on silly string. Her most active recollection was of slicing up a boy named Ryan Silva. It was on permanent replay, looping around other strange images of gambling at a casino and driving with Lin. Big holes in her thoughts from big holes in her head – *beautiful and annoying* – smaller than bicycle tires and just as black.

Her Jadaraa Soo clanged so loudly that it become its own punk band. She needed to feed. The 'lil bastard couldn't even heal it was so fucked up. Her face was an enduring display of damage and she'd begun to lament killing the soulful songbird. Out here in the pristine open, full moon smiling down creeping below the tree line, the smell of pine and dirt, echoes of wings flapping and crickets' violin, calm and undisturbed; it was nice.

She remembered the taste of him and how he felt against her once smooth skin, and all of a sudden being outed at the club didn't seem like such a big deal anymore. Definitely not worth killing somebody over, but she had, and his body lay rotting in her garage back in LA – *a waste of fluids, a waste of life, a waste of a beautiful voice*…she sighed, *a waste.*

"Fuck it, Z. Snap out of it," she said to nobody but the wind, continuing to trek across the mountain.

1930. Chicago.

Benjamin Douglas Raines let Z beat him at a game of chess. She yelled at him for it and he took it on the chin with a smile as she egged him to give her his best shot, as she set up the board. For nearly a month she'd been confined with the vampires, but she wasn't anybody's chump and didn't need any handouts.

"You know he intends to have you turned," Benjamin said after his third consecutive win.

"That is what he keeps saying." Z positioned her bishop to slay his horse.

He moved a pawn to protect his steed. "What do you want?"

Z opened her mouth to tell him, but just like her bad penny, Cross entered the room. He took a seat in one of the chairs that formed a ring around a mound of melted wax where a dozen candles burned. He winked at her and smiled. Though they still shared a room, it had been a few days since they had spent any time together. The soldier had been off doing one thing or another and he'd even missed joining Z for her meals. Quietly, he cracked open a book and began reading.

She fell silent over the game and the matter dropped. Leinil Goode took up his violin and began playing music as Tyler and Alayna danced. By now, Zia had met almost everyone except the native and Ms. Kebel. They seemed to never be around when she investigated the tunnels or joined Benjamin for their daily chats and chess.

She'd grown particularly fond of a homely vampire named Vanessa Reed, who was a Chicago housewife until the vampire, Bernard Kegg, fell in love with her. Bernard was killed in the Omjadda attack of '28 and since then Vanessa had been alone. She and Z were fast becoming friends, and the widow soon found that with meeting and learning about so many interesting people she grew comfortable in her bizarre lodgings. But she still yearned for the great outdoors.

Cross continued to try and appease his strange guest. She'd ask for a "lousy drink", whining about the speakeasies above, and he went so far as to procure two luxurious crates of alcohol during the country's prohibition. By the quality of the hooch, it looked like it would have been a fun heist if he'd allowed her to tag along. Thoughts of running from the coven came less and less frequently even though Cross still denied her access topside.

He also never joined her for drinks, but there were a few others in the coven that did. In particular was her best pal Vanessa, whom Z had to coach into joining the wet stinging mirth, and of course Gavin, who boasted the local taverns as his regular haunts, and a vampire named Robert Keoning. Keoning was a mix – *American and Chinese*, Z thought, *the great American melting pot*, though she never asked him his true ancestry. He was originally from San Francisco, one of those vampires that came to Chicago to get out from under the web of The Council.

From what Z was learning, they were all considered pretty young in vampire years, and retained some interest in the leathery brew. On more than one occasion Cross was made to carry his lithe female back to their room and subsist on her intoxicated blood, which of coarse, he found uninviting. It was a consummate joy to the widow, despite the pounding in her head, hearing about the rancid taste of her blood in the mornings when she woke with a hangover. The bad lieutenant may not have liked her revelries in intoxication, but he took no actions to make her stop.

There were only a few members of the coven that Z shied away from entirely for one reason or another. They were Selina, at Benjiman's obvious suggestion, and Emily Rosenthal, whom Z had taken an immediate dislike to on that first night in the Grande Hotel. The grubby vampire always seemed to flaunt herself around Cross when they were in the same room together, like it was supposed to make Z jealous. She also avoided a cunningly sharp looking vamp named, Tristin Faust. Faust was handsome in a way that she most definitely liked. He had a long thin face, a defined nose, a strong chin, and dark, bushy eyebrows that made him look thoughtful and brooding.

He appeared almost regal in Z's eyes, having such classic lines. It wasn't the fact that he'd begun to hang out with the dangerous Ms. Pillar in Cross's dominant absence that she steered clear of him. It was the fact that she felt a curiosity toward him that she wanted to investigate. If it was what she feared, clawing at her belly in her most primal core, then it did not bode well. *Nope, not at all.* So, until she better understood her billowing flame she thought it best to keep some distance from the blond-haired man, lest she lose what little ground she had gained with the confederate.

Though Z feared a chance meeting between her and Selina in one of the lair's many dark passages it had not yet happened. The catacombs under Rosehill Cemetery with its twisting lanes were ripe for an ambush and Z could tell from Selina's malevolent glares that the day was fast approaching. The widow anticipated the event and began carrying a concealed knife upon her person. She didn't know if she would be able to kill her if it came down to it. Gauging how durable vampires were, based on Benjamin's stories, Z wasn't even sure she could hold her own, let alone take her down a notch or two. But if it came down to it, she was certainly going to try.

Having finished Winesburg, Ohio Z had found Alice in Wonderland, vaguely recalling it from her youth. Reading it now helped her to cope with the strange and unusual circumstances of her surroundings. She was stuck in the rabbit hole, alright, and she never knew just how far down it went.

"Z," informed the Union soldier. "I don't think you should do that." Her eyes had glazed over, her attention was robbed, Benjamin could see the idea forming in her head when the line of men was led down the tunnels. "Let's finish our game."

But she got up and marched after them. Cross caught her at the mouth of the passage where she had seen them disappear. "It is best if you remain here with everyone else," he politely urged, blocking the entrance with his body.

She glared at him, and then tossing a look back at Benjamin that yearned for the big man's help, she realized she was alone. The vampire stood beside his board and pieces, a soldier through and through. "I know why they're here," she stated to Cross resolutely. "I want to talk with them."

"I cannot allow you to do that."

She grimaced and shook her head and tried to move around Cross, but he grabbed her by the arms, stopping her. She cursed and yelled at him to get off her, punching him in the collarbone. The confederate man pushed her away from the exit and she landed rudely on the hard, uneven floor. Panting and enraged, she stared up at the vampire. All activity in the room had ceased. Benjamin moved toward her until Cross signaled him to remain where he was.

"Zia, I am sorry for this," he began, "but I must insist–"

"Z. My name is Z." Her voice boomed in the cavernous gloom

as she rose. "How many times must I keep telling you." Her breath was an engine. "Of all the people in the gaddamn world you do not have the right to call me Zia anymore. Zia was married to man she loved. Zia had friends and a life above this rancid place. You took that all away when you made her pull the trigger, so don't you ever use that name on me again! Do you hear me? Never again."

The obstinate woman moved to outflank the Lieutenant once more and he moved to subdue his unruly guest for the last time.

"Cross, don't!" yelled Benjamin in his deep, penetrating voice and he stopped. "If she is to be one of us, then she should know."

As the South stared down the North, Z stormed through the darkened tunnel, searching for the live men that she had seen. Cross sighed and followed the widow. So did everyone else in the room. They all emptied into a smaller area where Z spied three men bound in the thrall of Vanessa, Perceval, Robert, and Emily. The men were black, of variable years, and by the looks of them poor. They'd been beaten and were scared.

Vanessa jumped when the widow found her lapping at the wound in the throat of one of the men. Even though she knew Z understood what she was, it was altogether different having her barge into the group feast. Her expression belied feelings of guilt at being caught.

Robert greeted her cheerfully, telling her that it'd be best if they got together some other time. Perceval also appeared guilt-ridden at having been caught drinking another man's fluids. Emily was the only one that did not seem to care if the newbie watched her eat or not. She gave no concern to Z's presence and continued sapping the man she held in her arms. When Cross and the others spilled into the room after the intruder, Vanessa begged for him to remove her. But Z wouldn't have it.

"You think I don't know what goes on here? You think I'm stupid or worse yet too dainty to understand while I suffer his teeth nearly every day?" She pointed at Cross with his stink all over her, and he found her tirade amusing. "I know what you are. I've known since the first night that he brought me here and you think I'm scared of that?" Z drove her eyes over each and every face that she'd come to know, landing on Selina Pillar in the back of the room. "That I'm afraid you'll kill me?"

They stood in silence, staring at the widow with their pale skins, doughy eyes, and burgundy veins wiggling under their flesh for her thrushing blood. She knew it. She was the live, loud thing on display. She was the lamb that lay with lions. The men in the vampires' captivity, conscious and bleeding, begged the woman with their eyes to set them free. But Z knew what they didn't. There was no freedom for the living under the earth. It was a cemetery after all. It housed the dead or those soon to die. There was only imprisonment and death – simple equations that the bank robber could deal with.

Z crossed to the Negro man that Vanessa had been feeding from when she busted in on them and rounded to his back so that everyone might get a good seat. She thrust his head to the side and he screamed in protest, pulling against the ropes tied around his wrists, bobbing on his wet knees. Z told him to shut up as she attacked Vanessa's wound in his neck.

Cross howled in laughter, watching his not-so-dainty-abbreviation suckle heartily the man's raw blood. His brood glared in awe at how the hot pink woman subdued the man's sweaty brown flesh. Her flat, round teeth bit into him. He yowled as the cannibal, pure and sadistic, who needed nothing but room to put on a show surprised them all. The confederate's cackles soon choked within his throat as the abbreviation ripped a chunk of meat out of the side of the man's throat. His yelps and last gasps of pain, arteries pumping out as he fell to the languid black floor twitching and convulsing, filled the dank room and tunnels. Above him his murderer glared at her southern tutor as he died.

The whole room drew silent except for the whimpering cries from the other live men and a broken engine laugh from Emily that wound to full mania. Cross glared at Z in disbelief, the edges of his little experiment cracking. Z stepped into his orbit and spit the chunk of flesh at him. It hit his chest and bounced onto the ground with a wet, papery thunk.

"If this what you want me to become…" she said, pausing as her gaze swept the room. "Then deal with it."

Emily's gleeful bubbles of crazy followed Z down the tunnel as she made for the space she used as a bathroom. Once there, away from the dark carnival of eyes, Zia Jean Boyd hurled into her poop bucket, regurgitating the unknown man's death. She cried in that awful silence and thickly sick smell, pressed into a corner of the earth. All the weight from years of rot and decay fermenting in the soil pushed down on her through the consummate dark.

305

A dreadful feeling crawled up her gut. Something Lin had said…
in a garage…different garage than where she'd stashed Ryan's corpse.
Wait a minute…not so much said as was alluded to. It took Z a few hard-
earned minutes to pull the fabric of past together into a jigsaw tapestry
that she could understand. *Sleeping.* She'd been sleeping. And Lin knew
it.

Something about sleeping was bad, though Z couldn't find that
particular little jagged piece to add to the puzzle box, so that she might
get a good look at herself. The vampire pushed her thoughts and they
exploded back at her in vivid color. She grabbed her head as searing
bright hot graduals of pain screamed across her mind. She fell to one
knee, woozy. Spiraling around a whirlpool of down, she remembered
shooting her husband, ripping a man's throat out, and a dozen other
deaths. The tastes of pain collided in her mouth, and all her injuries
pulsated and throbbed.

Panting heavily, immobile, exquisite torment – her head felt
like a big bass drum, expanding, contracting – thrumming in a flood of
memory. She'd murdered her husband. She killed Ryan, and before she
could even ask herself the question that was forming in her mind, unwrap
the hard to swallow truth like peppermint candy, she recalled killing a
vampire named Cross. She was vaguely aware of him being her lover at
one point and time. But there was more to it than that.

Damn! Do I kill everyone I know?

It was no wonder that Lin had left. *I am Shiva, the swallower of
souls!* Hindu pictures from books ran through her mind on tiny cartoon
legs. The memory of being at a tattoo shop getting the ancient goddess
of creation/destruction needled to her back settled in. Walking on, the
four corner winds shifted direction and Z caught the faintest hint from
the scents that she detected back at the bar. A ripple of terror fled up
her spine. Though for the life of her, she could not understand why. She
poked around the muted forest with her one good eye.

Nothing. Leaves, twigs, earth, pine needles – *would love to suckle a
little squirrel.*

Z pursed her lips together and made a wet, chittering noise like
the tree rodent. "C'mon out Rocky. C'mon and get some…I've got a
huge nut for you."

She called the critter with that noise again as she lifted her nose to the wind and sniffed. That scent from the bar was heavier and coming from two directions now. Z twirled around, panic moved within her shot up breasts, and her Cyclops gaze wreaked havoc across the landscape. Something deep, dark and terrible in the blank pit of her mind was coming for her and she couldn't put a face to it. That made the thing all the more terrible to imagine. Suddenly, she didn't feel that a casual stroll through the forest looking for Rocky & Bullwinkle was gonna cut it anymore. She needed to motor.

Gauging the distance from the strength of the bizarre scents in the air Z had little time. So, she ran as fast as she could. No idea as to where she was going – that hadn't changed. She just knew she needed to reach a certain part of nowhere that had a car she could jack, because that unknown hollow in her pucker-shot head was telling her she couldn't out run what was coming; that it was going to catch up with her sooner rather than later.

Crashing around the tall stalks of trees, branches whipping her mutilated face, Z pushed herself as hard as she could go. But it wasn't good enough. Adding to the plague of looping images of murdering past lovers and the putrescent punk rock tunes of her Jadaraa Soo were now two dark flashes flanking her on either side.

Fear danced on the twisted edges of Z's skin as she scrambled to make sense of the flustering musk odor that was baring down on top of her. Thick and smothering, a savage blanket, the two massive dark things headed off in front of her, criss-crossed, and disappeared. Z slammed on the brakes, kicking up the sandy, timberland ground. She trembled, afraid.

Her one good eye scanned the horizon. She knew they were out there. She could smell them. And it was there, on the tip of her mind's tongue…so notorious, yet gone. Riveted out of consciousness by a dozen lead pellets and a narcoleptic parasite. She couldn't picture what they were, but for some dismal reason their tang was awfully familiar. The approaching dawn was incredibly quiet. Even the static hum of mice, birds, walking insects, and cricket chirp that usually inundates the background was missing. The forest was stymied.

Z felt the light fingers of a breeze graze the back of her neck, rousing and cool.

Then suddenly, the ground detonated a few clicks beyond the ridge and something huge and hairy cast its shadow across the moon above her as another dark shape came barreling through the timber. All at once she remembered. *Dear God! I know what they are!*

1930. Chicago.

It was always the darkest part of the tunnels that made Z nervous. Dipping in and out of them like a shower of rain, the dark was bound to rub off. Moving through one of the dense patches, something tripped her and Z went crashing to the ground. She rolled over to stand and saw Selina Pillar unfold from the thick black. A tall wraith, silent and ghostly pale, her coal black hair hung down over an ebony dress and it was impossible to tell where she began and the darkness of the tunnel left off. They were one.

Z inched her hand closer to her concealed knife as the revenant moved toward her. Selina did not say anything. Doll eyes; open wide and staring down, the vampire extended her hand to help Z up. The widow looked from Selina's outstretched hook to the blank expression on her face and knew she meant no real kindness. Fear welled in Z's belly as she took the vampire's hand. Selina jerked her off the floor. Reaching into the pocket of her trousers Z whipped out the knife and aimed it for the vampire's gut, determined to use Selina's own force in the strike.

It was no use. Without a single facial twitch or change in the vampire's doll-like expression, or a tonal shift in her stance, Selina knocked the traveling blade out of Z's hand. It felt like a sledgehammer had hit her wrist. The force twirled Z around. She went dizzy and then suddenly stopped in a hard explosion of lightning pain. Spittle and groans flew from the widow's mouth as her back slammed against the brick of the tunnel wall. Before Z could even make sense of what was happening or catch her breath, Selina had one hand around her throat lifting her off the ground.

Z struggled to breathe, face going red, puny human fists railing against the steel grip of the vampire. It was useless. There was nothing Z could do and all the silent witch did was stare at her like an insect discerning a meal through glass. *Cold.* The coldest look that Z had ever seen. It chilled her through to the bones. Z felt herself slipping into the dark unconscious voyage of death. Head light and going numb, pin-pricks along her face, Z stopped struggling and everything closed in black around her.

The next thing she knew her legs shot pain across her back and she was on the floor again. Coughing through every gigantic breath, saliva dripping from her mouth, Z's vision slowly tuned and she glared at the feet of Selina Pillar. The vampire had nearly killed her — *easily, like a boxer picking a fight with a baby.* Z tried to stand on rubbery legs as her chest still heaved, grateful for each dank stink of oxygen that filled her lungs. Her head beat with an ache that was sure to stay with her for the rest of the day. A careful little reminder from the vampire to the widow: *I own you and I can take you out any time I want.*

"What did you hope to prove?" asked the ominous wench with a voice that sounded like it was covered in sandpaper.

"What makes you think I was trying to prove anything," spat Z through deep breaths, wiping saliva off her chin.

"You are as transparent as glass," the vampire charged.

"Then I guess that means you wont see me coming."

Selina chuckled at the threat, the tips of her teeth pocket curling into a devilish grin, as she recalled the sounds of Z's sobs in the dark. "So you want to be one of us?"

Z leaned against the cold, damp wall and rubbed her neck where Selina had her pinned. "Whoever said I wanted to be anything like you?"

"Hhmmpht," the pale cat grunted with a weird fondness and slowly wandered off.

Sauntering away, her tall slinking back getting smaller, Z could only stab the vampire with daggers of hateful glares. She peeled herself off the sticky wall and thought it best to stay in her quarters for the rest of the night, lest their tango have a fatal reprise.

In the shared abode with the confederate soldier, Z read another chapter of Alice's Adventures in Wonderland and talked with Cross about his life before the war on his father's plantation. The old soldier, imbued by the conversation, had dinner for her brought to their underground hovel and she dined listening to Cross's stories.

He had learned to ride horses by the age of nine and became an Overseer of his father's fields. He had three sisters and his mother died of consumption when he was very young. His father raised them in the large house on a Virginia Plantation. A Separatist, he was eager to succeed from the Union with the rest of his family. He told her tales of chivalry and youth, mastering the plantation's slaves, and about a 'lil southern belle that he'd fallen in love with from South Carolina. Between Z emptying a bottle of wine and his bygone memories as a plantation owner's son, Cross supped from the spitfire girl, drinking her rose fluid as she drank the wine. Having filled his veins on Z's rich bounty he pulled his blood covered lips from the bowl of her neck and kissed her.

Shocked, with all the pleasure and mirth suddenly gone, Z pushed him away. She wiped her own blood off her lips and ran from the room as he quietly apologized. Alone in his chambers, breathing out regret, Cross knew it was too soon. Z's life essence pumped through his calabash system, warm and loving. It was the only embrace he held from the woman, and in his veins it was already fading.

"Here ya go Vee. Us gals gotta stick together," said Z as she handed her a shot a few hours later.

Z hid in a game with the big man, drinking one of her last bottles of whiskey when Vanessa had wandered into the room, joining them at the widow's urgent requests. She did not want to drink alone and Benjamin had not stomach for the light tasting liquid.

"Bottom's up," Vanessa chimed as she threw the shot down her gullet and shivered in the fire water's warm embrace.

"You gotta help me whip this sorry sonnabitch just once," shouted Z as she stood, loud and drunk.

"Merle and Bernard used to play. I was never any good at it."

Z squished her face and waved a hand at her. "Neither am I. We'll defeat him with superior num…num…" She stifled a belch. "Mumbers."

Benjamin Douglas laughed at her drunkenness, called the game, and asked Vanessa to walk her back to Cross's place. The vampire agreed and with a few minor protests Z clung onto her shoulders as they left the room. Z spied Tristin again in his lonely perch as she left. She wanted to sit with him, but Vanessa steered her away, and Emily sauntered into the cute boy's orbit. Z scoffed and pursed her lips at the ugly vampire and then smiled a warm liquor grin at Tristin. She twirled her fingers in a not-so-elusive wave. He smiled and nodded back as Vanessa escorted the stinking drunk into the tunnel.

"He's sooo cute," whispered Z to Vee.

"Tristin?" Vanessa raised her eyebrows. "I'd steer clear of that one if I were you. Don't think Cross would take too kindly to you and him."

"Fuck Cr–" Z began in a loud roar.

"Shhhhhh," urged the vampire.

"Fuck Cross." Z lowered her voice to a tiny whisper. "He tried to kiss me you know." Vanessa saw the lieutenant's teeth marks healing at the base of Z's neck. "No, not that," Z corrected. "He does that…no. On the…" Z tapped her plushy lips.

"Oh."

"He likes me." Z wore a sorrowful face. "Too much."

"Perhaps, things will change for you once you are turned," Vanessa said, trying to persuade her drunken companion.

Z sighed and lumbered to the steady, nonmoving wall. She rested there as the room spun and she stared at the vampire for a long minute before she spoke. "He made me kill my husband, Vee." A tear streaked down the widow's face. "He had his faults, I'll give ya that, but he was mine and I loved him."

"I know Z. I know."

"At least Merle's out there with your son and their alive, you know." Z's scrunched up eyes penetrated through the dark as she spoke. "They're taken care of each other, living life." The widow grieved a huge sigh. "But they're out there you know. They're out there." Z took another swig from the whiskey bottle and wiped tears from her face.

"I miss them," stated Vanessa. "When Bernard first came to me and offered me this life in exchange for their wealth and freedom I thought I'd truly found hell. I absolutely believed that I was going to die apart from them. They were all I knew. The thought of leaving them for Bernard tore me up. But he helped me to understand and work through it. It was the right thing to do. We were starving and had practically lost everything by then. Merle and I…we knew we wouldn't have lasted the winter had I not…" She trailed off, looking into the face of the grieving widow, telling her things that she already knew. "I grew to love him, Z. I loved Bernard. Perhaps, you'll love Cross one day too."

"Yeah," mumbled Z, pushing herself off the wall and started walking. "You're a good friend, Vee. But I got it from here."

Z waved ta-ta and the vampire watched her leave. A solemn

feeling descended from Vanessa's shoulders to her feet. She knew how difficult it was for the woman. She'd been in her shoes. A live thing among a nest of hungry wolves, walking the thin veil between this world and the only one she ever knew, and all around old perceptions cracking. Letting go and accepting something strange and unknown wasn't easy.

"Z?" Vanessa called.

The girl twirled around on clanky feet. "Yup?"

A bright face. A gorgeous gal, hiding in alcohol and loneliness. Vanessa crossed the space between them, moving effortlessly, seeming to glide over the ground, as Selina had done. *The vampire's apparent grace* – another thing Z envied as she watched the hem of Vee's gown flitter quietly. She nestled in closely. "You mustn't come among us for the next few days."

"What?" Z scrunched her face, looking cock-eyed at the vamp.

"It is for your own protection." Z wasn't getting it. Vanessa was going to have to be blunt. "You're bleeding. You've begun your monthly cycle. I can tell. It's just started."

"Oh." Words embarrassingly slipped away.

"You need to stay in your chambers until it passes. That will, at least, allow us to better deal with the constant scent of fresh blood."

Z felt ashamed and dirty, "I'm sorry…I–"

"There are things we each endure in this company. But until it passes, stay in your chambers."

"Yes, ma'am," Z saluted, turned around, and stumbled home.

A deep pity for the widow sat in Vanessa's chest as she lowered her gaze following the woman down the tunnel with her eyes. Z sang a song that the vampire had never heard before, disappearing into the melodic dark. Vanessa's Jadaraa Soo twittered at the delicious scent seeping between Z's legs, and she decided to have a little chat with Tristin, before Z did something rash and stupid that could not be undone. The girl was generally unpredictable, highly passionate, and if she thought the young vampire was cute then Vanessa knew trouble loomed over the horizon of Rosehill Cemetery.

The werewolf fell from the sky toward her. It would land on her before the other one reached her position. Boxed in on either side, a quick pivot, and they had her pinned. Couldn't move back, couldn't go forward – *Checkmate!* Z dug in, spread her stance, and waited until the hairy beast was on top of her. Mouth gnarled and drooling, growling from two rows of nasty, spiked teeth, its massive paws stretched out with five thick piercing claws at the end of each arm. Shaped like a human hand only larger, coated in coarse gray and black hair, the beast's nails were so sharp they cut the air with song. Its body was like that of a wolf, ribcage distended, belly soft and weak. Its bulky thighs were drawn up for the pounce; elongated feet gleamed in the moonlight with razor sharp talons. The animal was a fast descending wrecking ball of death and suddenly, Z remembered what Kiyiya had told her.

"Their bodies are no stronger or weaker than yours. Air to breathe. Water to nourish. Same laws of gravity apply."

When in arms grasp, Z moved, charging forward. The clicks from the beast's claws missed her, grabbing air. The vampire shot her arm upward, extending her fingers like a knife. Using her own sharp talons, she cut the creature's belly wide open with its own force. A long, widening rift of pain and blood opened above Z's head and splashed wet gore over her as the wolf howled in anguish, crashing to the forest floor in a massive heap of its own twisted limbs.

Z kept running, straight for other one. *He's too close.* She didn't have time to bring her hand down and the werewolf plowed into her lithe, lanky frame with the impact of a Mac truck. Both of them went crashing back, over the other beast as it lay quivering, one leg in a spasm. The creature's momentum shot them through a dense crunch of branches as she fought to stay away from its powerful jaws. Snapping the hard green limbs like dried twigs, they fell to the ground in a rolling pile of slashing claws and biting teeth. The ground made a horrific mess of her, tossing the vampire over its rocky form.

Tumbling under the hairy smother and ardent odor of the wolf they both skidded to a stop, beaten and bruised. Z rushed to her feet, panic pumping her nerves to flee. If she stayed down she was dead. That much she knew. Z stood and the wolf took a swing at her with one of his mammoth hands. Jumping back, she was too slow, and five points of black razor-sharp ivory tore through the left side of her chest, slicing her arm, ribs, and breasts. Z screamed bloody murder and it was just as loud inside of her head from the wailing Jadaraa Soo as it was outside.

She punched the wolf in the eye, a clean hard tap, and nearly got her forearm bitten off. She had to even out the odds a little. Two against one and she was already pretty mangled to begin with. *These federal boys don't play fair!* Z scooted back with every lunge and snap of the werewolf's death trap, doing her best to stay on the creature's blind side. She knew this tactic wasn't going to last. The terrain was bumpy – too many fallen branches, rocks, and ledges that plummeted straight down into the jagged cut across the valley. She couldn't out pace the thing by backing up forever. It was just bad odds, as a gambler, she knew instinctively that it was a loosing bet. She needed to break it up. Boxing with the wolf was doomed to get her killed.

"Hey scruffy?" She popped him in the snout. "You stink; need a bath!"

Z kneed the beast hard under the jaw as he snapped bitter air, crawling on all fours toward her, and it nearly bit its own tongue off. Feeling cocky, the buckshot, dyed redhead landed a combo on the wolf's face, but he grabbed one of her tiny fists in its huge paw and tossed her into a tree. Pain, lighting up with the sky, made her one good eye fuzzy and she tried to kick the creature as he swiped her thigh. The beast cut a bloody path of twisting, writhing veins through the thick meat of her leg. She winced in agony and belted the thing in its other eye causing it to shake its enlarged head. The wolf snorted and stamped its feet.

"You silly little girl," he growled through a muzzle hot with hate. "I'm going to enjoy watching you die."

"Yeah?" She gritted her teeth, holding back the pain, unable to put her weight onto the damaged leg.

"Yeah," it said and rose.

Climbing onto his hind legs and unfurling its broad shoulders the wolf easily towered over the vampire, exposing its delicate undercarriage. The beast snapped his head from side to side, undoing the kink in the muscles that rippled through his thick neck as he stretched both grappling arms down to the gleaming points of his fingernails.

"And how do you plan on doing that, Lassie?" Z egged him on.

"By feasting on your–"

The wolf never got to finish telling Z how he was going to kill her and eat her corpse. As soon as he started jaw wagging Z lunged for his soft, fragile underbelly, as weak as any other mammal's, and grabbed two fistfuls of hair and clamped onto his throat with her own sharp teeth. She shook her head to get a better bite, chomping down through all that rancid hair until she felt the werewolf's hot fluid pump into her mouth.

Gorgeous and wet, a banquet to her starving and bruised Jadaraa Soo, the creature's sour blood would go a long way to healing her mutilated flesh. Z knew it would be a quick bite when she launched at the hairy buffet. *Fast food service.* Agent Johnson ripped her off him, tearing two, small fistfuls of hair from his thick pelt and threw her across the forest's grade.

It was exactly what she wanted – *a bit of distance from the animal.* The only flaw in her singular logic to survive so that the sun might get a chance to burn her up was the crash landing. End over end, ass over elbow, knocking on all her edges, she had to move quick, dawn and Special Agent Hairy Death were racing toward her!

Road's
End

Kate crossed off another road with the red marker. They'd already scouted Wagon Mound, Levy, Mills, and now Roy. Playing it by their guts, working on a theory that the perps only drove from Slim's bar until just before dawn, calculating for erratic speeds to arrive at distance, they had a few options open to them and no way of doing it except the hard way. Driving. Back and forth, criss-crossing the earth looking for a needle in a haystack – *a big baby blue Cadillac sized needle.* By late afternoon the trash was piling up inside of the cruiser and it was beginning to smell of body odor, cigarette smoke, and fast food.

Their backs were achy so Wallace pulled over before turning back onto County Road 3-S, NM 39. Refueling, stretching outside of the car, breathing the air, Kate's cell phone lit up again like a Christmas tree. It was the Chief. Second time today. The detectives were sure by now that the friendly federal boys had informed their Captain that they had taken over the case. He would be wondering why his people hadn't checked in yet. So, Mauldune did what she did the last time he called. Nothing. And let it go to voice mail.

Back on the road, scenic if you hadn't been looking at it all day, miles spun on and on, barreling down tarmac that cut through landscapes that looked like dirty dried ice crystals from space. The license plate came back registered to the Juniper Loran Corporation. It was a company car. *A personalized license plate for a company car?* That didn't jive. The Lieutenant did some more digging on the computer and found out that the Juniper Loran Corporation was a subsidiary of the Lanyard Group, a financial organization with strong real-estate holdings up and down the whole West Coast. When she dug even further into the Lanyard Group, she discovered that it was a limited liability partnership of Delacroix Enterprises, International. Beyond that the cyber trail went cold.

The detective had to dig to find a phone number listed for the Juniper Loran Corporation. It wasn't easy. When she called it she got an automated answering machine and left a message. The Lanyard Group didn't list a number, only an address, and DEI didn't list either. Neither one of the detectives knew if the FBI Agents had scooped any of this info or not. It all looked fishy, random and unconnected, but every jaunt and scrape of intelligence they gathered seemed to propel them deeper down an ever-strange rabbit hole that, somehow, felt right. Besides, it wasn't like they had anything better to do with their time, except drive. Fuel the cruiser, drink more coffee, and drive.

Pressing on, into the later part of the afternoon Kate was finding it hard to stay awake. She needed to hit the head, and informed John to find either a gas station or a very private tree. But that never happened. Rolling past a little tucked away motel, Sergeant Wallace thought he saw something bluish behind some trees, on the South side of the building. He hit the brakes and backed up.

After all day in bed neither one of them wanted it to end. They were enjoying each other's company too much. Conversations were as voracious as sex. Lin told her about her life in Brazil with Dominique and what it was like to be a vampire when she was first turned. Sarah was surprised to learn that all she had to do to become a hybrid revenant was to ingest some black blood from some other creature. All the films she'd ever seen showed vampires turning others by either biting them on the neck or sharing their blood with them. They were campy rejects to a true scientific wonder. Sarah was fascinated by what Lin revealed. Her mind reeled to learn about an ancient race that was responsible for the creation of a new species. It was beyond her wildest imagination.

"Vital fluids are consumed by the Omjadda blood during transference," described Lin. "They act as a catalysis that initiates the growth of the parasitic organism, thereby diluting and altering the source blood."

"So, you are neither 'Onjamma' nor human anymore."

Lin nodded. "Dominique calls us the Children of Evensong."

Sarah laughed.

"What's so funny?"

"A bit flowery, don'tchya think?"

The vampire cocked her eyebrows and made a face. *Z never liked that term either.* Lin was indifferent.

"Is that it?" the live girl asked, hoping for more. "Is that all that takes place besides the need for blood after the transference?"

Lin thought about it for a second, lazily holding the girl after their second blissful union. "Over time the Jadaraa Soo rebuilds skin and muscle tissue, from the inside out."

"Into what?"

"It retains an inherent understanding of itself, so–"

Sarah sat up. "It's sentient?"

"Yes," Lin answered, liking the term. "It dominates the human circulatory system, causing cardiac arrest and suffocation as the parasite centralizes in the fibrous tissue of the lungs."

Sarah leaned in and examined Lin's eyes. The vampire just stared at her not sure what the girl was up to and explained how painful the transference could be until Sarah sat back down. "There are minute traces of petechial hemorrhaging in your eyes." The look on Lin's face told the medical student that she didn't understand. "It's these tiny little dots in the white parts of the eyes as a result of strangulation."

"I remember not being able to breathe."

Sarah laid her hand to Lin's bare chest, thinking about having a veiny creature writhing through her body cutting off air supply. It did not sound pleasing in the slightest. Gently, she planted a kiss on Lin's chest where the beast lay inside. The parasite wiggled toward her face, hungrily

"So that's the only way, huh?" commented Sarah a bit crestfallen that Lin could not change her.

"It is the best way," replied the vampire. "The closer one is to original source the stronger the bond is between host and blood parasite."

"Symbiosis," uttered the medical student, lying against the vampire's chest.

"Yeah, I guess," agreed Lin. "There have been catastrophic results with attempts at bonding hosts to secondary blood. Dominique mentioned something about it."

"Like what?" Lin smirked and Sarah knew she wasn't going to tell her. "Let's just say…it's not pretty."

"So…" Sarah maneuvered, trailing a light finger around the nipple of one of Lin's breasts. "I'd have to drink that 'Onjamma' blood to be with you forever."

The vampire lay still. Quiet. Eventually, Sarah rose and looked her in the eye. "I want to be with you."

"Sarah…" urged Lin, rising, and a million good times were instantly crushed in the descending mood.

Lin wanted to be with her too, but she couldn't escape the truth. Sarah's scent was all she could think about. Wrapped up in it, her beast starving through the few moments of touch and normalcy that the vampire craved. Lin's desire for the dancer was insatiable and it scared her to think what she'd be like once she had consumed her blood, had that special taste of her in her mouth, in her veins, beating her dead heart alive, and knowing she was out there without her. Imagining it only brought about pain. *But it's the only way.* Sarah had to live – *Apart.* Lin was a killer. A subtle monster that Z helped to cultivate. Lin moved to the edge of the bed to get dressed.

Exhaling, Sarah's presence painted a clear picture. *That which was born on that dark day in the desert is who I am. A butcher. No good will ever come from loving me.* Whether confined in the locket as a black and white photograph or sitting on the bed besides her wearing the jewelry of herself – *breathing* – Lin loved the girl. She always had, waiting for her throughout her long life. There was nothing that could compare to her in dream or body. Even the love she had for the Vam Pŷr in her youth as a mortal woman was nothing short of a childhood crush in comparison. And yet…Lin knew she had to let her go. She did not know why she felt this. But it was strong and it was clear. Everything else about the girl in the locket was an enigma of the soul. The only simple truth that drilled through Lin's head over and over again with each pang and violent shudder of her Jadaraa Soo for Sarah's blood was that despite it all Sarah had to, *Sarah must…*live apart from her.

"Huh?" spoke the vampire as if waking from a dream.

"I said I was getting hungry," restated Sarah. "We've been shut in all day. Aren't you hungry? I'm starved."

Lin just stared at the easy comment. Eyes gaunt, her face restless under the thinly pale epidermis; Sarah wondered how often vampires fed. "You have no idea," replied Lin with breathy urgency, accenting each word and staring uncomfortably at the woman.

A tingling threat pricked the hairs along Sarah's arms and both of them ignored the elephant in the room. Tusks gleaming, they moved to get dressed. Stepping onto the tight knit nap of the carpet, Sarah left the island bed and tried to find her pants and underwear. The room was a toss. Pitching clothes back and forth, each woman, quiet in her own swell, started to delight in the memories of how the garments had gotten strewn all over the motel room in the first place. But Lin's smile quickly vanished as she heard the screeching squeal of tires on tarmac close by.

Turning, she said to Sarah sharply, "Get dressed."

Suddenly, it was like all the oxygen had been sucked out of the room. They moved quickly, putting on clothes that stunk of yesterday and last night. Lin told Sarah to check the window as she squeezed into her boots. The young woman crossed to the edge of the curtain and pulled it back, unaware of where Lin was sitting in the room. Bright light smacked Sarah's face. She'd been cooped up all day in the darkened motel and the sudden glare of sunshine hurt her eyes, making her squint. Sarah reeled back and tore the curtain open further than she'd initially intended. Rancid light spilled into the room and the vampire cursed.

"Sorry," Sarah uttered quickly as she corrected the cloth hanging so that she could peer out without any undo harm to Lin. She felt embarrassed by her own stupidity.

"What do you see?" asked the vampire.

"Just some guy and his wife pulling into the parking lot."

Lin was unsure. Tires locking up on tarmac made her jumpy. "Where are they going?"

"Nowhere," said Sarah, turning from the curtain gap. "They just stopped in the center of the lot."

Burning hot lead dropped in Lin's gut. Sarah saw the look on her face clearly in the dim light. Worry crept onto the dancer's face, transported there from Lin's gaunt expression as fear wove into the fabric of her unsullied skin.

"Okay. We're checking out," Lin said as she rose.

"But what about the —"

"Sun?" Lin finished the live girl's sentence for her and thought for a moment. "Yeah…" Crossing to Sarah, she kissed her. "It's only skin."

But deep down in the gnawing pit of her self-conscious gut Lin knew otherwise. The band was striking up the orchestra, the curtain lights had dimmed; the tendril fingers of fate were not going to leave it up to chance like she had hoped. Destiny it seemed had come riding in, all shiny white horses and the apocalypse – *gotta pay for what I've done.* She grimaced. She wasn't even going to be allowed the opportunity to walk away from the girl. The vampire suddenly realized what fate already knew: That left to her own devices, Lin was too weak. She'd eventually cave. She'd give in. And just like last time…*Kill them all.* She was nothing short of a monster and Sarah had to get as far away from her as she possibly could.

❧❦

Stepping from the cruiser, the detectives looked around. A soft wind blew in juniper scent; birds chittered in the woods around them. Kate went to the manager's office as Wallace went to the side of the building where he thought he saw an antique car parked. They needed confirmation. Confirmation and a room number. Confirmation, a room number, and a bathroom – four cups of coffee and two pit stops later were having an effect on the lieutenant's bladder. Of all the slow urgency to finally creep up on them so suddenly – *It figures!*

The glass door to the little motel office chimed as the detective entered. The thirty-something owner poked his head out from behind the door that separated his living quarters from the office. A mash of smells emanated from the unseen tiny kitchen as the television blared in the background.

"May I help you?" the dark haired man named Kevin asked as he entered the room, noticing Sergeant Wallace moving toward the side of his building through the large plate glass windows that made up one of the office walls.

"Yes," affirmed Kate, flashing her badge with a smile. "I'm looking for the owners of a vintage Cadillac that you may have on the premises. Possibly two women; arrived late last night or early this morning?"

The man's heart sank. *Knew it was too good to be true.* There just was no such thing as easy money. He told the detective all he knew, which wasn't a whole lot. Confirming that he had two women who checked in last night, he described how they arrived just before dawn, asked for a room, paid in cash, and that was that. They'd been inside all day, as far as he could tell. Kate asked for the room number and a spare key. The man groaned, practically begging her not to mess up the place as he'd just completed a very costly renovation. Whatever his worry, the detective hadn't noticed any new wood or additions. From the outside the place looked like it'd been standing in the same spot, in the same condition, for twenty years.

Wallace crept away from the cruiser with a hand on his holstered gun, peering at the blind-drawn eyes of the motel. Arching around the side of the building, the Caddy's fins came into view. *Baby Blue.* It was a beautiful ride. He breathed on the glass and noticed the ramshackle backseat. Focusing on the junk pushed down to the floorboards, hard edges and black jagged ends, a few security tapes popped from the wreckage. His heart sunk thinking about the deaths he knew of and worried about all the ones that he didn't. He was determined to find out the answers when he confiscated the vehicle and searched it for evidence. Moving to the rear of the '63 Cadillac, the letters on the license plate pulled it together in an abbreviated focus: ETRNL BTCH! *They're really taking this whole vampire thing seriously.* He drew his gun and headed across the lot.

Mauldune exited the manager's office, tossing her partner some hand signals as she drew her gun. Room one-forty-three. They moved in, synchronized and flanking both sides of the door. Wallace had that look. Kate had seen it before. He was ready to bust the door down, guns blazing. It was what she and the Chief was worried about. She signaled for him to hold back and produced the key that the nervous, little owner had given her.

From his perch on the sidelines, Kevin watched as the two cops moved across his gravel strewn lot. He caught the license plate on their vehicle and it had Arizona tags. He wrinkled his face. *Not even New Mexican police and they have their guns drawn?* Fear gripped his addled mind and he forgot about the macaroni and cheese and pork chops he had on the stove, thankful that bookings were light. If the out of state cops decided to opened fire, or worse yet, if the criminals who paid him cash up front started shooting it would be a mess. *At least there wasn't a full guest book to suffer casualties.* Kevin imagined lawsuits that made him sweat and wondered what the two girls had done in Arizona to piss off the police officers to where they'd tracked them way out here.

Quietly, Kate slid the key into lock and checked to see if it would turn. Hard on the tumblers, the little bronze lock opener didn't budge. Kate exhaled noisily and made a face – *rueful mechanics, its always the hard way.* So, despite the Sergeant's silent hand gesturing protests and lip smack telling her to bust the door down, she knocked.

Straining to listen, Lin heard the latch of the car doors scrape against metal. Clinking open. Closing with a thud. Two sets of shoes on gravel, one walked in the direction of the manager's office and the other, away from it. They weren't a husband and a wife. She could smell lubricant oil and gunpowder, cigarettes and cheeseburgers, perspiration and urine in the bladder. The heart of the old man tapped in his chest with expectancy, alarm, and fear. Whoever he was, he was excited. They were here for her. That much was obvious.

"You've got to get out of here."

But Sarah clung to her orbit, spiraling down with her tainted past, caught in its gravitational pull. Satellites convalesced, winding up for the inevitable pitch of karmic retribution. It was odd; for a creature that had lived so long without a care about the tick of time Lin suddenly found herself with so little of it. She felt pressured, squeezed, as if the room was a giant juice box.

She looked Sarah dead in the eyes. "No arguments. Just go." And thrust the keys to her Caddy into a protesting hand and led the girl to the bathroom. "Get as far away from here as you can. Don't look back."

Lin leaned in and kissed her, quick and jerky, pushing her toward the small window at the rear of the tiled room. Confusion framed Sarah's face. She wasn't sure as to what was going on, but Lin was deathly serious and that scared her.

"I'll find you," Sarah told her as she opened the narrow portal.

"It won't matter." Lin stepped away from the light as the dancer cranked the window open. Everything was happening too fast. Only seconds now. Lin pushed her hearing past the motel room door to what was happening beyond. Her invisible players were drawing near. Sarah hung by the window, hesitating.

So Lin stuck her arm into the path of daylight and pulled her shirtsleeve back. She wanted Sarah to know. To understand. That very soon there would be no reason for her come back. The veins in her balled hand and taught forearm viciously reacted to the light. Instantly, the parasite ran, pulling down into the dark shadow of bones and organs. The skin and muscle of Lin's limb shriveled, becoming corpse-like. Sarah was shocked and repulsed. "Get outta here," Lin ordered, listening to footfalls heading her way.

The dancer didn't want to leave the vampire alone. She didn't fully understand. She thought of Z biting into that bartender and getting shot and knew that whatever was going on most likely had to do with that. But leaving Lin here...*It's not right.*

Lin pulled her estranged limb out of the sun and shook the parasite back into her hand and arm, hearing a key slip quietly into the lock of their door, tumblers clicked into cut notches. Her Jadaraa Soo slithered back into comfortable hovels around muscle, bone, and tendons. She could smell machine oil in the lock. *This is it.* "Now," she urged through clenched teeth, a violent whisper, practically begging.

There was a knock at the door.

Encapsulated in the knell of three fast beating hearts, Lin looked into the eyes of the girl for the last time and started backing up into the rented room's main space. She felt the tendril fingers of fate resting comfortably on her shoulders as Sarah finally started climbing out the bathroom window. Another knocking on the door quietly exploded Lin's nerves.

"Who is it?" she sang, eyes faraway and dead.

Through the wooden barrier a woman's voice responded. "Metro Police. We'd like to talk with you for a moment."

Lin exhaled. She was ready. It'd come due. "Yeah," she announced like she'd just been woken up, bothered by the intrusion. "Sure. Lemme get dressed and I'll be right there." She paused, listening to their breathing and the soft terse words passing between them, trying to think of another way out. "Say...what's this all about, anyway?

"Ma'am," The word shot back from the blank wooden door in a tight polite feminine voice. "It'd be easier to talk with you once you open the door."

"Yes, of course. I'm coming."

The vampire snapped her neck to both sides, heard Sarah running through the woods behind the motel and an eerie calm took a seat within her. "It's only skin, it's only skin, it's only skin..." she kept repeating in a whispered mantra.

As she stepped toward the door, to greet the police on the other side and welcome the blistering smile of the sun, confusion erupted outside. Shouts from the officers and the familiar roar of her Cadillac detonated beyond the wooden veil. Its tires cut, heavy and fast, through parking lot gravel. Lin strode to the door, quickly. *It isn't about her,* she thought; *it's about me. You want me! Forget about her!* But a gunshot rang out, and then another. Lin's calm fled from her fingertips to the floor as a tight ball of fear clutched her stomach with steel hands and twisted. The vampire opened the door as another shot blistered her ears.

The roof of the wrap around porch diffused most of the sudden blast of sunshine. Vision hazy, her parasite retreated deeper into her body cavity and Lin saw what the police officers saw. Sarah wasn't driving away toward freedom and getting the hell out of here. She was heading straight for them. She was barreling down the small stretch of parking lot, right into them. Right into…*Shit!* Lin jumped out of the way, just as Lieutenant Mauldune turned and saw her standing in the opened door. Kate turned and raised her pistol to the woman. But it was too late. Cadillac grill and roaring metal. She too jumped out of the way as she heard John fire off another shot.

Sarah fell from the bathroom window with a hard thump and rolled down the sharp incline behind the motel. It stank. Laundry vents and leaking pipes, there was a compost pile out back somewhere where Sarah couldn't see. She listened for a minute as Lin talked with whoever it was at the door. Her belly knotted and twirled rotations around the stripper's pole in her heart. She felt like ejected trash, and she wasn't having it!

Confused, she ran a few steps into the sparse forest behind the building and then stopped. This wasn't what she wanted. It may have been what Lin wanted. But it definitely wasn't what she wanted to do. Running away made her feel like a coward. She'd been running away since she was sixteen and all of a sudden she wanted to stop. It never took her anywhere. For all her vain efforts she was no better off than her momma stuck in that trailer with Derrick. Meeting the vampire was the best thing that had ever happened to her and she knew it. Sarah stared down at the keys in her hand. Black eyes and a yellow face grinned at her, laughing. Happy!

She tossed a look back at the tiny, opened window and peered to the far end of the motel where the Cadillac waited. It really wasn't a choice anymore. She wasn't going to run away. Sprinting along the backside of the building, she poked her head around the blunt curve of the painted brick and saw the vintage, baby blue luxury vehicle resting in the swath of sunlight and swaying churn of shadowy leaves.

Quietly, she unlocked the door and climbed in. She pumped the gas pedal like she had seen Lin doing earlier and stuck the vampire's smiley face key chain into the throat of the steering column. Sarah exhaled. The dangling yellow grin said that everything was going to be all right. She hoped so. She had no idea what she was doing, adrenaline pumping. Her heart was a percussion line at a football game, banging in her ears. She turned the key and the beautiful machine thundered to life. She didn't hesitate. No time to think. She slammed it in gear and backed up. Peeling out, spitting stones into the forest, Sarah tore out from behind the building and saw the two plain clothed detectives turning in her direction.

One of them, an older man, began running at her like he was gonna catch her. Stop her with words, yelling harsh language, commanding her to stop. He was shouting, but she couldn't hear him. It was all a blur. As she reached the edge of the parking lot, ready to continue her escape down the faded, black tarmac of the street she cut the wheel sharply. Turning back into the motel, rounding around the stationary unmarked police car a bullet smacked the windshield. *Jesus Christ!* A *phfttfp* of white glass, a round speck of disaster splintered her view. She never even heard the shot. The motel room was the only thing she could see. Another *phfttfpt* of white glass breaking and an impact in the front seat that she felt vibrate her back. She was really doing it!

Sarah let out a scream and floored the gas pedal as she saw Lin open the door, standing directly in front of the moving vehicle. She hit the horn as two more shots destroyed the windshield. Ducking under the tiny explosions of lead, the next thing she felt was the jolting crash rocking her in the big, flat boat of a seat. Shattering wood, the munch of glass, visibility was nil. Sarah slammed on the brakes. She reached across the front seat and opened the passenger side door. All around her the building wheezed and coughed like a dying old man. Though, it would all be for naught if she'd managed to plow Lin under while attempting to rescue her from the fuzz.

"Get in!" Sarah yelled, hoping the vampire would hear.

Her eyes flitted over the sparking rumble, waiting. In just a quick breath a pile of debris moved and Lin crawled out, tucked under a bed sheet. The vampire jumped into the car, trailing the sheet like a cape. Sarah's face lit up, a beacon of light.

"Stay down!"

The former medical student, former dancer, now official fugitive from the law, gunned the car in reverse and pushed the pedal to the floor. She backed up in a cloud of burning rubber and smoke that caused the female cop to jump out of the way again. Seeing it out of the corner of her eye, Sarah had to admit, it felt good. Out of the wreckage, she whipped the steering wheel around and barely missed the police cruiser sitting in the center of the lot.

Sarah didn't look back, just as Lin had told her. Ducking down, she gazed at the bundle of woman under the jerky Santa Fe design that twisted across the bed sheet. Two more taps of lead against the back window. Tiny cracks from little guns. Sarah was on the road now, pedal to the metal. There was no retreat from this, no surrender. She'd swooped in desperado-style and saved Lin's bacon. Desperately in her heart, Sarah knew that she wasn't so much as running away from something anymore as she was running toward it. Hell bent and full of fury things had definitely gotten weird. The crazy girl from nowhere New Mexico finally knew what she wanted. It was right here with her tucked down between the front seat and the dashboard hiding from the light of the sun. The only rub was that Sarah didn't know if she was going to be able to keep what she'd won. Were the two cops throwing lead at them gonna let it go or beat them down with spinning wheels? Everything was up in the air and falling fast.

Time looked short on the horizon. Sarah knew she only had to go until nightfall, then the vampire could be unleashed. It wasn't that far off. She told herself she could do it and that it was a small sacrifice to make for love and immortality. These two cops that were chasing Lin, spitting hot lead at her in their anger, they had no idea who and what they were chasing. They looked blind standing there on the front porch, screaming at Sarah behind the wheel.

"Just sit tight," she told Lin, gripping the steering wheel tightly. "I'll find us a place in the shade."

Lin smiled underneath the blanket, a full crescent moon grin. "You're one crazy chick, you know that?"

Sarah maniacally chuckled, a nervous, jittery laugh. "Yeah. I guess I am."

She flicked her eyes to the rearview mirror and the laugh cut from her throat. "Aw, Shit."

"What is it?"

Desperate to know, imprisoned in bad linen that was full of the gorgeous scents of the two of them making love, Lin felt helpless. She lifted the edge of the sheet. She was entangled in it like a fishing net and part of it was stuck in the closed door. The vampire stole a burning glance into the sun.

"Nothing," Sarah answered with her shoulders leveled to the street.

Lin knew she was lying. She gave it away in her voice, in the look on her face, and her stench of fear that permeated the cab of the Cadillac. The vampire could only guess at what she was fibbing about, though she was pretty sure she was right. The cops were following them. They hadn't escaped. They had only begun the chase. Obviously, fate wasn't done with them yet. And for some reason that Lin couldn't fathom, that thought scared the hell out of her.

Mauldune hit the deck as the Caddy launched into the motel. The building exploded around her, a hail of blistering noise and cracking and twisting wood. She rolled out of the way just as a section of the porch roof smacked onto the concrete walkway that would have surely broken her legs had she continued to lie there. Heaving mouthfuls of air she struggled to her feet and peered into the rubble. Tailpipe exhaust and red brake lights, Kate didn't have her gun.

She looked for it and found it a few feet from where she'd thrown herself. She ran to the weapon and saw the motel's owner running from the office, shocked and dazed, mouth gaping open in sheer awe. *I don't have time for this!* Picking up the handgun she headed back to the huge, gaping whole where a motel room had once been. She spied Wallace on the ground on the opposite side of the damage. He wasn't moving. *Son of a Bitch!*

As she began to climb through the mangled wreckage to the rear of the vehicle it spun out and backed up in a fuming mist of sickly rubber stench. And for the second time today, Kate had to dodge the classic car, tossing her lithe frame to the ground or else get trampled.

Cursing, she rose to her feet as the fin-tailed rear vanished down the road. Kate squeezed off two shots before they cleared the lot. But they weren't good enough. The driver, the girl in the door, the car – *they were gone!* Pouting, Kevin wandered up to the wreckage shaking his head in disbelief at the damage he'd unfortunately witnessed.

"Aw Maan!" he moaned. "Who's going to pay for this? Hey!

Who's going to pay for this?!"

"Damn," breathed Kate, kicking the dirt as they sped off, ignoring the proprietor.

The angry Lieutenant heard the Sergeant moan as she crossed to him and the disgruntled motel owner followed her surveying the huge hole in the middle of his establishment.

"Stupid Son of a Bitch; had 'em dead to rights..." lamented Wallace as he tried to get up. But he yelped in agony and grabbed his leg.

"What happened?" Kate kneeled beside him.

"Clipped me," Wallace muttered through hot breaths of searing pain.

"Is he all right—" began Kevin.

"Listen," Mauldune said, cutting him off. "I need you to stay with him. I've got to call it in. We need an ambulance fast."
The man looked lost – bewildered. He was thinking about his insurance premiums. "Can you do that?" The Lieutenant asked forcibly.

He stammered and nodded yes as Wallace pulled on Kate's coat, trying to lift himself up and meet her gaze.

"No Ambulance," he grumbled. "I'm fine. Just help me up. Help me up!"

"We've got to get you to a hospital. You're hurt."

"I didn't come all this way to sit on the damn sidelines while they get away again. C'mon, help me up."

Kate exhaled bitterly and, against her better judgement, helped Wallace to stand. The motel owner was gripping his head, confused. One minute she was gonna call an ambulance and local authorities, the next she was helping the cop walk. Somebody needed to call somebody; *there's a gaping hole in my motel!*
Wallace's face was a twisted mess of hurt. His pant leg was damp with sticky blood. He saw Kate staring down at his leg, gleaned her worried countenance, and attempted to allay her fears. "I can make it."

"John, that leg looks pretty bad."

"I can make it," he uttered through gritting teeth, accenting each word as if his life depended on him getting out of the crumbling damage and back on the road. "Every second we stand here we lose 'em."

He was right, they were getting away. *These sonnabitches are getting away with murder!* Kate knew she should've just left John with the motel manager and followed pursuit. That was the best protocol. *Call it in. Get back up.* She knew it. She was the ranking officer on the scene, *gaddammit,* why couldn't she just order him to the hospital, jump in the cruiser and be done with it? Instead, she carried John to the passenger seat of the car and helped him in, his face a tight scowl, biting back the pain.

Kevin, dismayed at the actions of the officers went back inside, deciding to call the police, *the local police,* and then his insurance company. He couldn't handle standing around while they debated their next blundering move.

Wallace shoved the car keys into Kate's hand, and as she closed the door she saw the wet, red trail of blood on the small stone gravel that had oozed from his clipped leg. She did her best to push it from her mind. *We made this trip to together.* Resolute, she climbed behind the wheel, fired up the unmarked police car, jammed it into gear, and tore out of the motel parking lot in hot pursuit, doing her best not to look at her partner suffering in the seat beside her.

"911 Emergency. How may I help you?" said the sanitized voice on the other end of the phone.

But Kevin just stood there too awestruck for words. His mouth had suddenly gone bone dry. The receiver dangled from a loose wrist as he watched the two out of state cops speed away from the damage that they had caused. Everything was happening too fast. In all the haste and worry, he didn't even have the chance to write down their license plate number and now they were gone. His insurance company was never going to believe any of this.

Landscape sped away in dotting blurs, an impressionist painting; it passed across the cracked windshield. Air whistled through bullet holes and miles kicked off from fast spinning wheels. Around each bending curve, over inclines and down descending hills, the cops were tight on them. No siren. Just two dirty vehicles rolling along at breakneck speeds. Dust and debris flew off the Cadillac as a small bit of bed sheet flapped violently in rushing winds, stuck in the passenger side door, clamping Lin in place.

Each car passed other slower moving vehicles and road signs whizzed by with Sarah barely able to have enough time to read the lettering. She couldn't shake the tenacious bastards on their tail. They were glued and there didn't seem to be any way around it.

"Those cops are right behind us," Sarah finally admitted.

"Can you ditch 'em?" came Lin's response muffled from the bed sheet.

"I'm trying."

Lin caught the doubt in Sarah's voice and she cursed herself for getting the girl into this twisted mess. None of it was her problem to begin with. They tumbled through time, karmatically linked together. The vampire systematically destroyed the poor girl's world over and over again. First the desert, in a raging sandstorm, and now this. Lin despised her damnable heart. It wouldn't let her walk away, would it? *No.* She had to court the dancer, play a big drama to give Sarah the locket, and now because of that she was going to most likely wind up dead on the side of the road in a ditch or shot through the head by some ignorant cops who were chasing them because of what she and Z had done. It wasn't fair. Rancid and cold, Lin hated herself.

Wallace grimaced from the pain as he adjusted himself in the seat, using both hands to move his bad leg. He grabbed the first aid kit and decided to mend what he could. Cutting open his bloody pant leg he stiffened with shock as he saw the brutal extent of his pain.

"How bad is it?" Mauldune immediately asked. But he scowled and held his tongue, feeling like a chump. "Dammit, John. Don't play with me."

"It's fucked, okay." He bit back at her. "Is that what you want to hear? But it doesn't matter. Do you hear me? It doesn't matter." He pointed at the car they were chasing. "They do!"

Ever John Wayne! He made a big show of it to take the attention off his leg. He thrust an angry paw at the speeding Cadillac in front of them and glared razors at Kate. Sergeant Wallace bandaged the cut from where his pinched skin had burst and tied a makeshift tourniquet across his thigh to slow the bleeding.

"I'm gonna call it in," he gruffly muttered as some time worn on.

"What about McCallister?"

"Hhrrmm," he scowled. "Fuck McCallister. I'm calling it in. We need to end this and bring those Sonnabitches to justice."

The old, grumbling, seasoned homicide detective grabbed the CB, turned the dial to the local channel, and raised a dispatch. He wired it in, gave the details and requested Back Up and a blockade. He saw the signs for Logan and knew that with a coordinated effort they could easily box them in. One way or another he was going to get his killers. *Dead or Alive.* Either way was fine with him.

"Where's the sun?" asked Lin.

"Starting to set."

A red sky was beginning to burn at the tips of the mountains, taking its seat in the dusk. Lin lifted the blanket a bit to test the light in the air. It was darker ducked down here on the floor and she had a little more wiggle room, but it wasn't an accurate gauge of the light in the sky. So, she figured it was best to hold out down there on the floor until the sun set a little further. The last thing she wanted to do was scare Sarah with a vampire sunbathing. Things were out of control already.

"Hold on," Sarah mentioned, eyeing a dirt road up ahead, marking the distance from where they were to the cops behind her. "I'm gonna try something."

Sarah didn't slow down. She kept the throttle full and jerked the wheel hard to the right. The back end fished, but she kept the Caddy on the dirt road, speeding away in a cloud of miserable dust. Lin banged her head on the dashboard and inside of the door. She cursed, feeling that it was all too familiar. Her roll had switched to that of Z, hunkered between the seat and the metal dashboard hiding from the sun. In her mind, she heard fate laughing.

The terrain was roughly jagged and uneven over the hilly road. The Cadillac furiously bounced. Rocking Sarah in her seat, she had a hard time keeping her hands on the wheel and her foot on the gas. She hit her head on the roof of the cab and spied the open desert before them. She ignored the pain with the knowledge that she only had to reach the flat plain horizon where the sun slowly sank. *Then the vampire could be released.*

Topping the hill, the Cadillac wasn't visible anymore. Panicking, both pairs of the detectives' eyes scanned the road and its varied sides. A poof of dust lingered in the air above a dirt road and Mauldune told John to hold on.

Slowing down to take the turn, she cut the wheel to the right, but Wallace still groaned as his injured leg banged against the inside door panel and dash. Visibility was shit. Banging around in a cloud of exhaust and dirt, all Lieutenant Mauldune could do was pray that they were on the poor excuse for a road. She crested a hill with altitude and landed hard, spraying sand and sagebrush across the windshield. John lit the cab up with noisy pain, bright screaming agony as his fractured knee jammed into this thigh and his thigh jammed into his twisting hip. The Lieutenant slowed her roll, hit the windshield wipers, and pressed on spewing sandy grit from spinning back tires.

After a few minutes Kate was able to discern the dirt road by following a string of far off power lines in her peripheral vision. She gunned the cruiser up a dune, but had to cut the wheel sharply as they came down hard to avoid hitting the rear end of the Cadillac. The police cruiser came to a stop in a jerking lurch.

"Sarah? Sarah?" called Lin, wedged tightly between the seat and the smashed in dashboard.

There was no response. The dancer leaned against the steering wheel unconscious, a trickle of blood streamed down her forehead. Harshly, Lin struggled with the blanket, trying to free herself as the lure of blood enticed her starving parasite. Breaking a hand free, Lin reached out to the unmoving dancer and grabbed her thigh.

"Police!" Lin heard someone shouting. It was that same female voice from behind the motel room door. "Come out with your hands raised above your head!"

Shit! This isn't good. Lin pulled against the stuck bed sheet and her trapped body with more force and vigor. They had plowed into a dune when Sarah lost control of Lin's big baby blue boat. Now, the Cadillac rested cock-eyed in a mound of sand, the engine dead, as radiator fluid leaked out through a huge wound in her baby's metal face.

Sarah groaned.

The policewoman fired off her orders again as Lin pulled her head free from the bedding. Sun-glare from the setting orb streamed down and bit the vampire's eyes. Lin could feel her inner beast shrinking away from the almighty light as Sarah groaned awake, disoriented.

Mauldune was tiny and visible in the bent angle of the rearview mirror standing behind the opened door of the police cruiser.

Half awake and head thumping, Sarah opened her door. Lin protested, begging her to stay in the car, trying to get her to recognize her voice. But all the little dancer from Albuquerque could hear was her own heart pounding in her skull and the rush and ringing of blood coursing through her veins. Lin reached out for her as Sarah inched toward the opened door. The vampire tried to grabbed onto Sarah's leg, but the girl slipped through her grasping fingers. Lin desperately fought to free herself.

Kate turned to Wallace as she climbed out of the vehicle when they had come to their abrupt stop. "You alright?"

"Yeah. I'm comin'," the old man mused not wanting to miss the collar of his life.

"I'm going in."

He waved her on and had to work to steady his breathing. His leg shot torture up his spine like the grand finale at a Fourth of July fireworks display. "Right behind you," he charged, struggling to open his door.

Mauldune moved off to subdue their culprits and secure the scene as Wallace attempted to stand. She shouted her orders to the back of the hunched over driver and the unseen passenger and suddenly the driver's door creaked open. Kate raised her gun, training it on the open portal and glanced back at John. He wasn't looking too good and was barely in position.

Shouts erupted from the unseen passenger for Sarah to stay in the car. *So the driver's name is Sarah.* The Lieutenant watched as Sarah rolled out of the crashed Cadillac and into the dirt.

"Stay on the ground," Kate ordered.

She didn't want things to get more out of hand then they all ready were. Shakily Sarah stood. Mauldune noted a possible head injury and she still couldn't see the passenger who was screaming for the girl to get back into the car. *Listen to her! She's talking sense.* Though, not seeing the passenger was a possible threat. With John hurt as badly as he was Kate couldn't take any chances. She had to subdue the perps...*by any means necessary.*

"Stay down!" the Lieutenant ordered again. "Hands on your

head; knees to the ground. Do it now!"

Everything was a blur, vision spinning, sounds hollow and echoing. Bits of recent memory plagued Sarah's jostled mind and she was finding it hard to get her bearings. Her feet felt like they were slipping on a treadmill.

Lin pushed and pulled herself forward, fighting for every single inch that she could get against the taught and captured bedspread. She'd wrapped it around herself hastily when the car came careening through the front door, and was now trapped under its twisting folds and the compacted crunch of the dashboard and front seat. In her frantic haste, she began pounding on the hard metal dashboard with her fists. Sarah was out of the car and the lady cop was giving commands. Everything was happening too fast!

Lumbering forward, Sarah advanced up the hill toward the cop. She was stressing the Lieutenant out. The girl was either injured too much to respond, drugged up, or she was trying something stupid. *Fucking Prick, Stay Down!*

"Drop to your knees; hands on your head, NOW!" Kate ordered. "Do it! I'm not playing. I will shoot. Stop! Stop moving! Do you hear me?! Stop moving and fall to your knees." *Damn!*

Kate started advancing forward, ready to take her down by force when two things happened at once. The first was Lin breaking free from the massive hold of the caved in dashboard. The vampire popped into Kate's line of sight with an aggressive thrust. The second was how Sarah swung her arm advancing up the hill. *Ambush.* "GUN!" the Lieutenant yelled and fired.

As dimming sunlight panicked her parasite Lin couldn't believe what she saw. Exposed flesh shriveled like a prune as she fought with her own muscles and tissues to work. Her bones reacted to the horror that she was witnessing. Her own voice, a blistering outrage, was deaf in her ears as she witnessed her last chance at salvation falling to her knees.

Sarah felt something hard hit her in the gut and she went down. Slowly, she pulled her hands up and they were covered in some kind of warm, red liquid. It took her a minute to realize that it was her own blood and she wondered what had happened.

Mauldune stood there in shock for a second, watching Sarah fall. Both hands of the girl swung around and suddenly she didn't see a gun anymore. The passenger was screaming wildly, a bright, deafening shrill, and eerily it seemed faraway as if from a dream.

Lin, enraged, tore open the passenger side door, commanding her Jadaraa Soo to brave the dying light and move. It took everything she had to budge the retreating puppet master. But she found the will, the heartsick will to advance on Sarah's killer, trailing swirls of light-gray smoke behind her.

"Stop or I'll shoot!" commanded Mauldune turning toward the woman whom she had seen in the doorway just before the Cadillac crashed into the motel. But the woman didn't stop. Kate took aim as Wallace righted himself with the help of the car door.

BLAM!

The shot rang out and clipped the dark-haired, tattooed woman in the right shoulder. But she didn't stop. She still kept coming. "Cease and Desist!" Kate yelled not wanting to put her down.

BLAM!

Sergeant Wallace's shot missed and hit the ground near Lin's feet. Neither shot seemed to persuade or alarm the woman in the slightest. *She must be hopped up on some serious shit.* The thought of a drugged out lunatic released the fear chemical in Mauldune's neural net to float through her system. She turned to Wallace quickly. He was sagging on the door for support. The look on his grim countenance was an easy read. *We have to bring her down.* The perp was forcing their hand.

Kate fired again, but it still had no effect. John fired too and winged her in the arm, scraping a chunk of smoking, shriveled flesh out of her. His aim was off. Delirious and hazy, sweat fell into his eyes as his head and leg banged a great big drum. Nothing was slowing the woman down. She appeared impervious to bullets like a damn action movie star.

Panic set in as Kate raised her gun again and aimed for a clear, between the eyes, bang yer dead, head shot. She sighted the zone, but the target kept moving. Off in the distance, John called out Kate's name. He used her first name. Not her last name. *He so rarely does that.*

Lin slapped the gun out of Mauldune's hand and in one fluid movement, before the policewoman could even react or plead for mercy, the vampire grabbed her head and twisted. Wallace's eyes went wide as the body of Kate Mauldune fell limp and dead to the ground.

The surviving detective fired at the woman again who hadn't

lost a beat over killing his partner. She was probably the one that had killed his nephew Stephen. In Sergeant Wallace's pain-spitting mind Lin definitely was. His finger moved, light over the trigger, squeezing off shot after shot. Most of them missed, hitting the ground in front of her. He had to aim and hold himself up with the opened door at the same time. He was worthless and he knew it.

The meat of one of Lin's thighs exploded in a bright red bloom. It didn't slow her down. It just didn't make any sense to the Sergeant. She'd taken numerous hits. Even junkies on PCP couldn't take this much heat. She should not be walking around, gaining a physical advantage on them. Then, it churned in his brainpan what Deputy Barney Fife had leaned in and said, *"Like vampires."* The thought was too absurd to comprehend. *Kate was dead. She brought one of 'em down before this maniac broke her neck.*

Wallace fired again through the passenger side window. The bullet shattered the glass and hit Kate's murderer square in the belly. The unstoppable fiend rounded the opened door and Wallace, turning on his bum knee, fell. He landed hard on the inside runner of the car and screamed his discomfort. He raised his gun again and pulled the trigger. It only clicked regretful empty noise.

The haggard vampire stood over him, staring down at the cop, briefly pausing in her assault. *Gloating*, most likely thought Wallace, a mean scowl twisting down the corner's of his mouth. He wasn't going to give her the satisfaction of begging for his life, but he had to know. Up close and dirty with the setting sun washing over her, bullet holes glaringly obvious red dots of decay, he had to know if she was a thing from some Hollywood nightmare or just another druggie who'd probably check out from her wounds after she had her way with him.

"What are you?" he asked, shaking with fear.

"Death," Lin roared, a thundering beast in the back of her throat, exposing her fangs to the wounded police detective.

In that brief instant, before she pounced on him, with such intense viciousness and ferocity, Sergeant John Wallace knew with a clear certainty that vampires roamed the earth. At roads end, dying wasn't all that bad, but in his gut he knew that he had let his nephew and his sister down. He let Sally, the woman he loved who was waiting for him back in Arizona, and Kate down. He'd gotten her killed. As the undead thing tore out his throat, and he choked on his own blood, it feasted. He wondered if there would ever be any sort of redemption for what he had done to those that he'd loved. His final thought, at the twilight of his existence, called out to God in the simplest, most silent voice asking for forgiveness.

Lin rose from the drained cop's corpse a bloody, stinking mess. Bits of the Sergeant's flesh and splattered gore decorated the passenger seat and inside door panel. They had hurt her precious Sarah, her timeless gift, and because of that she'd shown no mercy. The starving and injured Jadaraa Soo drank voraciously of the man's fluids. It had already begun to absorb the cop's blood that had splashed across Lin's flesh from her savage butchery as she crossed to the dancer.

Sarah was lying on the ground bleeding out, a single gunshot wound to the abdomen. She heard the girl's heart beating from atop the hill and as she fell down beside her lover the knock from that plum organ still sounded distant and weak. She had to get her to a doctor or she wasn't going to make it.

There's another way.

Lin pushed that thought out of her head. *That isn't gonna happen!* She brushed the dancer's hair out of her face. Sarah had a knot on her forehead from where she'd hit it on the steering wheel when they'd crashed. Lin bemoaned the situation and told the unconscious girl that she was going to be all right, not having a clue as to what she was going to do. The locket struck Lin's eye. It was bent around Sarah's neck, and the vampire knew that she had to do everything in her power to keep the young woman alive. Lin pulled the silver jewel out of the sand and laid it delicately on Sarah's chest.

Then turning, the wounded vamp peered down the dunes, across a flat stretch of mesa and saw a small subdivision about a mile or so off. It appeared her only hope to get Sarah the kind of attention and treatment that she so desperately needed. Lin picked her up. The poor thing was weightless in her arms. Lin headed toward the tiny dots of houses that rode the darkening horizon.

The subdivision was beginning to alight as the sun lazily dived behind this horrible side of the earth – specks of yellow glow from porches, windows, and streetlights. Someone, somewhere in the housing development, was having a cook out. The smell of chlorine from a couple of pools wafted on the air and mingled in a hard-to-swallow cocktail of motor oil, sewage, dog hair, and cat shit. The scents clamored in Lin's nostrils under the delicious fragrant bloom of Sarah's rich, pungent aroma. She was bleeding out, spilling her vital fluids all over the vampire and the only thing the parasite wanted to do was feed.

Better To Burnout

1930. Chicago.

When Cross learned that Z's unused womb was leaking a treasure of silky red nourishment he told her the same thing that Vanessa did: To stay in their chambers until it had passed. Then surprisingly, he volunteered to leave her in peace, alone in the room, while she took care of her womanly duty. Day after day, alone, she would never have expected it, but she missed the lieutenant's solid company, playing that awful game with Benjamin, drinking whiskey with Gavin and Robert, and talking with Vee.

No sooner had she finished reading Alice's Adventures in Wonderland did she start over again, feeling that she missed something the first time around. Cross delivered meals to their chamber while she remained shunned by the whole coven of blood-lusting vampires. She was a leaking gist. His meal drops were the only time she saw anybody and even then he didn't stay. She wondered how he was subsisting away from her. *Did he have another girl tucked away in the lair that he ran to? Had Selina pulled back the sheets on her bed for him again?* Zia's imagination ran the gauntlet.

Hours of crushing boredom, the likes of which she had not endured since she was a child living with her mother and father in Detroit. The tedium of school and chores, helping to take care of her little brothers, the neighborhood girls were insufferable twats, and the whole city slowly decaying around her. She had to run away. If there were laundry lines running through her room Zia knew she would have just upped and killed herself. Get it over quick and avoid the slow painful death of monotony.

Bouncing around, polishing off the whiskey, because she'd already finished the wine, signing songs at the top of her rent voice, out of tune and obnoxious, the alcohol only increased the regularity of her flow. It thinned her blood. Yet, the alcohol curbed each repetitious second of her ho-hum life buried in the largest grave in the whole damn cemetery. Dancing around, sweaty and loud, she saw Cross standing in the doorway out the corner of her eyes.

"Surely, it is not that bad?"

Z stopped bouncing, panting profusely to catch her breath, all red faced and a huge grin. "Tell ya what…you let me out of here for a night and I'll answer that question in the morning." Z chuckled and up-ended the last bottle of hooch in the joint.

"I must admit that I had not intended to keep you down here for so long. Circumstances, being what they are, have forestalled my plans."

"Yeah? And what plans are these?" Z sashayed over to him. "What do your 'lil ole plans have to do with 'lil ole me, Franky?" All roused up in his stagnant oxygen, she stank of booze and blood, an aromatic aphrodisiac bottled in the licentious curves of the woman. "What do you wanna do with me? Why am I here?"

The gentleman, on edge by her proximity, moved deeper into the room. "Per our arrangement, Miss Z. Per our arrangement."

Zia shook a wily finger at him and stifled a huge "Fuck You" in her chin and exhaled her hyper-tedious energy. Z wandered back into the center of the room, tipping the bottle once or twice before she set it down, feeling comfortable with her liquor buzz, humming in all the right places.

"I've got a few questions for you, Mr. Cross," she said overly accentuating the formal use of his name, pandering to his politeness. "That I want answers to."

"All right," the man obliged hearing a challenge from his prize. "I will see if I can accommodate."

"Oh you will, Mr. Cross, you will." Z rubbed her hands together, pulling the bullshit out of thin air. "First off...you used to be human right?"

"Yes, that is correct."

"Okay. And near as I can tell everything works like it used to. Is that right?"

"Mostly."

"Agreed. Agreed," Z answered with her hands. "So, what I want to know is, can you get it up?" Z glared at the Lieutenant with a cocky grin as he held the pitch of this tongue. "Well, come now Mr. Cross." She over accentuated his name again, tauntingly. "Are you a man or all monster?"

His eyes drew small and beady. "I think you are too drunk and don't know what you are saying."

"Oh, no," Z answered with earnest infraction. "I know exactly what I'm sayin'. You just don't like what I have to say. You tell me to be myself, all sequestered away in your dank, little prison, but look…being myself just offends you. So, why do you keep me locked up here? Am I too much woman for your ghostly senses?" She ran her hands over her breasts and pushed her brows up and down. "I'm tellin' you right here and now, Mr. Cross, I wanna know if you're man enough to get it up. Does that fit in to your '*plans*', Mr. Cross?"

Z smiled through her galvanizing, fun-loving, yet bitter tirade, making quotation marks with her fingers. She had never seen the Lieutenant angry before, so she didn't know that he was actually upset. He spoke firm and slowly. "You have such a foul mouth for such a beautiful woman."

"A mouth that you tried to kiss, if I remember correctly." Z matched his tone. "So, all I want to know is if you can back up your advance Mr. Cross. What's waiting in the wings of all this madness? You either got the cavalry in the rear ready to charge or you're cannon fodder shooting blanks?"

Z chuckled at her metaphor, picking up little bits of war jargon from her chats with Benjamin Douglas Raines. "So, what's it gonna be?" She cocked her eyebrows again and held them high, setting the challenge and the measure of the man, driving his own actions back at him.

His embarrassing kiss was thrust out there in the open, daring him with her flavor. It kept his feet ground to the spot long enough that he did not run when Zia Jean Boyd began removing her clothes as she walked toward him.

The rush of sickly-sweet blood hit him like a cloud, a massive vapor scent that made his head swoon, knees weaken – *the woman offers herself in so many tantalizing ways.* Z stood in front of him, purely naked, wet with blood, staring up at him, and he felt the sting in his forehead where she had shot him on that first night and wiggled into his soul. "Either bite me or fuck me," she said, "but just don't stand there."

The vampire grabbed her with both hands, lightning quick, sending a ripple of fear across Z's spine and kissed her. All manly and hard, he picked her up, carrying her to the bed. He did not set her down gently and delicate. He tossed her with a violent force of passion and she bounced, rocking the springs with loud squeaks. From her perch on his bed, she watched him undress, exposing more pale flesh that was divided by a million tiny rivers of veins. Each tentacle of the Jadaraa Soo was alive with his lust as he rushed to remove his garments like there was no time left in the world.

Z's head swooned from all the liquor. She closed her eyes to find balance in the tilting room and saw the face of her husband – *first alive and then dead.* Bile felt like a force that raced up the back of her throat. But she shook the vision of him out of her mind, out of her head. He didn't need to be there for what was going to happen. Z was intent on spiraling down. She wasn't dying, so she got busy with the nasty business of living.

Cross climbed onto the bed, bleached white and naked, and positioned the hot, flushed woman in front of him on her back, tummy flat, face looking at his. He stared down at her for a moment, pausing in his quickened state to enjoy the woman: her gorgeous form, luscious breasts, and honey brown eyes so deep they dripped like molasses with every stare. She stunk of nothing but blood and he entered her. His vile parasite absorbed Zia's vaginal secretions through the pores of his skin.

At first, Z felt the intoxicating twinge of hate as Cross's hard member slipped inside of her. Though, hour after hour, as he answered her rude questions with pounding vitality hate fell away to twisted pleasure. By the end of it she was too delirious and numb to continue and eventually begged him to stop. Her whole body pulsed in waves, vibrating, and it turned out to be the best sex she had ever had.

Exhausted and sweaty, Z lay on the bed unable to move, unable to count the steady streams of orgasms that had caused her feeble body to tremble. She invited the crazy, cock-mad confederate to lay beside her as she drifted off to sleep. The two commingled lovers didn't spoil their ride with words. Quietly, he held her. Her warm, thrumming back spooned along his cold front, and for the time being, it was all right. *Just alright.*

The creature ran at her on all fours, tearing up the ground with its tremendous arms, pulling its great bulk forward as its hind legs propelled it at a breakneck pace. She barely had enough time to grab a suitable branch from the forest floor. Scrounging in a pinch, Z reached behind herself and picked up the thickest felled limb that she could fit her hands around. Pulling it around her side to use as a lance the thing threatened to snap in half if she breathed on it improperly. Years of laying on the high desert floor, drying in the sun, losing all its moisture and vitality to the arid winds, the branch was not going to be able to impale a charging gnat, let alone a two hundred pound beast. Z had to change her tact. And fast!

Fear boiled in her veins. Thoughts of being left wide open to a raging blender did not help matters any. Images of werewolves rendering flesh from bone in movies and that sickening day in Chicago flittered across her internal home theater as the beast charged. Teeth flung drool from pulled back lips. Its head was down too low for her to reach its soft underbelly. Z felt it down to her toes – *I'm so utterly screwed!*

Holding out for that last incredible second, the vampire scooped up a handful of dry brittle soil and shot into the air over the barreling wolf. She tossed the dirt into the Agent's hairy, snarling face as scary claws reached out to pluck her from the air. Pulling her legs in tight, thankful for the springy coiling action of the Jadaraa Soo, Z sailed over the raving beastie. As she watched the creature plow under her with its tiny tail up a silly idea popped into her brain. She acted on it, whacking the wolf on its exposed rear with the useless branch that she still held in her hand.

The branch splintered to dust and the wolf yelped, not so much from any pain, but from the shock of being hit in its delicate bunghole. Humiliated, Agent Jonston fell off the edge of the mountain's ridge, leaving a wide skid mark trailing over the rocks.

Z landed with a bit more grace than the last time she was flying through the air. The grinning rascal scoured her present location for anything she could use as a weapon. Finding nothing more than the same brittle limbs on the ground she sought something with more heft. Pulling down a branch from a live tree, she spied the other agent. He was holding his split belly, trying to stand. The skinny part of his shape-shifting legs shook from the pain. It wasn't going to be too much longer before she had more than she could handle coming at her again from two fronts. Suddenly, Z realized how quiet it had gone.

Listening…

She didn't hear the thing – not its muzzled breath, nor the touch of light padding paws. She exhaled a wrenching groan dreading the thought that the wolf was laying low to draw her in. *God forbid the thing pummeled off the side of the mountain and killed itself.* Z knew the impossibility of that. The mountain was more like a long gradual pimple pushed up from the earth, cut with jagged ravines and gouging trenches that took millennia to form from seasonal rains. *No! That'd be too easy.*

Z sprinted over to the other FBI Agent and tested the mettle of her limb. Whether he wanted to stand or not, get himself into the fray, or crawl away, it didn't matter. Z swatted him twice against the head. Once when he turned and saw her coming and the other when he hit the ground. She heard a crack and would have clocked his melon again, for a third brain-splattering-round, but the low growling rumble behind her changed her tune.

Z turned as the wolf, close to the ground, stepped out from a thicket of trees, its face mean and hurtful, rolling a steady growl in the back of its throat. *Okay, here we go. Fun time's over.* She had definitely pissed it off.

1930. Chicago.

Z awoke with a start, alone in bed, having thought she heard something that jarred her sleep. As she lay her woolly head back down on the pillow, groggy with eyes half closed, and the sound erupted again. Z's eyes popped open. It was unmistakable: A wolf's howl. Its meaty braying echoed through the cavernous lair, amplified by the tunnels of brick. *A timberland beast must have found its way into the vampire's den.*

Z dressed and headed out of the room looking for Cross. Cold damp, trodden earth padded underneath her bare feet as another howl startled her. It ripped through her spine and it did not occur to her that a wolf, loose in the lair, might present some measure of trouble. She heard Leinil's violin echoing around the tang of the creature's moan and followed the illustrious sounds of the fiddle. Cross and Benjamin were otherwise engaged in a game of chess, the maestro played as the lovers, Delgado and Paige, were embroiled in books of poetry. Selina, Perceval, and Gavin kept company at the far side of room as Z approached Cross. But Emily intercepted her.

"What brings the little Miss out?"

"Did you not hear it?"

"Hear what?" whispered Emily playfully, stroking Z's long hair as the wolf called again. Emily grinned, a devilish smile of rotting teeth, and laughed at Z's wrinkled face, leaving the girl to stew in her confusion and disgust.

"Red Riding Hood, Red Riding Hood through the forest dark and deep," sang the demented ghoul as she wandered down the tunnel. "The big bad wolf is coming to Grandma's house it creeps."

Emily cackled and howled like a wolf, and the beast responded in kind. Z did her best to ignore her and crossed to the soldiers playing their game of pieces.

"I thought you resting when I left?" reprised Cross upon seeing her.

"It must be trapped down here." began Z to a room full of eyes. "It woke me. Can you not hear it?"

The girl was visibly phased and breathing hard. But she was more worried as to why nobody else seemed too concerned that a woodland creature was lost among them. Cross gazed at his concubine, understanding her distress.

"Excuse me, Benjamin," he added as he stood. "Might we continue some other time?"

"Yes, of course."

Cross held out his hand for the widow, inviting her to walk with him to their room. Another moan escaped from the muzzled lips of the unseen animal and Cross informed her that Arielle and Kiyiya had arrived during her absence earlier that day. He assured her that she would meet them tomorrow after she had rested fully. The feeding that he had with her, only a few hours ago still kept her weak.

For four and half days the widow had been locked away from the northern brood, tending to her womanly wound. She barely had the chance to escape the small confines of their shared cell when the vampire began feeding from her again. His teeth were heavy like a starved child against her skin. The last of the liquor was gone and she had reread the book over again, all she wanted was time away from the small den, but she was continually led back.

A month and a half had passed with the vampires and Z figured there wasn't much else to learn. But she was wrong. Little Alice's journey down the rabbit hole was never-ending and twisting with regular oddities. Cross told the girl that Kiyiya was a shape-shifter, calling him a Windigo. But Z scarcely understood the word or how it had anything to do with the howling noise ripping through the tunnels.

He sat with her on the bed and explained that it happened on occasions when the native and Arielle lodged with them and intertwined in the flesh. Having never grown up with ghost stories or weird tales as a child Z did not fully understand the intricate qualities of a shape-shifter. What Cross described to her sounded beastly and god awful – *a four legged dog between the legs of a woman*. The sheer mechanics of it did not seem possible. The wolf's howl echoed through the din of the lair again, and it was hard for Z to picture how the man's lustful cries of passion transformed him into a timberland creature.

Run Alice Run! The place was strange indeed. Kiyiya was not like her. He wasn't even like them. He was something all together different, a man that could change into the body of a wolf. If any last remnants of Z's old world thinking still clung to her shattered bonnet then the knowledge of such a bizarre beast, that she could no more imagine than understand, destroyed them. Her world…had gone…completely insane.

She bid the man to return to his game with Benjamin and leave her to her absolute segregation. His explanations of the baleful howls left the widow with a nagging gut, feeling utterly lost. She lay in the bed, knees pulled tight to her chest, listening to the cries of passion from a man that was not a man and a wolf that was not a wolf. Absentmindedly, her fingers fidgeted with Cross's bite marks until sleep finally took her.

In dreams…her mind struggled to make sense of it all.

They met in the common room. Z had been awake for awhile. She and Benjamin had already completed their daily game when the creature and his bride came sauntering into view. The widow was immediately struck by Arielle's beauty. She wore a stunning silk blue dress with dark navy brocade and a necklace of sparkling sapphire. The dress was a modern cut and she looked as if she were going out on the town. Her blond curls fell around her shoulders and cherubic face. She lightly held the hand of the man beside her as she walked confidently into the room.

Kiyiya looked human. Z didn't know what to expect upon seeing him, but he resembled her own delicate species, even though she knew that he was not. The Objiwe tribesman was tall, broad shouldered, had sun-dried olive skin, and wore his shimmering black hair long. He had it pulled back, wore a fashionable suit, and his braid ran down his length to the small of his back. As he neared, Z was instantly aroused by the native's masculine presence. Vanessa gently laid her hand to Z's back, leaned in, and whispered, "Steady yourself."

That was another thing Z envied the undead – *their gifted smell.* Nothing was private in their company. Even the smallest expression was detected through their enhanced physical senses. It was annoying sometimes. So, Z greeted the vampire and her gorgeous man, trying to make a quick exit before she did anything stupid to embarrass herself.

"So, you are the one for Cross," Arielle said politely. "Z, I am told?"

"Yes," the widow claimed, enraptured in the man's delicious pheromones.

The vampire smiled knowingly and Z saw her teeth. Those gnarled, canine teeth, set within her pale complexion and crisscrossing veins of the parasite. Kiyiya took her hand and pressed his lips to her fingers in a gentlemanly bow, as he said hello. Z was a flutter. She could barely contain her heat. The man was a magnet of charisma, and it didn't matter anymore if he turned into a dog or not, she wanted to bed him.

"Such a short affirmation for such a lovely creature," he told her in reference to her name.

But all she could muster was, "yeah."

"You look pale, child," grieved Arielle, taking Z by the shoulders. "How long have you been down here?"

The widow pulled her attention to the ravishing woman. "Don't rightly know. Feels like forever."

The vampire flashed a toothless smile, full of sympathy, and turning to Cross said, "Franklin, this will not do. We can not have her becoming sick on her big day."

"Most true," the confederate added.

"Very well then. It is agreed," the ravishing vampire spoke. "Tonight we venture out." She patted Z's shoulder. "Now, let's get you dressed."

Z wasn't sure what was happening, but she followed the lady as she led her from the room. Kiyiya lifted a hand to his chest and bowed slightly, saying a blessing in his native tongue as they departed.

In the vampire's chambers the widowed Mrs. Boyd spied slashes in the stone wall near the couple's four-post bed. It looked as if some one, or something, had gouged their claws in a raging fury. A ball of fear welled up in Z's belly, knotting. She didn't understand. Looking at the grooves in the wall, at least an inch wide with a foot spread, she shivered and thought it best to keep her questions about the native to herself. But the vampire noted the woman's rank curiosity and encouraged her to speak to Kiyiya if she had any questions.

"Better to know," Arielle said, "than to let fear fester." Gazing at the woman through the mirror she moved Z's hair this way and that to find the perfect style. "You are very pretty, my dear. But you dress unflatteringly."

"Haven't really felt like gettin' dolled up."

"Yes, I can imagine." The vampire found a suitable style and began pinning up the woman's hair. "You did not come to this of your own accord?"

"No," Z answered flatly, fearing that she'd spoil the moment with banal truths if she said more. It had been ages since she had been pampered, and it simply felt nice.

"I know it is difficult," the vampire sympathized, catching the hard glint in her eyes. "But Vanessa says you are wearing it rather well." She applied makeup to Z's face "I have known Cross for a very long time and if there is anything you want to know, just ask." She smiled with knowing eyes.

"Thank you." It was all Z could muster to say.

When Arielle had finished accentuating the widow's beauty, she fit her into one of her frocks, a lavish green dress from a different era, and told Z a little about her life to pass the time and ease comfort and friendship between them. The woman was amazed to discover that Arielle was one hundred and twenty one years old. An only daughter of a traveling preacher, formerly out of Philadelphia, she grew up on the road and had a love affair with a being called R'Aan that she referred to as an Omjadda.

The implication of the affair was astounding, the rabbit hole kept slipping, kept getting wider and wider. There was no fixed point to the ground, her compass spun wildly, she was falling and it was the most dolled up that she had ever been in her entire life. Z looked at herself in the mirror – transformed.

"It's beautiful," the girl added, commenting on the gown. It was a new mask for the hardened bank robber.

"You wear it well."

Despite the woman's frequent compliments, Z did not feel as radiant as the vampire that stood beside her. Arielle's features even paled the striking beauty of Selina Pillar and suddenly the math of years that they had been discussing took relevant shape. "That makes you the oldest one in the coven."

"Not quite," she informed, affixing a pin into the widow's hair.

"Cross is only a hundred and one. You out pace him by twenty. It has to be weird living so long."

"It takes some getting used to," the vampire confessed.

"So, who is it then? Who's older than you? Is it Selina? I don't think I've ever heard how old she is."

"No. Selina has yet to crown her first century." The vampire stepped back to admire her work on the live girl. "It is Kiyiya."

"Kiyiya?" Z didn't understand. "He barely looks a day over thirty."

"Yet he was born several years before I." The preacher's daughter liked her handiwork. "1792 I believe. Not too far from where we are now."

Z turned and faced the regal woman. "Cross told me about him."

"Good. I am sure he spoke well."

"He did." Z hesitated not wanting to corrupt the fun she was having, but she needed to know. "Does he…you know, does he always turn into an animal when you and he…"

Arielle laughed, a brightly feathered thing that lifted Z's fears away. "So that is what he has been telling you." She bubbled sensibly in her mirth, a jewel among Z's entire experience under the cemetery. "I see now your hesitation."

"I'm sorry. I don't mean to pry. It's just that…"

"It is fairly hard to take in at first," she surmised. "I understand."

Z kept hearing that. That they understood. Almost everyone in the coven had told her, at one time or another, that they understood what she was going through. Confusion was normal for their kind as they entered into night, and they wanted her to know that she was not alone in its rough ways and hard embrace. Yet, in their cold, dispassionate smiles, lit in their far away eyes, set within a ghostly condition that drank the blood of the living, Z found it hard to accept.

Again, Arielle suggested that she take her questions directly to the shape-shifter, even though the vampire knew that he made Z hot. "He is kindly and will help you to understand," she bade. "Now, let's see if the others are ready."

Z nodded and followed Arielle to a main section of hallway where they were waiting. Tyler Delgado, Alayna Paige, Robert Keoning, Kiyiya, Cross, and Vee were there dressed to the nines, looking sharp and ready to kill. Cross complimented the widow on her stunning appearance, giving praise to the vampire that had assisted the mortal woman with looking so replete with splendor.

The old soldier wore a fashionable suit instead of his formal military grays and he enveloped his prize in an arm as Robert pressed against the wall. A stone grating from behind Z pulled her attention to the smell of fresh air as it hit her in the face. She was awestruck at the feel of the night on her cheeks. The vampires glided through the opened portal, obstructing her view. Z looked back down the tunnel from where they had come and had absolutely no recollection as to how she'd gotten there. She was too enraptured in her conversations with Arielle to detect distinct markers.

The opened portal let out into a mausoleum. Beyond its windows, marble walls, and door the world waited breathlessly. It was so close that she could taste it. Evening danced on her skin as she strode past the rows of tombs, completely beside herself, never noticing how the vampire's watched her. It had been weeks since she last asked about going outside, and now here she was only seconds away from the bright lights of the big city. As she stepped out of the monolith structure, setting her feet firmly on the tender grass of terra firma, all her chiding little questions about Kiyiya and Arielle's past, who Cross truly was, and why she was here among the vicious brood fell away to the joyful fact that she was simply, and positively, outside.

Finally…the ground and the sky the above. Cool wind blew about her shoulders. Z did not hurry to place the shawl around her neck that Vanessa had given to her to wear when they had met in the tunnels. The vampires absorbed Z's wonder as she took the night into her lungs, closed her eyes, stretched her arms out wide, and twirled under a gaping glitter of stars. A crescent moon dangled from the sky's earlobe and, in all her imaginings, Zia Jean never thought that such a plain thing, as the fresh outdoors, would feel so incredibly good.

"Look at the girl, Franklin," lectured Arielle to the grim master. "You must take her out more, from now on. Show the lady the town."

The stalwart lieutenant did not reply. Instead, he asked the mortal woman to entreat them with a little of her life and history as they strode through the cemetery. Under twilight scents and moonlit zephyr she unfurled her song. Thinking, at first, that it held nothing as dramatic as she had heard from the pale lady this afternoon, Z soon found out that her audience was most eager and interested in her life.

Crossing the old railroad tracks for the belly of Chicago, passing monumental headstones from some of Second City's most wealthy, lumbering guests, the vampires deepened Z's tale with probing questions. The woman found out things about herself through the ripe vein of conversation that she had taken for granted.

In the vampires' eyes, she was a marvelous thing, exciting and full of vibrant energy. She was a highwayman, whose love affair with the criminal, Mr. Boyd, was as enrapturing and delightful as Cross's and Benjamin's days in the war, or Arielle's escape into the mountains with an Omjadda prince. Z's tale nourished them. They were astonished at her daring feats of thievery and found kinship in her reasoning as to why she and Simon Ray defied the law, cutting a path of swashbuckling antics through a country that steadily declined, steering away from its original independent values. They kept the woman talking long into the night, visiting smelly, back alley gin-joints that howled with jazz and the vigor of the city, until eventually the party dissected and dispersed.

Vanessa left with a man that Z would have sworn worked for the Outfit and Robert found a whore, bidding them ado. Tyler and Alayna departed for a walk around Lincoln Park so they too could find their own delicious snacks. The rest gained access to one of the city's growing skyscrapers and spilled out onto the roof. The wind was murderous. Whipping and alive, the vampires did not want to stay in its pushy embrace, but Z didn't want to leave. The scope of the cityscape was breathtaking. The winds, though fierce, were better than the stagnant pools of dead air in the lair.

So she was glad that Cross conceded to remain with her on the top of the world when Kiyiya and Arielle took there leave. Z knew she would have to return soon to that dank place, but not yet. *Not yet.* It was just the two of them now, whittled down by the affairs of the evening, and it was all that tethered the poor widow to the earth.

"They have all agreed," said Cross as he stood next to the woman who peered over the ledge of the building.

"Agreed to what?" Z pulled a piece of hair out of her mouth that had blown there.

"To have you as one of us."

"I thought that was your plan all along."

"True. But I required the consent of the whole coven." He stared at her earnestly. "Bringing a new member into our fold is not something that I can do alone."

"Aren't you the big cheese? Boss man? Numero Uno?"

Cross laughed. He enjoyed her frank humor, wicked as it was at times. "This was a decision that effected us all. So, we each had a say in it."

Z just looked at him until finally the gravity of what his words meant settled within her. "I had to wait for Arielle and Kiyiya to return," he continued. "Before I would know for sure." He paused as the wind whipped between them, a steady thundering of hooves. "She's returned with the blood."

At first Z didn't grab his meaning. *The Blood?* The hem of her dress twisted in the noisy blasts of gusty air until it slowly dawned on her. *The Blood.* She recalled Cross telling her that they were transformed by the blood of an Omjadda and as Arielle pampered her and dressed her in her fine things she told Z about her love affair with one of the ancients.

"Is it R'Aan's?" the woman asked.

"I do not know. And I do not think she will tell you if you ask. So please, do not."

Z stared at the twinkling lights below and the dark ebb of Lake Michigan. All of a sudden she grew very cold. She drew the shawl that Vanessa had given her tighter around her arms and inhaled the altitude. "I bet Selina didn't agree."

Cross smirked and shook his head diffidently. "I feared you'd think as much. I heard about your little scuffle with the knife and I'll have you know that she was one of your more staunch supporters."

Z's eyes flared wide with amazement. *If she was a supporter then who drew against me?* "She has a way about her," Cross added. "his can not be denied. But do not let it fool you."

Z bowed her head and chuckled. *All this time? Cowering from the woman and avoiding her like the plague and she turns out to be okay.* Z sighed. She had so much to learn. "What happens next?"

Cross pulled her close to him, placing an arm around her waist, nestling against the woman for her warmth as his Jadaraa Soo writhed comfortably between the embrace. "We enjoy the view."

He held her for awhile and he felt her shaking. He knew that it wasn't due to the wind. He'd opened a door for her that could never be closed and in it were all sorts of horrors and wonders that she could scarcely imagine. After a time, Cross bit her. There on the roof, gazing out on a living tapestry of stars and street lights, the din of the city roaring with the music of the gale. It was too enchanting a scene for him to refrain from his hunger and his passion, so he supped of her intoxicating red fluid. Not a lot, just a taste, a luscious little taste of the damnable woman that held sway over him

As they departed the roof through an unlocked access, Z asked, "What would have happened had the vote not been in my favor?"

Cross smirked, knowing how the girl had become his meter and centerpiece of this strange new age. "Then we would have started our own coven."

Z let him kiss her then. He held the door open for her to pass, and to the stars staring down at them from the heavens it might have looked romantic. But inside the widow, twanging pangs of guilt skirted the edges of her soul as she flirted with the man that had made her kill her husband. She pushed her hate down with the hopes of burying it forever. However cold the eyes of the stars were, the solid truth was colder: Simon Ray was dead. She was here and alive, struggling to hang on.

Life was too impermanent for her to stay tied to any one thing or person. The delicate Mrs. Boyd knew that, even if the timeless slow-decayers did not. She always figured that she and Simon Ray would go out together in a smoky hail of gunfire with some of Hoover's boys. *Better to burnout than fade away.* So, her time with the vampires was altogether different, startling and weird. The ruckus rascal was fading into the din of the city, the menagerie of the lair, and the widening gulf of her limited understanding of how the world spun crazy.

On the street, Cross hailed a taxi and they drove around the Loop for awhile before being dropped off at a nondescript location near the cemetery. It was a wonderful night. The city was magnificent with its tall press, lively spots, and bright lights. It pulsed in Z's ardent veins. *Perhaps it isn't all bad, this underground existence. Arielle seems akin to it. As does Vanessa and my silent buddy Selina Pillar.*

Z thought of living a life as long as the preacher's daughter, or even the native, and figured that if she were going to have time to kill that she'd spend some of it getting to know Tristin. His handsome charm had proven conspicuously absent of late since she spilled her drunken guts to Vee. *Yeah. Perhaps, it won't be so bad. Living timeless. Being around forever.* In the back seat of the yellow cab the widow snuggled against Cross's cold shoulders and dreamed.

Z stepped away from the felled beast, moving into a clearing to give herself some room to maneuver around the agent that growled behind her. The two creatures circled one another. Z held the branch like a baseball bat, recalling the last time she stared a big bad wolf down. Things were different then. Buried under the skin of the earth, in a darkened corridor, she wasn't even a vampire yet, just human. Regular meat tar-tar and only a tad more vulnerable than she was just now. Fear didn't pump the same back then. Under the cemetery, Z was numb to almost everything, teetering on the edge of death at every second from god knew where. She was spoiled in her grief over her dead husband, selling her body so that she could live just one more day.

Fear beat the hell out of her now, but she was calm in its maddening embrace. Her cares and concern were more focused on the rising sun that was creeping through the trees. The wolf's teeth glistened just as brightly now as it did in that darken hovel in Z's mind. Nasty and sharp, the thing yearned for the vampire's flesh. *So, this it? A hot meal for you while you chew my charring corpse? Okay. Better to burnout than fade away!*

Z charged the shape-shifter, and for a split second she thought she saw a flicker of doubt in the gauge of Agent Jonston's fiery yellow eyes; surprised that the vampire would rush headlong to her death. *Doesn't he know? I've been dying for years!* Late to the quick, the wolf ran at his target and jumped. *Thank you, Jesus.* Z jumped too. Twisting her body and positioning the tree branch, she jabbed the limb into the soft flesh of the creature's neck, just above its collarbone, as he grabbed her. They fell to the ground where gravity and earth did what Z's lack of leverage could not: Impale the limb all the way through the werewolf's thick pelt and muscular throat. He lay on top of her gurgling his own blood, unable to even moan or cry out in agonizing pain.

The werewolf's bright red fluid poured over Z, oozing into the valleys of her rendered flesh, giving the savage Jadaraa Soo something to lap up. Buried under a reeking carpet of Agent Jonston, Z struggled to breathe in her own right. Canine musk and the man's unique smell smothered her as she crawled from beneath the beast. But he wouldn't let her go.

Just like a G-Man. The wolf grabbed Z by her ankle with a weak and feeble hold as she sat up. Looking down at the dying animal, sunburst eyes pitiful and sad, choking on its own vital fluid, the vampire knew what she had to do. Reaching for a rock, she had to be sure. It was just a nagging feeling about her kind and other nocturnal creatures that smacked of unwanted sequels. Z intended for this dance to end.

"Hey..." she panted as she pulled a large flat stone toward her. "You ever see that Stephen King movie, Sometimes They Come Back?" The flat rock grated across the ground to her lap. "Well, it looks like you're not going to be able to either."

Z knew if she were a normal gal that she would feel some sense of remorse, some ounce of regret for snuffing out another life so indiscreetly. But Z had never been a normal gal. Even before she partook of the dark drink the thrill of violence enticed her, thrilled her; made her do evil things. She smirked, a vicious grin, as she brought the heavy rock down on its head, again and again. Bright red werewolf blood splattered and misted her face – *red kisses*. Agent Jonston flinched, body jolting with each thud. Z thought of The Fly. How Patricia Owens crushed the giant insect's head in the compactor and Vincent Price smashed the webbed insect before the spider could make it a meal.

She heard the Scientist's small voice in her ears, attached to the insect body. *"Help Me. Help Me."* Z slammed the flat, broad stone down on its head – over and over – *have to be sure* – smashing the Hoover boy's drawn-out jowls and massive head to a bloody, meaty, unrecognizable pulp. Her face and arms were a Pollock painting of death. The agent's cruel, black claws limply unfurled from around Z's ankle as its life ebbed away.

Roughly, she used the thin edge of the stone to saw the beast's head off. It was messy and grueling work. She had to put her back into it, grinding the stone against the earth to severe the mangled melon from its body. *Have to be sure. Have to be! Fuckin' bad pennies.*

Creatures with regenerative qualities were a pain in the ass. Better to spend time on the little copper Lincoln's and do the job right. As Z carried her killing rock over to the other writhing and injured wolf Agent Jonston's hair began to slowly fall away from his dead flesh. It lay in piles around his corpse like pine needles. Bones reset to their normal configuration, their normal size and shape, popping and cracking under mushy muscles that receded into the form of a naked man. His head severed, lying prone on the forest floor set affront a red rising sun.

Z whacked the other beast upside the head for good measure, to keep him down. His belly and lumps were healing. *Best not let him get an edge on me.* Z was tired, worn, she felt like achy hammered shit and wanted nothing more than a bottle of Johnny Walker Black, a Sanglant, and a couch to prop up her feet. She wanted to kick back and soothe her ugly wounds with alcohol and blood. Yet, here she was stuck in the middle of nowhere. *With you ugly sonnabitches on my heels while Lin and Sarah are...*

She held the rock in mid swing as a face formed from her returning memories; holes the size of bicycle tires spinning in her head. It was the same face that she had seen a time or two in Lin's locket. The hussy was on a stage and in the relic. Suddenly, it all came crashing back in a tidal wave of two bad days and an interfering brat that stole Lin's affection. *That bitch!* Z glared down at hairy Agent Johnson as he struggled to rise.

"I know Dominique sent you. I wanna hear it outta your mouth." She kicked the beast. "C'mon. Say it boy. Say it." She clicked her tongue along the back of her teeth just as if she was calling her favorite pooch. "Say it."

But she could see it in his eyes that she wasn't going to get anything out of him. His anger was bleeding through in waves. "Ah hell!" she said. "I know it's her." She smacked the creature with the flat side of the rock again and tossed the stone to the ground. "Fuckin' bitches, I tell you what. Lin sure knows how to pick 'em."

The stone landed with a thud on the ground close by and cracked in half. Z crouched down and jammed her arm into the healing split of the werewolf's belly as it howled utter torture. "That's my ear!" she yelled and punched it in the snout.

The vampire yanked her arm out of the shape-shifter's body cavity, clutching onto a healthy handful of intestines. She pulled and out spilled the creature's guts. She rose and walked around to its backside bringing the fleshy rope with her. She wrapped it around the wolf's beefy neck, good–n–tight, and tugged. She even put her boot on the werewolf's furry, broad back and pushed as she wrenched the intestines tight, strangling the air completely out of the agent's throat.

All around her the ground began to take definite shape. Shadows around rocks and trees formed little pools of night, clinging to the earth defiantly. The sky she faced in somber, morning light was soft and clear. There were no clouds to offer retreat. She closed her eyes and jerked the intestines harder. As the creature's last wheezing gasps of air chortled through its muzzle the sun's warmth began to heat Z's back. *Fuck!* She could feel her Jadaraa Soo slinking away. *I'm toast.*

1930. Chicago.

Z was no good at it. She stunk. Pulling the rosined bow across the strings of Leinil's fine instrument she made noises that would frighten a sick cat. Vanessa and Gavin were laughing. They were no better, though, Gavin did pluck a nice melody before he abandoned the violin altogether for Z's out-of-tune ear. Leinil did show her how to hold the bow and lay her head on the chinrest. But he could not help her with what she lacked musically. That only the divine creator could account for and he apparently missed the young Zia Jean on her delivery day with the special gift of music.

Gavin and Vanessa applauded as the maestro retrieved his instrument in good cheer and played for them a sonata by Antonín Dvořák, a Czech composer whose romantic melodies Leinil had recently fallen in love with. In his hands the strings came alive, the body of hand-carved wood sang a lovely tune as soulful notes filled the antechamber and fled down the halls. His fiddling of waxed horsehair trailing over the bridge lighted the darkened tombs under Rosehill Cemetery and everyone knew what the sounds of heaven sounded like.

Benjamin told Z once that the maestro used to play for the Chicago Orchestra. That he, Emily, Cross, and others first heard him perform when the orchestra played their first concert on October 16, 1891. They were regulars of the symphonic exhibits then and watched with much glee Leinil's progress to first chair. Emily was enthralled with the young man and eventually claimed him for herself. The widow had never heard Leinil speak of this and was confused as to the relationship he had with the ghastly revenant, having never really seen them together. If the two were still a couple they did not flaunt their affections like Tyler and Alayna.

The violinist was a solitary man and away from his instrument he was often found alone with a book, or jotting down notes, capturing the music he composed silently in his head. Leinil's voice spoke through the tiny round purfling and curved body of the feminine-shaped instrument as if it were all he needed to connect with the world and communicate his heart and mind.

Both the big man and Cross came into the room as Leinil played. Cross touched Z's back lightly and silently bid her to come away with him. She followed the Lieutenant to the mouth of the tunnel away from the main group. Having finally gotten a handle on the layout of the underground catacombs Z began to feel a bit more at ease within the place.

There were three main rooms connected by one snaking tunnel that wound in a flattened triangle. The room they occupied was the smallest of the common areas and a favorite among the brood. Each common room was connected to another series of tunnels dedicated specifically to that room that either led to personal chambers, storage facilities, or looped back around. There were also those long, dark passages that led nowhere, having been sealed off in a collapse or left unfinished decades ago. The lair even supported crawlways that led to hidden entrances stationed throughout the cemetery in large stone crypts. As Cross explained several evenings earlier, he and Bellecourt designed additional ossuary passages and quarters so that it would not be easy for anyone to find their way through the winding lanes if they had accidentally stumbled upon the secluded den.

"Would you take the drink this evening?" Cross asked with an ear to Mr. Goode.

Since that night out, atop the skyscraper, overlooking Chicago they had not spoken of the Omjadda blood that Arielle and Kiyiya had procured from the Dalam Kha'Shiya J'in. Several days had passed. Z knew it was there. Her destiny as a revenant waited for her, so she did not rush headlong into its cold embrace. Instead, a calm knowing descended within her and she took compliment and pleasure in the company of the vampires like she had never done before.

Cross had taken to entreating the woman with long walks through the cemetery at night and she'd become more docile in his company. On more than one occasion Z had gathered up the nerve to talk with Tristin and things seemed promising. But she still found it difficult to locate the young vampire when she wanted or when Cross was most indisposed.

"What is it?" the southern soldier asked, reading her hesitation.

"There is something I want to do first." Z withheld the condition within her breast, chewing the flat inside of her lip as she looked at Cross.

"I can not help you with it if you won't tell me what it is."

"I want to leave. Out on my own for two days, maybe three… and then when I come back," she balked at saying it. "I will take the drink with you."

Nervously, Z fidgeted her fingers and scrunched up her brow trying to discern the thoughts that flitted through the confederate's wooly head. He had kept her so guarded since she arrived. Time had tempered many things between the two of them, in this it was assured, but the widow didn't know if it had also tempered the trust of her jailer.

But before the man could render a decision on the matter a loud wolf's yowl rippled through the winding labyrinths. It broke the tension that Z tightly held in her shoulders as she thought of Kiyiya and Arielle intertwined in their lovemaking, so rigorous and passionate that it called out the native's wolf to unsheathe his skin in wild forms.

But Cross did not share in Z's mirth. He held an unyielding countenance, and as Z looked around she noticed that the others also stood by quietly. Leinil Goode's slim instrument hung down at his side, his bow taught in his hand; all the vampires were listening.

Cross looked to the big man. "What do you think?"

"Aye," said Benjamin. "It is not our brother."

The military man's eyes dashed in their sockets as he quickly reigned his thoughts. "You stay here," he told Z, with a force of power. "Gavin, Leinil, Benjamin – you are with me. Vanessa?" he shouted as he grabbed Z's arm, bringing the mortal woman to her side. "Stay with Z. Do not let her out of your sight until I return."

"What is it?" Z inquired "What's going on?"

Cross didn't answer. He didn't look at her. He joined his crew walking with them at a brisk pace down the main tunnel. The widow turned to her friend, wondering where Arielle and the native had gotten off to.

"Vee?" she begged, more pissed off at being left behind than not knowing. "What's going on here?"

"I don't know Z. Best to leave them to it." Vanessa watched the unpredictable woman standing at the mouth of the tunnel, staring down its deep dark orifice. "Come away, Z. Come away. Let's go to our rooms."

Reluctantly, Z stepped away from the passage, crossing to
Vanessa, as the mouth of the carved out orifice glared dark unhappiness.
It irked Z that some sort of action was taking place without her while she
was being sequestered away like a common housewife. The highwayman
was used to being in the thick of it. She thrived on the adrenaline rush
of a good fight. Waiting in the wings like a good little girl was never her
style, never her scene.

A scream curled the tense silence around them. It sent shivers up
both their spines. But even the bustling fear could not hold Z back. She
sprinted to the mouth of the tunnel again. "Who was that?"

"I don't know," lied Vanessa, thinking that it sounded a lot like Alayna.

Then, gunshots pinged and echoed through the amplifying
tunnels. Vanessa's worries were confirmed and Z's fear grew intense. The
vampire grabbed Z by the elbow, pulling her away when a low rumbling
growl resounded behind them.

They spun around and glared into the dark mouth of the other
connecting tunnel, a huge gaping wound in the pit of their bellies.
Vanessa trained her eyes through the dark tube until she saw it. A
werewolf! It walked on all fours toward them. The hairs along its thick
back stood on end. It had caught their scents and bared its sharp teeth.
Madness gleamed in its eyes.

"Z? Z? Get behind me." Vanessa moved to cover her as the
huge animal spilled out of the darkened edge across the room. "Get
behind me now, Z!"

The widow didn't hesitate. The beast was huge. It looked
nothing like how she'd imagined Kiyiya looking based on wolves that
she had seen in nature magazines. Its arms were muscular and long like
a man's and it was covered in pure black fur from stem to stern, except
that this beast had a wisp of white hair on the top of its head. Its frontal
paws were hand-like with gnarled claws that clicked on the stone flooring
as it drew closer. Its rear legs were oblong, with elongated feet, but still
recognizable as that of a man's. It had massive thighs for jumping and
running. It had a slim waist and protruding ribcage like a fat dog, an oily
round head with pointy ears, and a short muzzle brimming with rows of
sharp, drooling teeth. It growled terrifying thunder in its throat.

"When I say," Vee instructed, "run; do you hear me?"

"Yeah," Z squeaked, more amazed at the reality of the beast she witnessed than having the forethought to be ripped with piping hot fear. "You're beautiful," he whispered aloud in a daze.

It looked as if it was about to jump when a yell from above pulled its attention upward. The women turned as Cross jumped from an opened doorway cut in the soil of the curved roof. His arms were splayed wide, chest flailing outward. He gripped his cavalry sword, screaming through the air as he fell.

The creature cowered as it gazed upon the man landing on it. It yelped in bright pain as Cross drove his sword between its ribcage. Vanessa didn't hesitate, she pushed Z to flee, but the widow was too mesmerized by Cross and the beast. The shape-shifter easily rolled the soldier off its back and stood upon its hind legs like a man. It towered over them, huge like a bear. Cross stood between it and his people. He did not shrink from the fight, going toe to toe with the nightmare animal.

"Get out of here!" he yelled as he lunged at it again with his puny blade.

Vanessa had to practically drag Z from the room, shouting at her that they needed to go. It didn't sit right with the woman to leave Cross alone in the attack. She felt like a coward, going the other way, but didn't have any say in the matter. Vee's firm grip pulled her along, too fierce to break. If she thought about it, even for an instant, she would have realized that there was nothing she could do against the canine intruders, except die or hide.

In a widening birth of the tunnel they passed Selina and Tristin fighting with another werewolf. This one had gray hair with tufts of black running oblong across its body. Vee dragged Z away quickly and the widow saw Selina out the corner of her eye, twirling like a Dervish, crouched low, slicing open the wolf's belly with the tips of her razorblade fingernails. Upon standing, the black haired wraith stabbed the beast with both hands in the chest as Tristin kicked the animal's legs out from under it. The calm, placid look on Selina's face was galvanizing; everything felt like a dream.

Running down the tunnel, pulled by the taught arm of her friend, Z heard a pounding thud behind them, bouncing off the limestone and brick. It echoed growls, grunts, and gunshots. Vanessa barely had enough time to push Z through a door to a storage closet before a set of massive jaws tore her from sight. Vee screamed wildly, being dragged down the tunnel away from her. Z rent the muscles of her vocal chords to a bitter ache, calling her name. But she was gone.

Leaving the little storage hold, Z ran after them, finding the creature gnawing on her dear, dead friend around the bend. "Get away from her," she quaked through shaking lips as she kicked the animal in the rear.

The wolf dropped Vanessa, turned about, and faced her. Its orange-yellow eyes burned with exquisite hate at the frail young thing standing before it. In the beast's nostrils, Z's scent was soft and pulpy, teeming with fresh, natural life. She was unlike the vampires. It made the wolf drool hungrily as it inched forward. Z trembled, but held her ground.

The creature lunged. Z steeled herself for the sharp pierce of its nasty teeth and claws when a dark brown shape moved across her from the side. It grabbed the werewolf in mid air. Snapping teeth clamped down a hair's breadth away from her nose as the hulking blur threw the creature against the far wall. It yowled in pain as the other wolf stepped in front of Z, defensively.

"Chogan, No!" the wolf shouted. "Enough of this! Tell my brother that I will meet with him."

Kiyiya? The wolf's mane was mostly brown in color and it had an unmistakable sable streak running down its back. Hearing words escape from its muzzled lips in a deep gravelly voice stunned the woman. It looked more animal than man; Alice was falling again. The smaller wolf picked itself up from the ground and stood on its hind legs with a menacing stance.

"That will *not* be enough."

"It will to do for now," growled the beast with the sable streak. "Or none of you shall leave here alive."

"You'd do that to your own waakaa'igan?"

"Go! Before you find out."

The werewolf snorted and stammered, but it ran off as a gigantic howl erupted from its galloping muzzle. The sound boomed throughout the caverns and twisting halls of the vampire's den. The brownish wolf with the sable streak turned to the widow and Vee as the vampire struggled to pull herself from the dirty floor. Vanessa's left shoulder was severely punctured and her right side was perforated by slashes where heavy claws had dug in.

"Are you all right?" Z asked, rushing to her.

"Mostly," Vanessa chuckled nervously as she tried to ignore the pain.

She helped Vee to stand; flicking her eyes to the wolf that watched them. Its musk was thick and brawny. Z wasn't sure what it wanted or if she should be concerned. At the moment the hairy beast just stood there until it rent its gigantic head toward the darkened ceiling of the tunnel, opened its long mouth, and cried a strange noise. Groans of pain shook its massive body. Bones popped and cracked back to the size and shape of a man in an agonizing metamorphosis. Brown fur slowly receded to sweaty olive skin and the sable streak that had ran down the length of the creature's back transformed into the flowing mane of Kiyiya's long hair. If Z had not seen it with her own eyes than she would not have believed it. Standing before her was the naked specter of the Objiwe native, where only a moment ago stood a wild beast.

"I am sorry," he said turning and walked away.

Z was too dumbstruck to utter a single sound. She moved to help Vee, but the vampire did not require her aid. Only the syrupy tang of blood would assist her to heal from the wolf's bites. Being so close to Cross's prize, the injured revenant was tempted.

They wound their way back through the winding tunnels to the common room, picking up a few others. Gavin had lost a hand and was taken to his quarters by Leinil who had lost his instrument when he saved Gavin from losing anything else. Benjamin had beat back two wolves on his own and Tyler shot several of them while rescuing Alayna.

It appeared that the wolves entered through a couple of the hidden entrances at once, flooding the lair with their stink, wreaking havoc wherever they could. Robert, Emily, and Perceval's whereabouts were not yet known and Selina and Tristin looked relatively unscathed from their ordeal. They followed the big man, Z, and Vee to where the others gathered.

By the time they arrived, those that were in wolf form had already transmogrified into their human guise. Arielle stood at Kiyiya's side at the far end of the room, and the native wore a wool blanket while talking with another native who was bigger than he. The man had a patch of white running through his hair from the top of his head and he held his side where Cross's sword had struck. Z recalled that the wolf that had first come upon them in the common room had a white mane trailing through its fur, just as Kiyiya had a black one. Their voices were animated and spoke a language that she did not understand. She assumed correctly that it was Kiyiya's native speech.

Cross stood behind them, a little ways from the native. He looked haggard, but none the worse for wear for his ordeal. At Kiyiya's advice he gave them room to council. The lieutenant stiffened as the others approached, watching the eyes of the wolf pack outline his coven members. Z went to him and saw a great big swath of torn clothing and ripped flesh along his abdomen and left side. He held a tight chin and kept his eye on the pack. His other hand held firm to his bloodstained sword.

The men and women gathered around the tall native had their wounds too. Though, to Z's untrained eye they did not look as bad as her ragged bunch. Selina's hands were stark red, dripping blood onto the floor. The widow tried to pinpoint the shape-shifter that had felt the vampire's viscous stings and thought she saw him near the back holding in his guts. Everyone paid their attention forward, drawn by the meeting that embroiled Kiyiya and Arielle.

Z felt Cross pull her toward him. She gazed into his chiseled blue eyes, and then looked down at his slashed side. Placing a hand over the rough wound, she felt the tingle and wiggle of his tiny parasitic veins rubbing against her flesh.

"You need to feed," she whispered.

"Aye," he softly spoke in her ear. "But there are others with more need than I."

Z thought about it, looking at Vee holding her shoulder. She saw the bite on Tristin's arm. She stared up at the lieutenant. He did not have to ask. "I'll do it."

Cross looked down at her with a piqued shock, his brow knotted and tired. He did not say a word. Arielle crossed to where they stood and Cross let go of Z, stepping out to meet the dismayed vampire.

"Kiyiya has agreed to go with them for now. End the hostilities." Arielle could see the look flash across the confederate's face, so she placed a hand to his shoulder, steadying him. "He has made the choice, Franklin.

He is set go. It is a family thing."

"We are his family," uttered Cross bitterly.

"I know," stated the preacher's daughter. Her eyes swept over her broken brood, welling with guilt for their troubles. Kiyiya's pack had never accepted his love for her and it was their intent to rid the coven of her person and pull him back into their fold. "I am so sorry," she said to the crowd, looking close to tears.

"Never you have to," Tristin inform. "Just tell us what we can do and it will be done."

Arielle cupped his face and kissed him tenderly. "For now... nothing. Let me do what I can to help."

She remained as graceful and regal as ever, returning to Kiyiya's side as the intruders left. The native and Ms. Kebel returned to their room where the werewolf could put on a fresh pair of clothes and rejoin his brother's pack with hopes of settling what differences he could.

"Did you get to wet your blade?" Selina asked the widow.

"She pulled a wolf off me," added Vanessa in Z's defense.

"Of course she did," smirked Selina, eyeing Z as she sallied up to Cross. "I will search for Emily and the others and seek Arielle's aid in procuring sustenance."

Z knew what she implied and wondered if she was being vague on her account. Cross nodded his agreement and as she left Tristin followed her. Cross pulled along side Z.

"You do not have to do this. Selina will return soon enough."

Z wondered why he'd even say such a thing to her at a time like this. "I want to help."

He wrapped his fingers around her arm and said, "Then, come."

But she stopped, refusing to move. "Vanessa first."

Cross nodded his head and Z met with her friend. Watching the widow speak with Bernard's lover, he could not but love her more. Z worked to convince the woman that she should sup from her with Cross's consent. But before Vanessa would bite into the widow's flesh she mournfully apologized.

Z cradled Vee's head against her warm bosom, so accustomed to the sap of ghouls at her neck. The former Mrs. Boyd was compassionate and kind, giving. It was a side of her that Cross had not seen previously. The vampire didn't drink from Z's well for that long before Cross took her to see Gavin. His hand was gone. Lost in the belly of one the beasts. He would not be getting it back.

He too had trouble drawing blood from Z at first. Having come to love and respect the woman, marked by Cross's scent, he felt it imprudent, despite his desperate need. But after prodding by both, the woman and Cross, he partook of Z's flavor, calming the ache at the end of his wrist. He sampled more than Vee and the widow felt lightheaded after he'd pulled his bloody lips away from her.

Cross prepared his wet nurse a meal so that she could reconstitute her strength. As she dined she and Cross learned that Alayna was soothed by Tyler's own dark fluid and Leinil flatly refused Z's generous offer, begging her to no take offense. Benjamin found the mangled bodies of Robert Keoning and Perceval Jones in a small hovel in one of the darkened tunnels. They died in the vicious attack and were nothing more than pieces.

Z did not understand how the vampires had died. It played against what she thought she'd come to know. She grieved for Robert's loss. He was a fun natured man that she'd come to adore. Though, she had not taken the time yet to get to know Perceval that well. Their loss saddened and hardened the soul.

Later that evening, Cross explained to her that they were not as immortal as she had thought. They lived exaggerated life spans propagated by the symbiont condition of their Jadaraa Soo, and there were, in fact, many ways to destroy a vampire besides the touch of daylight. He explained them all to her, stroking her hair while she lay in bed drifting off to sleep.

But the widow could not sleep just yet. Z removed her blouse and pulled Cross to the nape of her neck so he too could sup the healing nectar in her veins. He did not want to fight with in her already weakened state, so he fed from her lightly and bade her to rest. She had done enough for one day. In a torment of fitful dreams weaving through Z's amber bonnet, she did not sleep deeply or soundly. Under Franklin Cross's touch she trembled throughout the night.

Deplorable. To end without a kiss?

Viewing the morning with two "special" some ones and all Z had to show for it was a valley of corpses, slash marks over her body, and the start of a real nasty suntan. She wasn't like any of those vampires that she'd seen on the big screen at drive-in movie theaters, or at home playing on her DVD player where the unfortunate bloodsucker mourned his or her last glimpse of the dying light, becoming weepy and soft, a soulful puppy that was damned to lap at the neck forever. *Fuck that!* She'd seen her last sunrise in Chicago and had no special interest in witnessing the one that was happening this morning.

In fact, she wished that she wasn't even getting the chance to see as much of it as she was. Sunrises in general were overrated. Whether in tweeny-heartthrob-vampire novels, or romance novels, or cheap dates inside your car, or at some secluded vista with a bottle of wine and a packet of $3.00 rubbers from Walgreens, sunrises on the whole were a pain in the ass. Cursing all the while, Z scrambled for a place to hide. She couldn't escape the rancid illusion of the blessed sun. Farmers beware! It was Z's scream that shattered the light.

The fact was that people could get used to anything. Whether living an eternal night life without the touch of the sun, working a shit job for thirty years that they hated, remaining in a bad relationship, eating out of boredom, or watching reruns because nothing else was on TV, humans were adaptable creatures. So too are vampires. With no foreseeable future in the shade behind a rock or under the taught canopy of a Juniper Tree, Z chose the only other option available to her: She dug a hole.

Using her bare hands, a few yards out from where she had killed the Special Agents, looking to avoid roots and rocks, in the soft sandy soil of the high desert, Z dug. Tearing the earth open with frantic fingers she dug and dug, cursing the fact that she was so damned tall. The light bit her face, exposed arms, and shoulders. Hot and pungent, she could feel the veins contracting into the darkness behind her skin. Constricting like a python, the further they dived, the harder each movement became. She was going to seize up, become a flesh statue, and burn from the inside out, unable to scream bloody terror. *Fucking karma!*

All her injuries took effect, leaking the morning light through to her soul. She began throwing dirt on herself as quickly as she could and dug the hole around her body, squishing down until all she could see was the dark, and all she could smell was the earth, nestled around her with mothering arms. Pissed off and worn out, Z waited out the burn of the day. That was...until somebody dug her up.

It was just after noon, compacted in the ground with all her unbidden thoughts plaguing her immobile body. She could feel the Jadaraa Soo working to repair her damaged flesh. She didn't hold out for a speedy recovery. These things took time and a lot of blood for it to work. What little sustenance that Z was able to graft from Agents Johnson and Jonston during their fracas was a boast with its own regenerative qualities. Except the blood, racked with lycanthropic toxins, cancelled any healing potential that she might have been able to gain. Her Jadaraa Soo processed the wolf venom into a white cakey film that coated her skin and flaked off like dandruff. Stuffed in a suitcase of soil, the toxic waste pushed out through her pores, feeding the loose earth around her.

At first she didn't know what was happening. Something or someone was messing with the soil above her. Could have been a coyote that had sniffed her out. Hikers, thinking they'd found among the other carnage a dumped corpse in a shallow grave and called crime scene investigators. Whatever it was, it ripped Z from the soil pretty fast. She struggled to remain buried, kicking and cursing, as it lifted her up. There was little she could do. Before her eyes gave way to sun-blindness and her ears went deaf she saw the grotesque image of her attacker: Special Agent Johnson!

He was only partially transformed. His arms were like that of his wolf, hair trailing down his protruding spine. They looked irregular and out of proportion with the rest of him. His eyes burned with the maddening swirl of Lycanthropia venom, and he sported an ugly gnash of misshapen teeth. The split down his abdomen, that she gave him earlier, was now only a puffy, sore line. *Don't that beat all?* Kiyiya had told her that werewolves healed faster than vampires.

"C'mere, you little bitch!" the angry Agent roared. "I'm going to watch you—"

That was all Z heard before her ears went dumb from the retreating parasite. Though, she could guess at how he finished his sentence: *I'm going to watch you burn. I'm going to watch you fry. I'm going to watch you suffer for what you did to my partner. I'm going to watch you scream. I'm going to watch you shrivel into a burning husk until your eyes pop out of your head and your hair dances on fire.* Z could go on forever. She had a wild imagination. Unfortunately, she didn't have a whole lot of time to use it.

Before her limbs seized with doomed paralysis she kneed the

special agent in the jaw and pressed her thumbs into his eyes to gouge them out. *This fucker ain't gonna watch me do shit!* Next thing Z knew she was hitting the ground fairly hard and tumbling into a pile of skewed appendages. Pounding on the hard earth her vision rocked back and forth, jamming into use a few times, and she got a quick lay of the land.

There was a thicket of trees off to her right where a nice comfortable shadow clung to the ground with both hands waiting for her. Z never heard Agent Johnson walking toward her because her Jadaraa Soo was too busy freaking out. Pathetically attempting to crawl away, the half man/half wolf creature picked the smoldering vampire up by the ankle and tossed her with vicious indignation. Z slammed into an old twisting Juniper and bounced off it like a racquetball.

She was unaware that she was falling. Daylight confined her parasite to a fleshy prison that it could not escape. Her exposed skin began to blister as her internal organs heated up. She could feel the fire rising within her. Soon she would become her own sun. *So, this is what it was like for you Cross. Happy now, you bastard!?!*

1930. Chicago.

Z woke to the confederate vampire's absent company having slumbered for nearly thirty-six hours. The orgy of bites was healed from her skin and she set about her own tasks. A bath. A meal. She wanted to take stock of the coven. The wolves had smashed a great many things in their wake, and though late to the aftermath, she pitched in to clean up. To her dismay she learned the Arielle had gone. Nobody knew when she might return. Everyone was dower over Kiyiya's decision to leave with the pack. They understood why he went, being forced by his brother's rage, he did not want his chosen family to suffer. Though he was missed, the deaths of their brethren hung over them. The mood of the coven was dark. Cross came to her after meeting with Emily and told the widow that she could best serve them by taking her leave and then the dark drink.

It was an awkward time. Weeks kept down here like a prisoner with so many thoughts of the city above and the air outdoors. Now she was finally given the freedom to exit and…she didn't want it. She felt a need to be swallowed in the community's grief. But the attack had calcified the differences between them.

"From this moment on," said Cross, answering the confusion he saw splayed across her face, "you must find your own way."

He placed money her hands, politely informing her that an unnatural autumn chill had seized the spring air. He asked Vanessa to lead her out. The vampire obliged the woman that had healed her, taking Z down a passage that exited through a crypt on the lower level of the Rosehill Mausoleum.

She made sure that Z fully understood how to return down the same passage if she so chose after her affair with the billowy arms of Chicago. Vanessa did not join her in the crypt, even though her heart yearned to accompany the widow. She kissed Z on the lips as if she might never see her again and closed the marble panel that hid the doorway.

Z stood in the crypt for the longest time before making her way through the grandiose hall. It was fitted with Italian marble and had Doric columns that resembled the Greek Parthenon in Athens. Daylight streamed through stained glass windows designed by Louis Tiffany. Z was torn at what to do. Flushed and eager after the attack, feeling as if she belonged to the coven, she wanted to remain with the vampires and mourn the dead. She felt that she had earned that much. Yet, her own grieving heart tugged a bitter rope that still kept her tethered to the death of Simon Ray. So it was his face she envisioned when she closed her eyes, surfacing the strength necessary to open the huge bronze doors, and flee into the neoteric City of Big Shoulders.

Making her way across the inlaid plots, weeping stone angels, and gray hanging headstones she hoped they could hear her footsteps thundering below. Because despite Cross's ardent trust and loving grace to free her to the wilds of her own intentions he'd done it at the wrong time. It was yet another thing that ground painfully in her heart and she felt a renewed vigor to loathe the man. Cursing to herself, she hailed a taxi, fully convinced that he expected her to run and never return. *Perhaps, it's what he truly wanted? Am I free?*

By the time Z ate her fill at a Chinese restaurant and found some hidden Jazz joint to sauce herself up she'd already reached her conclusion: The world was flat and dull gray, busying itself with inane lies. She could see that now, as clear as day. Bent over the arm of a leather chair, swilling down a fifth of somebody's nasty home brew, the tattooist worked on the intricate design on Z's lower back. It was her first ink. Something she concocted on the spot: Two Smith & Wesson pistols reaching out of a bed of flowers that framed the face of a weeping girl and Simon Ray's name scrolled in cursive lettering along the top of her bum under the design.

The tumble of the past few months ran through her head as she soothed the skin-painter's needle with drink. All the events from Detroit to Jacksonville, where Simon Ray got shot up that first time, to getting arrested in Georgia and Missouri, and robbing banks in Ohio strung together a destructive thread that had led her lost, rambling soul to the habitat of the damned. The girl had blazed a trail of love and unrequited longing, spitting a hail of gunfire and pathetic glory. She had a voracious appetite that equaled the pithy veins of the cloistered creatures whose company she kept. *Yes. I could run. Could hop a train and be so far gone that neither the law nor the vampires would ever find me. But where would I go? Where is there on this plot of Earth that equals the coven?*

Z was a fugitive at a time when states were giving up their jurisdiction to Hoover's boys. He was musclin' for more political power and getting it by the headlines that screamed from the mouths of skinny, snot-nosed paperboys. Soon there would be nowhere in the U.S. that his arm could not reach. The days of gangsters and rumrunners were nearing an end, *yes-siree.* Z recognized her limitations. She was an outmoded relic waiting for death. Her husband had already found his bullet with his name etched on it in her hands. Without him to lead her on that turbulent road that they'd walked together for so long, where was the fun? What would she do with herself on the beaches of Mexico without him?

She closed her eyes for a spell and listened to the sweaty man work, his electric pen buzzing along the base of her spine. In all the time that she was with the vampires, knowing full well that they confiscated the car that she and Simon Ray stole and drove to the Great Lakes city, Z never dredged up the nerve to ask what they had done with his body. *Perhaps he lay there still in the burned out void of the Grande Hotel?* She vowed to check on that.

Though, for now, whether he lay on that dirty unhallowed ground, reeking of death and decay, or had been taken somewhere and buried, most likely, in the cemetery yard where she spent her days and nights Z realized that she would forever be his tombstone, his final *requiescat in pace.* His name would be etched in her skin as a reminder of what she'd lost in her pursuits to savor life. To break beyond the boundary of her stagnant upbringing and attain something great and unreal she'd lost what mattered most. Ironically though, she found something they both sought for in vain – *Infamy and Immortality.* Both of which she would soon divine.

Taking another swig from the bottle of bathtub gin (two parts tub, one part gin), listening to the refined hum of the tattoo gun immortalize her only love, Z twisted into her 'lil ole head that she was done pussy-footing around with that hunky boy-toy Tristin. Whether

Cross liked it or not she was gong to test his mettle against her skin. Fiery and dangerous were her thoughts as she drew her guns and saw the smoky edges of the city's cloudy sunrise. It was tinged with the scent of rain and it held no less sparkle than what she'd come to suppose as a last hurrah. She admired the tattoo artist's work in a mirror as she finished her bathtub gin and it began to rain, casting a gloom over the whole city. Z felt the change boiling in her veins. She paid the man for his ink and his time and hailed a taxi to the final resting stop.

She was gone less than twenty-four hours from the lair, and returned to bury herself underground. Enclosed with all the other freaks and social dejected vagabonds, buried deep with her dark dreams and reckless tongue, the fiery widow bent her thoughts toward lust and forever. The rain beat against the sullen concrete headstones of Rosehill Cemetery. It drove its wet embrace into the green ground and seeped down through the roots to the catacombs below. Amid the liquid spilling from the earthen ceiling, clanging on the cobblestone floor, Z drank the blood of the ancients, wishing that Arielle and the native were still among them.

Z landed on the rocks below in a crevasse of a ravine. She didn't hear her bones breaking, but she felt them snap. The humerus bone in her left arm and the femur in her right thigh shattered like toothpicks. Slowly, she felt her Jadaraa Soo slither into her extremities as her vision faded into sight. She became aware that she was in a darkened cleft of one of the mountain's many chasms. She did not hesitate. Sluggishly, body screaming oh holy fucking agony, her ears so jammed by the parasite's whine that she could scarcely make out the sounds of Agent Johnson going full wolf at the top of the ridge. She wasn't out of it yet. Beat to a pulp, body thrumming like a head-on car crash, she pulled herself under the lip of a hanging rock and waited.

Sure enough he came. *Dutiful little soldier.* The werewolf landed on a rock below her perch, crouched low, and looked around. He raised his muzzle to the air and sniffed.

Biting back the agony of standing on a shattered limb, Z hurled herself onto the wolf's back and bit down as hard as she could. With her one good arm she reached around Johnson's massive neck and grabbed his windpipe and started clawing.

The beast howled in pain as Z bit, gnashing her teeth into its hardened flesh, ripping the soft side of its neck. Its lamenting bray echoed across the ravine walls, amplified on the mechanics of the rocks, and caused the ears of a Jackrabbit to perk up two miles away. The wolf swung around wildly, trying to reach around and toss her off his back. But all it accomplished was tearing her already pitiful, raggedy clothes.

Z held firm to the creature's windpipe, so by the time he grabbed her around the wrist and threw her with all his might, she did not let go of his most needed organ. Flung with full force, the wolf managed to enact more damage onto itself than what the vampire was able to do on her own. It was one of the things that she had learned from Kiyiya when he returned to the coven.

"A wolf's mind is in a constant state of rage and aggression. It hampers its ability to think and reason properly. This rage can be used as a weapon against itself. Only those with a strong will and mind can tame the beast when they wear its mien."

It was a lesson Z never forgot. Though, she scarcely thought she would have any cause to use it until yesterday. *Time's a funny master.* As she picked herself up from the ground, cradling her side and arm, she hobbled down the ravine to where the Special Agent suffocated. Three ribs had snapped when she landed from his toss. Just another thing to add to her laundry list of suffering. Z tossed the tip of Agent Johnson's esophagus into the dirt as she approached him.

With all her most recent and unpleasant memories returning doing their best to kick her ass along with the wolves she could have done with a kind face or a loving voice thrown her way. She thought she had that with Lin. But it turned out she was wrong. *Bitch abandoned me for that slag, Sarah.* It was times like these that Z didn't envy being a vampire. Outliving the ones you love or living long enough to see them stab you in the back – *it's a nightmare, a special room in hell!*

As Z climbed onto the rock where the FBI Agent lay she felt like she wanted to puke upon seeing him. He had thrown her so hard, railing against the pain, that his windpipe had acted like an internal ripcord slicing through his left collarbone. It lodged in the ball joint of his shoulder's rotator cup, almost severing the limb from his body. *Nasty.*

Z glared down at the tangled meat. There weren't any other fresher sources of blood out there that she could see. Dead Johnson was her best bet at a meal if she was ever going to walk out of here. Gauging the tip of the sun above the lip of the ravine she had about four or five hours tops before it lit the dark crevasse and gave her cause to move.

Z threw herself on the wolf's mangled, transforming corpse and suckled as much blood as she could. There was a time or two that she had to stop and remove globs of clotted hair out of her mouth. It was the worst meal she ever tasted and wore a sour face through the whole ordeal.

Afterwards, she pulled her mutilated corpse up the ravine and nestled under the lip of the hanging rock. It would give her the most shade throughout the rest of the day than any other place that she noticed along the huge gouge in the earth. *Might even be able to hang out here long enough until a patch of clouds moves in to obscure the sky or dusk lines the horizon low enough for me to scuttle up the cleft chin of rocks and retreat into the shade on the opposite side of the ridge.* Time would tell. It always did. Z balled into a hurt locker of red pulsating nerves. She wasn't going anywhere anytime soon and it was torture to breathe.

Sooner or later, she knew she was going come down from this mountain and find some scrap of civilization that she could sink her teeth into, and then there would be hell to pay. *Oh yes!* With each grating breath, each bright rivet of misery and pain, each mangled part of her that made her look grotesque, she cultivated her vengeance against the three persons responsible for her unlucky predicament: Dominique, Sarah, and Lin.

That stripper is gonna get it first. Oh yes! I'm gonna make you pay sweetheart. Z's fangs ached viciously for Sarah's nubile blood. Z calmed her fraying nervure on images of feasting slowly on that whimpering whelp. *The audacity of her to even think that she can come in and muscle up my affairs. Oh, yeah. She's gonna pay alright. Down to the very...last...drop!*

Lord
Death

Lin carried Sarah toward the lights of the subdivision below. The dancer's breathing was weak and shallow, but she was alive. At least, for now, but she was bleeding out. A rich, pungent bronze taste filled the air between them. Lin hated smelling Sarah's blood as it leaked onto her stomach and extremities, but she loved the aroma of the girl. She couldn't help it. Carrying her to some faint hope, Lin's body quickly absorbed Sarah's vital fluid as it pumped raw from the gunshot wound, sucked down through her pores by the greedy parasite. She hated herself for imbibing the girl's sanguine broth against her will.

Funny thing about the desert...everything was always further than it looked, or smacked dab on top of you. Reaching that first house took Lin just passed nightfall. A smorgasbord of homes, each identical, yet different in their own unique, little ways: A lawnmower here. A kiddie pool there. A shaggy, yapping dog. Xerascaping. A barbecue grill. There was nothing too distinct or obvious about the house Lin chose. It was fairly close to the edge of the subdivision, but not right on the outer ring where it might cause suspicion if someone were to find the wrecked cars and drained corpses of the two homicide detectives. She would have some warning if people started sniffing around.

The fenced backyard was average enough. It dropped at a steep incline, a wall of railroad ties and pleasantly placed shrubbery that braced an in-ground pool and stone tiled patio. It afforded some camouflage if Lin needed it. An automatic light came on when she reached the fence. Hurrying to climb over it, Lin almost dropped Sarah a couple of times. Muscles frayed by bullet holes, the pain was setting in. She'd gone and gotten herself shot up. Now that the rush of the high-speed chase and rescuing Sarah was all sewn up on the hill in a heap of broken metal and dead flesh, the only thing left for the vampire to deal with was an aftermath of ache and blood. *Oh, yes! The blood. Sarah's blood.* Lin wished that the bleeding would stop. Sarah's lips were drawing thin and pasty.

She set the girl down, staring into her quiet face. That same face she held as she lay sleeping only a few hours ago, when they were making love, watching planes fly across the stars, and every time Lin opened her locket. That face was with her for so long and now it looked like it was going to leave. Lin glanced down at the silver jewel around Sarah's neck and couldn't help but think that it was still her Albatross, still her sterling guilt as she carried her across the desert. *Sarah never should have been here.*

Lin wandered over to the sliding glass doors and peered inside the home. A quaint room, sofa, lounge chair – *both empty.* The TV was on. News. Bland carpeting. A fire place – *unlit.* Brick and fake wood paneling. More lights were on beyond the room and there was a little boy, about five or six, playing with some toys. *Fuck.*

Just then a man walked into the room. Slightly balding, late thirties, about six two, two hundred and twenty pounds. He wore beige slacks and a starched collared shirt. His attention was on the television as it switched to a commercial. Lin quickly stepped away from the sliding glass doors and paced, thinking. The man sat in the recliner and sipped a drink in a liquor tumbler. Lin stared down at the dancer. A small pool of red goo was leaking onto the stone tile. *I have to stop the bleeding!*

A woman's voice rang out from inside, calling her husband, Doug. He yelled back and Lin's eyes trailed to the kid playing with a set of matchbox cars on the carpet.

"Could you come in her for a minute?" asked the voice.

"Be right there."

The man lingered on the tip of the evening news, moved to the edge of his seat. It was obvious to Lin that he didn't want to get up, that the banality of the nightly gossip was where he wanted to be. She inched forward, thankful for nagging wives, and peered inside. *Sarah's bleeding out. Gotta do something. Gotta…* A young girl stepped into the room. Lin leaned back, out of sight, behind the folds of the curtain. The girl never looked up from the electronic game she held in her hand.

"Dad…" she whined. "Mom wants you in the kitchen."

Lin watched as the girl exited through another entryway and climbed a staircase – *the room has no main doors that open and close.* Exposed portals. She could see a closet door when she strained her neck around the half-drawn curtain. Doug set his drink down and got up. Going to the kitchen, he left the little boy alone in the room. The kid was seriously absorbed with playing and only looked up once when his father had walked away.

Lin ran her fingers through her hair and pressed her palms against her temples and groaned through tightly mashed teeth as she heard the clanging knoll of high desert winds rattling through her brain. The telephone rang and the pubescent voice of the pre-teen yelled throughout the house that she had it and picked it up in the middle of its next ring. Lin picked Sarah up. She was limp in the vampire's arms, a sagging blanket. She needed to get her inside. She didn't have a choice. This was the way it had to be.

Lin crossed to the sliding glass door and popped the inadequate lock, opening it. The little boy turned and stared at her. For a moment Lin thought he was going to yell and then it'd be nothing short of a mad dash to quell the house before somebody did something stupid, like call the cops. She stood still and waited a couple beats of his tiny active heart and he spoke.

"Hi."

"Hi," Lin responded and crossed to the couch, setting Sarah down. "Your Mommy and Daddy home?"

He shook his head yes and looked at Sarah. "What's wrong with your friend?"

"She's sleeping." Lin's eyes swept the room, listening to who else might be in the house that she had not seen.

She stepped to the opened glass door and slid it closed as the kid went over to Sarah. Standing up he just passed eye level with the dirty, prone stranger. A quick flash of memory tormented Lin and she turned away from the boy. Reminiscent of William before she sent him to live with his father in Africa; they were roughly the same height. In over two hundred years the vampire had never kept the company of one so young, and now she knew why.

"She okay?" he asked.

"What's your name?"

"Henry."

"Henry. That's a nice name." Lin crouched down to his size to better reason with him. "Listen, I need you stay with my friend here while I–"

Lin didn't get the chance to finish her sentence. Just then Doug re-entered the room. Eyes down, he was sucking off a tidbit of juice that was left on his thumb from the meaty morsel he'd confiscated from Carolyn's roasted chicken. When he saw the filthy, blood-splattered woman kneeling next to his son he pulled up quick near the center of the room. Lin slowly rose, eyes locked on Doug. The man's eyes bounced from the intruder to his son and then to Sarah, bleeding and stretched out on his couch, and then back again.

"Look Daddy," piped Henry with a cheerful voice. "There's a lady."

Doug struggled to control his breathing, glaring at the stranger so near to his son, *in his home.* Lin could smell his fear, ripe like a farmer's market in the early morn. "Yes," he said calmly, not wanting to alarm the boy. "Daddy sees the lady. Now, come here."

"She needs help," expressed Lin urgently. "She's been shot."

Doug's eyes drifted over the reclining girl as he moved forward to see the gunshot wound in her belly. *It doesn't matter.* They didn't belong in his house, standing so close to his son. "Henry?" he called with a controlled, firm voice. "Henry? Come here."

Lin moved forward, around the boy, lightly touched his head. "Please," urged Lin. "I only want to patch her up."

Doug's nerves pulsed a screaming fire engine. *How dare she?* Repulsed that the stranger had touched his son, fingers so gently lain harshly directed her point. "If it's as bad as you think, then call the police and get her to a hospital."

Douglas Bradley was a practical man. He devised practical solutions that usually got high dollar corporations out of impractical technical and/or construction problems. The company he worked for praised his practicality. They even gave him a plaque for it last year and a raise that helped him to buy his house.

Lin was not in a practical mood. "No police. No Hospital."

Henry waved one of his toy cars in sleeping beauty's face. "Look what I got. Hey, Miss wake up." He shook her unaware of the tense glare between his father and the strange-looking woman. "Look what I got."

"Sorry," Lin simply said.

Before Doug could cry out or move to grab his son or take any action against the intruder at all, she crossed the neutral-colored carpeting, clamped her hand over the man's mouth, and took him down to the floor. She bit him. Henry turned to see his Daddy wrestling with the other lady. He didn't know what to think or feel about how his Daddy was playing with her. Distracted by the action on the floor, Henry missed it when Sarah opened her eyes. He heard her moan and turned back to the lady on the couch.

Seeing Sarah's eyes opened, he smiled. He had a bright, cherubic face that lit up like gold when he grinned, at least, that is what his parents always called him: *"little, golden treasure."* They said his eyes beamed as bright as the sun. Sarah's eyes fluttered like a bird and the warmth of Henry's positive gaze was a pleasant surprise. Her belly throbbed and her head ached and she felt incredibly weak. Her throat was parched and she wanted a drink of water.

"Hello," she eked out on a sandpapery voice. "Who…who are–"

Henry shoved his toy car in her face. "Lookie what I got."

Lin supped from the man's throat until his thrashing subdued. She sat on top of him, knees pressing his arms, gulping rapidly to hasten his unconsciousness. She didn't want to kill him. She didn't want to hurt anyone. She just wanted to make Sarah's wound stop bleeding, so she could focus on saving her life.

When she climbed off the man he was still breathing, a slow, steady breath, and he'd wake with a hangover, but he was still alive. His gorgeous, warm fluid coursed through her injured Jadaraa Soo and it was salvation. Plump and lively, Lin felt renewed. She spied the little boy talking to Sarah. He showed her his toy and Lin knew what she had to do in order to patch up her girl. She didn't like it, but they were here now. *No turning back.* And, if she didn't move quickly she'd loose Sarah forever because of her ignorant carelessness.

So many thoughts crammed through Lin's head as she left the room with a purpose. Internal brain surgery, each guilt-stricken accusation and bitter memory since she sent William away in 1781 sliced her up. It botched her befuddled reasoning, and through the grind of nagging fault Lin felt the warmth of this home – pictures on the wall, a tight-knit family, and the smell of a scrumptious meal being prepared by loving hands…*did I do the right thing? Sarah wouldn't be in this predicament if I had taken William to Nsia myself. All those people might have never died had I not traveled with Ramielle. I should have never loved Dominique. If I lose you now… there is no going back. You are my redemption, my soul, and I let Z ruin it.*

All I touch is death.

Carolyn was in the kitchen when she heard the knocking about in the living room and assumed Doug was pulling out the Pilates machine. She was exceptionally happy about how the bird was turning out. The last one was too dry, and the Rosemary she added to this one not only enhanced the flavor of the broth, in which she basted the whole chicken, but it filled the room with delicious scents.

Her neighbor Kimberly, three houses down, told her how her Gran used to roast chicken with Rosemary and how she started using Sage, once or twice, when they moved to New Mexico. She said it tasted the same. Talking with Kim gave Carolyn an idea and she surfed online for a recipe that she liked. Two days ago she took the chicken out of the freezer to thaw. It'd been in there about a week and half and the meal looked like a great dish to make with Madison. Considering the damage she did to the last bird, Carolyn was hoping for vindication with tonight's dinner.

Getting Madison to assist her in the kitchen was an altogether different matter. *Hard to get two sentences out of her these days about anything.* The girl was either on the phone to one of her friends from school, on the computer with her friends from school, watching TV, or playing with that damned videogame. *Girl Time* used to mean spending mother and daughter moments together away from Henry and Doug. Shopping at the mall, milkshakes in the park, a manicure and new hairdo, they used to spend time with one another and enjoyed their company. *Now, Girl Time means Madison going out with her friends.*

Carolyn was taken aback last Saturday when her daughter barred her from her room. Melanie and Veronica were over and Madison had the gall to say that "they" needed "their" *Girl Time.* Carolyn was so put off that she left the hallway with her mouth hanging open and eyebrows raised. Doug told her that Maddy was just going through a phase, she'd come back around. He kissed her on the forehead and said that it would be okay. Carolyn understood it once the shock wore off. She was once a twelve-year-old girl too. *But damn. It just seemed to happen so fast and come out of nowhere.*

Now, the only girl time they shared alone was when Carolyn drove Madison to one of her friend's houses, to the movie theater, or to the mall. She missed their special moments together and wondered if her daughter missed them too. Though, it was hard to be understanding when she felt like it had become such a chore for them to be in the same room together. To Carolyn it seemed like they were missing each other more and more and the word "Mom" had definitely taken on a new tone or two that Carolyn did not like.

Setting the oven mitts down, she punched in fifteen minutes on the timer, grabbed the charger for the Gameboy that Madison had left in the kitchen, and turned around. She never even heard the soles of

Lin's shoes on the tile. She was in mid stroke of calling her husband's name and cut it off with curt an "oh" when she saw the stranger standing behind her.

"Who are you?" she asked the woman like she was a surprised dinner guest. "Where's my husb—"

Lin smashed her palm against Carolyn's face and the woman went down like a sack of wet potatoes with a bloody nose. The heavy block end of the Gameboy charger made more noise hitting the tile floor than Carolyn did. Lin crossed the kitchen, through the hall and foyer and climbed the stairs.

Henry rolled his matchbox car over Sarah's shoulder, going "Vroom, vroom, vroom" with his mouth, until he saw the shiny silver oval. He let go of his toy car and picked it up.

"This is pretty. Did your Mommy give it to you?"

Half in a daze, eyes slivers of listless sight, Sarah reached out and grabbed Henry's hand and tried to smile. It came out lopsided like someone was shoving glass in the bullet wound. "Where's Lin?"

Henry pulled his hand away, drew in his chin, and wore his thoughtful face. He looked down at the woman lying on the couch. Her face was all messy. She needed a bath. Henry hoped that he'd get a bath tonight. He liked playing with the water in the tub and had some cool toys that he hadn't played with for awhile. The lady looked very sleepy.

Lin heard the music coming from the upstairs room once she reached the foyer. It wasn't very loud. The girl was talking on the phone. Climbing up the stairs, the vampire avoided looking directly at the pictures on the wall. Family vacations at the beach. Wedding photographs. Baby pictures. Kids building a snowman. It was all very quaint and homey and Lin didn't want to think about it.

"No really, that's what she said." Madison's voice fell from her room. "If you don't believe me ask Laura Hodges. She was standing right there."

Even if the girl wasn't yakking on the phone Lin wouldn't have any trouble finding her room. It had a poorly constructed collage of pictures of her hanging out with her best friends and a 'Keep Out Henry' sign tacked to the outside of the door. Lin wondered if the little boy was even old enough to read. The door was slightly ajar and Lin pushed it gently open with the same hand she used to clock Madison's mother. Stepping into the room, Lin never noticed that she smeared Carolyn's blood on the door.

"Nuh uh! Really?" The girl twirled a lock of her walnut brown hair, embarrassed. "He said that?" She listened as Veronica repeated it again. "I guess. He's kinda cute." Madison's shoulder's slumped. "Can you hold on a sec? I think my little brother's in my room again."

Madison turned, ready to give Henry what for, but instead drew upon the smothering proximity of a foul looking woman. Lin shot her hand out, covering Madison's mouth, and pinched her nose with an iron grip. The young girl's screams were buried in the vampire's palm. Lin pulled the telephone receiver out of Madison's hand.

"She'll have to call you back," Lin said blandly and ended the call with a flick of her thumb.

She dropped the phone and it fell to the floor with a plastic clank. Picking the girl up, Lin held her with both hands restricting her airflow and dragged her from the room. Madison kicked and jerked until she fell unconscious in the hall. Setting her down, Lin opened the closet door. It had a lock on it and the vampire figured that they'd be safer in there than in one of the bedrooms. *There could be something, anything, in one of the rooms that might inspire them to be a hero.* Lin didn't need anyone thinking they could play the part. Things were bad enough as they were and with any luck they'd be gone long before morning. She just needed time and a quiet place to work.

Moving a few items out of the closet, Lin made room for the whole family, tossing the junk to the other end of the hall. Then, she set the sleeping girl in the closet and shut the door. She'd wake in a few minutes with a splitting headache.

Lin carried Carolyn upstairs and set her in the closet too. She was groggy and slowly coming around. Lin thought that she might have broken the woman's nose. The bags under her eyes were turning purplish-black. Once the cook was neatly tucked away, she moved Doug upstairs and got a quick lashing from the mother's tongue as she labored to push the man's bulk into the small space and keep Carolyn from rushing out the door.

"Calm down for the sake of your kids," Lin told her. "Or I'll be forced to teach you a lesson."

Lin slammed the door on the woman's wide eyes and traversed the steps one more time to gather up the little boy. He'd been such a good child that Lin hated the thought of putting him in there with the rest of his family. But she needed him out of mind and out of sight. She needed, *no!* Sarah needed Lin's full focus and concentration. As much as she hated it, Henry had to go in the closet. He would be a distraction otherwise.

When Lin returned to the livingroom the boy was back to playing with his toys, just how she had found him when they first arrived. Crossing to him, she passed Sarah's slim field of vision.

"I don't feel so good," the dancer moaned.

Lin crouched beside her and caressed her forehead and cheek. She was cold. "It's okay. I'm going to make it better."
She stood and held a hand out for Henry. "Come with me."

"Don't..." groaned Sarah. "Don't hurt him..."

Lin looked down at her. The vampire's eyes were bunched and she was hurt that she would even say something thing like that. "He'll be fine. Rest."

Lin led the little boy away.

Sarah called after her, repeating the same thing over and over again. "Don't hurt him. Don't hurt him..."

What kind of person does she think I am? Though, buried under the superficial hurt Lin knew. She told Sarah about the farmhouse the other night. They stood in the ruins of lives. Lin and the company she kept murdered a whole village of folk: *Men. Women. Children.* She looked down at Henry and heard the congealed voices of those terrified families clamoring for their lives and the lives of their loved ones.

For years Lin took solace in the fact that she did not take place in the wholesale slaughter, that she did not join Prophet and Ramielle in their glee to feast wildly upon them, or taunt and tease them as Jordan had done. She went hungry. She knew it was wrong. She begged them to stop. For many years after that horrible storm this knowledge of thinly veiled separation was a comfort. Though deep down, where her soul sat, Lin knew it was a lie. She did feast – *eventually*. She did take place in the slaughter – *eventually*. She murdered people to stuff her veins or else she would have died a pointless death like the rest of them. Just because she reasoned that the others were going to kill them anyway wasn't an excuse for what she had done.

That was when the trips started. Late fifties. Z went with her and they had their own little brand of mayhem and fun. *Z's kind of fun*. That's what she told herself. Z had a different perspective, a different outlook on it all, and she was so flush with life. Lin was, after all, a vampire. As Z told it, everyone else was just meat. Their position on the food chain was simply higher up than everybody else. All Lin needed to do was reconcile herself with that simple fact and the desert trips would soon stop.

But decade after decade, trip after trip, each furore into the darkside of her condition with the wild one didn't solve anything. The trips never stopped. They became their own regular, little horror shows, a dance in the darkness of her soul splintered in those two sandy, raging days, stuffed in that large house in 1934. Sarah was on the couch with a bullet in her gut because of that fact. Lin couldn't look away from it now. It stared her in the face. She couldn't delude herself any longer. She partook. She imbibed. She killed. *Often*.

Feeling Henry's little hand in hers folded back the eons of time to when she held her own son's hand. Walking with him along the roads and fields of Casa del Rio Dulce, basking in the sweltering heat of the day, and riding in the Orange carts. She recalled pushing him on the swing that the native Thiago had made for him in the front yard. She never forgot the scent of William or how he felt cuddled against her breasts suckling as an infant. Lin could no more harm this little boy than she could her own son. *Sarah doesn't know that*.

The vampire smiled down at Henry as they climbed the steps, hiding her fangs behind a thin line of flesh. Her heart panged to see her son again. *Foolish*. Standing on the windswept grounds of Africa, staring at the fresh mound of dirt where his body was interned, Lin listened to Ana Luzia under a great huge canopy of stars about how William had grown into a good fighter, a good father, and a good son. But all Lin could think about, staring at the mound of earth, was how her little boy looked on the day he boarded the ship. His small hand in hers, they walked up to the plank together. Lin hugged and kissed him madly. She held him longer and tighter than she'd ever done and then gave him to Anna Luzia for all time. He waved goodbye to her while standing on deck. He looked so sharp in his little suit. Lin watched the boat sail away until it was a dot on the distant horizon.

She cried when she returned home to Dominique. For three days she cried…and the Vam Pŷr consoled her, lovingly. Standing at his grave in 1822 Lin never shed a tear. She felt the call, the pull to go to the motherland, as if the child himself had come down from heaven and whispered in her ear. But at William's graveside Lin did not weep. Around her was the village where he and his father had lived. The children that he had sired – *her grandchildren* – were asleep around her. Nsia had told her countless stories about it when they were together in London, embroiled in ardent love, and Lin often imagined his words as if they were little time capsules of bottled.

William was buried next to him. Anna Luzia, bent and wrinkled with age, showed the vampire the mounds where her loved ones lay. That was all that was left. *It is all that is ever left.* Her little boy was revered as a warrior among the tribe. *He was not an outsider. He had a home.* Lin was content to see that all the graves of the tribesmen were neat and decorated - *tidy*. That they were shone honors, commitment, and love by generations of progeny honed in the mantle of their age-old war with the Omjadda. A duty that Lin gave her son over to when she put him on that ship. A duty which she later learned she had given birth for in the first place.

William never was hers. He always belonged to the tribe. *He was his father's son.* She was a consort to the spawn of their enemy. An enigma in their secret war to cleanse the earth of the ancient Omjadda ilk. Her love for Nsia was cultivated by the Vam Pŷr to sire a lasting peace between the warriors and the Children of Evensong. Back then, Lin felt a special alliance to the former blood slave. She loved Dominique. The woman held purchase over her heart. At the time, it was an honor to give Nsia a son. She had loved him too. Though now, walking with the little boy, coming to rest beside the closet door, Lin wished that she could have loved Nsia just a little more. Then perhaps, she would have taken her own son to meet his father in those distant lands, instead of giving him over for a vial of black fluid and the arms of a woman that were always cold.

"Henry?" Lin crouched beside him. "I need you to stay with your mommy and daddy for a little while and be quiet. Can you do that?"

He nodded.

"Good."

Lin opened the closet door and the sobbing ran out. She led Henry around to the opened end and he stepped into the closet.

"Oh my God, Henry!" Carolyn announced, face streaking with tears. Madison was in her arms and they were both crying. Carolyn had found some tissues on one of the shelves to clean her nosebleed. A messy wad of it was crumbled in her outstretched hand, begging her son to come to her. "What do you want from us?" begged the mother as she tightly held her son.

Groggily, Doug lurched forward, gripping the side of his neck with one hand. "You can't do this. You can't keep us locked up in here..."

Slowly, Lin closed the door.

Head down, eyes drawing in no particular detail, she pulled away. Doug's wet hand sluggishly slapped against the inside of the door. Their humbled cries and wailing laments beat like avatars of the long dead in the vampire's ears, pressing down hot and flush.

She went to the kitchen first and grabbed some rags, a thin tong, and a pot of hot water. While walking out of the kitchen the buzzer went off. It jolted Lin and she turned around, glared at the annoying sound, and turned the rancid thing off. The roasted rosemary chicken stayed in the oven to cook a bit longer. The potatoes on the stove softly boiled and the asparagus waited to be fried. Lin kneeled down on the floor next to Sarah.

"You've lost a lot of blood," she told her, lifting her shirt. She grimaced. "It should be all right."

Sarah struggled to keep her eyes open. She was tired. Lin drew a nasty face and pulled the cloth out of the water. She laid it against Sarah's parched lips first and squeezed. Water trickled across the desert of her tongue and ran down the side of her cheeks. Her mouth moved in a small circle as the liquid ran over it. Then Lin cleaned the area around the gunshot hole.

Wringing the towel out, the water in the pot turned red. The blood had begun to congeal around the edges of the wound and the bleeding had nearly stopped. By the look of Sarah's pallor that wasn't a good sign.

The vampire listened to the girl's beating heart. *Slow. Feeble.* Lin rolled her onto her side and looked to see if the bullet had punctured her backside. It hadn't. Lin felt around Sarah's lower back to see if she could feel the bullet lodged anywhere back there, but she didn't. Rolling her over, the girl was an indolent doll, almost spiritless, and a trickle of blood ran out of the perforated hole. Lin cleaned it up. Her veins were enflamed against the walls of her skin, pressing for the mere scent of the red liquid.

Lin looked into the hole, but couldn't see the bullet. Grabbing the tongs she moved to use them to extract the little lead element, but the head of their pinchers were too big. Lin tossed them aside and used her fingers.

"Sorry."

Sarah woke up yowling in the pain. The vampire held her down with one hand and dug around with the other. She found it, thinking of a dozen other times that she had done the very same thing during the slave revolts in Brazil when Portuguese soldiers had opened fire on the half-armed crowds. Lin pulled the bullet out with her fingers. Sarah collapsed in an exhausted heap. The tiny, hard head of the shell was wet between Lin's mashers. She tossed the bullet in the pot of water and it clanged on the copper bottom.

Lin cleaned up the wound again with the murky water and wished she had some gunpowder, salts, and a healing salve. She looked around the room, didn't see any rifles hanging on the walls. The TV chatted its irritating gaze and Lin figured that they had to have some kind of med-kit, somewhere in the house. She wrung out the cloth and pressed it lightly against Sarah's mouth again and then laid it on her gut. Leaving the girl on the couch, Lin went in search for anything medicinal in the house to bandage the destructive little hole.

She ransacked the kitchen first. Found some Band-Aids and Hydrogen Peroxide in the downstairs bathroom. They were mostly for little cuts and scrapes. *Ineffectual.* She hoped they had something better upstairs. Hearing Lin's feet pad down the hallway, both Doug and Carolyn shouted that the kids had to go to the bathroom and needed to be let out. Their crying and pleas followed Lin as she went from room to room looking for stuff to use. Tossing the bottle of Peroxide onto the master bed, Lin found some Johnson & Johnson Topper Dressing Sponges, Aspirin, and gauze tape in the master bathroom. Someone had been seriously injured in this house at some point. She guessed it was the husband.

As she gathered the stuff up from the master bath she heard

Doug kick against the door and yell that his kids had to use the toilet. Lin stood there listening to both of the children crying under the booming violence of Doug. The vampire rubbed her eyes and set the stuff down on the huge master bed. *Keeping them alive is becoming irritating.* As she passed the hall closet Lin banged the door loudly. "Hold it!"

Sarah was light as a feather, ghostly pale like Lin, and fought to remain conscious. Lin carried her upstairs where she could keep a better eye on the family. The dancer's eyes fluttered open, Lin kept telling her to hold on, that they were almost there, that she was going to be all right. She laid the dancer down on the master bed delicately and removed the soiled rag from the wound.

Spinning the top off the Hydrogen Peroxide bottle, Lin doused the bloody orifice with foam-activating liquid. Tearing open a Johnson & Johnson Sponge she laid it over the hole and fastened it with a Band-Aid and some gauze tape. She procured a glass of cool water from the bathroom spigot, crushed a few Aspirins into the water, and lifted Sarah's head gently so that she could drink the dry tasting concoction. The girl gulped half of it before she begged Lin to set her down. That was really all she could do for her now. The rest was up to Sarah. The girl looked so blanched and gaunt, lying there breathing shallow and slow, Lin feared to move her. *Best to wait a few hours and see how things turn.*

"Pleeassee…" Madison sorrowfully whined. "I can't hold it."

Lin sighed heavily, a noisy, grating wheeze, and crawled beside Sarah. Pressing herself against the woman, she lay down and held her. Lin listened to the dancer's heartbeat as the family cried out. It was laggard and steady for awhile, but eventually, it began to wane. The people in the closet also grew quiet after a time, resided to their cramped fate, huddled in the small darkness. Lin was alone in a gigantic room with the girl, in a bed that wasn't hers, wearing clothes that were a few days old and stank with sweat, gunshot residue, and dried blood. She stroked Sarah's hair and prayed for her to come through, whispering in her ear about how lucky she was to have met her and how much she enjoyed being with her over the past few days, and how much she *needed* her.

The vampire's encouraging words, though bottled as they were from a deep fountain of love, kissed softly to the acoustical spiral, could not quicken the pulse of the dying woman. Slowly, Lin came to realize this. She had lost too much blood. She needed an infusion. Sarah would be dead before morning and it was her fault that she had gotten hurt. *My fault!* Soon, the dancer would become just another face in the gallery of souls that Lin kept locked away in the back of her mind. Another set of eyes staring at her from that dark place where she kept the people that she had caused to die. There were many of them. *Too many to count.* Always watching her, always there – *staring.*

The vampire peered down at the fading woman and could think of no other means to save her than what had damned her own anxious soul. *Salvation by inches in the cruel hand of fate.* Tendril, sticky fingers brought them both to this point of retched circumstance, but they would not massage Sarah's heart. Fate had drained her engine's cup, forcing the vampire's hand to the solution which she so ardently fought against. Damned by every angle, turned away at every point, a pawn of constant abuse. Lin's blood was second generation. It wasn't Omjadda blood anymore. She was the daughter of the Vam Pŷr. A Child of Evensong. The Council had laws against this kind of thing. Even if she were to survive, she'd be hunted. An outlaw. An outcast. *We'd be alone together.*

It smacked against her immediate need as Lin recalled the time when Dominique offered to give her some of the vials of Ornn's blood to take with her after they had broken up. Mother Night wanted her to be able to choose for herself a companion from future ages. So that at some far flung day Lin could find a soul that would help her to connect to that distant time. Lin told her no. She told Dominique that she would never have cause to use it. She turned her back on Jaci's most generous offer. *So arrogant! So, ignorant! So vain!* Sarah was dying in her arms and there was little more she could do than watch her slip slowly into the great expanse.

*Damned if I do. Damned if I don't...*Lin stared down at the Jadaraa Soo trailing through her arms, moving under her skin. *Second Gen. Bad Blood.*

She had to do something. She just couldn't let Sarah die. *Not now.* Not after all these years of waiting to find her. The girl had returned from the prison of the silver locket. *Not now... Not like this!*

Maybe second gen turns weren't as bad as she thought? Others had done it, turning a mortal from one's own veins. She had heard it about being done. *Dominique wasn't always a virtuous fountain of truth.* The queen bee was a well-honed manipulator, a seducer, a temptress – *A Vampire! She always said I had strong blood. Can I be enough?*

Can I be enough for now?

Lin didn't know what to do. The thumping in her ears from Sarah's ribcage was getting faint, a paper drum beating its last hurrah in a cavernous tomb to a lowly spectator of one. Sarah didn't have a whole lot of time for Lin to think about it. *Salvation by inches…death immortal…*

"Ppllleeeeaasseee," Madison cried again from beyond the bedroom wall. "I have to go to the bathroom. Please, let me out. Please!"

The girl subsided in a hail of sobs. Doug pounded on the door and asked for Lin to come speak with him. He said that he *just* wanted to talk. That he knew a way to save her friend. He wouldn't try anything. He begged until his voice went hoarse and scratchy and he coughed. Then Lin could smell urine in the closet and they drew quiet again.

Quiet.

In the big house with all the windows for eyes, lights on like every one was home and everything was fine. The big house where children ran up the steps and mom made dinner; kids went to school, and a husband watched the nightly news. The house with its big bed smelling of sex and laundry detergent, was where Sarah lay dying.

Everything felt numb and strange as if Lin was encased in a bubble inside of a living dream. She wanted to wake up. She wanted to wake up. She wanted to wake up. Lin turned back to Sarah and didn't know what else to do.

The water in the potatoes finally boiled away and the mushy, white kernels of earthen grub began to burn. Their black scent wafted upstairs and pulled Lin from her cruel thoughts. She heard the family whispering. They weren't even sure that Lin was still there anymore. Mom and Pop were considering the woman's silence. They thought of kicking the door down and getting the hell out of the closet.

Lin touched Sarah's cheek before she rose and crossed silently to the locked closet door. She listened to them debate for a second or two, allowing them to come close to a grand decision before she ruined their escape plans. The vampire slapped the front side of the barrier once with her flat palm and whispered through the hairline seal between the white wooden door and the jamb. "Kick this door down and so help me God, I'll make you regret it. In the worst possible way."

Carolyn's tears and Doug's useless comforts fell on Lin's stiff shoulders as she descended the stairs to the kitchen below. She removed the smoldering matter from the burner and turned the stove off. Already a smoky cloud filled the top of the modern appliance and it was only minutes before a smoke detector somewhere in the house blared loud angry sudden alarm. Lin didn't need that. She had enough to worry about. Her reality was cracking, all her edges were frayed and she felt like they were being pulled apart.

Staring into her faint, black reflection in the microwave door above the stovetop, Lin snapped. She punched her dark image, cracked the glass, and bent the door. She hated what she had become. She was a monster...*yet again.*

Walking back up the steps to sit next to Sarah felt like years. Watching the dancer's chest rising and falling a couple of times felt like it took hours. Lin's own heart stopped pumping and her own breath ceased. She was a shell. Her Jadaraa Soo was so deftly silent and void-like that Lin felt as if she were floating in space. Then slowly, she cut a long sliver down her wrist with her thumbnail. The pain brought her back to the room.

"Sarah?" she bade the girl to wake. "Sarah? I need you to drink this."

Sarah's eyes fluttered open with the soft beating wings of funeral birds.

"Here." Lin turned the cut toward her mouth. "Drink."

A small drop fell into the mouth that Lin loved to kiss and splashed on the inside of her cheek. Black fluid fell on the girl's dry cracked lips and spotted her chin. Sarah's mouth quaked for the rancid solution, chewing air. She coughed and groaned from the spasms of pain in her hole.

"Don't fight it. You'll be fine."

Lin pressed her sliced wrist tight against Sarah's cold lips and told her to drink. She squeezed her arm with her other hand to coach the vile liquid out of her body. Once the engine of Sarah's tongue began lapping at the valley of the cut skin dark blood began to flow. She curled around Lin's body, pulling at the vampire's arm with renewed strength and vigor.

Despite Lin's resistance she was excited to see some verve in the girl again. Sarah hungered for life, supping from the vampire's veins. Soon Lin's Jadaraa Soo began to quake from its extreme loss of self, but Lin held firm. She had to make sure. Images of death riffled through the vampire's mindscape as the parasite conveyed a volley of fear to the symbiont. At last, Lin pulled her wrist away, heaving huge gulps of air.

The feeding was as intense as their earlier love and passion!

Sarah's body shivered. Her mouth still worked like a vacuum, rotating on the memory of the vampire's arm and slowly the blood did its dastardly work. Seeping through the membrane of the esophagus wall, eating the acids in the stomach and soaking through the lining of tissue and organs, Lin's black blood spread throughout Sarah's entire body. Every vital liquid and viscous nectar that it came in contact with was consumed.

Sarah grabbed her gut and howled in pain. Vicious agony twisted pointy, invisible knives and she began convulsing as the black blood started to eat her circulatory system. Her discomfort was intense, a fire raged across her skin; her internal plumbing succumbed to liquid jaws. Sarah pulled at her clothes, tearing them. She shook the bed, violently. Lin watched her with a sober scowl, from a dejected perch, having undergone the exact same thing over two hundred years ago. The memory of it was still warm and fresh as the day she writhed in the throes of torment on the floor of Dominique's chambers. Sarah's heart sounded good, beating madly as the blood entered it.

Already Lin could see the stable veins of the parasite forming under Sarah's bleached skin. The girl's eyes fluttered wildly and her body grew stiff and rigid as stone as Lin's black blood squeezed the heart and raced through the rippling channels of Sarah's brain. Her breath choked in her throat as the parasite moved into her lungs and the dancer's heartbeat slowed rapidly. Bent like an arch, feet pushing into the lavish comforter that covered Doug and Carolyn's bed, Sarah gasped her last breath and fell.

Her heart beat once…twice…it lingered on a rhythm…thrice… and then, died. Sarah lay immobile. Lin's brow furled, a storm cloud over her eyes, as she gazed at her lover's death. The vampire drew her hands up to her mouth and waited. The twisting, gnarled veins of the parasite continued to creep through Sarah's body, re-mapping her entire structure. It weaved into places hidden and unknown. It curled around bone and tied knots in the fibers of dead muscles.

Lin hoped.

Hanging on eager prayers, she heard the family rustling around in the tight confines of the closet and stared down at Sarah. Every second it took for the parasite to revive her was another step she took toward death. *IF…the parasite was going to revive her?* Scientists were starting to prove what the Omjadda had learned a long, long time ago. Human death was not sudden and permanent, as the species liked to believe. Bodily organs retained residual life energy for up to twenty minutes. The brain took anywhere from five minutes to two hours to die after heart death. Cellular decay in the skin's tissue can begin within two to ten minutes after the body heaved its last gasp. Life lingered. Life held on. Everything, including death, had a process.

Lin waited. Her blood, though born of Omjadda blood was not that precious exotic liquid. She did not know if its sentient qualities would be enough. *Symbiosis. That's the word she used when we were in bed together.*

"I need you," she whispered and took Sarah's hand, holding it as Doug called from his darkened prison.

"What's going on out there? What's happening? Just tell us something. You can let us out; we won't call the cops. We want to help." He knocked on the wall a few times. "Do you hear me? We can help. You don't have to keep us locked in here anymore..."

Lin looked into Sarah's death face as the veins moved across the whites of her eyes, sucking the moisture out of the desert girl's gaze. The vampire witnessed how the wiggling little bastards broke through the gums of Sarah's upper palate and wound into the familiar shape of fangs. So young, and having never plucked the bloom of blood from another's throat, the woven vampire teeth were still reddish in hue, like that of the rest of its intricate system. But Sarah did not breathe. She lay still on the purchase of death, a white pawn in the tapestry of violent lies.

"C'mon," Lin urged. "C'mon..." She laid a hand to Sarah's unmoving chest. The Jadaraa Soo inside the girl's core was dormant. "C'mon." Blood tears welled on the ledges of Lin's eyelashes, gathering momentum to fall. "I need you."

But nothing moved within the girl anymore and a thin red stream streaked down the vampire's face. Sarah's mouth was agape and her pupils were rolled back. She looked like a tossed doll that a child had thrown away. The life and love in Lin's veins were not enough. *Not Enough!* Lin felt Sarah's death, shattering, and slumped in agile defeat as pulsating numbness pounded against her being.

Then suddenly Sarah's back arched, a violent eruption – a bitter, expectant quake. Her eyes smacked open and screamed at the ceiling as her lungs sucked in a gallon of air. She squeezed Lin's hand as if to break the vampire's fingers. She lived. *Dear God, Thank You; she was alive!*

Lin wept. Not for sorrow or for loss, but for love. The Jadaraa Soo in the woman's heart squeezed her delicious organ with a new life, kick starting it with thunderous salvo. Lin laid her head against Sarah's torso and cried. But her elation was premature.

Sarah grew sallow again. Her heart rapidly decreased to a funeral drum. The fingers of her hand that, only seconds ago, curled tightly around Lin's veiny digits relaxed and slipped away. She was dead weight on the bed. Lin panicked. Eyes beat against the sides of their fleshy cage. Lin's mind raced at what to do.

Pulling her arm up, the vampire glared at the cut in her wrist that Sarah suckled. She renewed the slash in a bright, painful flick of her thumbnail. She held the limb over Sarah's opened mouth, but the parasite refused to deliver anymore of its precious body. Lin pushed and squeezed her forearm. She strained to get a few drops to fall into Sarah's mouth. But it was no good. The little smattering of blood that she rent from her own selfish flesh was useless. *I'm not enough.*

Sarah needed more. *She needs blood.* The whole of the house caved in on Lin as her eyes drew upon the silver jewel, languid and dangling from Sarah's limp neck. Time folded back on itself and Lin was stuck again between a maddening feast, unquenchable thirst, and innocent bodies rife with a storehouse of nourishment.

The idea repulsed her just like it had in the infuriating winds of the tempest and she flew off the bed. Standing in the lonely dark of the room there was no Ramielle to order vile actions, there was no Prophet to keep the villagers from fleeing into the storm and wild night, there was no Jordan to bait the victims with cruelty. There was only Lin and she had already bottled a banquet of blood in the closet.

Slowly, she turned to the bedroom's opened doorway and the hall beyond. *Has my sorrowful mind known all along what I instinctually intended? I was a fool to think that we would just be able to drive away from here and leave it at that. Foolish. Foolish. Foolish. I am the lord death and I dance the dance of destruction.*

Z's Shiva tattoo flew across Lin's harried mind as her feet ate the carpeting. A dank wall of blackness receded into her…away from her… into her. She was a pulsating suitcase of misery. The whines and cries from the closet grew to a deafening pitch in the vampire's ears. Sarah's sallow breath clanged like a school bell.

"SHUT UP!" she screamed at the top of her lungs and crashed to the floor.

For awhile her own weeping obscured everything else in the house as she lay crumpled in a heap of weak, tormented flesh.

Fingers dug into the carpet wanting something to grab. Finding nothing, a tight knit, Lin pulled herself to where Sarah lay on the bed. The girl's breathing was coarse. A slow whispering grate that wheezed into the plush darkness of the room. Desperate not to feel, harrowing thoughts matriculated through cold synapses of hot memory. She buried her face in the girl's hip.

"The scent of the sea is crisp," Lin told her. "Sailors called it their mistress. You can loose yourself in its wet arms as you gaze out across its endless folds. Ever shifting. Ever changing. At night, standing on the bow of the ship with your eyes closed is the closest I have ever come to flying. I want you to see this. I want you to know this. I want to take you to the sea." Lin stretched her arms across the girl's thighs. "I don't want to have to do this." She bit back the sting of tears. "But I don't want to lose you. I've waited so long just to find you."

"Yearn for it my sweet," recalled Lin. Ramielle's words as the Vam Däm Mu jabbed her in the forehead. *"Teach her truth. Feed and live. Or, stay here and die."*

Lin hugged the dancer's body.

"Pathetic," commented the ghost of Ramielle. "Still unable to face what you are when it matters most."

Lin looked up and standing on the opposite side of the bed, where light from the master bathroom spilled onto the empty carpet, was the timeless specter of Ramielle Eirinhas. She was dressed as Lin last remembered her as she disappeared into the desert with Jordan and Prophet.

"I'm not like you," Lin told the vision. "I never was."

"Yes. How unfortunate. But you've changed. You've become more like me than what you care to admit."

Wanting to deny it, Lin watched the apparition cross to the bed and brush Sarah's hair back. "She's dying."

"I know."

"So what are you going to do about it?" The ghost shot her a hard glance. Taunting her like she used to. Lin heard knees knocking on the closet walls and turned toward the noise with a hard look all her own.

"What are you waiting for? You are only prolonging the inevitable."

"Have you no shame?!" She glared at the apparition.

"This is beyond shame. Beyond your pitiful notions of redemption and sacrifice. It cuts to the core of what you truly are." Ramielle's lips curled into a smile.

"If that were true you never would have killed yourself."

"I was murdered," the ghost said accenting each word specifically.

"Yeah. I heard." Lin scrunched her face in a disapproving glare. "You lost it and terrorized an English hamlet until the inhabitants hunted you down and killed you."

"They cut off my head and then burned me. Do you have any idea how that feels?"

"Nobody does what you did unless they *want* to get caught."

The specter of the Vam Däm Mu raised her eyebrows fittingly. "You're one to talk."

"We should've left those people alone."

"But we didn't."

"No. We didn't."

Ramielle stepped away from the outstretched woman on the bed, looking mournful. "Why did you bring her here?"

"She was shot."

Ramielle cocked a single eyebrow high and knowing and glared at Lin. She didn't buy the vampire's bullshit. "Why are *they* locked up?"

She nodded her head in the direction of the compact family and before Lin could respond she switched her tactics. "Are you going to let her die?"

Lin looked up the breadth and gait of the girl before answering, "No."

The spirit watched Lin. With her lover dying on the bed, the vampire was balled in a jangle of doubt. The ghost would have felt something compassionate, akin to sympathy, if she were real. If her form had weight, or left an impression on the tight knit carpeting the Vam Däm Mu might have been moved by Lin's dilemma. But as it were, she was not. "Do you think Dominique would have let you suffer like this?"

Lin turned to the ghost. "I don't know."

Ramielle's eyes popped. "You don't know?" She glared dumbfounded at the vampire. "You were together for how many hundreds of years and you *'don't know'*?" The offended phantom shook her head. "She deserved better than you." Ramielle exhaled and refined her point. "Do you think Dominique would have stopped, for even one moment, if your life depended on it?"

"No." Lin felt ashamed.

"You're damned right she wouldn't. There was nothing that she would not have done for you. And here you are spoiled in that good woman's devotion claiming to love this girl, and yet you still fail to act when necessary."

"I do love her," defended the vampire in a soft, heavy whisper.

"Just not enough," she uttered, standing with her arms crossed, glaring down at the haggard soul with an accusatory stance, towering over her.

In Lin's arms Sarah felt cold and distant, a fading light, her tiny soul crushing as if under the hard heels of Vam Däm Mu. The weight of this moment was stretching; bitter taffy and condemned.

"The choice is very simple, Little One…" Ramielle leaned across the bed. "If you love her do what you have to do to save her. If you don't…walk away."

The ghost of the Vam Däm Mu stood. Lin turned away from the specter and stared at Sarah for a terse minute. No cascading memories clouded her vision. No ardent denial clogged her mind. Lin felt a simple truth blossoming within, and she knew what she had to do.

Standing up, she breathed slow and steady. Turning, she walked slowly out of the room. Passing the locked closet where the family of four huddled, scared and cramped, boxed in with their sweat and stink of urine, crying an ocean of tears together, Lin grabbed the door handle and popped the lock as the little metal knob turned.

A crevasse of light formed in the closet across frightened faces and got wider, hurting their eyes. With a stern manner, Lin noticed that the little boy was sleeping, curled in his mother's lap. She was thankful that his eyes could not fall on her. The pre-teen leaned against Doug's shoulder, his arm held his child and both of their eyes squinted against the dim brightness of the hallway. Lin pointed at the tall man. His knees were bent with his back hunched over. He was too large for the confined space.

"You. Come with me."

"After my wife uses the restroom and we get some food for the children and clean them up."

Lin didn't blink. She didn't twitch a muscle. "Don't force me to make you in front of them."

Carolyn turned to her husband and began crying again. "No. No"

Each word became a broken whine of tears and Henry groaned and moved in her lap. She was on the verge of waking him. Madison's face withered to tears as she told to her father not to go. He assured her that everything was going to be all right and patted her hand. The man's solemn eyes looked up at the vampire as he stood. Carolyn grabbed onto his pant leg and begged him to stay.

"It'll be all right." He repeated the message to send it home. He searched Lin's hard scowl for any sign that he spoke truth. "Please, let them eat and use the facilities. It's only decent and human."

Lin stepped aside for him to squeeze by. She wasn't human. "Downstairs. Now." She hadn't been human for a very long time.

Carolyn's breathing skipped as she held her daughter. Tears streamed down her face as snot clogged her sore nose. Lin closed the door on the three of them and was thankful that Henry still slept, that his mother's awful braying had not woken him. The vampire wouldn't have remained as calm and controlled if his little eyes were looking up at her. Eyes that held that same innocence as her son, William. It would have been too much. Too much, indeed.

"It's not too late, you know," began Doug as Lin nodded for him to get moving. "We can still help your friend. The police don't even have to know about you. I...I can drive her to the hospital myself and if anyone asks I can say that I found her on the side of the road. That I was driving home and, and I saw her walking along and she fell and I stopped to offer assistance."

Doug turned and looked at Lin for some hint, some glimmer that his idea could work. She was a blank slate, a cold fish. Perhaps his idea would have worked an hour ago. It sounded convincing enough. But they were past all that now. Sarah had crossed over, and in her current condition she would raise too many questions. It simply wasn't an option anymore.

Carolyn pulled her children closer and repeated the mantra that her husband had used, saying that everything was going to be all right. She wanted to believe the words, because she needed to believe them. Slowly, her husband's voice trailed off below, heading downstairs. She strained to listen. After a few moments she heard some kind of knocking about coming from the kitchen and it took all her will to keep from violently shaking. Doug's words came out of her feeble lips and were nothing more than numb symbols in her mouth. She hugged her children as tightly as possible and prayed that everything was going to be all right. Prayer was the cup of loneliness that begged to be fulfilled. Carolyn drank from that lonely cup, filling it with tears.

Lin attacked Doug from behind. They were in the foyer, near the small hall that connected to the kitchen and she pounced on his back. Doug went down hard and clanky as she bit into his jugular and held on. In less than a minute he stopped thrashing. In less than two minutes Lin and her precious Jadaraa Soo were full. Normally, she would have stopped. But this time wasn't normal. She was eating for two now. So, she gorged herself, becoming fat and ruddy. Her eyes turned black from the amount of blood that filled her system. The veiny arms of the parasite grew flat and warm and Lin felt as if she'd thrown on a couple of pounds.

When she left, Doug's corpse was sprawled against the back wall of the foyer, alone downstairs, his skin shriveled and his muscles had atrophied. His body was skeletal and gaunt, a husk of his former self. Carolyn heard Lin's footfall coming down the hall. There was a place upstairs that squeaked. Doug was always talking about tearing up the carpeting and fixing it. But he never got around to it. The grieving woman heard that squeak, that singular, lone noise that sounded like family. Only now it sounded as if someone had pulled her spine out.

"Doug?" she called as the footfall passed the closest door. "Where's my husband?" Carolyn listened. "Doug, are you out there?" she shouted. "Doug?"

Panic broke in her voice at the silent reproach. She could not help but to tremble and shake. She was terrified and she knew. In the pit of her gut, Carolyn knew that the horrible fiend had killed her man. "Where's my husband?" she screamed over and over again, tearing her voice to pieces.

Madison's tears and sobbing grew more hysterical as her mother lost it. "I want my Daddy… I want my Daddy…Gimmie my Daddy…"

The young girl and little boy cried, begging to have their father returned to them. All of the confusion and terror, wailing and shrieks beat against Lin's back as she crossed to the bed. The din from the closest was palpable, and the vampire did her best to ignore it.

She rubbed fresh blood from her face onto Sarah's lips, moving her hand slowly around the girl's mouth as the family cried their growing laments. Sarah's parasite reacted. It was weak, but hopeful. Lin stuck her bloody fingers in Sarah's mouth and the dancer began sucking. Hungrily, the parasite cleaned the murderous digits with Sarah's tongue.

Lin pulled her wet fingers out of Sarah's mouth, leaned down, and kissed her. She left a bloody smooch on the girl's plum blue lips. The vampire bit her own wrist, tearing a gaping hole where she'd previously cut a slit with her thumbnail. Placing the bleeding wound on Sarah's hungry mouth, Lin pulled her forward, onto her lap. After a few seconds of suckling, the girl's limbs became active – *alive* – and Sarah curled into the space around Lin, as if the center of the universe was the hole in Lin's arm and the life essence, the goo that made everything go, was the bloody nectar that seeped from the wound.

Lin could feel Doug leaving her. His blood was cleansed and purified in her body. Consumed by her Jadaraa Soo it used his vital fluid to make its own flesh, its own being. Even when her parasite screamed in her ears, joining the mournful bashing of the surviving family, to pull back from the youngling's lips Lin held on. She wanted Sarah to feast from her parasite's flesh and not just consume the overflow.

The vampire's veins grew thin and long again. Lin's eyes returned to a roadmap over deathly pale optics and everything lost that dark red tint. Sarah did not grow as plump as the vampire had with Doug's blood in her system. The girl's new Jadaraa Soo was still forming and consumed the viscous liquid with a ravenous appetite. When Lin pulled her wrist away from Sarah's mouth she could tell that the parasite still wanted more.

More…

The family wept together, having stopped shouting for Lin to tell them what had happened to their husband and daddy. In the maddening silence they came to their own conclusions. It was simple math. The only confusion that slammed through each of their heads was why. *Why Now? Why Me? Why him?* Nothing deteriorated the mind more quickly than that singular, engulfing word and question. Why shattered sanity. Why made them feel alone. Why was a ball of hurt that never ended.

Sarah groaned a breathy grate, yawned and stretch. Well fed and moving the blood throughout its system, her parasite reached as far and as wide as it could go. It shook a little at the tips of its universe and then curled within itself, pulling its host's limbs into a fetal position. Yet through it all, Sarah never woke. Her puppet master moved its strings, but she was not conscious to dance. Lin stood and rubbed her sore wrist. *Now…only time will tell.*

"Please…" Carolyn whined. Her voice was cracked, hoarse, and dry. "Bring him back. Bring him back….Bring him back… He was a good man."

The woman sobbed and repeated herself endlessly, lost in the painful narcotic chaos. The children clung to the feeble husk of their mother because they didn't have anything else to hold on to. Each of them was alone, bound together in a single space, adrift in dreadful turmoil that none of them understood.

"You know it already, don't you?" the specter of Ramielle asked, walking around to Lin's eyesight.

"It doesn't matter. This will work."

The ghost chuckled. It was the kind of slow bitter laugh that made Lin feel like a fool. Both the illusion and the undead woman watched the young vampire as she panted wildly, breathing like a rabid dog in quick, short bursts of fervid breaths.

"The trees in the forest fall one by one. One by one. One by one." The hallucination sang Lin's old nursery rhyme. "The trees in the forest fall one by one. All…day…long–"

"Stop it." But the Vam Däm Mu laughed viciously, baring her vampiric teeth and started the rhyme all over again.

"I said, stop it." Lin charged the specter of malfeasance and attempted to grab her. But her hands passed completely through the seemingly whole body of Ramielle Eirinhas as if she were nothing more than air. "What the…"

Lin tried again, falling into a splintered shock, and when her tendril digits curled upon the emptiness of her own palms, yet again, she backed away, horrorstricken and shaken, muttering the word, no, over and over again. She pressed the large bowl of her thumbs tightly against her temples as the vision laughed and laughed a heartless cackle that wouldn't cease.

The vampire's back found the flat wall as she pushed against it to crawl inside of the wood and sheet-rock and hide from the ghostly vision. But it was of no use. The storm raged and the pitch of the house tilted.

"Don't lose your head," Ramielle told Lin, and picking hers up from the cradle of her neck she tossed it to the crazy vampire.

Lin reached out to grab it. Instinctual, a motor response, a reflex, but there was nothing to hold, nothing to catch. Ramielle's severed head still cackling like a forest of monkeys passed through Lin's outstretched hands and disappeared into the cavity of her chest. The ghost vanished, but her insane laughter lingered on, drilling through Lin's ears like a hurricane.

"No,no,no,no,no,no,no,no,no,no,no…." muttered the vampire as she slid down the wall.

She grabbed her knees and rocked back and forth. She slammed the back of her head against the wall a few times, leaving an indentation and a few strands of raven-black hair lodged in the cracked plaster. Carolyn heard Lin's pleas of anguish and revived her calls with vigor, screaming at the top of her lungs for Lin to return her husband and free them.

Lin pressed her palms over her ears to push the vile woman's torrid rants out of her mind, to push Ramielle's awful cackling out of her mind. All she wanted was Sarah. All she needed was Sarah to look up at her again with those gorgeous green eyes and that tender glow of life flushing through her young pink skin. Lin wanted to go back. Lin needed to go back. She pounded her head against the wall, unable to stop the feeling that she was falling, fast and furious, through a ring of fire!

Sarah panted and sweated a tarnished red liquid. She was alive…
though barely. Her Jadaraa Soo struggled to reconstitute and form a
cognitive bond. The vampire knew what she had to do if she wanted
to save the girl from the locket, but its weight was too much to bear.
Lin started singing, rocking back and forth, as she cradled her own pale
shoulders with her own limp arms. She was a cup of loneliness mouthing
prayers in the only way she knew.

"The trees in the forest fall one by one. One by one. One by
one. The trees in the forest fall one by one. All…day…long… The trees
in the forest go chop, chop, chop. Chop, chop, chop. Chop, chop, chop.
The trees in the forest go chop, chop, chop. One…by…one…"

The ground yielded to each step, soft and sandy, spreading outward by the weight put into it and filled partially as each footstep was evacuated, leaving wide impressions. The sun beat down gold and glorious. A crystal blue sky. Cloud mountains, billowy and white, hovered over the high desert landscape, vast and endless. Special Agent Ian McCallister listened to Special Agent Gorman as she gave her report.

"Two local boys, Todd E. Darryl and Jake Carmens, discovered the site earlier this morning when they were out riding their motorcycles. Witnesses came upon the deceased remains of Sergeant John Wallace and Lieutenant Katelyn Mauldune of the Phoenix Metro Police, Homicide Division, and called 911."

"These the same two as the other night?"

"Yes Sir."

McCallister looked down at the mangled corpse of the Arizona Sergeant. Wallace's throat had been torn out, his chest clawed. Dried blood splatter coated everything along the inside door panel, front seat, windshield, and down the front of the detective's shirt. *Made a real mess of it.*

"The boys spoke with an Officer Jimenez," she continued. "He was the first to arrive on the scene. They told him what they saw. He checked it out and called it in."

"It's a damn mess."

"Yes Sir." Gorman followed her superior to the other body.

"Hard to contain."

"Davy's worked a cover story. Seems plausible considering that the M.E.'s estimated time of death was around 6 or 7pm yesterday. All night exposure would attract coyotes."

The special agents stopped at the top of Kate Mauldune's twisted head and looked down. The front of her body lay prone in the sand, but her head looked up from the back. Her eyes were open, like they were staring at the gorgeous sky beyond the nodding brows of the FBI. She looked calm, restful - a broken doll.

"Any signs from the other vehicle?"

"No Sir. Not yet."

Special Agent Ian McCallister drew his attention to the housing development below. It was about a mile and a half off by his estimation. He raised his nose to the wind and sniffed. But there nothing for his highly acute sense of smell to grab. Too much time, sand, and wind had rolled passed this place since the carnage had happened for him to get a decent fix.

"All right," he said. "Let's secure the scene. Get statements from everybody and send them on their way. I'll call a clean up crew for 0800. I want our cover story working by morning. And nobody else is allowed on site."

"Yes, Sir." She moved to follow orders.

"Heard anything from Johnson?"

The underling paused. "Not yet. Will let you know first thing."

Special Agent McCallister sighed and glared back down at the ruined body of Kate Mauldune. Sandy grit lodged in the folds of her clothing. It took root in the corners of her twisted mouth and had begun to clog her opened eyes. The sun was starting to bake her dead skin, dehydrating the corpse. He crouched down beside her and the scent of gunshot residue and urine was stronger. He turned toward the cock-eyed Cadillac stuck in a mound of earth and without checking the detective's gun he had a fairly good idea about how the events had played out.

He stood and walked down the dune as behind him his team carried out his orders. He knew the local boys never liked it when the FBI came waltzing in, flashing their big badges, telling everybody what to do and how to do it. That was one of the reasons why he joined the Federal Bureau of Investigation in the first place. He liked muscling in and telling people what to do. Special Agent Ian McCallister was good at giving people a purpose, or at least a job function. He had a knack for assessing situations quickly and applying the right need. Though this job had already sprung a few surprises that he hadn't anticipated. It was a grade-A cluster-fuck. What was supposed to have been an easy grab and elimination with a quick turn around had become a full-blown catastrophe.

The special agent made the clean up call and then dialed another number. *She's not going to like it. Though this is more her mess than mine.* Bodies were piling up. The job got harder once bodies started piling up. Too many of them and the operation went bust. The Bureau had procedures to follow. *The Vam Pŷr knew that. I was clear with her about the conditions.* Even for someone who was as specialized and distinguished as Special Agent McCallister he still had a boss that he answered to. Despite what the client wanted there was a chain of command that he had to follow. *We aren't animals to be unleashed.*

She answered on the fourth ring. "Well? Did you find her?"

Not even a hello. "We found her car. It was abandoned at least eighteen hours ago."

"And what about her mongrel friend?"

"We're in pursuit."

"What does that mean, exactly?"

"We'll find her. Two of my best agents are on it. She won't get far."

Dominique stopped dead in her tracks. Her entourage came at rest behind her. Everyone was dressed to the nines. Some wore dark sunglasses or held parasols against the setting sun. Clyde held a parasol over the Vam Pŷr. Dusk skirted the edges of the East Coast. The burning orb was a dim red ball, mostly hidden on the other side of the earth. The private jet at the end of the runway waited for Dominique and her party. A long red carpet had been rolled out for her that led to the sleek airliner, and a whole side of JFK Airport was rented specifically for this one flight.

The taught modern lines of the waiting Leer Jet were accentuated by the established logo of Delacroix International, which was a subsidiary of Delacroix Enterprises, and the man that owned this secluded aircraft wanted Dominique to fly in style. It was his way.

"This is very disappointing," scolded Mother Night "You came highly recommended and yet you can not dispatch one annoying little flea."

"The job is more complex than you let on. It is going to cost extra."

"Of course it is. Anything else?"

"Yes. We have a problem."

"What is it?"

"The police from Arizona—"

"Yes?" interrupted Dominique, upset, and very close to yelling. "What about them?"

"They're dead. Your daughter killed them both."

Dominique gasped. "Oh, mon ami."

Those that had been with Dominique the longest pulled closer to her. They hung on her every word and gasp. They comforted her, gave her support. Though, only two of the seven members of the group stood apart. They were her guests, Joshua and Prophet.

Each member of Dominique's entourage that were joining her on this foray overseas to attend the Tournament and meet with the enigmatic vampire Michele Delacroix, had their own agendas to serve in the great lady's company. Dominique knew it. She held no illusions about her prominence, position, and wealth. She'd grown strong on The Council and could no longer afford the luxury of real friendships. Lin's lost love was the last true connection that she had known, and even it had been strained for nearly a hundred and fifty years.

Joshua had known the Vam Pŷr since her days as a blood slave among the Tien Däm Mu. He simply loved her as a friend, but he did not pander to the tides of her moods. Prophet, on the other hand, had come at Dominique's request to help save Linnet's soul and had remained in her orbit to council her pain. Though he strove to rescue the Vam Pŷr's most favorite pet he sought to envelop the grand matriarch into the lavish folds of the Bithtaran rites. She was a coveted prize if the religious sect were to expand as he planned.

Everybody wanted something from her now-a-days. It made it hard to know what was true or not. But hearing of Lin's acts of brutal murder took more from her than what any other could take. It would surely get back to The Council and some reckoning would commence. They were, after all, police officers. They had families and the loyal fraternity of the force. Mistakes like these always created hassles. Lin had finally gone beyond Dominique's tight sphere of control. *I might not be able to save you this time, my love.*

For the longest time the phone lay dead against his ear, pumping stale air on both sides of the speakers. "What do you want me to do?" asked the special agent, jarring the pensive shade.

Dominique's face twisted into a loathsome scowl and she cast a worried eye at Prophet. She knew she had to let Lin go, but she didn't want to. *Be strong.* "She made her bed. Let her lie in it."

Mother Night closed her cell phone abruptly and continued down the path of plush red carpeting, a knitted river of blood, and boarded the plane with her entourage in tow. It was in God's hands now. *Lin is off the rails.* It was something that Dominique had always feared might happen in the loose wiles of that Chicago harlot. *Nothing good ever came out of that coven! I'd sooner see the whole lot plowed under before anymore of their mischief breeds anymore loss.* The Vam Pŷr was ill tempered and disposed to worry. All she could do now was sit and wait; let Lin's horrid debacle unfold, let her learn. There was little else she could do at the expense of her own broken spirit. It was a dark time, indeed.

Special Agent Ian McCallister closed his phone and put it away. The Children of Evensong were nothing more than arrogant, pampered brats, filled with their own vainglory; they disgusted him. Which was partly why he enjoyed his job. Working in the field often afforded the special agent the opportunity to kill those arrogant, self-righteous bloodsuckers. It was a perk that came with the suit and the paycheck at the end of the week. He turned his nose to the wind again and inhaled. There had to be a scent somewhere on this crash site where he could get a fix as to where his quarry had wandered.

His eyes scanned the horizon. It wasn't hard to figure out that they'd taken off toward the subdivision. It was the most logical spot. His intel on the clients showed high intelligence and innovative thinking. Linnet Pevensey would have sought transportation in suburbia. *We'll check that out once we get this site secure.* Special Agent McCallister climbed back up the small hill just as the Coroner began bagging and tagging the bodies.

Sarah woke to the sounds of birdsong and a trash compactor. Picking up plastic cans in the street, the metal arm moved slowly as it grabbed the waste with its pinchers, lifting it to where it dumped the blue cans in a hole at the truck's top. One house at a time it moved down the block, collecting each bin in the cul-de-sac, the entire neighborhood, keeping the place clean and tidy.

Sarah tried to move but there was something on top of her. She lifted her head and peered down the length of her body, seeing Lin stretched across her lap. Her raven hair shimmered in the intruding light that sneaked through the edges of the curtains.

Sarah felt as if she had tied one on the night before. Her body pounded a unique numbness and she felt strangely distant within her skin. Rising onto her elbows, her whole body tingled, thrumming in the darkened room. And outside? She could hear everything. Not just the tweet-tweet of the flighty creatures, but the flapping of their wings and their flittering little hearts; she heard a neighbor, a few houses down, washing her car and the song playing on the radio as if it were just beyond the frame of the window.

She didn't recognize where she was and wasn't particularly concerned about it at the moment. The place smelled different – *new*. Burnt potatoes from last night's meal clung to the ceiling, a decaying funk lingered in the carpet downstairs, and old clothes from throughout the house mixed with other strange scents. A delicious dried coppery aroma collided amid the other dozen smells that Sarah couldn't place.

"Morning sunshine," she said, but talking took more effort than it should have. Her special ray of goodness didn't reciprocate. Lin lay prone across Sarah's midsection. She felt her move – a tiny wiggle. But the woman still stared at Sarah's feet with the crown of her head glaring at the dancer. "Hey?" she called. "I thought you said vampires don't sleep."

The jocularity in her tone soon abated as she stared at Lin. "Hey?" Sarah reached out and shook her shoulder, rising, and Lin slid off her. Sarah thought she was joking until the vampire crashed in a horrid heap onto the floor beside the bed with a dead cascading thud.

Lin's body puffed a thin cloud of dust. Specks of dried rotten flesh danced around Lin's shriveled husk and the impact of her hitting the floor knocked her jaw out of whack. Lin's mouth grotesquely hung open, glowering at the frightened woman. Sarah screamed, a coarse shrill shriek that rent throughout the whole upstairs of the house, as she jumped backwards on the bed.

Suddenly, a biting memory ripped through her body as if her skin was peeling off. It felt like something was pressing hard against her skull. It wasn't a memory that Sarah recalled, because she was looking at herself without a mirror, unconscious and lying on the bed. Dirty and covered in blood, Sarah panted like a rabid animal, her chest bobbed up and down in rapid successions. From the eyes of the spectator, Sarah witnessed biting her own wrists and shoving it over her other self's mouth. Then she bent down and kissed herself, curling up with her on the bed. These weren't her memories, from her mind's eye. They were Lin's memories! *But why? How?*

All at once she felt smothered, unable to breath, like she'd forgotten how it was done. Her chest felt constricted, strangulating from her center, as her muscles pinched in a tightening sharp pang. It was exactly how she always imagined falling off a cliff in outer space would feel if she were forced to abandon her rocket ship. Sarah ran her hands over her mouth to remove the flesh that covered it in her mind. Nothing was there. Dried blood flakes caked around her speaking hole chipped off and flittered in the air. Her breath returned as she watched them. Floating...

Then Lin's face, gaunt and pale, eyes engorged black, her mouth swathed in fresh blood was flush in Sarah's mind staring at her. *"I'm sorry. I love you."*

Sarah's eyes popped and she fell off the bed, crashing to the floor with more volume and mass than that of the sunken shell of her vampire lover. Shaking, Sarah quickly climbed to her feet and stood. Another strangulating pang riveted her whole body in crushing pain as she stumbled around the girth of the master bed. She was starving. Falling onto her knees beside Lin's corpse another blood memory shook her frame: She...no Lin, was rocking her back and forth, crying blood tears. *"Stay with me. Stay with me forever."*

Sarah was frightened, truly afraid. She didn't know what was happening. The last thing she remembered was driving. *No? There was an accident. We crashed.* Vaguely, it came into wakefulness. There were police. Gun fire. *I was shot.* Sarah had a difficult time pulling her eyes off Lin's withered corpse. *You're dead?*

She pulled back and lifted her tattered shirt and found the bandage that Lin had placed over the wound in her gut. Sarah peeled it off. The bandage was dry, caked in old, brown blood. Underneath the soiled cotton, the wound was almost healed. There was some slight scaring, star shaped. She put her hand to it and it felt hard.

Looking down at her belly, Sarah saw something else too. Underneath her anemic white skin, trailing out in all directions were dark burgundy veins. *Oh my God...* Slowly, she lifted her arms into view and saw them there too. She turned her hands over, palms up, and the nasty little veins snaked through to the tips of her fingers. *What happened?* No sooner did she ask the question internally than she got an internal response. Another memory that wasn't hers, Lin slit her wrist and put it on Sarah's mouth.

"Drink this," the vampire had said in the wee hours of morning. *"Don't stop. Take it all. Take everything. You mean that much to me."*

A lightning bolt of pain ripped through Sarah's spine. It bent her neck and fled out through the pores, down her forearms, as she witnessed herself feeding from the vampire, sucking the moist blood and veins of Lin's Jadaraa Soo. The vampire's self-preserving tentacles abandoned the sinking ship of its body and stuffed themselves down Sarah's throat. The girl gagged on the memory as if the vile thing was, again, crawling through her opened orifice, melding with the sickly beast that already lay within her chest.

Sarah crumbled to the floor, panting and worn out. "What did you do to me?"

Another strangulating pang tore through her alien system and all of a sudden it made sense as to what it was: *Hunger.* The vampiric veins wanted blood. *So, this is how it feels.* Sarah looked again at her extremities. The veins thrashing beneath her skin were different, more gnarled and fat. She didn't remember Lin possessing such pronounced rivers under her skin. The unions of their flesh passed across her mind and nothing resembled the wicked concoction that boiled under her flesh now.

Then, just as if she had asked the question, why, a series of blood memories paraded across her mind's eye and she knew that Lin had manipulated her veins so that she could appear more normal when she was among humans. But there was more too it. She had memories from Lin's before they had met...hundreds of years before she was even born. Sarah felt the spray of the sea, smelled the dew in a jungle forest, recalled giving birth, and fought in war.

Remarkable. The name of her parasite sprang to mind: *Jadaraa Soo.* Though, Sarah had only heard it spoken once in the motel room, she completely understood what it meant and what it was and where it came from. Her mind stretched back, over thousands of years. Faces and images from bygone eras paraded before her feeble senses faster than she could handle.

Times were different then. Violent and foreign. She was a male, pale skinned warrior fighting Turkish soldiers around 3 BCE. She flayed them with a sword, hacking off limbs, and crushing skulls of frightened men. Then suddenly, she became somebody else and she was racing through a dense dark forest that no longer existed along the shores of the African continent. *The Lanz Gur Mae.* It was the ancient name of her home, the place of her birth. Strange rituals cascaded through her mind; a waterfall of bizarre cultures clashing in the maelstrom of so many lives lived. Her sight was impeccable in the near darkness of a glade, a forest, and deep earthen caves.

She imbibed incense at ancient altars while at the same time sampled cakes at a bakery in Paris, France in 1774. Sarah's interior self tracked an antelope under thick jungle leaves. The moon, *Layal*, shone above her. The night sky was a minefield of stars more brilliant than she had ever seen, glistening wet after a rain. The darkness was as clear and luminous as a fine summer's day. She smelled the animal's scent, followed its quickening hooves as brightly and as strong as if it were in the room now with her and Lin's corpse. She jumped, landing on its back, and sunk her teeth into its pungent throat as she brought it to the ground. It tasted *So…Good.* So hot and delicious, blood flowed into her mouth. Sarah became aroused by its simple tastes and lust bristled over her delicate limbs like a volcano.

She convulsed and curled into herself, whimpering under the strain of such torrid imagery. Again she was a man, but he was not a man. *What did Lin called it? Oh yes, Omjadda.* She was a king. She ruled a vast and primal people in the mountains of the world. She walked through *his* keep, made love to *his* concubines, slaves, and wife. Handled matters of the clan and partook of roasted human flesh. Through *his* eyes, she died at the hands of a lover named Fizza. Yet, who was also known by another name, a different time – *Dominique* – and suddenly Sarah had a face to go with the name.

Life with Jaci burned to the surfaced of her skin, across eons and continents, released from a dormant place within the blood, Sarah felt a devastating love for the Persian woman from two main sources: Lin and Ornn Däm Mu. There was so much longing and hurt clashing within that she thought she would crumble and die. A wall of feelings so vivid and ripe towered over her and broke, falling into the crashing hunger that beat upon the shores of her flesh.

Without any control over her own bodily functions, the Promethean creature began crying blood tears. She pulled herself off the floor into a sitting position. She felt tired, exhausted, and without asking the question, just thinking about it, she understood, with the deepest capacity, how Lin had loved the woman and how Ornn had led Dominique's hand to slit his own throat.

Sarah reacted to the killing stroke, rushing her hands to her uncut neck as she felt *his* blood seep through her nimble fingers, accepting the karmic tide of *his* quiet death. In the fiery synapses of Sarah's coiled, parasite-addled brain she understood a strange and limitless history, experienced by a gallery of lives that she knew nothing about. But she was lost in this great knowing, suffocating on the prophecies that were now spoken to her by a scraggly white-haired woman, who wasn't a woman, that scared the hell out of her.

Fedah Maalj was the seer of the people, the Jaddat. She had a pronounced forehead, no eye sockets and no eyes, a small nose, and two rows of sharp teeth behind thin lips. She was bent with age, gruesome looking, pale white, and was born to the Fedah Layal J'in long before Ornn had been birthed into his clan. The old woman was Layal's messenger on earth. Born into the fifth clan of the tree-dwelling people, the Fedah Layal was named for the goddess's halo, those three luminescent rings that surround the moon. But the seer belonged to all Omjadda, not just one J'in.

Sarah didn't understand how she knew any of this, but she did. Her fear and perplexity at the rich tapestry of interlocking memoirs took her further into the cellular logic of the blood. It was like opening a door to a room filled with doors, and each one was flung open transporting experience and stories in ancient tongues that Sarah had never heard. The Jaddat's power was awesome and immense with Gai'Anaka. The old crone spoke through Ornn to her as the bubble of an eight hundred year-old memory burst.

Sarah fell through the oily hands of time. Maalj's face moved closer, reaching an index finger, and touched Ornn's forehead, penetrating Sarah's third eye. Bright electric pain ruptured from that singular point on her skull. Her vision went hot and stark white as if she'd been jabbed with a searing poker and Maalj's word rung deeply in her ears.

"Ah, the Sylph. I see your eyes have been opened. Though, you are not yet ready for what is to come, my child. We will soon talk, you and I, and upon ashes and death rebuild. Soon, my young one. Soon."

As the blinding light and gripping agony faded from Sarah's vision she found herself staring at the ceiling, surrounded by the closed curtains of a dull gray afternoon. She lay on her back with both legs bent under her and her arms splayed wide. She felt her Jadaraa Soo crawling under the skin of her face, down her thighs, and under her breasts. It felt weird. Bizarre. Sarah rolled over onto her side and stared at the dried husk of Linnet Pevensey.

She recalled the vampire speaking to her about blood memories at the motel, but it was nothing like she had just experienced. Full connectivity through cognizant recognition and hidden knowledge that spoke directly to her from the past. *What the fuck?* Lin never told her about that! She said the parasite only showed images of feeding and sex to convey its hunger along with feelings of pleasure and pain. What she had just experienced was so much more than that.

"What did you do to me?"

No sooner did the words escape her lips did her mind showcase some of the same memories that she had already seen of Lin feeding Sarah her blood. They were vivid, but this time around the imagery and sensations were not as intense. *Dulled by knowing, perhaps?* Sarah reached out her hand and touched Lin. The weight of her trembling fingers caused the skeleton to break and Lin's dried bones crumpled before Sarah's inimical eyes.

The poor girl shook with fear, withdrew her hand, sat up, and wrapped herself in her frail arms next to the deteriorating corpse. She cried great big sobs, pulling her knees tightly against her chest. Sarah wanted to fade away. To squeeze into a speck of atom-dust and never be. Another strangulating pang ripped through her system and she knew with unfailing certainty: There was no going back. She would be this way forever. Whatever she was, whatever Lin had done to her had made her different. Blood memories had been stitched through time, sewn into the canvas of her muscles and bones, reaching further back than what she could scarcely comprehend.

Slowly, Sarah pulled herself off the floor and wandered into the bathroom. She fumbled for the light switch, eventually found it, and turned it on. The bulbs over the vanity flickered its sluggish illumination and Sarah made the mistake of looking directly into the light. Searing white blindness stabbed her eyes and she turned away. She slowly felt her Jadaraa Soo moving across her eyeballs as her vision restored. *Fuck! That hurt. Is there anything about being like this that doesn't cause pain?!*

The answer to her internal musings was another strangulating thirst pang. It rocked her limbs. *Great!* Sarah turned on the tap and the scent of the filtered water smelled good. Her lips were parched. Her throat felt sore and dry. She made a cup of her hands and the liquid felt exquisite running over her arms. She drank three handfuls and felt something new rippling through her body caused by the Jadaraa Soo. *Pleasure.* It felt as if the thing purred and Sarah felt warm all over.

"So, blood's not the only thing you crave."

She chuckled sardonically and gazed at her reflection in the mirror. But suddenly the corners of her vision dimmed. The room took on a shade of night and Sarah felt sadness, an intense remorse, and Lin stared back at her reflection in the mirror as she spoke.

"I'm sorry that when you wake up, if you wake up, that I won't be here with you." It looked as if the vampire were standing directly in front of Sarah. *"I'm sorry that I've gotten you into so much trouble. I never meant for you to get hurt. Finding you has meant more to me than I could ever express. Know this…I did what I had to do to save you."* Blood tears ran down worn streaks from previous outpourings. *"Dominique always said that I had strong blood. Well, we're going to find out."* She smiled meekly. *"I love you."* Lin bent her head down for a minute and then looked up and touched the mirror. *"Above all else… remember that."*

A message writ in the blood. Sarah gripped the sink with both hands and nearly snapped it off the wall. She let go. Water poured in the sink, a constant wet splashing from the mouth of the spout. It ran down the drain with a deep gurgling sound. Sarah touched the mirror in the exact same place where Lin had touched it. In her mind's eye they were touching each other through the looking glass, through time, and through blood. She did not see her vampiric reflection anymore. She only saw Lin.

Lin's remorse subsided with the vision as Sarah's great loss dropped to the cracking in her belly. *Lin is gone. She's never coming back.* Through gaping sobs Sarah pulled her arms around the painful hole in her gut. It wasn't where the gunshot wound had been. It was in the core of her being – a gigantic loss and wailing confusion. Sarah stumbled from the bathroom and fell to her knees in front of a curtain-covered window just as another thirst pang seized her.

Accompanying the violent shudder was the vision of Lin, accompanied by Z, attacking a cashier and manager at a convenience store. Their deaths were brutal – vicious and cruel. But she understood these memories to be nothing more than the parasite's desire to feed. It was hungry. *Baby wants a bottle.* It was communicating its need to her just how Lin had explained it the other night. *The other memories…the other visions…Maalj? They are something else.*

Foolishly, Sarah pulled on the curtain to help her stand and daylight flooded her new vampiric eyes. It was more intense than the bathroom light. Hot white searing pain bit at her skull. Though before everything vanished she could see little bits of the neighbor's backyard in the setting sunlight, trailing desert dunes, and tiny specks milling about

Lin's car. The crash site was crawling with men...*with police*. Daylight was a hard thudding pound that striped Sarah of her sight. In her blindness, she stumbled backwards hoping that she was able to close the heavy cloth curtain.

A few minutes later, she was on her knees again facing the bedroom door. Her whole body was bracketed in a sea of floating pain and violent memories. It was more horror than she ever witnessed in her entire life. Her mind felt crowded, as if legions had moved in and taken permanent residence. She literally could not stop shaking.

In the small adjunct hallway that led to the master bedroom Sarah noticed a long trail of blood on the wall as if someone with messy fingers had smeared them. Instantly, Sarah remembered doing it. Though, she was not herself. She was Lin. She felt gorged and satiated on fresh blood and lazily pulled her fingers across the wall as she entered the bedroom to feed Sarah, because...*I was dying.*

Sarah turned to the bed where she saw herself lying in the memory and knew that Lin believed that she was checking out and that all her attempts to save her were failing. Utter hopelessness spread into the carpet through her fingertips as Sarah began to understand the fear that the vampire had about losing her. Lin was a rack of guilt. She blamed herself. It was a cold wrong feeling to know such a thing. *A cold wrong feeling indeed!*

Another thirst pang rippled across her body, a wave of veins grabbing puerile, undead flesh. Sarah, spitefully annoyed, bit into her arm. There was a slight muffled sensation of pain, as if the signal had come from the other side of the world, as her teeth pierced her flesh. She felt movement in her mouth that she'd never felt before and was soon aware that she suckled her own dark blood. After a terse minute the Jadaraa Soo did not like consuming itself. It wasn't what it wanted, but in some odd way it calmed the rotten ache that was bashing her brain for blood.

After a minute or two, Sarah removed her fangs from her arm, climbing to her feet again, and walked out of the bedroom. She turned to look at the remains of her lover before they fell out of sight. Loneliness and grief tugged at her bones. Sarah's own feelings were a welcomed gift in light of all the other sensations and thoughts that were breaking upon her consciousness.

She felt small against the tide of time that had been opened within the dormant arms of her two Jadaraa Soo. It threatened to consume her. Her life seemed pathetic. Dancing to get ahead, struggling at school, living in Hobbs and Lovington, fucking Derrick, and running from her momma, was insignificant. She was lost amid a vast void within, a spiral as deep and wide as the cosmos. Its tendril fingers reached out to purchase more flesh than she had. It threatened to own more of her haggard soul than she could bear. Sarah staggered into the hall, but stopped short. Coming to the opened closest door, she saw smeared and splattered blood, red exaggeration on the white painted wood. It felt familiar.

Apprehension welled up. She didn't want to look inside of the closet. Something horrible had happened there. Instinctually, she knew. The vampire placed a hand to her trembling mouth. She was deftly afraid to peek within the dark, opened crevice. The door hung ajar, a gaping grin, blocking her way down the hall. Its wide invitation begged her to look within its hollow. There was no way around it. Curiosity pressed on her shoulders. The whole house was deathly silent, except for her shivering breaths of fear.

Sarah stepped around the corner and lifted her eyes to that rank space and beheld stark emptiness. Urine and feces marked the ground. Smatterings of blood decorated the walls. She exhaled. Her apprehension melted away as the parasite thrummed against her forehead, pulsed in her ears. Sarah tilted her head down and saw a foot. A tiny foot…and she knew. It was the emaciated foot of a child. Her brow knotted and her fear returned threatening to strangle her chest. She turned around and held a ghastly vision.

The sunken and drained corpses of a woman and a little boy lay in the hall. Misshapen. Posed. Lin had lain the child in his mother's lap after she had killed him. He looked as if he was sleeping and all the edges inside Sarah's mind were crumbling. She recalled the child standing over her when Lin had brought her to the house. He showed her his toy car. He was proud of it. He reached down and touched the necklace that Lin had given her and out of shock and remorse Sarah's own digits wandered to the silver locket that still adorned her neckline.

Simultaneous memory and live act grabbed the precious ornament and a door was flung wide open. All of Lin's memories about what had happened in New Mexico seventy-five years ago during that two day sandstorm crammed through her compressed skull at a breakneck pace. It was horrible. She felt dizzy. Her body shook from the visions. She nearly fell, propping herself against the doorjamb of the opened closet.

She slid down the decorative wood trim to a deathly seat near the corpses. She felt weak and sluggish, drained just like the two dead bodies. The events that took place in those ruins where Lin had taken her the other night were maddening. She witnessed the murder of her vestige at the hands of the vampire she had loved and cried. Blood tears, weeping from the flesh of her Jadaraa Soo, parachuted from her bowled cheeks. It was worse than what Lin had described. *Such cold terror dwelled within her.* The dancer could not escape its peerless gaze. It boiled in her skin, a karma tide. *How could Lin have been so cruel?*

The parasite answered her unspoken question by stepping through a window in time, holding the door wide open for Sarah to look. Her eyes fell on the corpses of the mother and child, but Sarah no longer saw them reposed in decaying slumber. They were breathing. They were screaming. The woman fought and punched Lin as she attacked. But Sarah witnessed each and every horror as if she were the one doing it. The mother's struggle was feeble against the vampire. Such cold detachment coursed through Lin's veins with a hardened resolve. *She kept thinking how she needed to save me.* All night long the woman had been yelling at Lin from the confines of the locked closet. She was obviously tired. Weakened. Abused. The little boy – *Henry – Dear God! Lin knew his name. I know his name. He cried in a pool of his mother's blood as Lin drained her dry to feed it to me...* Sarah was alive with the reality of it.

"I love you," Lin whispered as she murdered the boy.

"No," Sarah yelled, kicking her legs against the warm flush of his life in her veins. "No!"

"I love you." Lin pushed the memories of her son out of her mind as Henry's tiny heart ceased within her mouth.

Ardent love and self-disgust! The vampire had damned her soul to save the dancer. Sarah pushed against the jamb. She twisted and hit her head with her hands to make the memories stop. But in her mind she was the killer, reasoning that it was a kindness to send the boy on the same voyage that she had sent his family. *Leaving him alive would have been monstrous.* Sarah's own screams began escaping from her lips as she pulled on the bloody door handle, struggling to stand. She closed the closet door and walk away from the terrible visions of Lin killing the mother and child, but they were within her forever.

Sarah ran her fingers through her knotted hair, smearing blood stained tears across her face with the meat of her palms. She lifted her head, gazed down at the end of the hall and held another grueling sight. Lying in infinite slumber at the top of the staircase was another corpse.

It was the body of a young girl. She leaned against the wall at the mouth of the stairs; arms and legs akimbo as her head bobbed forward. Her brunette hair covered her face in a messy tangle. Sarah trembled like a motor boat. Breaths, panting in short gasping deaths. She was more terrified now than any other time in her life as she approached the body and fell down beside it.

In her mind, Sarah saw the girl alive. *She was pretty once.* Matted hair obscured her face. *She was in her room, on the phone.* The whole terrible sequence played out. The young girl's mother railed against Lin, trying to keep her safe, a hellfire of scratching fingernails and spit. But it did no good. The vampire smacked the woman across the bridge of her nose and she fell backwards, blood flying, as the closet door slammed closed again. Lin threw the girl down the hall and amid the wails of her family she did tear her throat out, gorging on her life at the top of the stairs. Lin pulled every last drop that she could muster from the prepubescent girl's petite frame.

"Dear God, what did you do? What did you do?"

Sarah reached a shaking hand to move the young girl's hair out of her face. But she knew what she'd find. *Eyes staring blankly open, face lean and sunken.* Shriveled flesh. Sarah could see it along the girl's arms. So she quickly pulled her hand away, bowed her head, and lamented the child's death: *Sorry that I could live.* It felt as if she would never stop crying. Her soul was a boundless harbor of waste. She was a simple girl from Hobbs, New Mexico. A nobody. She was just a stripper that dreamed of becoming a doctor, and the woman in her mind, who was ripping apart her soul, had murdered others so that she could live. *I don't deserve this. Nobody deserves this.*

"Nobody," she cried, falling into the hurt. "Nobody has ever loved me...like you."

Sarah found it hard to stand and fell beside the girl's corpse, asking why. Every turn around every corner in this mad house was yet another atrocious act committed for the sake of love. *My damnable love. Would it have been better to go into the earth having loved and known you than to awake to such an unceasing nightmare?* Sarah clashed against the brackets of death that held her prisoner. Yet, through all of Lin's violent memories of murder, through all the sweltering pain and grief that knocked the dancer down, one thing emerged with stark voracity: Lin had never given up. *She never gave up on me.*

The simple girl from nowhere New Mexico used the hand railing to help her stand. She craved fresh air away from the rotting stink of the house. Starting down the steps, her footing was loose, her body languid – it wasn't hers to run anymore – and she fell. Sarah tumbled, end over end, to the bottom of the stairs, landing hard in the foyer. The floor was made with inlaid sandstone tiles that led into the kitchen.

The young vampire barely felt any pain from her spill and laughed. She cried too through the absent gaiety, unable to get a handle on everything that was happening. It was coming at her too fast and vivid. She couldn't stop shaking. Her nervous system was a wreck. She was falling apart. Using the two bottom steps, after a time, Sarah pulled herself up.

She turned toward the front door, unsure of the light. The portal had tall tinted windows on either side of its wooden façade. It looked as if night was dropping its dress. Dusk could be settling over the land, but she glimpsed her ragged condition in a mirror. Her reflection hung on the wall, just past the potted plant. The looking glass was framed with a gold trim that had inlaid sandstone pieced together like a jigsaw puzzle. Jagged edges against cut jagged edges; each little speck of earth was like a million tiny eyes staring at her. She was a mess – ghostly pale and whiter than what she remembered Lin ever being. Her clothing was torn and dirty, her face and hair was covered in dried caked blood. *The blood of the family…through Lin's body!*

Her eyes were sallow and bleached. The veiny parasite ran throughout her face, just beneath her skin, a roadmap of outrageous memories. *I'm a hideous fiend!* Sarah crossed to the mirror, getting close, and peeled back her lips. She had two sets of teeth. One set, the larger ones, was colored more like teeth than that of the other smaller set. The tinier ones were a reddish hue and positioned directly behind the larger fangs. It was easier to tell from the backset of teeth that her vampire fangs were comprised of several veins woven together in a tight mesh. She pulled her lip further back and saw where the Jadaraa Soo had broken through her gums to form the canine mashers.

Lin only had one set of teeth. *I remember.* Confused, Sarah looked again. There definitely were two sets of fangs. *Whatever I am, whatever you did, I'm different than you.* This agonizing thought slammed through her brain as she stepped back from the mirror and turned to find Doug's corpse sprawled out at the back of the foyer, near the entrance to the kitchen.

Instantly, she recalled how Lin had killed him and fed his blood to her. He was the first. *It started with you.* The memory was just as horrible and gut wrenching as the others. In Sarah's mind she became the killer. She felt Lin's anger and resistance to the heinous crime as his life spilled into her. Her Jadaraa Soo thrummed and panged with her suffering throughout Sarah's limbs. They were now one and the same. Nothing but rancid love passed between them now. They were closer than God's breath in a baby; and the vampire had passed a whole family under her teeth so that Sarah could survive. *You washed my gums in their blood, baptizing me with their deaths!*

It was larger than anything that had loomed in her eyes and its crushing weight was more powerful than what Sarah could take. Too much, just too much death and destruction screamed through her head in a conflux of raw emotions – and it wasn't enough! Another hard shuddering pang tore outward from her chest. A strangulating need as the whole of the parasite shook its host to feed…to feed it now!

Sarah never even felt the doorknob in her hand as she turned it. She never felt her arms flinging the wooden portal wide open or the glass breaking upon her body as she ran from the house through the frail outer door. Sarah never heard the violent shrieks that tore from her mouth as she ran down the street. All she knew was that she had to get away, that the savage inhumanity barreling through her head had to stop. But it kept coming. Rolling over her like a tidal wave of persistent domination, Sarah was a slave to the eons of cruel hunger that had awakened within the parasitic blood.

The poor girl never felt the pounding of her feet slapping against the asphalt in the dimming light, or the overture of evening caressing her thin pale flesh. Sarah was unaware that as she ran from the house screaming holy terror she tore off her clothes. All she knew was that she was covered in the blood of the family. She was covered in Lin's blood and its stain had darkened her soul. She had to get away. It had to stop. Screeching in the final seconds of daylight Sarah ran from the monster she'd seen in the foyer mirror. She ran from the monster living in her head. She ran from herself, a crazy ashen thing fleeing down the suburban street toward the crisp, fresh scents of dry earth and open desert.

Special Agent Ian McCallister turned in the direction of the scream as it shattered the humble dusk in rueful horror. He had gotten the crash site fairly contained. His team was just finishing up their statements as the noise reached him. He passed a look with Special Agents Gorman and Davy. The vile shrieking was nonstop. It was not the pitiful sounds of someone being attacked and squealing offense. This was worse than that. This was painful howling through a mouth of madness. All three of the special agents turned toward the blaring wails and the few remaining local cops didn't get what the federal boys were staring at. The far off subdivision had been there all day.

To the human ears that were there and listening to the wind scraping across the desert on top of the hill its whine through the cars and people were all that they could hear. That and the abrasive sounds of the tow truck as it loaded the Arizona police cruiser onto its flat bed. The screaming yowl was too far away for human ears to detect.

"Davy. Gorman," called McCallister with a quick pulse in his voice. "Check that out."

As Gorman passed her superior, he grabbed her arm and whispered. "If it's what I think it is, box it up tight. Top priority. I don't want the locals involved. Got it?"

"Yes Sir."

Her black, mid-length, regulation hair bounced above her shoulders as she climbed the dune, joining Special Agent Davy as he headed toward the car. "Looks like we finally caught our break."

"You think?" he asked.

"Oh yes." A vicious smile curled one end of her mouth. "Can't you taste it?"

Special Agent McCallister turned his nose into the wind and sniffed. This time the air gave him something good. He closed his eyes to discern the multiple scents. *A vampire. Only one. And blood. Lots of blood.*

He opened his eyes and felt the titillating pulse of the hunt bristling under his skin. It was a delicious bloom. He glared down at the streetlights and house lights taking abstract shape along the horizon of the thickening night. His ears pricked alive with the vampire's screams and the deathly scents fired the thrill of the chase. Automatically, his heart quickened and he felt the hairs on the back of his neck rise.

He had already given up hope, thinking that the trail had grown cold and uninteresting, amassing to a week's stack of paperwork. *Now it's become fresh. Now, it gets exciting.* The case opened up for him like a flower. He inhaled the breeze flowing from the subdivision again: The cool taste of the scared creature's fear. She was riff with it and it ignited the ire of his wolf. McCallister shivered with anticipation to rip a real scream from that wailing throat, one especially made for him. He straightened his tie and exhaled his exhilaration, looking finely professional in his tailored black suit. After all, he had a job to do and he especially liked doing it when he got to kill a vampire or two – *They're a nasty, arrogant lot with more pull than they deserve.*

Special Agent Ian McCallister walked back up the hill of the sandy dune to finish sweeping the scene and clear the human riffraff out. He was a professional, after all. He could hold his excitement in check until his team called in. There were procedures to follow and his clean up crew had only just arrived, early he noted, and they were doing their thing.

Oh, yes, he grinned. Things were looking up. *Run while you can, sweetheart, because I'm going to catch you. Who ever you are. Wherever you go. I'm going to catch you and tear your fucking throat out and watch you die!*

Lexicon

Ankh – (*Angk*) Master Symbol of Life. Ones leader; ruler.

Ankh Shisk – (*Angk Sheesk*) Female robes of office. Worn by Omjadda female J'in Ankhs.

Ankh Shūr – (*Angk Shur*) Male robes of office. Worn by Omjadda male J'in Ankhs.

Araci – (*AhRaa cee*) Native Guarani term for Spirit of the dawn. *South America.*

Asli – (*Ahzlee*) 1. Original. 2. The People.

Bithtaranism – (*Bith Tear Raan-ism*) The only known and recognized religion of the Children of Evensong. Developed in the late 1600's by the freed blood slave, Shev Taran, formerly of the Qamar Däm J'in. Named after the *Bithtara*, the ceremonial, medical garments worn after members of the religious sect expose themselves to sunlight as a purification ritual, usually every one hundred years. The followers of Bithtaranism are normally called *Bithtarans*. In the Twentieth Century Bithtaranism rose in popularity among vampire covens and even garnered a few Omjadda members into their fold.

Brood – (*Brood*) 1. The initiated members of one's family or coven. 2. Lesser vampires with weaker symbiotic bonds, usually deformed by the symbiotic transformation.

Bruxsa – (*Bruxsah*) A feminine vampire of Portugal. The Bruxsa is believed to transform into a creature of the night by the means of witchcraft, and goes out in the shape of a bird. Also believed to possess a normal life during the day; Bruxsas are known to torment lost and tired travelers, and feed primarily on children. *Portuguese.*

Chaya Ip – (*Chaa Yaa'Ep*) An unusual and grotesque Omjadda dish, traditionally served at high functions, attributed and developed by the Tien Däm Mu J'in. The Chaya Ip is comprised of six human beings, three male and three female, bound together around a stuffing of fruit and vegetables where a precious jewel, the Ip, hides. The Chaya Ip is slow roasted while its ingredients are alive to capture its exotic flavor. It is considered an honor and treasure to be the first one that breeches the Chaya, the outer wall of flesh, and secures the jeweled Ip.

Casa del Rio Dulce – House on the Sweet River. Built in 1687 by Dominique De'Paul and Isabela da Nóbrega. *Portuguese/Spanish.*

Children of Evensong – A loose term of those belonging to the symbiont species derived from the mixing of Omjadda and Human blood.

D'oeuvre Fetish – A particular obession toward the binge eating and purging of food stuffs by vampires. *First note of a D'oeuvre advocate was in 1621; Louis DeBloomrugé. He also discovered the toxic potency of blueberries. French/English.*

Dalam Kha'Shiya – (*Daa Laam Kha She Yaa*) That which waits in the pitch of darkness is the traditional understanding of this moniker for the Seventh J'in (Clan) of the Omjadda. However, the phrase can also be interpreted as, *Dangerous Night Water Spirit.* The Dalam Kha'Shiya J'in is one of two Omjadda clans to emerge from the Dalam Vala'Shiya J'in after the Great Migration.
> *Dalam* = Night; Darkness. *Kha* = Danger; Dangerous. *Shiya* = Water Goddess; Ocean Spirit: Mistress/Servant of the Night Mother God/ Goddess, Layal.

Däm'Um – (*Daa'Oomm*) One Blood; first blood. *Dam* = Blood. *Um* = One; first. Other forms of the word *Dam* that have emerged into the African and Arabic Languages from the Omjaddas are: *Dama, Damma, & Dammu.*

Directorate – An advocate for the Accused in a Council Tribunal. One who speaks on behalf of another.

Eras of Slavery – Traditionally considered to range from 692 BCE to 1546 ACE. Though it is widely accepted in known circles that Vam (*Blood Slaves*) were created for the distinct purpose of human herding prior to this dating. Normac, a Vam Shiya of northern European descent, squelched the last remnants of symbiont slavery in 1546. Normac's revolt lasted nearly half a century aided in part by members of the N'um Vala'Shiya J'in. Normac is chiefly remembered for brilliantly shielding the decades long war from human knowledge by masking with the Schmalkaldic League* and Protestant Reformation.

In total, the conflicts that ended the Omjadda's Vam trade lasted over two centuries. Beginning as modest slave revolts that were primarily quelled, no actual progress toward liberation was established until the fall of the Tien Däm Mu J'in's slavery system in 1494. This was accomplished by two blood slaves, Fizza and Ramielle Eirinhas, orchestrating a simultaneous Vam revolt with an external attack led by the symbiont, Joshua, of the N'um Vala'Shiya J'in.

> ***Schmalkaldic League*** – A defensive alliance of Lutheran princes within the Holy Roman Empire during the mid 16th Century. Although originally started for religious motives soon after the start

of the Protestant Reformation, its members eventually intended for the League to replace the Holy Roman Empire as their source of political allegiance. While it was not the first alliance of its kind, unlike previous formations, such as the League of Torgau, the Schmalkaldic League had a substantial military to defend its political and religious interests. It receives its name from the town of Schmalkalden, in the German province of Thuringa. German: *Schmalkaldischer Bund*

Fedah Layal – *(Fey Daah Lay Al)* The three silvery rings of moonlight surrounding a bright, full moon, can also be interpreted as *God Light*. Name of the fifth J'in (Clan) of the Omjadda. The Fedah Layal J'in emerged from a split within the Rom Pŷr J'in prior to the Great Migration.

> *Fedah* = God's/Goddess's Light. The word *Fedah* found primary rooting in the Arabic Languages to mean, silvery. Over time the *'h'* was displaced to strengthen the accentuation of the *'a'* as the language progressed with a new tonal structure. *Ex: fed-ha.*

Gai'Anâka – *(Guy ann Akaa)* The Force, essence; Mother of all things. A later derivative of this word is *Gaia*, which means Mother Earth or Plant Life. Later development of early human civilizations misused this term for a name for the Earth.

Great Migration, The – An important time in the history of the Omjadda that denotes when the ancient race was force to flee their dying homelands and venture across what are now known as Africa, Europe, and Asia. The Omjadda term for this was Rånon Ŭd'ertz *(raNon Ood'rts)*, though all deeper meanings are lost.

Ja – *(Ja or Jaa depending on meaning and expression)*. Ja *(Ja)* = Source. Jā *(Jaa)* = Spiritual Essence, Spiritual Source.

Ja Rů Tộk – *(Jaa Roo TeOok)* The Omjadda Blood rite of passage that transforms a Mar into a Vam when Omjadda Blood is introduced into the bloodstream of a Mar (Human Being). This intermingling of bloods creates a (symbiotic) parasitic/host relationship in the infected organism creating a new species that is neither Human nor Omjadda, who feeds off the blood of other highly evolved living organisms.

Jaci – *(eYaa cee)* Native Guarani term for Spirit of the moon. *South America.*

Jad – *(Jaad)* Tree.

Jadda – *(Jah Daa)* The Tree of Life. Deep Rooted Essence. The word *Jadda* is also used as a term of endearment to one's mother.

Jadda Asli Roh - *(Jah Daa Ahzlee Row)* Royal Blood of the People of the Jadda Tree. Modern term of the eldest J'in (Clan) of the Omjadda. Originally derived from the *Asli Pyl* tribe, People West of the Onnaki River. Ancient lore states that in the *War of No Fist* the Asli Pyl met with their neighbors, the *Om Pÿr*, People East of the Onnaki River, to do battle and that in the settlement of the conflict the Asli Pyl took the moniker *Jadda Asli*, which meant: *Original People of the Jadda Tree*. The suffix Roh, *Royal Blood*, was added after the Omjadda's first and only recorded civil war; see *The Legend of Marh*.

Jadaraa Soo – *(Jah Daa Raa Soo)* Omjadda term for the vampiric parasite veins of a blood slave.

Jaddat – *(Jaa Dat)* Seer; Mother of the people of the Jadda Tree; Listener and Speaker with Gai'Anaka. A Jaddat is a spiritual elder born to the people. One can not ascend to the position of Jaddat, it is preordained by birth. A Jaddat is born without eyes, eyebrows, or eye sockets, so the term, Seer, is in reference to a Jaddat's gift of spiritual sight and prophetic visions.

J'in – *(Geh'In)* Clan: Family. One's Gathering: Those one chooses or is born amongst.

J'in Ankh – *(Geh'In Angk)* Familial Head; leader of the J'in (Clan); symbol of his or her people.

Kulak – *(Koo Lak)* A Russian term, now part of the English lexicon, for a peasant with a prosperous farm and a substantial allotment of land that worked the agrarian parcels with the help of hired labor. In the Soviet period the term became an ambiguous Party construct with mostly negative connotations. In the mid to late 1800's, with the formation of the symbiont council, the term was applied to petitioners that wanted access into The Council's jurisdiction under the laws of its domain among one of its many covens. Over time, with use, the term developed slang undertones to reflect one's subordinate state and position among the caste of their coven's rank; usually associated with a lowly status. *Ukranian: kurkul, hlytai.*

Layal – *(Lay Al)* Night Mother, the God/Goddess aspect of the Omjadda people. The word *Layal* is one of the original words passed down from Omjadda to humans that has changed very little in spelling and pronunciation. Though the word still retains a meaning of Night, all references to its dual nature of mother/sister and the God/Goddess aspects of its Omjadda origins have completely vanished with human use. In Hebrew and various Indian Languages the spelling of Layal has changed slightly. Arabic is the only human language to retain its original spelling.

Lanz Gur Mae – (*Laanz Grrr May*) Omjadda expression for *the land from here to there*. Original home of the Omjadda before the Great Migration. It is traditionally believed to be where the desert of the Senegal and Gambia regions now exist, today. Early misinterpretations of the Lanz Gur Mae with the astral body, Nibiru, have resulted in its exclusion from ancient references.

Legend of Marh, the – The modern understanding of the Arabic word, Mar, which means Human Being has its origins based on the Omjadda legend of Jadda Asli Marh. Marh was a prince of the royal J'in, Jadda Asli. To the Omjadda, Marh and his followers were believed to be the sole source of the Human Race, however, there is no proof to that claim.

The legend states that Jadda Asli Marh broke from time honored traditions by seeking an alliance with Layal's vengeful father/brother, Rah, who governed the day. Marh's communion with Rah is believed to have transfigured him, wherein he lost his normal bodily sheen and could now walk in both the day and the night. Marh began teaching others how to commune with Rah and gained a large following. This caused unrest and dissention among the J'ins of the time and a huge rift tore the Omjadda apart. Civil war broke out to quell these new cultural influences. This war is the Omjadda's first and only recorded blood war in their long and glorious history.

The result of the conflict led to the banishment of Marh and his followers from the Lanz Gur Mae. The Jadda Asli added the suffix, Roh, to their name, which meant, cleansed from the golden light, retainer of the pure essence, and all utterances of Marh and his teachings were forbidden. It was not until the encroachment of human beings, in the death days of the Lanz Gur Mae, that Jadda Asli Marh's title was resurrected. Common belief of the time held that Marh and his followers perished in the Anon *(translation lost)*. Privately among the Jadda Asli Roh J'in, however, there survived a prophecy from the clan's reigning Jaddat that foretold of Marh's return in transcended form.

The new humanoid creatures were met with speculation and wonder because they spoke with an Omjadda tongue, calling themselves Mar, for Children of Marh. Again, rumors and dissention rippled through the J'ins and it was believed that Marh, in an unholy union with Rah, birthed these creatures to be his instrument of destruction and revenge against Layal and the Omjadda people.

Mar – (*Mar*) Omjadda word for Human Being. Later development from the Omjadda term, *Marh Pÿr*, which translates into *Marh's Children from the East*. The word *Mar* developed its modern roots in Arabic and the Greek Languages. Though in Greek, *Mar* further developed into a godhead term to denote the

God of War, aka *Mars*.

Mu – (*Moo*) Conjunction word used like the English word, of.

Nibiru – (*Né Bé Roo*) 1. A technical term of Babylonian astronomy, translating to 'crossing' or 'point of transition'; passage between heaven and earth. 2. Marduk's star. 3. An early name for Jupiter. 4. An astral body with an elliptic orbit theorized to have collided with another astral body that formed the Earth, Moon, and asteroid belt. 5. An undefined time of Omjadda wandering.

N'um Vala'Shiya –(*NN oom VahLaa She ya*) People of the Golden Treasure: fourth J'in (Clan) of the Omjadda. The N'um Vala'Shiya J'in is one of two Omjadda clans to emerge from the Dalam Vala'Shiya J'in after the Great Migration.

> *N'um = Dawn, Shiya* = Water Goddess; Ocean Spirit: Mistress/Servant of the Night Mother God/Goddess, Layal.

Ob'seak – (*Ob Seek*) A ceremonial sword owned by the Omjadda house of Jadda Asli. It is a symbol of the Asli's power and authority to rule over the other Omjadda J'ins.

Ohanao – (*O Ha Na O*) This is mine. I claim it for myself

Om – (*OM*) Original Sound; first word.

Omjadda – (*Omm' Jah Daa*) Original People of the Jadda Tree. A nocturnal, humanoid species that predates all known spoken and written human languages. Early civilized writings appear to have attributed this primordial race with godhead status. Other known names: Annunaki, Nephillim, Malaika, Kula Malaika Shaytan Khalid.

Onnak – (*Oh Nak*) Long river. An 'i' is added when the word is used in conjunction with what it is: <u>Ex</u>: *Onnaki River*.

Pun – (*Pun'*) North.

Puun – (*Poonn*) South.

Pyl – (*Peel'*) West.

Pŷr – (*Pur*) East. Later developments of the word Pŷr became known as *Son* or *Children of*.

Qamar – (*K'Mar*) The Moon.

Qamar Däm – (*K'Mar Daam*) Blood Moon. Often referred to as an eclipse or a red moon and the third J'in (Clan) of the Omjadda Race, believed to have originally sprouted as a sect of healers from the Jadda Asli and the Rom Pyr. Traditionally noted to have birthed more Jaddats than any other J'in.

Rom Pŷr – (*Rah'M Pur*) Strong People to the East; second J'in (Clan) of the Omjaddas. In the beginning there were two distinct Omjadda J'ins. The *Asli Pyl*, People of the West, and the *Om Pŷr*, Sound from the East. Each tribe was separated by the Onnaki River in the Lanz Gur Mae, developing independently, choosing their own leaders, governing structure, and unique cultural customs. As legend goes, when the *Om Pŷr*, Sound from the East, came to war with the *Asli Pyl*, People of the West, the J'in Ankh of the Asli Pyl meet with the J'in Ank of the Om Pyr, embraced him and called him *Rom*, strong. The J'in Ank of the Om Pŷr returned the embrace thus ending the *War of No Fist* and the term Rom Pŷr was used ever since for the people east of the Onnak.

Sanglant – (*Sang Lant*) Modern term for a blood lender. Sanglants usually work for The Service and sell their precious bodily fluid, allowing symbionts to feed off of them for money. Original French pronunciation for a Sanglant is *Prêteur de Sang*.

Shrij 'Tẹk Aůr – (*Shree'G Tik ArUr*) An Omjadda call for challenge. Usually delivered when one wishes to challenge the line of succession to the throne of J'in Ankh.

Sylph – (Sil'eff) A slender and graceful air spirit.

Tet Däm'vah (*tet Daa Vaa*) – Sacred Blood. Omjadda ceremonial term for the blessed life fluid within one's J'in.

The Council – A secret ruling body comprised of twelve members, from varying symbiont covens, throughout the world, established in 1838. The freed Vam Pŷr, Dominique De'Paul, is credited with conceiving the initial plans of the elite governing body.

The Service – Independent organization originally developed by Dominique De'Paul and Ramielle Eirinhas in the early 1800's as a way for symbionts to meet the needs of their particular feeding habits without causing harm to other individuals or raise suspicion of their existence and activity. With the establishment of The Council in 1838 the function of The Service was absorbed into the governing body.

Tien Däm Mu – (*Tee En Daa Moo*) People of blood: later, People of Ill Blood when the Vam Pŷr, Dominique De'Paul, interceded the Omjadda line of succession as J'in Ankh of the Clan. The sixth J'in of the Omjadda. The Tien Däm Mu J'in resulted from a split between rival family members of the Qamar Däm J'in just prior to leaving the dying lands of the Lanz Gur Mae. The Tien Däm Mu J'in are credited with starting the Rånon Ŭd'ertz (*Great Migration*), and renown for the *Chaya Ip*.

Vam – (*Vam*) A blood slave of the Omjadda, created when a human being partakes of Omjadda Blood in the Ja Rů Tŏk. The use of Vam were only used within four of the seven Omjadda j'ins and ended with the Eras of Slavery. See *Eras of Slavery* for more detail.

Vam Däm – (*Vam Daa*) Slave to the people of the Moon. Those Vam belonging to the Qamar Däm J'in. Though the term actually exists as a misnomer in the literal translation, it still denotes ownership of the slave to the rightful J'in.

Vam Däm Mu – (*Vam Daa Moo*) Slave to the people of Blood. Those Vam belonging to the Tien Däm Mu J'in.

Vam Pŷr – (*Vam Pur*) Slave to the People of the East: Slave Son; property of the Rom Pŷr J'in. *Vam* = Slave. *Pŷr* = Eastern People; Children of. The Rom Pŷr J'in are credited with discovering the sentient properties of their Tet Däm'vah to resurrect Mar into blood slaves through a symbiotic bond between host and parasite. The modern term of this is commonly known as a *Vampire*. In the Nordic/Austrian regions of Europe and Asia the term Vam Pŷr became one word, *Vampyr*, later developing into the spelling of *Vampyre*, which was commonly believed to be a child born from the sexual coupling of a vampire and a human. Since the reproductive organs of an infected Mar no longer function normally the production of such a child could never exist. Thus the modern term for Vampyre is completely incorrect and mythical. The sexual coupling of an Omjadda and a Human is quite possible, though, to date there are no known couplings between these two races other than the creation of Vam.

Vam Shiya – (*Vam She Yaa*) Slave to the people of Water. Those Vam belonging to the Dalam Kha'Shiya J'in.

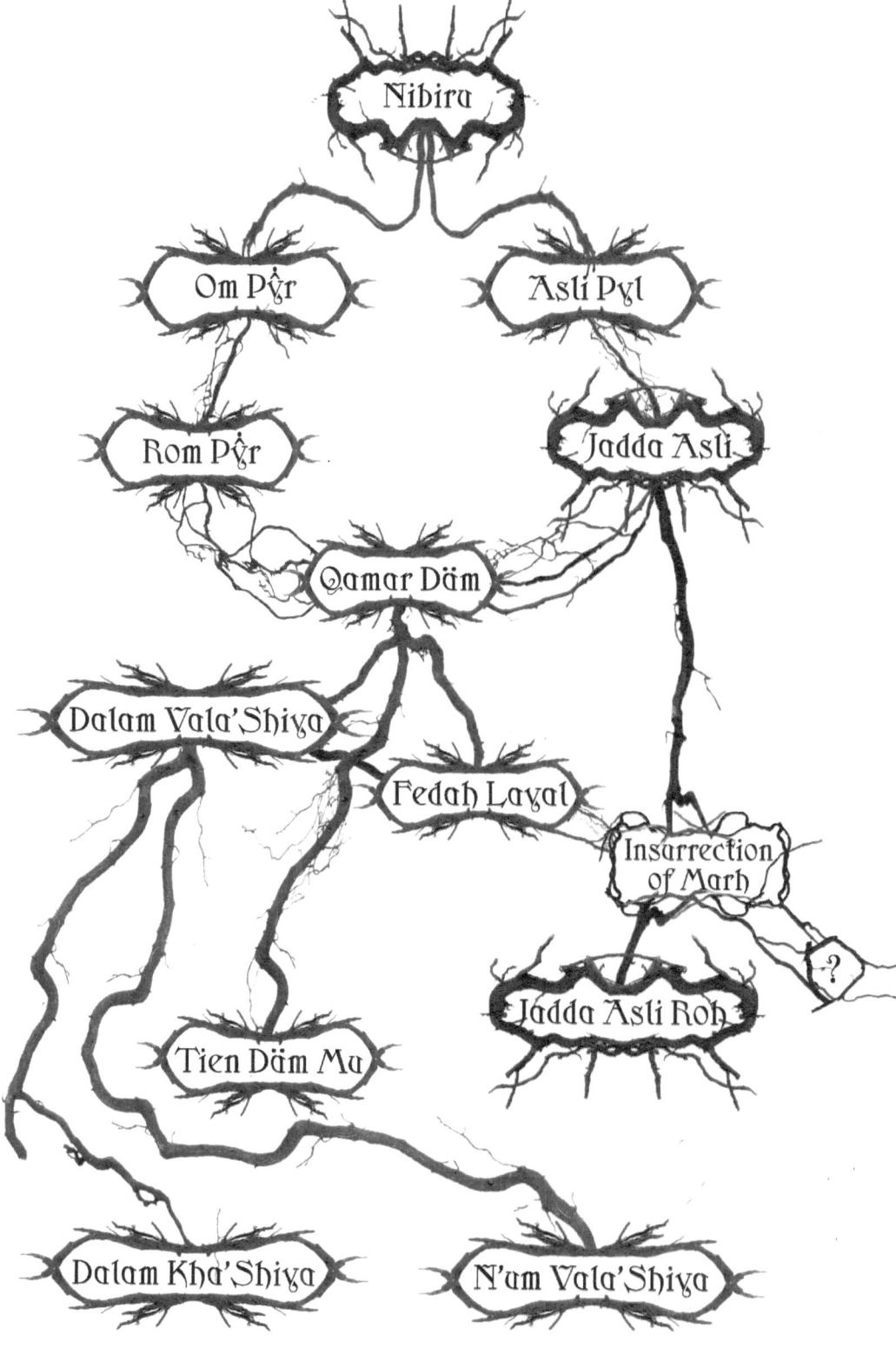

Publisher's Note

Photo: Jacquie Coté

This one was easier to write than the first one. Not sure if it's better. But it was definitely easier to pen. Could be because I'd spent a few years tooling the film script to a well-honed blunt instrument and all I had to do was follow that and fill in the spaces in between. Or, it could be that by finally finishing that first novel something opened up inside and I changed into a fatter butterfly, reached typing nirvana, or understood the writer's long lost mystery of fulfilling that first gigantic step. Whatever it was...a tad easier and more fun. Hope the fun shows through more than the easy. If not...well, I promise to make the next book better.

Author's Studio Site:
www.StudioOnTheSquare.net

Cool eStore:
www.CrazyDuckPress.com

On Facebook:
https://www.facebook.com/stavros.cockrell
https://www.facebook.com/ogbloodjunky
https://www.facebook.com/ogdeadgirl
https://www.facebook.com/loveinveinmovie
https://www.facebook.com/CrazyDuckPress
https://www.facebook.com/StudioSquared
https://www.facebook.com/KaosKustomFangs

Twitter: @VisualLyricist
Twitter: @CrazyDuckPress

Custom Fangs, Tusks, & Zombie Teeth:
www.kaoskustomfangs.com

Stavros Wishes to Thank:

Special Thanks to Lindsey, Julia, and Emily for the initial inspiration
to take my vamp world and graph it to a bunch of wacky photo shoot
ideas, which finally ended a continuos cycle of re-writing the same damn
chapters over and over again.   Mucho Props to God for putting me
here on this journey; Mom, "J", Val, Cousin Mike, Darlene, Grandma,
the Fathers and Mothers at Our Lady of Kazan Skete, Jersey Dan, Just
N'Gage, Mamma T, LW, L.A. Nantz, Lisa, Elizabeth, Horror Show Jack,
KT for art & inspiration, all you wonderful people out there
reading my books, and PB 'cause in truth…
All Thank Yous To Grace Pena!

YOU ARE THE VAMPRE REVOLUTION!
Live. Love. Create.

Stavros

Also Available by the Author!

Fiction:

Love in Vein

Dead Girl:
A Romantic Zombie Tale Revenge

NonFiction:

Vampire News: volume one
Tasty Bits For You To Sink Your Fangs Into!

Vampire News: volume two
The (not so) End Times Edition

Vampire News: volume three
Really...Vampires Suck!

Documentary Film:
Committing Poetry in Times of War

Upcoming Books:

Blood in Vein
Firefly's Kiss
Spoken Word
Baltimore

More from the author at:
www.crazyduckpress.com
www.studioonthesquare.net
www.kaoskustomfangs.com